Fairy Tales

Hans-Christian Andersen

Fairy Tales

With 167 Drawings,
Etchings & Woodcuts by great
European Illustrators

CHARTWELL
BOOKS, INC.

Translated by H.P. Paull (1875), selected by Hanne Harbo Andersen,
C. Burgauner and Peter Seitz,
illustrations supplied by Illustra-Agency, Munich.

Published by Omega Books Ltd.,
1 West Street, Ware
Hertfordshire, England

ISBN 0-89009-671-6

Printed by Brepols, Turnhout, Belgium

The Brave Tin Soldier

There were once five-and-twenty tin soldiers, who were all brothers, for they had been made out of the same old tin spoon. They shouldered arms and looked straight before them, and wore a splendid uniform, red and blue. The first thing in the world they ever heard were the words, "Tin soldiers!" uttered by a little boy, who clapped his hands with delight when the lid of the box, in which they lay, was taken off. They were given him for a birthday present, and he stood at the table to set them up. The soldiers were all exactly alike, except one, who had only one leg; he had been left to the last, and then there was not enough of the melted tin to finish him, so they made him stand firmly on one leg, and this caused him to be very remarkable.

The table on which the tin soldiers stood, was covered with other playthings, but the most attractive to the eye was a pretty little paper castle. Through the small windows the rooms could be seen. In front of the castle a number of little trees surrounded a piece of looking-glass, which was intended to represent a transparent lake. Swans, made of wax, swam on the lake, and were reflected in it. All this was very pretty, but the prettiest of all was a tiny little lady, who stood at the open door of the castle; she, also, was made of paper, and she wore a dress of clear muslin, with a narrow blue ribbon over her shoulders just like a scarf. In front of this was fixed a glittering tinsel rose, as large as her whole face. The little lady was a dancer, and she stretched out both her arms, and raised one of her legs so high, that the tin soldier could not see it at all, and he thought that she, like himself, had only one leg. "That is the wife for me," he thought; "but she is too grand, and lives in a castle, while I have only a box to live in, five-and-twenty of us altogether, that is no place for her. Still I must try and make her acquaintance." Then he laid himself at full length on the table behind a snuff-box that stood upon it, so that he could peep at the little delicate lady, who continued to stand on one leg without losing her balance. When evening came, the other tin soldiers were all placed in the box, and the people of the house went to bed. Then the playthings began to have their own games together, to pay visits, to have sham fights, and to give balls. The tin soldiers rattled in their box; they wanted to get out and join the amusements, but they

5

could not open the lid. The nut-crackers played at leap-frog, and the pencil jumped about the table. There was such a noise that the canary woke up and began to talk, and in poetry too. Only the tin soldier and the dancer remained in their places. She stood on tiptoe, with her arms stretched out, as firmly as he did on his one leg. He never took his eyes from her for even a moment. The clock struck twelve, and, with a bounce, up sprang the lid of the snuff-box; but, instead of snuff, there jumped up a little black goblin; for the snuff-box was a toy puzzle.

"Tin soldier," said the goblin, "don't wish for what does not belong to you."

But the tin soldier pretended not to hear.

"Very well; wait till to-morrow, then," said the goblin.

When the children came in the next morning, they placed the tin soldier in the window. Now, whether it was the goblin who did it, or the draught, is

not known, but the window flew open, and out fell the tin soldier, heels over head, from the third storey, into the street beneath. It was a terrible fall; for he came head downwards, his helmet and his bayonet stuck in between the flagstones, and his one leg up in the air. The servant-maid and the little boy went downstairs directly to look for him; but he was nowhere to be seen, although once they nearly trod upon him. If he had called out, "Here I am," it would have been all right; but he was too proud to cry out for help while he wore a uniform.

Presently it began to rain, and the drops fell faster and faster, till there was a heavy shower. When it was over, two boys happened to pass by, and one of them said, "Look, there is a tin soldier. He ought to have a boat to sail in." So they made a boat out of a newspaper, and placed the tin soldier in it, and sent him sailing down the gutter, while the two boys ran by the side of it, and clapped their hands. Good gracious! what large waves arose in that gutter! and how fast the stream rolled on! for the rain had been very heavy. The paper boat rocked up and down, and turned itself round sometimes so quickly that the tin soldier trembled; yet he remained firm; his countenance did not change; he looked straight before him, and shouldered his musket. Suddenly the boat shot under a bridge which formed part of a drain, and then it was as dark as the tin soldier's box.

"Where am I going now?" thought he. "This is the black goblin's fault, I am sure. Ah, well, if the little lady were only here with me in the boat, I should not care for any darkness."

Suddenly there appeared a great water-rat, who lived in the drain.

"Have you a passport?" asked the rat, "give it to me at once." But the tin soldier remained silent and held his musket tighter than ever. The boat sailed on and the rat followed it. How he did gnash his teeth and cry out to

7

the bits of wood and straw, "Stop him, stop him; he has not paid toll, and has not shown his pass." But the stream rushed on stronger and stronger. The tin soldier could already see daylight shining where the arch ended. Then he heard a roaring sound quite terrible enough to frighten the bravest man. At the end of the tunnel the drain fell into a large canal over a steep place, which made it as dangerous for him as a waterfall would be to us. He was too close to it to stop, so the boat rushed on, and the poor tin soldier could only hold himself as stiffly as possible, without moving an eyelid, to show that he was not afraid. The boat whirled round three or four times, and then filled with water to the very edge; nothing could save it from sinking. He now stood up to his neck in water, while deeper and deeper sank the boat, and the paper became soft and loose with the wet, till at last the water closed over the soldier's head. He thought of the elegant little dancer whom he should never see again, and the words of the song sounded in his ears –

"Farewell warrior! ever brave,
Drifting onward to thy grave."

Then the paper boat fell to pieces, and the soldier sank into the water and immediately afterwards was swallowed up by a great fish. Oh how dark it was inside the fish! a great deal darker than in the tunnel, and narrower too, but the tin soldier continued firm, and lay at full length, shouldering his musket. The fish swam to and fro, making the most wonderful movements, but at last he became quite still. After a while, a flash of lightning seemed to pass through him, and then the daylight appeared, and a voice cried out, "I declare here is the tin soldier." The fish had been caught, taken to the market and sold to the cook, who took him into the kitchen and cut him open with a large knife. She picked up the soldier and held him by the waist between her finger and thumb, and carried him into the room. They were all anxious to see this wonderful soldier who had travelled about inside a fish; but he was not at all proud. They placed him on the table, and – how many curious things do happen in the world! – there he was in the very same room from the window of which he had fallen, there were the same children, the same playthings standing on the table, and the pretty castle with the elegant little dancer at the door; she still balanced herself on one leg, and held up the other, so she was as firm as himself. It touched the tin soldier so much to see her that he almost wept tin tears, but he kept them back. He only looked at her, and they both remained silent. Presently one of the little boys took up the tin soldier, and threw him into the stove. He had no reason for doing so, therefore it must have been the fault of the black

8

goblin who lived in the snuff-box. The flames lighted up the tin soldier, as he stood, the heat was very terrible, but whether it proceeded from the real fire or from the fire of love he could not tell. Then he could see that the bright colours had faded from his uniform, but whether they had been washed off during his journey, or from the effects of his sorrow, no one could say. He looked at the little lady, and she looked at him. He felt himself melting away, but he still remained firm with his gun on his shoulder. Suddenly the door of the room flew open, and the draught of air caught up the little dancer, she fluttered like a sylph right into the stove by the side of the tin soldier, and was instantly in flames and was gone. The tin soldier melted down into a lump, and the next morning, when the maid-servant took the ashes out of the stove, she found him in the shape of a little tin heart. But of the little dancer nothing remained but the tinsel rose, which was burnt black as a cinder.

Clod-poll

Away in the country there was an old manor, and in it lived an old squire who had two sons; and they were so witty they were too clever by half. They were going to propose to the king's daughter; and there was no reason why they shouldn't because she had announced that she would marry the man who could give the best account of himself.

Now the two of them spent a week in getting ready; this was all the time they had for it, but it was time enough since they'd had some previous education, and that's so useful. One of them knew the whole Latin dictionary and the local paper for the last three years off by heart, reading both from the front and from the back. The other had learnt up all the company by-laws and what every alderman ought to know; this enabled him to discuss State affairs, he thought, and besides he knew how to embroider braces, because he was so clever with his fingers.

'I'm going to win the princess!' they both said. And so their father gave them each a splendid horse, the one who knew the dictionary and the newspapers getting a coal-black horse, and the one who was as clever as an alderman and could embroider getting a milk-white one. And the next thing they did was to oil the corners of their mouths with cod-liver oil to make them work easier. All the servants were in the courtyard to see them mount their horses, when along came the third brother – for there were three, only nobody counted him as brother because he wasn't such a scholar as the other two, and they never called him anything but Clod-poll.

'Where are you two off to, dressed up in your Sunday best?' he asked.

'To Court, to talk ourselves into a princess! Haven't you heard the proclamation that's been read out all over the country?' And they told him all about it.

'Oh, I say! I'd better come with you!' said Clodpoll. The brothers, however, only laughed at him and rode on their way.

'Father, let me have a horse!' cried Clod-poll. 'I'm just in the mood for getting married! If she'll have me, she'll have me! And if she won't have me, I'll have her all the same!'

'Stuff and nonsense!' said his father. 'I'm not giving you a horse. You've got nothing to say for yourself! Now, your brothers – well, they're gentlemen!'

'If I'm not to have a horse,' said Clod-poll, 'I'll take the billy-goat. That's my own, and it can carry me!' And so he got astride the billy-goat, dug his heels into its sides, and made off along the road. Phew! What a speed! 'Here I come!' cried Clod-poll; and he sang out till the air echoed with it.

But his brothers rode on ahead in silence, never saying a word; they were busy thinking out all the clever sayings they were going to make, because it all had to be well worked out.

'Tally-ho!' shouted Clod-poll. 'Here I come! Look what I found on the road!' And he showed them a dead crow he had picked up.

'Clod!' they said. 'What are you going to do with that?'

'I'm going to present it to the princess!'

'All right, you do!' they said, laughing and riding on.

'Tally-ho! Here I come! Look what I've found now! You don't find this on the road every day!'

And the brothers turned round again to see what it was. 'Clod!' they said. 'Why, it's only an old clog with the upper missing! Is the princess to have that as well?'

'Of course she is!' said Clod-poll. And the brothers laughed, and rode on and got well ahead.

'Tally-ho! Here I am!' shouted Clod-poll. 'I say, but it's getting worse and worse! Tally-ho! It's wonderful!'

'What have you found now?' said his brothers.

'Oh!' said Clod-poll. 'There's no telling! Won't she be delighted, the princess!'

'Ugh!' said the bothers. 'Why, it's mud you've got straight from the ditch.'

'You're quite right!' said Clod-poll. 'And it's the finest sort; you can't hold it!' And he filled his pocket with it.

But his brothers rode off as hard as they could go, and by the time they reached the city gate they were a whole hour ahead. All the suitors were being given numbers as they arrived, and were placed in rows, six by six, and so close together that they couldn't stir: which was just as well, because one was standing in front of the other.

The rest of the country's inhabitants were gathered round the palace, right up to the windows, to see the princess receive the suitors; and the moment one of them entered the room he would lose his tongue.

'No good!' the princess would say. 'Off with you!'

Then along came the brother who knew the dictionary, but he had clean forgotten it while waiting his turn in the queue; and the floor creaked, and the ceiling was of looking-glass, which made him see himself upside down. And then, standing at every window, were three reporters and an alder-

12

man, all taking down everything that was said, so that it could go straight into the paper and be sold for twopence at the corner. It was dreadful; and what's more, they'd made up such a fire the stove was red hot.

'It's pretty hot in here!' said the suitor.

'That's because my father's roasting cockerels today!' said the princess.

Ooh! There he stood; and the talk wasn't a bit like what he'd expected. Not a word could he find to say, for he had meant to say something funny. Ooh!

'No good!' said the princess. 'Off with you!' And off he had to go. It was the other brother's turn now.

'It's awfully hot in here!' he said.

'Yes, we're roasting cockerels to-day!' said the princess.

'What – what's that?' he said. And all the reporters wrote down: 'What – what's that?'

'No good!' said the princess. 'Off with you!'

It was Clod-poll's turn now. He came riding his billy-goat straight into the room. 'It's as hot as blazes in here!' he said.

'That's because I'm roasting cockerels!' said the princess.

'This is a bit of luck!' said Clod-poll. 'Then I suppose I can have a crow roasted?'

13

'Yes, you can if you like!' said the princess. 'But have you anything to roast it in? Because I've neither pot nor pan!'

'Oh, but I have!' said Clod-poll. 'Here's a cooker with a tin handle!' And he pulled out the old clog and put the crow in the middle of it.

'There's quite a meal there!' said the princess. 'But where do we get the gravy?'

'I've got that in my pocket!' said Clod-poll. 'I've more than enough here!' And he turned a little of the mud out of his pocket.

'Now I like that!' said the princess. 'You always have an answer. And you can give a good account of yourself, so I'll have you for my husband! But do you know that every word we've been saying has been taken down and will be in the paper to-morrow? Look, at every window there are three reporters and an old alderman, and the alderman's the worst of the lot because he doesn't understand a thing!' Now, this she said only to frighten him. And all the reporters sniggered and made a blot on the carpet.

14

'They'll be the gentry!' said Clod-poll. 'Well then, here's one of the best for the alderman!' And he turned out his pockets and gave him the mud full in the face.

'Well done!' said the princess. 'It's more than I could have done! But I shall learn!'

And so Clod-poll became king, winning a wife of his own and a crown and a throne. And we have this straight from the alderman's newspaper – which isn't to be trusted!

The Little Match-Seller

It was terribly cold and nearly dark on the last evening of the old year, and the snow was falling fast. In the cold and the darkness, a poor little girl, with bare head and naked feet, roamed through the streets. It is true she had on a pair of slippers when she left home, but they were not of much use. They were very large, so large, indeed, that they had belonged to her mother, and the poor little creature had lost them in running across the street to avoid two carriages that were rolling along at a terrible rate. One of the slippers she could not find, and a boy seized upon the other and ran away with it, saying that he could use it as a cradle, when he had children of his own. So the little girl went on with her little naked feet, which were quite red and blue with the cold. In an old apron she carried a number of matches,

17

and had a bundle of them in her hands. No one had bought anything of her the whole day, nor had any one given her even a penny. Shivering with cold and hunger, she crept along; poor little child, she looked the picture of misery. The snow-flakes fell on her long, fair hair, which hung in curls on her shoulders, but she regarded them not.

Lights were shining from every window, and there was a savoury smell of roast goose, for it was New-Year's Eve – yes, she remembered that. In a corner, between two houses, one of which projected beyond the other, she sank down, and huddled herself together. She had drawn her little feet under her, but she could not keep off the cold; and she dared not go home, for she had sold no matches, and could not take home even a penny of money. Her father would certainly beat her; besides, it was almost as cold at home as here, for they had only the roof to cover them, through which the wind howled, although the largest holes had been stopped up with straw and rags. Her little hands were almost frozen with the cold. Ah! perhaps a burning

match might be some good, if she could draw it from the bundle and strike
it against the wall, just to warm her fingers. She drew one out – "scratch!"
how it sputtered as it burnt! It gave a warm, bright light, like a little candle,
as she held her hand over it. It was really a wonderful light. It seemed to the
little girl as if she were sitting by a large iron stove, with polished brass feet
and a brass ornament. How the fire burned! and seemed so beautifully warm

that the child stretched out her feet as if to warm them, when, lo! the flame of the match went out, the stove vanished, and she had only the remains of the half-burnt match in her hand.

She rubbed another match on the wall. It burst into a flame, and where its light fell upon the wall it became as transparent as a veil, and she could see into the room. The table was covered with a snowy white table-cloth, on which stood a splendid dinner service, and a steaming roast goose, stuffed with apples and dried plums. And what was still more wonderful, the goose jumped down from the dish and waddled across the floor, with a knife and fork in its breast, to the little girl. Then the match went out, and there remained nothing but the thick, damp, cold wall before her.

She lighted another match, and then she found herself sitting under a beautiful Christmas-tree. It was larger and more beautifully decorated than the one she had seen through the glass door at the rich merchant's. Thousands of tapers were burning upon the green branches, and coloured

20

pictures, like those she had seen in the show-windows, looked down upon it all. The little one stretched out her hand towards them, and the match went out.

The Christmas lights rose higher and higher, till they looked to her like the stars in the sky. Then she saw a star fall, leaving behind a bright streak of fire. "Some one is dying," thought the little girl, for her old grandmother, the only one who had ever loved her, and who was now dead, had told her that when a star falls, a soul was going up to God.

She again rubbed a match on the wall, and the light shone round her; in the brightness stood her old grandmother, clear and shining, yet mild and loving in her appearance. "Grandmother," cried the little one, "O take me with you; I know you will go away when the match burns out; you will vanish like the warm stove, the roast goose, and the large, glorious Christmas-tree." And she made haste to light the whole bundle of matches, for she wished to keep her grandmother there. And the matches glowed with a light that was brighter than the noon-day, and her grandmother had never appeared so large or so beautiful. She took the little girls in her arms, and they both flew upwards in brightness and joy far above the earth, where there was neither cold nor hunger nor pain, for they were with God.

In the dawn of morning there lay the poor little one, with pale cheeks and smiling mouth, leaning against the wall; she had been frozen to death on the last evening of the old year; and the New-Year's sun rose and shone upon a little corpse! The child still sat, in the stiffness of death, holding the matches in her hand, one bundle of which was burnt. "She tried to warm herself," said some. No one imagined what beautiful things she had seen, nor into what glory she had entered with her grandmother, on New-Year's day.

Little Tiny

There was once a woman who wished very much to have a little child, but she could not obtain her wish. At last she went to a fairy, and said, "I should so very much like to have a little child; can you tell me where I can find one?"

"Oh, that can be easily managed," said the fairy. "Here is a barleycorn of a different kind to those which grow in the farmer's fields, and which the chickens eat; put it into a flower-pot, and see what will happen."

"Thank you," said the woman, and she gave the fairy twelve shillings, which was the price of the barleycorn. Then she went home and planted it, and immediately there grew up a large handsome flower, something like a tulip in appearance, but with its leaves tightly closed as if it were still a bud. "It is a beautiful flower," said the woman, and she kissed the red and golden-coloured leaves, and while she did so the flower opened, and she could see that it was a real tulip. Within the flower, upon the green velvet stamens, sat a very delicate and graceful little maiden. She was scarcely half as long as a thumb, and they gave her the name of "Little Thumb," or Tiny, because she was so small. A walnut-shell, elegantly polished, served her for a cradle; her bed was formed of blue-violet leaves, with a rose-leaf for a counterpane. Here she slept at night, but during the day she amused herself on a table, where the woman had placed a plate full of water. Round this plate were wreaths of flowers with their stems in the water, and upon it floated a large tulip-leaf, which served Tiny for a boat. Here the little maiden sat and rowed herself from side to side, with two oars made of white horse-hair. It really was a very pretty sight. Tiny could, also, sing so softly and sweetly that nothing like her singing had ever before been heard. One night, while she lay in her pretty bed, a large, ugly, wet toad crept through a broken pane of glass in the window, and leaped right upon the table where Tiny lay sleeping under her rose-leaf quilt. "What a pretty little wife this would make for my son," said the toad, and she took up the walnut-shell in which little Tiny lay asleep, and jumped through the window with it into the garden.

In the swampy margin of a broad stream in the garden lived the toad, with her son. He was uglier even than his mother, and when he saw the pretty little maiden in her elegant bed, he could only cry, "Croak, croak, croak."

"Don't speak so loud, or she will wake," said the toad, "and then she might run away, for she is as light as swan's down. We will place her on one of the water-lily leaves out in the stream; it will be like an island to her, she is so light and small, and then she cannot escape; and, while she is away, we will make haste and prepare the state-room under the marsh, in which you are to live when you are married."

Far out in the stream grew a number of water-lilies, with broad green leaves, which seemed to float on the top of the water. The largest of these leaves appeared farther off than the rest, and the old toad swam out to it with the walnut-shell, in which little Tiny lay still asleep. The tiny little creature woke very early in the morning, and began to cry bitterly when she found where she was, for she could see nothing but water on every side of the large green leaf, and no way of reaching the land. Meanwhile the old toad was very busy under the marsh, decking her room with rushes and wild yellow flowers, to make it look pretty for her new daughter-in-law. Then she swam out with her ugly son to the leaf on which she had placed poor little Tiny. She wanted to fetch the pretty bed, that she might put it in the bridal chamber to be ready for her. The old toad bowed low to her in the water, and said, "Here is my son, he will be your husband, and you will live happily together in the marsh by the stream."

"Croak, croak, croak," was all her son could say for himself; so the toad took up the elegant little bed, and swam away with it, leaving Tiny all alone on the green leaf, where she sat and wept. She could not bear to think of living with the old toad, and having her ugly son for a husband. The little fishes, who swam about in the water beneath, had seen the toad, and heard what she said, so they lifted their heads above the water to look at the little maiden. As soon as they caught sight of her, they saw she was very pretty, and it made them very sorry to think that she must go and live with the ugly toads. "No, it must never be!" so they assembled together in the water, round the green stalk which held the leaf on which the little maiden stood, and gnawed it away at the root with their teeth. Then the leaf floated down the stream, carrying Tiny far away out of reach of land.

Tiny sailed past many towns, and the little birds in the bushes saw her, and sang, "What a lovely little creature;" so the leaf swam away with her farther and farther, till it brought her to other lands. A graceful little white butterfly constantly fluttered round her, and at last alighted on the leaf. Tiny pleased him, and she was glad of it, for now the toad could not possibly reach her, and the country through which she sailed was beautiful, and the sun shone upon the water, till it glittered like liquid gold. She took off her girdle and tied one end of it round the butterfly, and the other end of the ribbon she fastened to the leaf, which now glided on much faster than ever, taking

little Tiny with it as she stood. Presently a large cockchafer flew by; the moment he caught sight of her, he seized her round her delicate waist with his claws, and flew with her into a tree. The green leaf floated away on the brook, and the butterfly flew with it, for he was fastened to it, and could not get away.

Oh, how frightened little Tiny felt when the cockchafer flew with her to the tree! But especially was she sorry for the beautiful white butterfly which she had fastened to the leaf, for if he could not free himself he would die of hunger. But the cockchafer did not trouble himself at all about the matter. He seated himself by her side on a large green leaf, gave her some honey from the flowers to eat, and told her she was very pretty, though not in the least like a cockchafer. After a time, all the cockchafers who lived in the tree came to visit her. They stared at Tiny, and then the young lady-cock-chafers turned up their feelers, and said, "She has only two legs! how ugly that looks." "She has no feelers," said another. "Her waist is quite slim. Pooh! she is like a human being."

"Oh! she is ugly," said all the lady cockchafers, although Tiny was very pretty. Then the cockchafer who had run away with her, believed all the others when they said she was ugly, and would have nothing more to say to her, and told her she might go where she liked. Then he flew down with her from the tree, and placed her on a daisy, and she wept at the thought that she was so ugly that even the cockchafers would have nothing to say to her. And all the while she was really the loveliest creature that one could imagine, and as tender and delicate as a beautiful roseleaf. During the whole summer poor little Tiny lived quite alone in the wide forest. She wove herself a bed with blades of grass, and hung it up under a broad leaf, to protect herself from the rain. She sucked the honey from the flowers for food, and drank the dew from their leaves every morning. So passed away the summer and the autumn, and then came the winter, – the long, cold winter. All the birds who had sung to her so sweetly had flown away, and the trees and the flowers had withered. The large clover leaf, under the shelter of which she had lived, was now rolled together and shrivelled up, nothing remained but a yellow withered stalk. She felt dreadfully cold, for her clothes were torn, and she was herself so frail and delicate, that poor little Tiny was nearly frozen to death. It began to snow too; and the snow-flakes, as they fell upon her, were like a whole shovelful falling upon one of us, for we are tall, but she was only an inch high. Then she wrapped herself up in a dry leaf, but it cracked in the middle, and could not keep her warm and she shivered with cold. Near the wood in which she had been living, lay a large corn-field, but the corn had been cut a long time; nothing remained but the bare dry stubble standing up out of the frozen ground. It was to her like struggl-

26

ing through a large wood. Oh! how she shivered with the cold. She came at
last to the door of a field-mouse, who had a little den under the corn-stubble.
There dwelt the field-mouse in warmth and comfort, with a whole roomful
of corn, a kitchen, and a beautiful dining-room. Poor little Tiny stood before the door just like a little beggar-girl, and begged for a small piece of
barleycorn, for she had been without a morsel to eat for two days.

"You poor little creature," said the field-mouse, who was really a good old
field-mouse, "come into my warm room and dine with me." She was very
pleased with Tiny, so she said, "You are quite welcome to stay with me all
the winter, if you like; but you must keep my rooms clean and neat, and tell
me stories, for I shall like to hear them very much." And Tiny did all the
fieldmouse asked her, and found herself very comfortable.

"We shall have a visitor soon," said the field-mouse one day; "my neighbour pays me a visit once a week. He is better off than I am; he has large
rooms, and wears a beautiful black velvet coat. If you could only have him

27

for a husband, you would be well provided for indeed. But he is blind, so you must tell him some of your prettiest stories."

But Tiny did not feel at all interested about this neighbour, for he was a mole. However, he came and paid his visit, dressed in his black velvet coat. "He is very rich and learned, and his house is twenty times larger than mine," said the field-mouse.

He was rich and learned, no doubt, but he always spoke slightingly of the sun and the pretty flowers, because he had never seen them. Tiny was obliged to sing to him, "Lady-bird, lady-bird, fly away home," and many other pretty songs. And the mole fell in love with her because she had such a sweet voice; but he said nothing yet, for he was very cautious. A short time before, the mole had dug a long passage under the earth, which led from the dwelling of the field-mouse to his own, and here she had permission to walk with Tiny, whenever she liked. But he warned them not to be alarmed at the sight of a dead bird which lay in the passage. It was a perfect bird, with a beak and feathers, and could not have been dead long, and was lying just where the mole had made his passage. The mole took a piece of phosphorescent wood in his mouth, and it glittered like fire in the dark; then he went before them to light them through the long, dark passage. When they came to the spot where lay the dead bird, the mole pushed his broad nose through the ceiling, the earth gave way, so that there was a large hole, and the daylight shone into the passage. In the middle of the floor lay a dead swallow, his beautiful wings pulled close to his sides, his feet and his head drawn up under his feathers; the poor bird had evidently died of the cold. It made little Tiny very sad to see it, she did so love the little birds; all the summer they had sung and twittered for her so beauti-fully. But the mole pushed it aside with his crooked legs, and said, "He will sing no more now. How miserable it must be to be born a little bird! I am thankful that none of my children will ever be birds, for they can do nothing but cry, 'Tweet, tweet,' and always die of hunger in the winter."

"Yes, you may well say that, as a clever man!" exclaimed the field-mouse, "What is the use of his twittering, for when winter comes he must either starve or be frozen to death. Still birds are very high bred."

Tiny said nothing; but when the two others had turned their backs on the bird, she stooped down and stroked aside the soft feathers which covered the head, and kissed the closed eyelids "Perhaps this was the one who sang to me so sweetly in the summer," she said; "and how much pleasure it gave me, you dear, pretty bird."

The mole now stopped up the hole through which the daylight shone, and then accompanied the ladies home. But during the night Tiny could not sleep; so she got out of bed and wove a large, beautiful carpet of hay; then

she carried it to the dead bird, and spread it over him, with some down from the flowers which she had found in the field-mouse's room. It was as soft as wool, and she spread some of it on each side of the bird, so that he might lie warmly in the cold earth. "Farewell, you pretty little bird," said she, "farewell; thank you for your delightful singing during the summer, when all the trees were green, and the warm sun shone upon us." Then she laid her head on the bird's breast, but she was alarmed immediately, for it seemed as if something inside the bird went "thump, thump." It was the bird's heart; he was not really dead, only benumbed with the cold, and the warmth had restored him to life. In autumn, all the swallows fly away into warm countries, but if one happens to linger, the cold seizes it, it becomes frozen, and fall down as if dead; it remains where it fell, and the cold snow covers it. Tiny trembled very much; she was quite frightened, for the bird was large, a great deal larger than herself, – she was only an inch high. But she took courage, laid the wool more thickly over the poor swallow, and then took a leaf which she had used for her own counterpane, and laid it over the head of the poor bird. The next night she again stole out to see him. He was alive but very weak; he could only open his eyes for a moment to look at Tiny, who stood by holding a piece of decayed wood in her hand, for she had no other lantern. "Thank you, pretty little maiden," said the sick swallow; "I have been so nicely warmed, that I shall soon regain my strength, and be able to fly about again in the warm sunshine."

"Oh," said she, "it is cold out of doors now; it snows and freezes. Stay in your warm bed; I will take care of you."

Then she brought the swallow some water in a flower-leaf, and after he had drank, he told her that the had wounded one of his wings in a thorn-bush, and could not fly as fast as the others, who were soon far away on their journey to warm countries. Then at last he had fallen to the earth, and could remember no more, nor how he came to be where she had found him. The whole winter the swallow remained underground, and Tiny nursed him with care and love. Neither the mole nor the field-mouse knew anything about it, for they did not like swallows. Very soon the spring time came, and the sun warmed the earth. Then the swallow bade farewell to Tiny, and she opened the hole in the ceiling which the mole had made. The sun shone in upon them so beautifully, that the swallow asked her if she would go with him; she could sit on his back, he said, and he would fly away with her into the green woods. But Tiny knew it would make the field-mouse very grieved if she left her in that manner, so she said, "No, I cannot."

"Farewell, then, farewell, you good, pretty little maiden," said the swallow; and he flew out into the sunshine.

Tiny looked after him, and the tears rose in her eyes. She was very fond of the poor swallow.

"Tweet, tweet," sang the bird, as he flew out into the green woods, and Tiny felt very sad. She was not allowed to go out into the warm sunshine. The corn which had been sown in the field over the house of the field-mouse had grown up high into the air, and formed a thick wood to Tiny, who was only an inch in height.

"You are going to be married, Tiny," said the field-mouse. "My neighbour has asked for you. What good fortune for a poor child like you! Now we will prepare your wedding clothes. They must be both woollen and linen. Nothing must be wanting when you are the mole's wife."

Tiny had to turn the spindle, and the field-mouse hired four spiders, who were to weave day and night. Every evening the mole visited her, and was continually speaking of the time when the summer would be over. Then he would keep his weddingday with Tiny; but now the heat of the sun was so great that it burned the earth, and made it quite hard, like a stone. As soon as the summer was over, the wedding should take place. But Tiny was not at

all pleased; for she did not like the tiresome mole. Every morning when the
sun rose, and every evening when it went down, she would creep out at the
door, and as the wind blew aside the ears of corn, so that she could see the
blue sky, she thought how beautiful and bright it seemed out there, and
wished so much to see her dear swallow again. But he never returned; for
by this time he had flown far away into the lovely green forest.

When autumn arrived, Tiny had her outfit quite ready; and the field-
mouse said to her, "In four weeks the wedding must take place."

Then Tiny wept, and said she would not marry the disagreeable mole.

"Nonsense," replied the field-mouse. "Now don't be obstinate, or I shall
bite you with my white teeth. He is a very handsome mole; the queen herself
does not wear more beautiful velvets and furs. His kitchens and cellars are
quite full. You ought to be very thankful for such good fortune."

So the wedding-day was fixed, on which the mole was to fetch Tiny away to
live with him, deep under the earth, and never again to see the warm sun,
because *he* did not like it. The poor child was very unhappy at the thought of
saying farewell to the beautiful sun, and as the field-mouse had given her
permission to stand at the door, she went to look at it once more.

"Farewell, bright sun," she cried, stretching out her arm towards it; and then she walked a short distance from the house; for the corn had been cut, and only the dry stubble remained in the fields. "Farewell, farewell," she repeated, twining her arm round a little red flower that grew just by her side. "Greet the little swallow from me, if you should see him again."

"Tweet, tweet," sounded over her head suddenly. She looked up, and there was the swallow himself flying close by. As soon as he spied Tiny, he was delighted; and then she told him how unwilling she felt to marry the ugly mole, and to live always beneath the earth, and never to see the bright sun any more. And as she told him, she wept.

"Cold winter is coming," said the swallow, "and I am going to fly away into warmer countries. Will you go with me? You can sit on my back, and fasten yourself on with your sash. Then we can fly away from the ugly mole and his gloomy rooms, – far away, over the mountains, into warmer countries, where the sun shines more brightly than here; where it is always summer, and the flowers bloom in greater beauty. Fly now with me, dear little Tiny; you saved my life when I lay frozen in that dark, dreary passage."

"Yes, I will go with you," said Tiny; and she seated herself on the bird's back, with her feet on his outstretched wings, and tied her girdle to one of his strongest feathers.

Then the swallow rose in the air, and flew over forest and over sea, high above the highest mountains, covered with eternal snow. Tiny would have been frozen in the cold air, but she crept under the bird's warm feathers, keeping her little head uncovered, so that she might admire the beautiful lands over which they passed. At length they reached the warm countries, where the sun shines brightly, and the sky seems so much higher above the earth. Here, on the hedges, and by the wayside, grew purple, green, and white grapes; lemons and oranges hung from trees in the woods; and the air was fragrant with myrtles and orange blossoms. Beautiful children ran along the country lanes, playing with large gay butterflies; and as the swallow flew farther and farther, every place appeared still more lovely.

At last they came to a blue lake, and by the side of it, shaded by trees of the deepest green, stood a palace of dazzling white marble, built in the olden times. Vines clustered round its lofty pillars, and at the top were many swallows' nests, and one of these was the home of the swallow who carried Tiny.

"This is my house," said the swallow; "but it would not do for you to live there – you would not be comfortable. You must choose for yourself one of those lovely flowers, and I will put you down upon it, and then you shall have everything that you can wish to make you happy."

"That will be delightful," she said, and clapped her little hands for joy.

A large marble pillar lay on the ground, which, in falling, had been broken into three pieces. Between these pieces grew the most beautiful large white flowers; so the swallow flew down with Tiny, and placed her on one of the broad leaves. But how surprised she was to see in the middle of the flower; a tiny little man, as white and transparent as if he had been made of crystal! He had a gold crown on his head, and delicate wings at his shoulders, and was not much larger than Tiny herself. He was the angel of the flower; for a tiny man and a tiny woman dwell in every flower; and this was the king of them all.

"Oh, how beautiful he is!" whispered Tiny to the swallow.

The little prince was at first quite frightened at the bird, who was like a giant, compared to such a delicate little creature as himself; but when he saw Tiny, he was delighted, and thought her the prettiest little maiden he had ever seen. He took the gold crown from his head, and placed it on hers, and asked her name, and if she would be his wife, and queen over all the flowers. This certainly was a very different sort of husband to the son of the toad, or the mole, with his black velvet and fur; so she said, "Yes," to the handsome prince. Then all the flowers opened, and out of each came a little lady or a tiny lord, all so pretty it was quite a pleasure to look at them. Each of them brought Tiny a present; but the best fit was a pair of beautiful wings, which had belonged to a large white fly, and they fastened them to Tiny's shoulders, so that she might fly from flower to flower. Then there was much rejoicing, and the little swallow, who sat above them, in his nest, was asked to sing a wedding song, which he did as well as he could; but in his heart he felt sad, for he was very fond of Tiny, and would have liked never to part from her again.

"You must not be called Tiny any more," said the spirit of the flowers to her. "It is an ugly name, and you are so very pretty. We will call you Maia."

"Farewell, farewell," said the swallow, with a heavy heart, as he left the warm countries, to fly back into Denmark. There he had a nest over the window of a house in which dwelt the writer of fairy tales. The swallow sang, "Tweet, tweet," and from his song came the whole story.

33

The Flying Trunk

There was once a merchant who was so rich that he could have paved the whole street with gold, and would even then have had enough for a small alley. But he did not do so; he knew the value of money better than to use it in this way. So clever was he, that every shilling he put out brought him a crown; and so he continued till he died. His son inherited his wealth, and he lived a merry life with it; he went to a masquerade every night, made kites out of five-pound notes, and threw pieces of gold into the sea instead of stones, making ducks and drakes of them. In this manner he soon lost all his money. At last he had nothing left but a pair of slippers, an old dressing-gown, and four shillings. And now all his friends deserted him, they could not walk with him in the streets; but one of them, who was very good-natured, sent him an old trunk with this message, "Pack up!" "Yes," he said, "it is all very well to say 'pack up;'" but he had nothing left to pack up, therefore he seated himself in the trunk. It was a very wonderful trunk; no sooner did any one press on the lock than the trunk could fly. He shut the lid and pressed the lock, when away flew the trunk up the chimney with the merchant's son in it, right up into the clouds. Whenever the bottom of the trunk cracked, he was in a great fright, for if the trunk fell to pieces he would have made a tremendous sommersault over the trees. However, he got safely in his trunk to the land of Turkey. He hid the trunk in the wood under some dry leaves, and then went into the town: he could do this very well, for the Turks always go about dressed in dressing-gowns and slippers, as he was himself. He happened to meet a nurse with a little child. "I say, you Turkish nurse," cried he, "what castle is that near the town, with the windows placed so high?"

"The king's daughter lives there," she replied; "it has been prophesied she will be very unhappy about a lover, and therefore no one is allowed to visit her, unless the king and queen are present."

"Thank you," said the merchant's son. So he went back to the wood, seated himself in his trunk, flew up to the roof of the castle, and crept through the window into the princess's room. She lay on the sofa asleep, and she was so beautiful that the merchant's son could not help kissing her. Then she awoke, and was very much frightened; but he told her he was a Turkish angel, who had come down through the air to see her, which pleased her very much. He sat down by her side and talked to her: he said her eyes were like beautiful dark lakes, in which the thoughts swam about like little mermaids, and he told her that her forehead was a snowy mountain, which contained splendid halls full of pictures. And then he related to her about the stork who brings the beautiful children from the rivers. These were delightful stories; and when he asked the princess if she would marry him, she consented immediately.

"But you must come on Saturday," she said; "for then the king and queen will take tea with me. They will be very proud when they find that I am going to marry a Turkish angel; but you must think of some very pretty stories to tell them, for my parents like to hear stories better than anything. My mother prefers one that is deep and moral; but my father likes something funny, to make him laugh."

"Very well," he replied; "I shall bring you no other marriage portion than a story," and so they parted. But the princess gave him a sword which was studded with gold coins, and these he could use.

Then he flew away to the town and bought a new dressing-gown, and afterwards returned to the wood, where he composed a story, so as to be ready by Saturday, which was no easy matter. It was ready however by Saturday, when he went to see the princess. The king, and queen, and the whole court, were at tea with the princess; and he was received with great politeness.

"Will you tell us a story?" said the queen, – "one that is instructive and full of deep learning."

"Yes, but with something in it to laugh at," said the king.

"Certainly," he replied, and commenced at once, asking them to listen attentively. "There was once a bundle of matches that were exceedingly proud of their high descent. Their genealogical tree, that is, a large pine-tree from which they had been cut, was at one time a large, old tree in the wood. The matches now lay between a tinder-box and an old iron saucepan, and were talking about their youthful days. 'Ah! then we grew on the green boughs, and were as green as they; every morning and evening we were fed with diamond drops of dew. Whenever the sun shone, we felt his warm rays, and the little birds would relate stories to us as they sung. We knew that we were rich, for the other trees only wore their green dress in summer, but our family were able to array themselves in green, summer and winter. But the woodcutter came, like a great revolution, and our family fell under the axe. The head of the house obtained a situation as main-mast in a very fine ship, and can sail round the world when he will. The other branches of the

family were taken to different places, and our office now is to kindle a light for common people. This is how such high-born people as we came to be in a kitchen.'

"'Mine has been a very different fate,' said the iron pot, which stood by the matches; 'from my first entrance into the world I have been used to cooking and scouring. I am the first in this house, when anything solid or useful is required. My only pleasure is to be made clean and shining after dinner, and to sit in my place and have a little sensible conversation with my neighbours. All of us, excepting the water-bucket, which is sometimes taken into the courtyard, live here together within these four walls. We get our news from the market-basket, but he sometimes tells us very unpleasant things about the people and the government. Yes, and one day an old pot was so alarmed, that he fell down and was broken to pieces. He was a liberal, I can tell you.'

"'You are talking too much,' said the tinder-box; and the steel struck against the flint till some sparks flew out, crying,' We want a merry evening, don't we?'

"'Yes, of course,' said the matches, 'let us talk about those who are the highest born.'

"'No, I don't like to be always talking of what we are,' remarked the saucepan; 'let us think of some other amusement; I will begin. We will tell something that has happened to ourselves; that will be very easy, and interesting as well. On the Baltic Sea, near the Danish shore' –

"'What a pretty commencement!' said the plates; 'we shall all like that story, I am sure.'

"'Yes; well, in my youth, I lived in a quiet family, where the furniture was polished, the floors scoured, and clean curtains put up every fortnight.'

"'What an interesting way you have of relating a story,' said the carpet-broom; 'it is easy to perceive that you have been a great deal in women's society, there is something so pure runs through what you say.'

"'That is quite true,' said the water-bucket; and he made a spring with joy, and splashed some water on the floor.

"Then the saucepan went on with his story, and the end was as good as the beginning.

"The plates rattled with pleasure, and the carpet-broom brought some green parsley out of the dust-hole and crowned the saucepan, for he knew it would vex the others; and the thought, 'If I crown him to-day he will crown me to-morrow.'

"'Now, let us have a dance,' said the fire-tongs; and then how they danced and stuck up one leg in the air. The chair-cushion in the corner burst with laughter when she saw it.

"'Shall I be crowned now?' asked the fire-tongs; so the broom found another wreath for the tongs.

"'They are only common people after all,' thought the matches. The tea-urn was now asked to sing, but she said she had a cold, and could not sing without boiling heat. They all thought this was affectation, and because she did not wish to sing excepting in the parlour, when on the table with the grand people.

"In the window sat an old quill-pen, with which the maid generally wrote. There was nothing remarkable about the pen, excepting that it had been dipped too deeply in the ink, but it was proud of that.

"'If the tea-urn won't sing,' said the pen, 'she can leave it alone; there is a nightingale in a cage who can sing; she has not been taught much, certainly, but we need not say anything this evening about that.'

"'I think it highly improper,' said the tea-kettle, who was kitchen singer, and half-brother to the tea-urn, 'that a rich foreign bird should be listened to here. Is it patriotic? Let the market-basket decide what is right.'

"'I certainly am vexed,' said the basket; 'inwardly vexed, more than any one can imagine. Are we spending the evening properly? Would it not be more sensible to put the house in order? If each were in his own place I would lead a game; this would be quite another thing.'

"'Let us act a play,' said they all. At the same moment the door opened, and the maid came in. Then not one stirred; they all remained quite still; yet, at the same time, there was not a single pot amongst them who had not a high opinion of himself, and of what he could do if he chose.

"'Yes, if we had chosen,' they each thought, 'we might have spent a very pleasant evening.'

"The maid took the matches and lighted them; dear me, how they sputtered and blazed up!

"'Now them,' they thought, 'every one will see that we are the first. How we shine; what a light we give!' Even while they spoke their light went out."

"What a capital story," said the queen, "If feel as if I were really in the kitchen, and could see the matches; yes, you shall marry our daughter."

"Certainly," said the king, "thou shall have our daughter." The king said *thou* to him because he was going to be one of the family. The wedding-day was fixed, and, on the evening before, the whole city was illuminated. Cakes and sweetmeats were thrown among the people. The street boys stood on tip-toe and shouted "hurrah," and whistled between their fingers; altogether it was a very splendid affair.

"I will give them another treat," said the merchant's son. So he went and bought rockets and crackers, and all sorts of fireworks that could be thought of; packed them in his trunk, and flew up with it into the air. What a whizzing

40

and popping they made as they went off! The Turks, when they saw such a sight in the air, jumped up so high that their slippers flew about their ears. It was easy to believe after this that the princess was really going to marry a Turkish angel.

As soon as the merchant's son had come down in his flying trunk to the wood after the fireworks, he thought, "I will go back into the town, and hear what they think of the entertainment." It was very natural that he should wish to know. And what strange things people did say, to be sure! every one whom he questioned had a different tale to tell, though they all thought it very beautiful.

"I saw the Turkish angel myself," said one; "he had eyes like glittering stars, and a head like foaming water."

"He flew in a mantle of fire,' cried another, "and lovely little cherubs peeped out from the folds."

He heard many more fine things about himself, and that the next day he was to be married. After this he went back to the forest to rest himself in his trunk. It had disappeared! A spark from the fireworks which remained had set it on fire; it was burnt to ashes! So the merchant's son could not fly any more, nor go to meet his bride. She stood all day on the roof waiting for him, and most likely she is waiting there still; while he wanders through the world telling fairy tales, but none of them so amusing as the one he related about the matches.

The Story of a Mother

A mother sat by her little child; she was very sad, for she feared it would die. It was quite pale, and its little eyes were closed, and sometimes it drew a heavy deep breath, almost like a sigh; and then the mother gazed more sadly than ever on the poor little creature. Some one knocked at the door, and a poor old man walked in. He was wrapped in something that looked like a great horse-cloth; and he required it truly to keep him warm, for it was cold winter; the country everywhere lay covered with snow and ice, and the wind blew so sharply that it cut one's face. The little child had dozed off to sleep for a moment, and the mother, seeing that the old man shivered with the cold, rose and placed a small mug of beer on the stove to warm for him. The old man sat and rocked the cradle; and the mother seated herself on a chair near him, and looked at her sick child who still breathed heavily, and took hold of its little hand.

"You think I shall keep him, do you not?" she said. "Our all-merciful God will surely not take him away from me."

The old man, who was indeed Death himself, nodded his head in a peculiar manner, which might have signified either Yes, or No; and the mother cast down her eyes, while the tears rolled down her cheeks. Then her head became heavy, for she had not closed her eyes for three days and nights, and she slept, but only for a moment. Shivering with cold, she started up and looked round the room. The old man was gone, and her child – it was gone too! – the old man had taken it with him. In the corner of the room the old clock began to strike; "whirr" went the chains, the heavy weight sank to the ground, and the clock stopped; and the poor mother rushed out of the house calling for her child. Out in the snow sat a woman in long black garments, and she said to the mother, "Death has been with you in your room. I saw him hasting away with your little child; he strides faster than the wind, and never brings back what he has taken away."

"Only tell me which way he has gone," said the mother; "tell me the way, I will find him."

"I know the way," said the woman in the black garments; "but before I tell you, you must sing to me all the songs that you have sung to your child; I love these songs, I have heard them before. I am Night, and I saw your tears flow as you sang."

"I will sing them all to you," said the mother; "but do not detain me now. I must overtake him, and find my child."

But Night sat silent and still. Then the mother wept and sang, and wrung her hands. And there were many songs, and yet even more tears; till at length Night said, "Go to the right, into the dark forest of fire-trees; for I saw Death take that road with your little child."

Within the wood the mother came to cross roads, and she knew not which to take. Just by stood a thorn-bush; it had neither leaf nor flower, for it was the cold winter time, and icicles hung on the branches. "Have you not seen Death go by, with my little child?" she asked.

"Yes," replied the thorn-bush; "but I will not tell you which way he has taken until you have warmed me in your bosom. I am freezing to death here, and turning to ice."

Then she pressed the bramble to her bosom quite close, so that it might be thawed, and the thorns pierced her flesh, and great drops of blood flowed; but the bramble shot forth fresh green leaves, and they became flowers on the cold winter's night, so warm is the heart of a sorrowing mother. Then the bramble-bush told her the path she must take. She came at length to a great lake, on which there was neither ship nor boat to be seen. The lake was not frozen sufficiently for her to pass over on the ice, nor was it open enough for her to wade through; and yet she must cross it, if she wished to find her child. Then she laid herself down to drink up the water of the lake, which was of course impossible for any human being to do; but the bereaved mother thought that perhaps a miracle might take place to help her.

"You will never succeed in this," said the lake; "let us make an agreement together, which will be better. I love to collect pearls, and your eyes are the purest I have ever seen. If you will weep those eyes away in tears into my waters, then I will take you to the large hothouse where Death dwells and rears flowers and trees, every one of which is a human life."

"Oh, what would I not give to reach my child!" said the weeping mother; and as she still continued to weep, her eyes fell into the depths of the lake, and became two costly pearls.

Then the lake lifted her up, and wafted her across to the opposite shore as if she were on a swing, where stood a wonderful building many miles in length. No one could tell whether it was a mountain covered with forests and full of caves, or whether it had been built. But the poor mother could not see, for she had wept out her eyes into the lake. "Where shall I find Death, who went away with my little child?" she asked.

45

"He has not arrived here yet," said an old grey-haired woman, who was walking about, and watering Death's hothouse. "How have you found your way here? and who helped you?"

"God has helped me," she replied. "He is merciful; will you not be merciful too? Where shall I find my little child?"

"I do not know the child," said the old woman; "and you are blind. Many flowers and trees have faded to-night, and Death will soon come to transplant them. You know already that every human being has a life-tree or a life-flower, just as may be ordained for him. They look like other plants; but they have hearts that beat. Children's hearts also beat; from that you may perhaps be able to recognise your child. But what will you give me, if I tell you what more you will have to do?"

"I have nothing to give," said the afflicted mother; "but I would go to the ends of the earth for you."

"I can give you nothing to do for me there," said the old woman; "but you can give me your long black hair. You know yourself that it is beautiful, and it pleases me. You can take my white hair in exchange, which will be something in return."

"Do you ask nothing more than that?" said she. "I will give it you with pleasure."

And she gave up her beautiful hair, and received in return the white locks of the old woman. Then they went into Death's vast hothouse, where flowers and trees grew together in wonderful profusion. Blooming hyacinths, under glass bells, and peonies, like strong trees. There grew water-plants, some quite fresh, others looking sickly, which had water-snakes twining round them, and black crabs clinging to their stems. There stood noble palm-trees, oaks, and plantains, and beneath them bloomed thyme and parsley. Each tree and flower had a name; each represented a human life, and belonged to men still living, some in China, others in Greenland, and in all parts of the world. Some large trees had been planted in little pots, so that they were cramped for room, and seemed about to burst the pot in pieces; while many weak little flowers were growing in rich soil, with moss all around them, carefully tended and cared for. The sorrowing mother bent over the little plants, and heard the human heart beating in each, and recognised the beatings of her child's heart among millions of others.

"That is it," she cried, stretching out her hand towards a little crocus-flower which hung down its sickly head.

"Do not touch the flower," exclaimed the old woman; "but place yourself here; and when Death comes – I expect him every minute – do not let him pull up that plant, but threaten him that if he does you will serve the other

46

flowers in the same manner. This will make him afraid; for he must account to God for each of them. None can be uprooted, unless he receives permission to do so."

There rushed through the hothouse a chill of icy coldness, and the blind mother felt that Death had arrived.

"How did you find your way hither?" asked he; "how could you come here faster than I have?"

"I am a mother," she answered.

And Death stretched out his hand towards the delicate little flower; but she held her hands tightly round it, and held it fast at the same time, with the most anxious care, lest she should touch one of the leaves. Then Death breathed upon her hands, and she felt his breath colder than the icy wind, and her hands sank down powerless.

"You cannot prevail against me," said Death.

"But a God of mercy can," said she.

"I only do His will," replied Death. "I am His gardener. I take all His flowers and trees, and transplant them into the gardens of Paradise in an unknown land. How they flourish there, and what that garden resembles. I may not tell you."

"Give me back my child," said the mother, weeping and imploring; and she seized two beautiful flowers in her hands, and cried to Death, "I will tear up all your flowers, for I am in despair."

"Do not touch them," said Death. "You say you are unhappy; and would you make another mother as unhappy as yourself?"

"Another mother!" cried the poor woman, setting the flowers free from her hands.

"There are your eyes," said Death. "I fished them up out of the lake for you. They were shining brightly; but I knew not they were yours. Take them – they are clearer now than before – and then look into the deep well which is close by here. I will tell you the names of the two flowers which you wished to pull up; and you will see the whole future of the human beings they represent, and what you were about to frustrate and destroy."

Then she looked into the well; and it was a glorious sight to behold how one of them became a blessing to the world, and how much happiness and joy it spread around. But she saw that the life of the other was full of care and poverty, misery and woe.

"Both are the will of God," said Death.

"Which is the unhappy flower, and which is the blessed one?" she asked.

"That I may not tell you," said Death; "but thus far you may learn, that one of the two flowers represents your own child. It was the fate of your child that you saw, – the future of your own child."

47

Then the mother screamed aloud with terror, "Which of them belongs to my child? Tell me that. Deliver the unhappy child. Release it from so much misery. Rather take it away. Take it to the kingdom of God. Forget my tears and my entreaties; forget all that I have said or done."

"I do not understand you," said Death. "Will you have your child back? or shall I carry him away to a place that you do not know?"

Then the mother wrung her hands, fell on her knees, and prayed to God, "Grand not my prayers, when they are contrary to Thy will, which at all times must be the best. Oh, hear them not;" and her head sank on her bosom.

Then Death carried away her child to the unknown land.

The Nightingale

In China, you know, the emperor is a Chinese, and all those about him are Chinamen also. The story I am going to tell you happened a great many years ago, so it is well to hear it now before it is forgotten. The emperor's palace was the most beautiful in the world. It was built entirely of porcelain, and very costly, but so delicate and brittle that whoever touched it was obliged to be careful. In the garden could be seen the most singular flowers, with pretty silver bells tied to them, which tinkled so that every one who passed could not help noticing the flowers. Indeed, everything in the emperor's garden was remarkable, and it extended so far that the gardener himself did not know where it ended. Those who travelled beyond its limits knew that there was a noble forest, with lofty trees, sloping down to the deep blue sea, and the great ships sailed under the shadow of its branches. In one of these trees lived a nightingale, who sang so beautifully that even the poor fishermen, who had so many other things to do, would stop and listen. Sometimes, when they went at night to spread their nets, they would hear her sing, and say, "Oh, is not that beautiful?" But when they returned to their fishing, they forgot the bird until the next night. Then they would hear it again, and exclaim "Oh, how beautiful is the nightingale's song!"

Travellers from every country in the world came to the city of the emperor, which they admired very much, as well as the palace and gardens; but when they heard the nightingale, they all declared it to be the best of all. And the travellers, on their return home, related what they had seen; and learned men wrote books, containing descriptions of the town, the palace, and the gardens; but they did not forget the nightingale, which was really the greatest wonder. And those who could write poetry composed beautiful verses about the nightingale, who lived in a forest near the deep sea. The books travelled all over the world, and some of them came into the hands of the emperor; and he sat in his golden chair, and, as he read, he nodded his approval every moment, for it pleased him to find such a beautiful description of his city, his palace, and his gardens. But when he came to the words, "the nightingale is the most beautiful of all," he exclaimed, "What is this? I know nothing of any nightingale. Is there such a bird in my empire? and even in my garden? I have never heard of it. Something, it appears, may be learnt from books."

Then he called one of his lords-in-waiting, who was so high-bred, that when any in an inferior rank to himself spoke to him, or asked him a question, he would answer, "Pooh," which means nothing.

"There is a very wonderful bird mentioned here, called a nightingale," said the emperor; "they say it is the best thing in my large kingdom. Why have I not been told of it?"

"I have never heard the name," replied the cavalier; "she has not been presented at court."

"It is my pleasure that she shall appear this evening," said the emperor; "the whole world knows what I possess better than I do myself."

"I have never heard of her," said the cavalier; "yet I will endeavour to find her."

But where was the nightingale to be found? The nobleman went upstairs and down, through halls and passages; yet none of those whom he met had heard of the bird. So he returned to the emperor, and said that it must be a fable, invented by those who had written the book. "Your imperial majesty," said he, "cannot believe everything contained in books; sometimes they are only fiction, or what is called the black art."

"But the book in which I have read this account," said the emperor, "was sent to me by the great and mighty emperor of Japan, and therefore it cannot contain a falsehood. I will hear the nightingale, she must be here this evening; she has my highest favour; and if she does not come, the whole court shall be trampled upon after supper is ended."

"Tsing-pe!" cried the lord-in-waiting, and again he ran up and down stairs, through all the halls and corridors; and half the court ran with him, for they did not like the idea of being trampled upon. There was a great inquiry about this wonderful nightingale, whom all the world knew, but who was unknown to the court.

At last they met with a poor little girl in the kitchen, who said, "Oh yes, I know the nightingale quite well; indeed, she can sing. Every evening I have permission to take home to my poor sick mother the scraps from the table; she lives down by the seashore, and as I come back I feel tired, and I sit down in the wood to rest, and listen to the nightingale's song. Then the tears come into my eyes, and it is just as if my mother kissed me."

"Little maiden," said the lord-in-waiting, "I will obtain for you constant employment in the kitchen, and you shall have permission to see the emperor dine, if you will lead us to the nightingale; for she is invited for this evening to the palace." So she went into the wood where the nightingale sang, and half the court followed her. As they went along, a cow began lowing.

"Oh," said a young courtier, "now we have found her; what wonderful power for such a small creature; I have certainly heard it before."

"No, that is only a cow lowing," said the little girl; "we are a long way from the place yet."

Then some frogs began to croak in the marsh.

"Beautiful," said the young courtier again. "Now I hear it, tinkling like little church bells."

"No, those are frogs," said the little maiden; "but I think we shall soon hear her now:" and presently the nightingale began to sing.

"Hark, hark! there she is," said the girl, "and there she sits," she added, pointing to a little grey bird who was perched on a bough.

"Is it possible?" said the lord-in-waiting, "I never imagined it would be a plain, simple thing like that. She has certainly changed colour at seeing so many grand people around her."

"Little nightingale," cried the girl, raising her voice, "our most gracious emperor wishes you to sing before him."

"With the greatest pleasure," said the nightingale, and began to sing most delightfully.

"It sounds like tiny glass bells," said the lord-in-waiting, "and see how her little throat works. It is surprising that we have never heard this before; she will be a great success at court."

53

"Shall I sing once more before the emperor?" asked the nightingale, who thought he was present.

"My excellent little nightingale," said the courtier, "I have the great pleasure of inviting you to a court festival this evening, where you will gain imperial favour by your charming song."

"My song sounds best in the green wood," said the bird; but still she came willingly when she heard the emperor's wish.

The palace was elegantly decorated for the occasion. The walls and floors of porcelain glittered in the light of a thousand lamps. Beautiful flowers, round which little bells were tied, stood in the corridors: what with the running to and fro and the draught, these bells tinkled so loudly that no one could speak to be heard. In the centre of the great hall, a golden perch had been fixed for the nightingale to sit on. The whole court was present, and the little kitchen-maid had received permission to stand by the door. She was now installed as a real court cook. All were in full dress, and every eye was turned to the little grey bird when the emperor nodded to her to begin. The nightingale sang so sweetly that the tears came into the emperor's eyes, and then rolled down his cheeks, as her song became still more touching and went to every one's heart. The emperor was so delighted that he declared the nightingale should have his gold slipper to wear round her neck, but she declined the honour with thanks: she had been sufficiently rewarded already. "I have seen tears in an emperor's eyes," she said, "that is my richest reward. An emperor's tears have wonderful power, and are quite sufficient honour for me;" and then she sang again more enchantingly than ever.

"Than singing is a lovely gift," said the ladies of the court to each other; and then they took water in their mouths to make them utter the gurgling sounds of the nightingale when they spoke to any one, so that they might fancy themselves nightingales. And the footmen and chambermaids also expressed their satisfaction, which is saying a great deal, for they are very difficult to please. In fact the nightingale's visit was most successful. She was now to remain at court, to have her own cage, with liberty to go out twice a day, and once during the night. Twelve servants were appointed to attend her on these occasions, who each held her by a silken string fastened to her leg. There was certainly not much pleasure in this kind of flying.

The whole city spoke of the wonderful bird, and when two people met, one said "nightin," and the other said "gale," and they understood what was meant, for nothing else was talked of. Eleven pedlars' children were named after her, but not one of them could sing a note.

One day the emperor received a large packet on which was written "The Nightingale." "Here is no doubt a new book about our celebrated bird,"

said the emperor. But instead of a book, it was a work of art contained in a casket, an artificial nightingale made to look like a living one, and covered all over with diamonds, rubies, and sapphires. As soon as the artificial bird was wound up, it could sing like the real one, and could move its tail up and down, which sparkled with silver and gold. Round its neck hung a piece of ribbon, on which was written "The Emperor of China's nightingale is poor compared with that of the Emperor of Japan's."

"This is very beautiful," exclaimed all who saw it, and he who had brought the artificial bird received the title of "Imperial nightingale-bringer-in chief."

"Now they must sing together," said the court, "and what a duet it will be." But they did not get on well, for the real nightingale sang in its own natural way, but the artificial bird sang only waltzes.

"That is not a fault," said the music-master, "it is quite perfect to my taste," so then it had to sing alone, and was as successful as the real bird; besides, it was so much prettier to look at, for it sparkled like bracelets and breast-pins. Three and thirty times did it sing the same tunes without being tired: the people would gladly have heard it again, but the emperor said the living nightingale ought to sing something. But where was she? No one had noticed her when she flew out at the open window, back to her own green woods.

"What strange conduct," said the emperor, when her flight had been discovered; and all the courtiers blamed her, and said she was a very un-grateful creature.

"But we have the best bird after all," said one, and then they would have the bird sing again, although it was the thirty-fourth time they had listened to the same piece, and even then they had not learnt it, for it was rather difficult. But the music-master praised the bird in the highest degree, and even assert-ed that it was better than a real nightingale, not only in its dress and the beautiful diamonds, but also in its musical power. "For you must perceive, my chief lord and emperor, that with a real nightingale we can never tell what is going to be sung, but with this bird everything is settled. It can be opened and explained, so that people may understand how the waltzes are formed, and why one note follows upon another."

"This is exactly what we think," they all replied, and then the music-master received permission to exhibit the bird to the people on the following Sunday, and the emperor commanded that they should be present to hear it sing. When they heard it they were like people intoxicated; however it must have been with drinking tea, which is quite a Chinese custom. They all said "Oh!" and held up their forefingers and nodded, but a poor fisherman, who had heard the real nightingale, said, "It sounds prettily enough, and the melodies are all alike; yet there seems something wanting, I cannot exactly tell what."

And after this the real nightingale was banished from the empire, and the artificial bird placed on a silk cushion close to the emperor's bed. The presents of gold and precious stones which had been received with it were round the bird, and it was now advanced to the title of "Little Imperial Toilet Singer," and to the rank of No. 1 on the left hand; for the emperor considered the left side, on which the heart lies, as the most noble, and the heart of an emperor is in the same place as that of other people.

The music-master wrote a work, in twenty-five volumes, about the artificial bird, which was very learned and very long, and full of the most difficult Chinese words: yet all the people said they had read it, and understood it, for fear of being thought stupid and having their bodies trampled upon.

So a year passed, and the emperor, the court, and all the other Chinese knew every little turn in the artificial bird's song; and for that same reason it pleased them better. They could sing with the bird, which they often did. The street-boys sang, "Zi-zi-zi, cluck, cluck, cluck," and the emperor himself could sing it also. It was really most amusing.

One evening, when the artificial bird was singing its best, and the emperor lay in bed listening to it, something inside the bird sounded "whizz." Then a spring cracked. "Whir-r-r-r" went all the wheels, running round, and then the music stopped. The emperor immediately sprang out of bed, and called for his physician; but what could he do? Then they sent for a watchmaker; and, after a great deal of talking and examination, the bird was put into something like order; but he said that it must be used very carefully, as the barrels were worn, and it would be impossible to put in new ones without injuring the music. Now there was great sorrow, as the bird could only be allowed to play once a year; and even that was dangerous for the works inside it. Then the music-master made a little speech, full of hard words, and declared that the bird was as good as ever; and, of course, no one contradicted him.

Five years passed, and then a real grief came upon the land. The Chinese really were fond of their emperor, and he now lay so ill that he was not expected to live. Already a new emperor had been chosen, and the people who stood in the street asked the lord-in-waiting how the old emperor was; but he only said, "Pooh!" and shook his head.

Cold and pale, lay the emperor in his royal bed; the whole court thought he was dead, and every one ran away to pay homage to his successor. The chamberlains went out to have a talk on the matter, and the ladies'-maids invited company to take coffee. Cloth had been laid down on the halls and passages, so that not a footstep should be heard, and all was silent and still.

But the emperor was not yet dead, although he lay white and stiff on his gorgeous bed, with the long velvet curtains and heavy gold tassels. A window stood open, and the moon shone in upon the emperor and the artificial bird. The poor emperor, finding he could scarcely breathe with a strange weight on his chest, opened his eyes, and saw Death sitting there. He had put on the emperor's golden crown, and held in one hand his sword of state, and in the other his beautiful banner. All around the bed, and peeping through the long velvet curtains, were a number of strange heads, some very ugly, and others lovely and gentle-looking. These were the emperor's good and bad deeds, which stared him in the face now Death sat at his heart.

"Do you remember this?" "Do you recollect that?" they asked one after another, thus bringing to his remembrance circumstances that made the perspiration stand on his brow.

"I know nothing about it," said the emperor. "Music! music!" he cried; "the large Chinese drum! that I may not hear what they say." But they still went on, and Death nodded like a Chinaman to all they said. "Music! music!" shouted the emperor. "You little precious golden bird, sing, pray sing! I have given you gold and costly presents; I have even hung my golden slipper round your neck. Sing! sing!" But the bird remained silent. There was no one to wind it up, and therefore it could not sing a note.

Death continued to stare at the emperor with his cold, hollow eyes, and the room was fearfully still. Suddenly there came through the open window the sound of sweet music. Outside, on the bough of a tree, sat the living nightingale. She had heard of the emperor's illness, and was therefore come to sing to him of hope and trust. And as she sung, the shadows grew paler and paler; the blood in the emperor's veins flowed more rapidly, and gave life to his weak limbs; and even Death himself listened, and said, "Go on, little nightingale, go on."

"Then will you give me the beautiful golden sword and that rich banner? and will you give me the emperor's crown?" said the bird.

So Death gave up each of these treasures for a song; and the nightingale continued her singing. She sung of the quiet churchyard, where the white roses grow, where the elder-tree wafts its perfume on the breeze, and the fresh, sweet grass is moistened by the mourners' tears. Then Death longed to go and see his garden, and floated out through the window in the form of a cold, white mist.

"Thanks, thanks, you heavenly little bird. I know you well. I banished you from my kingdom once, and yet you have charmed away the evil faces from my bed, and banished Death from my heart, with your sweet song. How can I reward you?"

"You have already rewarded me," said the nightingale. "I shall never forget that I drew tears from your eyes the first time I sang to you. These are the jewels that rejoice a singer's heart. But now sleep, and grow strong and well again. I will sing to you again."

And as she sung, the emperor fell into a sweet sleep; and how mild and refreshing that slumber was! When he awoke, strenghtened and restored, the sun shone brightly through the window; but not one of his servants had returned – they all believed he was dead; only the nightingale still sat beside him, and sang.

"You must always remain with me," said the emperor. "You shall sing only when it pleases you; and I will break the artificial bird into a thousand pieces."

"No; do not do that," replied the nightingale; "the bird did very well as long as it could. Keep it here still. I cannot live in the palace, and build my

nest; but let me come when I like. I will sit on a bough outside your window, in the evening, and sing to you, so that you may be happy, and have thoughts full of joy. I will sing to you of those who are happy, and those who suffer; of the good and the evil, who are hidden around you. The little singing bird flies far from you and your court to the home of the fisherman and the peasant's cot. I love your heart better than your crown; and yet something holy lingers round that also. I will come, I will sing to you; but you must promise me one thing."

"Everything," said the emperor, who, having dressed himself in his imperial robes, stood with the hand that held the heavy golden sword pressed to his heart.

"I only ask one thing," she replied; "let no one know that you have a little bird who tells you everything. It will be best to conceal it." So saying, the nightingale flew away.

The servants now came in to look after the dead emperor; when, lo! there he stood, and, to their astonishment, said, "Good morning."

Ole-Luk-Oie, the Dream-god

There is nobody in the world who knows so many stories as Ole-Luke-Oie, or who can relate them so nicely. In the evening, while the children are seated at the table or in their little chairs, he comes up the stairs very softly, for he walks in his socks, then he opens the doors without the slightest noise, and throws a small quantity of very fine dust in their eyes, just enough to prevent them from keeping them open, and so they do not see him. Then he creeps behind them, and blows softly upon their necks, till their heads begin to droop. But Ole-Luk-Oie does not wish to hurt them, for he is very fond of children, and only wants them to be quiet that he may relate to them pretty stories, and they never are quiet until they are in bed and asleep. As soon as they are asleep, Ole-Luk-Oie seats himself upon the bed. He is nicely dressed; his coat is made of silken stuff; it is impossible to say of what colour, for it changes from green to red, and from red to blue as he turns from side to side. Under each arm he carries an umbrella; one of them, with pictures on the inside, he spreads over the good children, and then they dream the most beautiful stories the whole night. But the other umbrella

has no pictures, and this he holds over the naughty children, so that they sleep heavily, and wake in the morning without having dreamed at all. Now we shall hear how Ole-Luk-Oie came every night during a whole week to a little boy named Hjalmar, and what he told him. There were seven stories, as there are seven days in the week.

Monday

"Now pay attention," said Ole-Luk-Oie, in the evening, when Hjalmar was in bed, "and I will decorate the room."
Immediately all the flowers in the flower-pots became large trees, with long branches reaching to the ceiling, and stretching along the walls, so that the whole room was like a greenhouse. All the branches were loaded with flowers, each flower as beautiful and as fragrant as a rose; and, had any one tasted them, he would have found them sweeter even than jam. The fruit glittered like gold, and there were cakes so full of plums that they were nearly bursting. It was incomparably beautiful. At the same time sounded dismal moans from the table-drawer in which lay Hjalmar's school books.

"What can that be now?" said Ole-Luk-Oie, going to the table and pulling out the drawer.

It was a slate, in such distress because of a false number in the sum, that it had almost broken itself to pieces. The pencil pulled and tugged at its string as if it were a little dog that wanted to help, but could not.

And then came a moan from Hjalmar's copy-book. Oh, it was quite terrible to hear! On each leaf stood a row of capital letters, every one having a small letter by its side. This formed a copy; under these were other letters, which Hjalmar had written: they fancied they looked like the copy, but they were mistaken; for they were leaning on one side as if they intended to fall over the pencil-lines.

"See, this is the way you should hold yourselves," said the copy. "Look here, you should slope thus, with a graceful curve."

"Oh, we are very willing to do so, but we cannot," said Hjalmar's letters; "we are so wretchedly made."

"You must be scratched out, then," said Ole-Luk-Oie.

"Oh, no!" they cried, and then they stood up so gracefully it was quite a pleasure to look at them.

"Now we must give up our stories, and exercise these letters," said Ole-Luk-Oie; "One, two – one, two –" So he drilled them till they stood up gracefully, and looked as beautiful as a copy could look. But after Ole-Luk-Oie was gone, and Hjalmar looked at them in the morning, they were as wretched and as awkward as ever.

As soon as Hjalmar was in bed, Ole-Luk-Oie touched, with his little magic wand, all the furniture in the room, which immediately began to chatter, and each article only talked of itself.

Over the chest of drawers hung a large picture in a gilt frame, representing a landscape, with fine old trees, flowers in the grass, and a broad stream, which flowed through the wood, past several castles, far out into the wild ocean. Ole-Luk-Oie touched the picture with his magic wand, and immediately the birds commenced singing, the branches of the trees rustled, and the clouds moved across the sky, casting their shadows on the landscape beneath them. Then Ole-Luk-Oie lifted little Hjalmar up to the frame, and placed his feet in the picture, just on the high grass, and there he stood with the sun shining down upon him through the branches of the trees. He ran to the water, and seated himself in a little boat which lay there, and which was painted red and white. The sails glittered like silver, and six swans, each with a golden circlet round its neck, and a bright blue star on its forehead, drew the boat past the green wood, where the trees talked of robbers and witches, and the flowers of beautiful little elves and fairies, whose histories the butterflies had related to them. Brilliant fish, with scales like silver and gold, swam after the boat, sometimes making a spring and splashing the water round them, while birds, red and blue, small and great, flew after him in two long lines. The gnats danced round them, and the cockchafers cried "Buz, buz." They all wanted to follow Hjalmar, and all had some story to tell him. It was a most pleasant sail. Sometimes the forests were thick and dark, sometimes like a beautiful garden, gay with sunshine and flowers; then he passed great palaces of glass and of marble, and on the balconies stood princesses, whose faces were those of little girls whom Hjalmar knew well, and had often played with. One of them held out her hand, in which was a heart made of sugar, more beautiful than any confectioner ever sold. As Hjalmar sailed by, he caught hold of one side of the sugar heart, and held it fast, and the princes held fast also, so that it broke in two pieces. Hjalmar had one piece, and the princess the other, but Hjalmar's was the largest. At each castle stood little princes acting as sentinels. They presented arms, and had golden swords, and made it rain plums and tin soldiers, so that they must have been real princes. Hjalmar continued to sail, sometimes through woods, sometimes as it were through large halls, and then by large cities. At last he came to the town where his nurse lived, who had carried him in her arms when he was a very little boy, and had always been kind to him. She nodded and beckoned to him, and then sang the little verses she had herself composed and sent to him, –

"How oft my memory turns to thee,
  My own Hjalmar, ever dear,
When I could watch thy infant glee,
  Or kiss away a pearly tear.
T' was in my arms thy lisping tongue
  First spoke the half-remembered word,
While o'er thy tottering steps I hung,
  My fond protection to afford.
Farewell! I pray the Heavenly Power
To keep thee till thy dying hour."

And all the birds sang the same tune, the flowers danced on their stems, and the old trees nodded as if Ole-Luk-Oie had been telling them stories as well.

Wednesday

How the rain did pour down! Hjalmar could hear it in his sleep; and when Ole-Luk-Oie opened the window, the water flowed quite up to the window-sill. It had the appearance of a large lake outside, and a beautiful ship lay close to the house.

"Wilt thou sail with me to-night, little Hjalmar?" said Ole-Luk-Oie; then we shall see foreign countries, and thou shalt return here in the morning."

All in a moment, there stood Hjalmar, in his best clothes, on the deck of the noble ship; and immediately the weather became fine. They sailed through the streets, round by the church, and on every side rolled the wide, great sea. They sailed till the land disappeared, and then they saw a flock of storks, who had left their own country, and were travelling to warmer climates. The storks flew one behind the other, and had already been a long, long time on the wing. One of them seemed so tired that his wings could scarcely carry him. He was the last of the row, and was soon left very far behind. At length he sunk lower and lower, with outstretched wings, flapping them in vain, till his feet touched the rigging of the ship, and he slided from the sails to the deck, and stood before them. Then a sailor-boy caught him, and put him in the hen-house, with the fowls, the ducks, and the turkeys, while the poor storks stood quite bewildered amongst them.

"Just look at that fellow," said the chickens.

Then the turkey-cock puffed himself out as large as he could, and inquired who he was; and the ducks waddled backwards, crying, "Quack, quack."

Then the stork told them all about warm Africa, of the pyramids, and of the ostrich, which, like a wild horse, runs across the desert. But the ducks did not understand what he said, and Quacked amongst themselves, "We are all of the same opinion; namely, that he is stupid."

"Yes, to be sure, he is stupid," said the turkey-cock; and gobbled.

Then the stork remained quite silent, and thought of his home in Africa.

"Those are handsome thin legs of yours," said the turkey-cock. "What do they cost a yard?"

"Quack, quack, quack," grinned the ducks; but the stork pretended not to hear.

"You may as well laugh," said the turkey; "for that remark was rather witty, or perhaps it was above you. Ah, ah, is he not clever? He will be a great amusement to us while he remains here." And then he gobbled, and the ducks quacked, "Gobble, gobble; Quack, quack."

What a terrible uproar they made, while they were having such fun among themselves!

Then Hjalmar went to the hen-house; and, opening the door, called to the stork. Then he hopped out on the deck. He had rested himself now, and he looked happy, and seemed as if he nodded to Hjalmar, as if to thank him. Then he spread his wings, and flew away to warmer countries, while the hens clucked, the ducks quacked, and the turkey-cock turned quite scarlet in the head.

"To-morrow you shall be made into soup," said Hjalmar to the fowls; and then he awoke, and found himself lying in his little bed.

It was a wonderful journey which Ole-Luk-Oie had made him take this night.

Thursday

"What do you think I have got here?" said Ole-Luk-Oie. "Do not be frightened, and you shall see a little mouse." And then he held out his hand to him, in which lay a lovely little creature. "It has come to invite you to a wedding. Two little mice are going to enter into the marriage state to-night. They reside under the floor of your mother's store-room, and that must be a fine dwelling-place."

"But how can I get through the little mouse-hole in the floor?" asked Hjalmar.

"Leave me to manage that," said Ole-Luk-Oie. "I will soon make you small enough." And then he touched Hjalmar with his magic wand, whereupon he became less and less, until at last he was not longer than a little finger. "Now you can borrow the dress of the tin soldier. I think it will just fit you. It looks well to wear a uniform when you go into company."

"Yes, certainly," said Hjalmar; and in a moment he was dressed as neatly as the neatest of all tin soldiers.

"Will you be so good as to seat yourself in your mamma's thimble," said the little mouse, "that I may have the pleasure of drawing you to the wedding."

"Will you really take so much trouble, young lady?" said Hjalmar. And so in this way he rode to the mouse's wedding.

First they went under the floor, and then passed through a long passage, which was scarcely high enough to allow the thimble to drive under, and the whole passage was lit up with the phosphorescent light of rotten wood. "Does it not smell delicious?" asked the mouse, as she drew him along. "The wall and the floor have been smeared with bacon-rind; nothing can be nicer."

Very soon they arrived at the bridal hall. On the right stood all the little lady-mice, whispering and giggling, as if they were making game of each other. To the left were the gentlemen-mice, stroking their whiskers with their fore-paws; and in the centre of the hall could be seen the bridal pair, standing side by side, in a hollow cheese-rind, and kissing each other, while all eyes were upon them; for they had already been betrothed, and were soon to be married. More and more friends kept arriving, till the mice were nearly treading each other to death; for the bridal pair now stood in the doorway, and none could pass in or out.

The room had been rubbed over with bacon-rind, like the passage, which was all the refreshment offered to the guests. But for dessert they produced a pea, on which a mouse belonging to the bridal pair had bitten the first letters of their names. This was something quite uncommon. All the mice said it was a very beautiful wedding, and that they had been very agreeably entertained.

After this, Hjalmar returned home. He had certainly been in grand society; but he had been obliged to creep under a room, and to make himself small enough to wear the uniform of a tin soldier.

Friday

"It is incredible how many old people there are who would be glad to have me at night," said Ole-Luk-Oie, "especially those who have done something wrong. 'Good little Ole,' say they to me, 'we cannot close our eyes, and we lie awake the whole night and see all our evil deeds sitting on our beds like little imps, and sprinkling us with hot water. Will you come and drive them away, that we may have a good night's rest?' and then they sigh so deeply and say, 'We would gladly pay you for it. Good-night, Ole-Luk, the money lies in the window.' But I never do anything for gold." "What shall we do to-night?" asked Hjalmar. "I do not know whether you would care to go to another wedding," he replied, "although it is quite a different affair to the one we saw last night. Your sister's large doll, that is dressed like a man, and is called Herman, intends to marry the doll Bertha. It is also the dolls' birthday, and they will receive many presents."

"Yes, I know that already," said Hjalmar, "my sister always allows her dolls to keep their birthdays or to have a wedding when they require new clothes; that has happened already a hundred times, I am quite sure."

"Yes, so it may; but to-night is the hundred and first wedding, and when that has taken place it must be the last, therefore this is to be extremely beautiful. Only look."

Hjalmar looked at the table, and there stood the little cardboard doll's-house, with lights in all the windows, and drawn up before it were the tin soldiers presenting arms. The bridal pair were seated on the floor, leaning against the leg of the table, looking very thoughtful, and with good reason. Then Ole-Luk-Oie dressed up in grandmother's black gown married them. As soon as the ceremony was concluded, all the furniture in the room joined in singing a beautiful song, which had been composed by the lead pencil, and which went to the melody of a military tattoo.

"What merry sounds are on the wind,
As marriage rites together bind
A quiet and a loving pair,
Though formed of kid, yet smooth and fair!
Hurrah! If they are deaf and blind,
Well sing, though weather prove unkind."

And now came the presents; but the bridal pair had nothing to eat, for love was to be their food.
"Shall we go to a country house, or travel?" asked the bridegroom.

69

Then they consulted the swallow who had travelled so far, and the old hen in the yard, who had brought up five broods of chickens.

And the swallow talked to them of warm countries, where the grapes hang in large clusters on the vines, and the air is soft and mild, and about the mountains glowing with colours more beautiful than we can think of.

"But they have no red cabbage like we have," said the hen, "I was once in the country with my chickens for a whole summer, there was a large sand-pit, in which we could walk about and scratch as we liked. Then we got into a garden in which grew red cabbage; oh, how nice it was, I cannot think of anything more delicious."

"But one cabbage stalk is exactly like another," said the swallow; "and here we have often bad weather."

"Yes, but we are accustomed to it," said the hen.

"But it is so cold here, and freezes sometimes."

"Cold weather is good for cabbages," said the hen; "besides we do have it warm here sometimes. Four years ago, we had a summer that lasted more than five weeks, and it was so hot one could scarcely breathe. And then in this country we have no poisonous animals, and we are free from robbers. He must be wicked who does not consider our country the finest of all lands. He ought not to be allowed to live here." And then the hen wept very much and said, "I have also travelled. I once went twelve miles in a coop, and it was not pleasant travelling at all."

"The hen is a sensible woman," said the doll Bertha. "I don't care for travelling over mountains, just to go up and come down again. No, let us go to the sand-pit in front of the gate, and then take a walk in the cabbage garden."

Saturday

"Am I to hear any more stories?" asked little Hjalmar, as soon as Ole-Luk-Oie had sent him to sleep.

"We shall have no time this evening," said he, spreading out his prettiest umbrella over the child. "Look at these Chinese," and then the whole umbrella appeared like a large china bowl, with blue trees and pointed bridges, upon which stood little Chinamen nodding their heads. "We must make all the world beautiful for to-morrow morning," said Ole-Luk-Oie, "for it will be a holiday, it is Sunday. I must now go to the church steeple and see if the little sprites who live there have polished the bells, so that they may sound sweetly. Then I must go into the fields and see if the wind has blown the dust from the grass and the leaves, and the most difficult

70

task of all which I have to do, is to take down all the stars and brighten them up. I have to number them first before I put them in my apron, and also to number the places from which I take them, so that they may go back into the right holes, or else they would not remain, and we should have a number of falling stars, for they would all tumble down one after the other."

"Hark ye! Mr. Luk-Oie," said an old portrait which hung on the wall of Hjalmar's bedroom. "Do you know me? I am Hjalmar's great-grandfather. I thank you for telling the boy stories, but you must not confuse his ideas. The stars cannot be taken down from the sky and polished; they are spheres like our earth, which is a good thing for them."

"Thank you, old great-grandfather," said Ole-Luk-Oie. "I thank you; you may be the head of the family, as no doubt you are, but I am older than you. I am an ancient heathen. The old Romans and Greeks named me the Dream-god. I have visited the noblest houses, and continue to do so; still I know how to conduct myself both to high and low, and now you may tell the stories yourself;" and so Ole-Luk-Oie walked off, taking his umbrellas with him.

"Well, well, one is never to give an opinion, I suppose," grumbled the portrait. And it woke Hjalmar.

Sunday

"Good evening," said Ole-Luk-Oie.

Hjalmar nodded, and then sprang out of bed, and turned his great-grand-father's portrait to the wall, so that it might not interrupt them as it had done yesterday. "Now," said he, "you must tell me some stories about five green peas that lived in one pod; or of the chickseed that courted the chick-weed; or of the darning needle, who acted so proudly because she fancied herself an embroidery needle."

"You may have too much of a good thing," said Ole-Luk-Oie.

"You know that I like best to show you something, so I will show you my brother. He is also called Ole-Luk-Oie, but he never visits any one but once, and when he does come, he takes him away on his horse, and tells him stories as they ride along. He knows only two stories. One of these is so wonderfully beautiful, that no one in the world can imagine anything at all like it; but the other is just as ugly and frighful, so that it would be impossible to describe it." Then Ole-Luk-Oie lifted Hjalmar up to the window. "There now, you can see my brother, the other Ole-Luk-Oie; he is also called Death.

72

You perceive he is not so bad as they represent him in picture books; there he is a skeleton, but now his coat is embroidered with silver, and he wears the splendid uniform of a hussar, and a coat of black velvet flies behind him, over the horse. Look, how he gallops along." Hjalmar saw, that as this Ole-Luk-Oie rode on, he lifted up old and young, and carried them away on his horse. Some he seated in front of him, and some behind, but always inquired first, "How stands the mark-book?"

"Good," they all answered.

"Yes, but let me see for myself," he replied; and they were obliged to give him the books. Then all those who had "Very good," or "Exceedingly good," came in front of the horse, and heard the beautiful story; while those who had "Middling," or "Tolerably good," in their books, were obliged to sit behind, and listen to the frightful tale. They trembled and cried, and wanted to jump down from the horse, but they could not get free, for they seemed fastened to the seat.

"Why, Death is a most splendid Luk-Oie," said Hjalmar, "I am not in the least afraid of him."

"You need have no fear of him," said Ole-Luk-Oie, "if you take care and keep a good conduct book."

"Now I call that very instructive," murmured the great-grandfather's portrait. "It is useful sometimes to express an opinion;" so he was quite satisfied.

These are some of the doings and sayings of Ole-Luk-Oie. I hope he may visit you himself this evening, and relate some more.

The Red Shoes

There was once a little girl who was very pretty and delicate; but in summer she used to go barefooted, because she was poor; in winter she wore large wooden shoes, and her little insteps became quite red.

In the village lived an old shoemaker's wife, who had some old strips of red cloth; and she sewed these together, as well as she could, into a little pair of shoes. They were rather clumsy; but he intention was kind, for the little girl was to have them, and her name was Karen. She received these shoes on the very day on which her mother was buried, and she wore them for the first time. They were certainly not suitable for mourning, but she had no others; so she put them on her bare feet, and walked behind the poor pine coffin.

There came by a large old-fashioned carriage, in which sat an old lady. She looked at the little girl, and felt pity for her; so she said to the clergyman, "Pray give me that little girl, and I will adopt her."

Karen thought all this happened because of her red shoes; but the old lady considered them horrible, and so they were burnt. But Karen herself was dressed in neat, tidy clothes, and taught to read and to sew, and people said she was pretty; but the looking-glass said, "You are more than pretty; you are beautiful."

Not long after, a queen travelled through the country with her little daughter, who was a princess, and crowds flocked to the castle to see them. Karen was amongst them, and she saw the little princess in a white dress, standing at a window, to allow every one to gaze upon her. She had neither train nor golden crown on her head; but she wore a beautiful pair of red morocco shoes, which certainly were rather handsomer than those that the old shoemaker's wife had made for little Karen. Surely nothing in the world could be compared with those red shoes.

The time arrived for Karen to be confirmed. New clothes were made for her, and she was to have, also, a pair of new shoes. A rich shoemaker in the town took the measure of her little foot, at his own house, in a room where stood large glass cases full of elegant shoes and shining boots. They looked beautiful; but the old lady could not see very well, so she had not much pleasure in looking at them. Among the shoes stood a pair of red ones, just like those which the princes had worn. Oh, how pretty they were! The shoemaker said they had been made for a count's child, but they had not fitted her properly.

"Are they of polished leather?" said the old lady; "for they shine as if they were."

"Yes, they do shine," said Karen; and as they fitted her, they were bought; but the old lady did not know they were red, or she would never have allowed Karen to go to confirmation in red shoes, which, however, she did. Every one looked at her feet; and as she passed through the church, to the entrance of the choir, it seemed as if the old pictures on the tombs, and the portraits of clergymen and their wives, with their stiff collars and long black dresses, were all fixing their eyes on her red shoes; and she thought of them only, even when the clergyman laid his hands on her head, and spoke of her baptism, and of her covenant with God, and that now she must remember that she must act as a grown-up Christian. And the organ pealed forth its solemn tones and the fresh, young voices of the children sounded sweetly, as they joined with the choir; but Karen thought only of her red shoes.

In the afternoon the old lady was told by every one that the shoes were red; and she said it was very shocking, and not at all proper, and told Karen that, when she went to church in future she must always wear black shoes, even though they might be old.

Next Sunday was sacrament Sunday, and Karen was to receive it for the first time. She looked at her black shoes, and then at the red ones; then looked again, and put on the red ones. The sun shone brightly, and Karen and the old lady went to church by the footpath through the fields; for the road was so dusty.

Near the church door stood an old invalid soldier, with a crutch and a wonderfully long beard, more red than white. He bowed nearly to the ground, and asked the old lady if he might wipe her shoes. And Karen stretched out her little foot also.

"Why, these are dancing shoes," cried the soldier. "I will make them stick fast to your feet when you dance." And then he slapped the soles of her shoes with his hand.

The old lady gave the soldier some money, and then went into church with Karen. Every one in the church looked at Karen's red shoes, and the pictures looked at them; and when she knelt at the altar, and took the golden cup to her lips, she thought only of her red shoes, and it was to her as if they passed before her eyes in the cup; and she forgot to sing the psalm, or to say the Lord's Prayer. Then all the people went out of church, and the old lady

76

stepped into her carriage. Karen lifted her foot to step in also, and the old soldier cried, "See what beautiful dancing shoes."

And then Karen found she could not help dancing a few steps; and when she began, it seemed as if her legs would go on dancing. It was just as if the shoes had a power over her. She danced round the corner of the church, and could not stop herself. The coachman was obliged to run after her, and catch her, and then lift her into the carriage, and even then her feet would go on dancing, so that she kept treading on the good old lady's toes. At last she took off the shoes, and then her legs had a little rest. As soon as they reached home, the shoes were put away in a closet; but Karen could not resist looking at them.

Soon after this the old lady was taken ill, and it was said that she could not recover. She had to be waited upon and nursed, and no one ought to have been so anxious to do this as Karen. But there was to be a grand ball in the town, to which Karen was invited. She thought of the old lady, who could not recover, she looked at her red shoes, and then she reflected that there could be no harm in her putting them on, nor was there; but her next act was to go to the ball, and to join in the dancing. But the shoes would not let her do as she wished: when she wanted to go to the right, they would dance to the left; or if she wished to go up the floor, they persisted in going down; and at last they danced down the stairs, into the street, and out of the town gate. She danced on in spite of herself, till she came to a gloomy wood. Something was shining up among the trees. At first she thought it was the moon, and then she saw a face. It was the old soldier, with his red beard; he sat and nodded to her, and said, "See what pretty dancing shoes they are."

Then she was frightened, and tried to pull off the red shoes; but they clung fast. She tore off her stockings; but the shoes seemed to have grown to her feet. And she was obliged to continue dancing over fields and meadows, in rain or in sunshine, by night or by day; but it was most terrible at night. She danced through the open churchyard; the dead there do not dance: they are better employed. She would gladly have seated herself on the poor man's grave, where the bitter fern-leaves grew; but for her there was neither rest nor peace. And then, as she danced towards the open church door, she saw before her an angel, in long white robes, and wings that reached from his shoulders down to the ground. His countenance was grave and stern, and in his hand he held a bright and glittering sword.

"Thou shalt dance," said he, "dance in thy red shoes, till thou art pale and cold, and till thy skin shrivels up to a skeleton. Thou shalt dance from door to door; and where proud, haughty children live, thou shalt knock, so that they may hear thee, and be afraid; yea, thou shalt dance."

"Mercy!" cried Karen; but she heard not what the angel answered; for her shoes carried her away from the door, into the fields, over highways and byways; but dancing, dancing ever.

One morning she danced by a door which she knew well. She could hear sounds of singing within, and a coffin, decked with flowers, was presently carried out. Then she knew that the old lady was dead, and she felt that she was forsaken by all the world, and condemned by an angel from heaven. Still must she dance through the long days and the dark, gloomy nights. The shoes carried her on through brambles, and over stumps of trees, which scratched her till the blood came. Then she danced across a heath to a little lonely house. Here, she knew, the executioner dwelt; and she tapped with her fingers on the window-pane, and said, "Come out, come out; I cannot come in, for I must dance."

And the executioner said, "Do you not know who I am? I cut off the heads of wicked people, and I perceive now that my axe tingles through my fingers." "Do not strike off my head," said Karen, "for then I shall not be able to repent of my sin; but cut off my feet with the red shoes." And then she confessed all her sins, and the executioner cut off her feet with the red shoes on them, and the shoes, with the little feet in them, danced away over the filds, and were lost in the dark wood. And he cut out a pair of wooden feet for her, and gave her crutches; then he taught her a psalm, which the penitents always sing, and she kissed the hand that had held the axe, and went away across the heath. "Now I have suffered enough for the red shoes," said she; "I will go to church, that I may be seen there by the people;" and she went as quickly as she could to the church door, but when she arrived there, the red shoes danced before her eyes so, that she was frightened, and turned back. Through the whole week she was in sorrow, and wept many bitter tears; but when Sunday came again, she said, "Now I have suffered and striven enough; I believe I am quite as good as many of those who go to church, and sit there showing their airs." And then she went boldly on, but she did not get further than the churchyard gate, for there were the red shoes dancing before her. Then she was really frightened, and went back, and repented of her sinful pride with her whole heart. Then she went to the parsonage and begged to be taken there as a servant, promising to be industrious, and do all that she could, even without wages. All she wanted was the shelter of a home, and to be with good people. The clergyman's wife had pity on her, and took her into her service; and she was industrious and thoughtful. Silently she sat and listened when the clergyman read the Bible aloud in the evening. All the little ones became very fond of her, but when they spoke of dress, or finery, or beauty, she would shake her head. Next Sunday they all went to church, and they asked her if she would like to go with them; but she looked sorrowfully and with tearful eyes at her crutches. And while the others went to listen to God's word, she sat alone in her little room, which was only just large enough to contain a bed and a chair. And here she remained with her hymn-book in her hand, and as she read in a humble spirit, the wind wafted the tones of the organ from the church towards her, and she lifted her tearful face, and said, "O Lord, help me." Then the sun shone brightly, and before her stood the angel, in the long white robes, the same whom she had seen one night at the church door, but he no longer held in his hand a sharp sword, but a beautiful green branch covered with roses, and as he touched the ceiling with the branch, it raised itself to a lofty height, and on the spot where it had been touched, gleamed a golden star. He also touched the walls, and they opened wide, so that she could see the organ whose tones sounded so melodious. She saw, too, the old pictures of the clergymen and their wives, and the congregation sitting on the ornamented seats, and singing out of their hymn-books. The church itself had come to the poor girl in her narrow room, or the room had become a church to her. She found herself sitting on a seat with the rest of the clergyman's servants, and when they had finished the psalm, they looked at her and nodded, and said, "It was right of you to come, Karen."

"It was through mercy I came," said she. And then the organ pealed forth again, and the children's voices sounded so soft and sweet. The bright sunshine streamed through the window, and fell clear and warm upon the chair on which Karen sat. Her heart became so filled with sunshine, peace, and joy, that it broke, and her soul flew on a sunbeam to heaven, and there was no one in heaven who asked about the RED SHOES.

Soup from a Sausage-Stick

I

Soup From a Sausage-stick

»That was an excellent dinner we had yesterday," said an old she-mouse to one who hadn't been at the party. "I sat twenty-first from the old Mouse-king; that wasn't bad, when you come to think of it. Now would you like to hear the different courses? They were extremely well put together. There was mouldy bread, bacon rind, tallow candle and sausage – all with second helpings. It was as good as having two meals. There was a pleasant atmosphere of cheerful nonsense, such as you get in a family circle. Not a crumb was left except the sausage-sticks and, while we were talking about these, the question cropped up of making soup from a sausage-stick. Everyone, of course, had heard about it, but nobody had tasted such soup, much less knew how to make it. A charming toast was proposed to the inventor: he deserved (said the speaker) to be master of a workhouse. Wasn't that witty? And the old Mouse-King got up and promised that the young mouse who could turn out the tastiest soup of the kind mentioned should become his Queen; they should have a year and a day to think it over."

"That's not so dusty!" said the second mouse. "But how do you make soup from a sausage-stick?"

"Yes, how's it made?" asked all the she-mice, young and old. They all liked the idea of being Queen, but they didn't fancy the bother of going out into the wide world in order to learn how to make the soup – which of course they would have to do. After all, it isn't everyone who is ready to leave their family and the old nooks and corners; away from home, you don't run across cheese-rind and sniff bacon-rind every day. No, you may starve sometimes – and even perhaps be eaten alive by a cat.

These no doubt were the thoughts that scared most of them out of sallying for in search of knowledge, and only four mice – young, nimble, but poor – turned up at the start. They were each of them ready to go to one of the four corners of the earth; the result would then have to be left to chance.

Each one took a sausage-stick with her as a reminder of why they were going; it would do for a pilgrim's staff.

Early in May they set out, and early in May the following year they came back ... but only three of them. The fourth one didn't report, nothing was heard of her, and today was the day of decision.

"There always has to be a touch of sadness clinging to our gayest entertainments," said the Mouse-King. Still, he ordered invitations to be sent out to every mouse for many miles around; they were all to assemble in the kitchen. The three mice who'd just come back stood lined up by themselves; and for the fourth one, who was missing, a sausage-stick had been brought wound about with black crape. Nobody dared to say what he thought until the Mouse-King had announced what might be said after that.

Now we're going to hear all about it.

II
What the First Little Mouse Had Seen and Learnt on her Travels

"When I set out into the wide world," said the little mouse, "I imagined, like so many of my age, that I knew all there was to know. Well, I didn't; it takes a year and a day for that to happen. I went straight away to sea; I

joined a ship bound for the north. I had heard that at sea a cook has got to know how to make things do; but it's easy enough to make things do; when you've plenty of sides of bacon, barrels of salt meat and mitey flour. You can like a fighting-cock – but you don't learn how to make soup from a sausage-stick. For days and nights we sailed along, rolling and drenched. As soon as we came to the port we were making for, I left the vessel; it was far up in the north.

It's a curious feeling to leave your own little hole at home, sail in a ship (which is also a kind of hole) – and then suddenly find yourself hundreds of miles away, standing in a foreign country. There were trackless forests with trees of spruce and birch; they smelt so strong – I don't like that – and the wild herbs smelt so spicy that it made me sneeze, and I thought of sausages. There were forest lakes with water that looked quite clear from close by, but inky black from a distance. White swans were floating there; lay so still that I mistook them for foam, though when I saw them fly and saw them walk I knew what they were. They belong to the goose family; once you see them waddle, there's no getting away from their relationship. I stuck to my own sort; I made friends with field-mice, who as a matter of fact know precious little, especially on the subject of good food, and that was just what I went abroad for. The very idea of making soup from a sausage-stick was to them so extraordinary that it was immediately passed through the

83

whole wood, but that it could actually be done they regarded as quite hopeless; least of all did I imagine that here this night I should be let into the secret. It was midsummer and that, they said, was why the perfume of the woods was so strong and the herbs so spicy, why the lakes were so clear and yet showed so dark against the white swans.

At the edge of the wood, among three or four houses, a pole as tall as a mainmast was put up, and from the top of it hung wreaths and ribbons. It was the maypole. Girls and boys danced round and round it, and their singing vied with the jigging of the fiddler. It was a merry party at sunset and in the moonlight, though I didn't join in – imagine a little mouse at a dance in the woods! No, I stayed in the velvety moss and held on to my sausage-stick. The moon shone on one spot especially, where there was a tree covered with moss as delicate – yes, I make bold to say, as delicate as the coat of the Mouse-King; but it was of a green colour that was most refreshing to the eyes. Then all at once there came tripping forward the sweetest little people not more than knee-high to me. They looked like human beings, though better proportioned. They are called elves and are elegantly dressed in flower-petals trimmed with the wings of flies and gnats: really quite smart. It was soon clear that they were looking for something, I couldn't make out what. But then a few of them came up to me, and the chief one pointed to my sausage-stick and said, "That's just the very thing for us. It's cut the right length; it'll be top-hole" – and he got more and more delighted, as he eyed my pilgrim's staff.

'You may borrow, but not keep,' I said.

'Not keep,' they all repeated. They took over my sausage-stick, as I let go of it, and they danced away with it to the beautiful mossy bit of ground; there they set up the sausage-stick in the middle of the glade. They, too, wanted to have a maypole, and the pole they now had might have been cut specially for them! Then it was dressed, and it looked an absolute picture.

Tiny spiders spun a thread of gold round and round it, hung up fluttering veils and pennants, so finely woven, so bleached and snowy in the moonlight, that my eyes were dazzled. The elves took colours from the butterfly's wings and sprinkled them over the white linen and, with flowers and diamonds glittering there, I didn't know my sausage-stick any longer. A maypole such as this had become was surely not to be found anywhere else in the world. And now at last came the arrival of the really important elves. They wore no clothes, which gave them an air of great distinction, and I was invited to look on at the show, but from some way off, as I was too big beside them.

Now the music began. It was like the deep clanging of a thousand glass bells.

84

I thought it was the swans singing; I even fancied I could hear the cuckoo and the thrush. At last it was as if the whole wood joined in: the voices of childen, the ringing of bells and the singing of birds, the most delicious melodies. And all that loveliness rang out from the maypole of the elves; it was a complete chime, and it came from my sausage-stick. Never had I dreamt that so much could come from it, but no doubt it all depends on who handles it. I was tremendously moved; I cried, as a little mouse can sometimes, tears of pure delight.

The night was only too short, but they always are up there at that time of the year. A breeze got up at dawn and ruffled the surface of the lake; all the delicate, hovering veils and pennants flew off into the air; the swaying kiosques of gossamer, suspension bridges and balustrades (or whatever they're called) which had been flung across from leaf to leaf, vanished into nothingness ... Six elves came and brought me my sausage-stick, asking whether I had any wish they could grant me. So I begged them to tell me how you make soup from a sausage-stick.

'How we do it?' said the principal elf, laughing. 'Well, you've just seen. I expect you could hardly tell your sausage-stick, could you?'

'Oh, you mean in that way,' I said, and told him straight out why I had come abroad and what was expected of me when I got back. 'What use,' I asked, 'will it be for the Mouse-King and the rest of our great empire to know that I've seen all this beauty? I can't shake it out of my sausagestick and say, Look, here's the stick, now comes the soup – though it might do, all the same, as a kind of dessert when you'd had enough.'

Then the elf dipped his tiny finger down into a blue violet and said to me, 'Now, mind! I'll rub your staff with magic, and then, when you get back to the Mouse-King's palace, touch your King's warm breast with the staff. At that, violets will come out all over the staff, even on the coldest days in winter. There, that's something for you to take home, and a bit extra as well ...'"

But before the little mouse said what this was, she turned her staff towards the King's breast and, sure enough, the loveliest bunch of flowers burst out, smelling so strong that the Mouse-King ordered the mice who stood next to the fireplace to put their tails at once into the fire, so as to cause a slight smell of burning; for the scent of the violets was unbearable, and not at all the kind that the mice cared for.

"But what was the bit extra you spoke of?" asked the Mouse-King.

"Well, you see," said the little mouse, "it's what's generally known as the 'effect'." And then she turned the sausage-stick round, and there were no flowers left. She simply held the bare stick and raised it like a conductor's baton.

"Violets are for sight, smell and touch – that's what the elf told me; but there must still be something for hearing and taste." So she began to beat time. It wasn't the music she heard in the wood at the festival of the elves – no, it was the kind you can hear in the kitchen … Well, well! What a hotch-potch! It came suddenly, as though the wind was roaring down all the chimneys: kettles and saucepans boiled over, the coal-shovel banged against the brass kettle – and then, just as suddenly, it quietened down. You could hear the faint song of the tea-kettle, so curious that you couldn't possibly tell if it was stopping or beginning. Then the little pot boiled, and the big pot boiled – they didn't take any notice of each other – it was as if a pot never had any brains. And the little mouse waved her baton more excitedly than ever, till the saucepans foamed and bubbled and boiled right over, the wind whistled and the chimney whined … Phew! it got so terrific that the little mouse even dropped her stick.

"That was a stiff soup!" said the old Mouse-King. "What about the next course?"

"There isn't any more," said the little mouse, and curtseyed.

"No more?" exclaimed the Mouse-King. "Very well; then let's hear what the next one has to say."

III
What the Second Little Mouse Had to Tell

"I was born in the Castle library," said the second mouse, "I as well as several of my family, who never had the luck to go into the dining-room, let alone the larder. Not until I left home and came here today did I ever see a kitchen. We were often positively starving in the library, but we got to know a great deal. Report reached us up there of the prize offered by the King for making soup from a sausage-stick, and then if my old grandmother didn't go and rout out a manuscript! She couldn't read herself, but she had it read to her – in which it said, 'If only you've a poet, you can make soup from a sausage-stick.' She asked me if I was a poet. I couldn't claim to be this, and she said that in that case I must set about becoming one. 'But what's wanted to become one?' I asked; for it was just as hard for me to find this out as to make the soup. However, Granny had listened to what others read; she said that three things were required, 'common sense, fantasy, and feeling; if you can only get these into you, then you'll be a poet and you'll manage all right with the sausage-stick'."
And so I went westward out into the wide world, in order to become a poet.

Common sense, I realized, is the most important thing of all; the other two don't seem to matter so much. So I began by searching for common sense. Now, where's it to be found? 'Go to the ant and become wise,' said a great king in Palestine; I knew that from my library, and I didn't stop till I got to the nearest big ant-hill, where I lay in wait watching for wisdom.

They're a highly respectable people, the ants; they're common sense itself. Everything with them is like a correctly done sum that comes out right. To work and to lay eggs, they say, is to live for the present and provide for the future; and that's just what they do. They divide up into clean ants and dirty ants, and they're numbered according to rank. The queen ant is number one, and what she thinks is always right, for she knows all there is to know, and this was an important thing for me to grasp. She spoke so much, and so cleverly, that it seemed to me nonsense. She said that their ant-hill was the highest thing in the world; but close by stood a tree that was taller, much taller. This couldn't be denied, and so the subject was allowed to drop. One evening an ant had strayed off in that direction, crept up the trunk, not as far as the top, and yet higher than any ant had ever been before; and when it turned round and found its way back, it told them in the ant-hill of something much higher, further off. But the ants all found this statement insulting to the whole community, and the ant was condemned to wear a muzzle and to serve a long term of solitary confinement. Then, not long after, another ant went to the tree and made the same climb and discovery, but its account (they felt) was given in a quiet level-headed way; and as, besides that, it was a much respected ant and one of the clean ones, they believed what it said and when it died they put up an egg-shell to its memory, for they always paid respect to knowledge. I noticed," said the little mouse, "that the ants frequently ran along with their eggs on their backs. I saw one of them drop hers, and she was making great efforts to get it up again, but she couldn't manage it. Then two others came and did all they could to help – in fact, they nearly dropped their own eggs – and this made them at once give up helping, for you have to look after number one; and the queen ant's comment was that it had been a good example of kindness and intelligence. 'These,' she said, are two qualities that set us ants highest among rational beings. Intelligence must and should outweigh everything, and it's I who have most of that.' With that she rose on her hind legs; she was so easy to recognize, I couldn't mistake her – and I swallowed her. 'Go to the ant and become wise?' I'd now got the queen.

I then went nearer to the big tree I've been speaking about. It was an oak of great age, with a tall trunk and a gigantic crown. I knew there was a living creature dwelt here, a woman called a dryad, who is born with the tree and dies with it. I had heard about this in the library, and now I was seeing such

a tree, such an oak-nymph, with my own eyes. She gave a terrible scream when she saw me so near, for like all women she was very frightened of mice, though as a matter of fact she had more excuse than the rest of them because I could gnaw right through the tree, on which of course her life depended. I spoke to her in a friendly cordial way, and she got back her courage and took me on her delicate hand. And when she heard why I had come out into the wide world, she promised me that perhaps that very evening I might come by one of the two treasures I was still looking for. She explained to me that Fantasus was a very good friend of hers, that he was as beautiful as the god of love, and that he often took a rest under the leafy boughs of her tree, which then rustled more than ever above their heads. He called her his dryad (she said) and the tree his tree; the oak – all gnarled, gigantic and beautiful – was just after his own heart, with spreading roots going deep down into the earth and with trunk and crown that rose high into the cool air and knew the drifting snow, the bitter winds and the warm sunshine as they should be known. 'Yes (she went on), the birds sing in the tree-top and tell of foreign lands, and there on that one dead bough the stork has built his nest; it looks very well and we get to hear something of the land of the Pyramids. All this appeals very much to Fantasus, though it isn't really enough for him. I myself have to tell him about life in the woods ever since the time when I was small and my tree was so tiny that a nettle could have hidden it, until now when it's grown so huge

89

and majestic. Sit down there, will you, under the woodruff, and mind!
as soon as Fantasus comes, I shall be sure to get a chance to pluck at his
wing and nip out a little feather. Take that – no poet ever had a better – then
you'll have all you need.'

And Fantasus came, the feather was twitched off, and I seized it," said
the little mouse. "I held it in water till it was soft … It was still difficult to
digest, but I managed to nibble it up. It isn't at all easy to nibble yourself
into being a poet; there's such a lot you must get inside you. Well, anyhow,
now I'd got two things, common sense and fantasy, and through them I
now realized that the third was to be found in the library, for a great man
once said and wrote that there are novels which are written solely that
people may be relieved of their unnecessary tears; in fact, they're a kind of
sponge to mop up feeling with. I called to mind a few of these books, which
had always seemed to me so tempting; they looked so used and greasy, they
must have soaked up no end of feeling.

I went home to the library and immediately devoured pretty well a whole
novel – that's to say, the soft part, the real book, whereas the crust, the
binding, I left alone. Once I had digested this novel and another like it,
I soon noticed their effect inside me; I ate part of a third and, lo and behold,
I was a poet! I said so to myself – and to the others, too. I had head-ache,
stomach-ache, and goodness knows what other aches. And when I thought

90

of all the stories that might be associated with a sausage-stick, my mind became full of sticks; the queen ant must have had a wonderful head. I thought of the man who put a white stick in his mouth, so that he and the stick both became invisible. I thought of a dry old stick, who was goldstick-in-waiting, and a stick-in-the-mud who wasn't; and of drumsticks and fiddlesticks. My whole mind seemed to run on sticks; and surely they would all make poems, if you were a poet, and I *am* a poet – I've worn myself out to become one. So, you see, any day of the week, sir, I shall be able to treat you to a stick – a story. There, that's the soup I'll make."

"Now let us hear the third one," said the Mouse-King.

"Pee-pee!" There was a squeak from the kitchen door, as a little mouse – the fourth of them, the one they thought was dead – come scurrying in and knocked over the sausage-stick with the black crape on it. She had run night and day, travelling on the railway by goods train when she had the chance, and even then she had nearly come too late. She pushed herself forward, looking rumpled and ruffled; she had lost her stick, but not her voice. She at once began speaking, as if she was the only one they were waiting for – the only one they would listen to – and as if nothing else in the world mattered to the world but herself. She began at once and said her say. Her arrival was so unexpected that no one had time to object to her or what she had to say, as long as she was saying it. Well, now let's listen.

91

IV

*What the Fourth Mouse, who Spoke before
the Third One had Spoken, Had to Say*

"It went straight to the largest town," she said. "I can't remember its name; I never can remember names. From the railway I went, along with some goods that had been seized by the Customs, to the town-hall, and there I called on the gaoler. He talked about his prisoners, especially about one who had been making rash speeches; and these had been quoted and quoted till he had to be made an example of. 'The whole thing's just soup from a sausagestick,' said the gaoler, 'but soup may well cost him his napper'."

"That aroused my interest in the prisoner," said the little mouse, "and I seized the opportunity to slip into his cell; there's always a mousehole behind every locked door. The prisoner looked pale; he had a long beard and big flashing eyes. The lamp smoked, but the walls were used to that and could hardly become blacker. The prisoner scratched both pictures and verses on them, white on black, but I didn't read them. I fancy he was bored, and so I was a welcome visitor. He coaxed me with bread-crumbs, with whistling and gentle words. He was very fond of me, I came to trust him, and so we were soon friends. He shared his bread and water with me, and gave me cheese and sausage. I lived in grand style, and yet it was more than anything our familiar intercourse (if I may put it that way) that appealed to me. He let me scamper on his hand and arm and even up his sleeve; he allowed me to creep into his beard and called me his little friend. I grew tremendously fond of him, and of course that sort of thing is mutual. I forgot my errand out in the wide world, forgot my sausage-stick that I left in a crack in the floor; it's still there. I only thought of staying where I was. If I went away, then of course the poor prisoner would have had no one left, and that's much too little in this world! So I stayed – but he didn't. He spoke to me so mournfully on our last day, gave me a double helping of bread and cheese-rind, kissed his fingers to me, and then he went and never came back. I don't know what happened to him. 'Soup from a sausage-stick,' said the gaoler; and to him I went, but I never ought to have trusted him. It's true, he took me on his hand, but then he shut me in a cage, on a treadmill. It's terrible! You run and get no farther; you're just a laughing-stock. The gaoler's grandchild was a sweet little thing with golden curls, merry eyes and a laughing mouth. 'Poor little mouse!' she said, peeping into my horrid cage. Then she drew back the catch … and I jumped down on to the window sill and out into the gutter. Free! Free! That was all I thought of, not what I had come away to find out.

It was dusk, and night was coming on. I found lodging in an old tower, where a watchman lived, and also an owl. I didn't trust either of them, least of all the owl. Owls are like cats and have one serious drawback, that they eat mice. You're bound to make mistakes sometimes, and that's what I did. She was a respectable old owl, most ladylike, who knew more than the watchman and just as much as myself. The young owls kept grumbling about one thing and another. 'Don't make soup out of a sausage-stick!' the old owl would tell them. That was the harshest thing she could say to them, so deeply attached was she to her family. I came to have such confidence in her that I said 'peep!' to her from the crack where I was, She seemed pleased with this trust and promised me her protection: no creature should be allowed to do anything to me – she would see to that herself next winter, when they were on short commons.

Yes, she was a downy old bird. She explained to me that the watchman couldn't hoot without a horn that hung loose from his shoulder. 'He fancies himself no end with that; he thinks he's an owl in the tower – thinks a big splash can be made by a small stone. Soup from a sausage-stick!' I begged her to jot down the recipe, and this is what she told me: 'Soup from a sausage-stick,' she said, 'is just a phrase among human beings; it can be taken in various ways, and every one thinks his way is the right way, though it's really nothing at all.'

"'Nothing at all!' I repeated. It gave me quite a shock. The truth's not always pleasant, but truth's the highest thing we know – the old owl agreed to that. I thought it over and realized that, if I brought back the highest thing we know, I should be bringing a good deal more than soup from a sausage-stick. So I hurried away to get home in good time, bringing with me the highest and best, namely, truth. Mice are canny folk and the Mouse-King is the leader of them all. He's in a position to make me Queen for the sake of truth."

"Your truth's a lie!" said the mouse who hadn't yet got leave to speak. "I can make the soup, and I shall."

V

How the Soup was Made

"I didn't go away," said the fourth mouse. "I stayed in this country; that's the right thing to do. There's no point in going abroad. You can get all you want just as well here. I stayed at home. *My* knowledge hasn't come to me from elves and dryads; I haven't nibbled my way to it, nor gossiped with owls. I've got mine by thinking things out for myself. Now please let's have the kettle on. Fill it up with water – right up. Light the fire, and let it burn till the water is brought to the boil – it must boil till it bubbles. Now throw in the stick. Next, will your Majesty please dip your tail into the seething pot and stir it round. The longer the stirring, the richer the soup. It costs nothing; no need of flavouring; just stir round."

"Can't someone else do the job?" asked the Mouse-King. "No," said the mouse. "Only the King's tail makes the right kind of stock."

The water boiled right over, and the Mouse-King came close up, almost dangerously near. And he whisked out his tail in the way that mice do in the dairy when they skim the cream from a bowl and then lick their tails. But his tail came no further than the hot steam before he jumped quickly down.

"Why, of course, you shall be my Queen," he said. "The soup can wait till our gold wedding; then our poor will have something to look forward to – and plenty of time to do it."

So the wedding took place. But a number of the mice, when they got home, said, "You could hardly call that soup from a sausage-stick; it was more like soup from a mouse's tail." One or two of the stories, they thought, weren't

94

half bad, though the whole might have been better done. "For instance, I should have said – so on and so forth!"

That was criticism, which is always so clever – afterwards.

The story went round the world. Opinion on it might differ, but the story itself remained entire. And that's just as it should be in things great or small, even in soup made from a sausage-stick – though you mustn't expect to be thanked for it.

The Little Mermaid

Far out in the ocean, where the water is as blue as the prettiest corn-flower, and as clear as crystal, it is very, very deep; so deep, indeed, that no cable could fathom it; many church steeples, piled one upon another, would not reach from the ground beneath to the surface of the water above. There dwell the Sea King and his subjects. We must not imagine that there is nothing at the bottom of the sea but bare yellow sand. No, indeed; the most singular flowers and plants grow there; the leaves and stems of which are so pliant, that the slightest agitation of the water causes them to stir as if they had life. Fishes, both large and small, glide between the branches, as birds fly among the trees here upon land. In the deepest spot of all, stands the castle of the Sea King. Its walls are built of coral, and the long, gothic windows are of the clearest amber. The roof is formed of shells, that open and close as the water flows over them. Their appearance is very beautiful; for in each lies a glittering pearl, which would be fit for the diadem of a queen.

The Sea King had been a widower for many years, and his aged mother kept house for him. She was a very wise woman, and exceedingly proud of her high birth: on that account she wore twelve oysters on her tail; while others, also of high rank, were only allowed to wear six. She was, however, deserving of very great praise, especially for her care of the little sea-princesses, her grand-daughters. They were six beautiful children; but the youngest was the prettiest of them all; her skin was as clear and delicate as a rose-leaf, and her eyes as blue as the deepest sea; but, like all the others, she had no feet, and her body ended in a fish's tail. All day long they played in the great halls of the castle, or among the living flowers that grew out of the walls. The large amber windows were open, and the fish swam in, just as the swallows fly into our houses when we open the windows, excepting that the fishes swam up to the princesses, ate out of their hands, and allowed themselves to be stroked. Outside the castle there was a beautiful garden, in which grew bright red and dark blue flowers, and blossoms like flames of fire; the fruit glittered like gold, and the leaves and stems waved to and fro continually. The earth itself was the finest sand, but blue as the flame of burning sulphur. Over everything lay a peculiar blue radiance, as if it were surrounded by the air from above, through which the blue sky shone, instead of the dark depths of the sea. In calm weather, the sun could be seen, looking like a purple flower, with the light streaming from the calyx. Each of the young princesses had a little plot of ground in the garden, where she might dig and plant as she pleased. One arranged her flower-bed into the form of a whale; another thought it better to make hers like the figure of a little mermaid; but that of the youngest was round like the sun, and contained flowers as red as his rays at sunset. She was a strange child, quiet and thoughtful; and while her sisters would be delighted with the wonderful things which they obtained from the wrecks of vessels, she cared for nothing but her pretty red flowers, like the sun, excepting a beautiful marble statue. It was the representation of a handsome boy, carved out of pure white stone, which had fallen to the bottom of the sea from a wreck. She planted by the statue a rose-coloured weeping willow. It grew splendidly, and very soon hung its fresh branches over the statue, almost down to the blue sands. The shadow had a violet tint, and waved to and fro like the branches; it seemed as if the crown of the tree and the root were at play, and trying to kiss each other. Nothing gave her so much pleasure as to hear about the world above the sea. She made her old grandmother tell her all she knew of the ships and of the towns, the people and the animals. To her it seemed most wonderful and beautiful to hear that the flowers of the land should have fragrance, and not those below the sea; that the trees of the forest should be green; and that the fishes among the trees could sing so sweetly, that it was quite a pleasure to hear them. Her grandmother called the little birds fishes, or she would not have understood her; for she had never seen birds.

"When you have reached your fifteenth year," said the grandmother, "you will have permission to rise up out of the sea, to sit on the rocks in the moonlight, while the great ships are sailing by; and then you will see both forests and towns."

In the following year, one of the sisters would be fifteen: but as each was a year younger than the other, the youngest would have to wait five years before her turn came to rise up from the bottom of the ocean, and see the earth as we do. However, each promised to tell the other what she saw on her first visit, and what she thought the most beautiful; for their grandmother could not tell them enough; there were so many things on which they wanted information. None of them longed so much for her turn to come as the youngest, she who had the longest time to wait, and who was so quiet and thoughtful. Many nights she stood by the open window, looking up through the dark blue water, and watching the fish as they splashed about with their fins and tails. She could see the moon and stars shining

faintly; but through the water they looked larger than they do to our eyes. When something like a black cloud passed between her and them, she knew that it was either a whale swimming over her head, or a ship full of human beings, who never imagined that a pretty little mermaid was standing beneath them, holding out her white hands towards the keel of their ship.

As soon as the eldest was fifteen, she was allowed to rise to the surface of the ocean. When she came back, she had hundreds of things to talk about; but the most beautiful, she said, was to lie in the moonlight, on a sandbank, in the quiet sea, near the coast, and to gaze on a large town close by, where the lights were twinkling like hundreds of stars; to listen to the sounds of the music, the noise of carriages, and the voices of human beings, and then to hear the merry bells peal out from the church steeples; and because she could not go near to all these wonderful things, she longed for them more than ever. Oh, did not the youngest sister listen eagerly to all these descriptions? and afterwards, when she stood at the open window looking up through the dark blue water, she thought of the great city, with all its bustle and noise, and even fancied she could hear the sound of the church bells, down in the depths of the sea.

In another year the second sister received permission to rise to the surface of the water, and to swim about where she pleased. She rose just as the sun was setting, and this, she said, was the most beautiful sight of all. The whole sky looked like gold while violet and rose-coloured clouds, which she could not describe, floated over her; and, still more rapidly than the clouds, flew a large flock of wild swans towards the setting sun, looking like a long white veil across the sea. She also swam towards the sun; but it sunk into the waves, and the rosy tints faded from the clouds and from the sea.

The third sister's turn followed; she was the boldest of them all, and she swam up a broad river that emptied itself into the sea. On the banks she saw green hills covered with beautiful vines; palaces and castles peeped out from amid the proud trees of the forest; she heard the birds singing, and the rays of the sun were so powerful that she was obliged often to dive down under the water to cool her burning face. In a narrow creek she found a whole troop of little human children, quite naked, and sporting about in the water; she wanted to play with them, but they fled in a great fright; and then a little black animal came to the water; it was a dog, but she did not know that, for she had never before seen one. This animal barked at her so terribly that she became frightened, and rushed back to the open sea. But she said she should never forget the beautiful forest, the green hills, and the pretty children who could swim in the water, although they had not fish's tails.

The fourth sister was more timid; she remained in the midst of the sea, but she said it was quite as beautiful there as nearer the land. She could see for so many miles around her, and the sky above looked like a bell of glass. She had seen the ships, but at such a great distance that they looked like sea-gulls. The dolphins sported in the waves, and the great whales spouted water from their nostrils till it seemed as if a hundred fountains were playing in every direction.

The fifth sister's birthday occurred in the winter; so when her turn came, she saw what the others had not seen the first time they went up. The sea looked quite green, and large icebergs were floating about, each like a pearl, she said, but larger and loftier than the churches built by men. They were of the most singular shapes, and glittered like diamonds. She had seated herself upon one of the largest, and let the wind play with her long hair, and she remarked that all the ships sailed by rapidly, and steered as far away as they could from the iceberg, as if they were afraid of it. Towards evening, as the sun went down, dark clouds covered the sky, the thunder rolled and the lightning flashed, and the red light glowed on the icebergs as they rocked and tossed on the heaving sea. On all the ships the sails were reefed with fear and trembling, while she sat calmly on the floating iceberg, watching the blue lightning, as it darted its forked flashes into the sea.

When first the sisters had permission to rise to the surface, they were each delighted with the new and beautiful sights they saw; but now, as grown-up girls, they could go when they pleased, and they had become indifferent about it. They wished themselves back again in the water, and after a month had passed they said it was much more beautiful down below, and pleasanter to be at home. Yet often, in the evening hours, the five sisters would twine their arms round each other, and rise to the surface, in a row. They had more beautiful voices than any human being could have; and before the approach of a storm, and when they expected a ship would be lost, they swam before the vessel, and sang sweetly of the delights to be found in the depths of the sea, and begged the sailors not to fear if they sank to the bottom. But the sailors could not understand the song, they took it for the howling of the storm. And these things were never to be beautiful for them; for if the ship sank, the men wer drowned, and their dead bodies alone reached the palace of the Sea King.

When the sisters rose, arm-in-arm, through the water in this way, their

youngest sister would stand quite alone, looking after them, ready to cry, only the mermaids have no tears, and therefore they suffer more. "Oh, were I but fifteen years old," said she; "I know that I shall love the world up there, and all the people who live in it."

At last she reached her fifteenth year. "Well, now, you are grown up," said the old dowager, her grandmother; "so you must let me adorn you like your other sisters:" and she placed a wreath of white lilies in her hair, and every flower leaf was half a pearl. Then the old lady ordered eight great oysters to attach themselves to the tail of the princess to show her high rank.

"But they hurt me so," said the little mermaid.

"Pride must suffer pain," replied the old lady. Oh, how gladly she would have shaken off all this grandeur, and laid aside the heavy wreath! The red flowers in her own garden would have suited her much better; but she could not help herself: so she said, "Farewell," and rose as lightly as a bubble to the surface of the water. The sun had just set as she raised her head above the waves; but the clouds were tinted with crimson and gold, and through the glimmering twilight beamed the evening star in all its beauty. The sea was calm, and the air mild and fresh. A large ship, with three masts, lay becalmed on the water, with only one sail set; for not a breeze stirred, and the sailors sat idle on deck or amongst the rigging. There was music and song on board; and, as darkness came on, a hundred coloured lanterns were lighted, as if the flags of all nations waved in the air. The little mermaid swam close to the cabin windows; and now and then, as the waves lifted her up, she could look in through clear glass window-panes, and see a number of well-dressed people within. Among them was a young prince, the most beautiful of all, with large black eyes; he was sixteen years of age, and his birthday was being kept with much rejoicing. The sailors were dancing on deck, but when the prince came out of the cabin, more than a hundred rockets rose in the air, making it as bright as day. The little mermaid was so startled that she dived under water; and when she again stretched out her head, it appeared as if all the stars of heaven were falling around her, she had never seen such fireworks before. Great suns spurted fire about, splendid fire-flies flew into the blue air, and everything was reflected in the clear, calm sea beneath. The ship itself was so brightly illuminated that all the people, and even the smallest rope, could be distinctly and plainly seen. And how handsome the young prince looked, as he pressed the hands of all present and smiled at them, while the music resounded through the clear night air.

It was very late; yet the little mermaid could not take her eyes from the ship, or from the beautiful prince. The coloured lanterns had been extinguished,

no more rockets rose in the air, and the cannon had ceased firing; but the sea became restless, and a moaning, grumbling sound could be heard beneath the waves: still the little mermaid remained by the cabin window, rocking up and down on the water, which enabled her to look in. After a while, the sails were quickly unfurled, and the noble ship continued her passage; but soon the waves rose higher, heavy clouds darkened the sky, and lightning appeared in the distance. A dreadful storm was approaching; once more the sails were reefed, and the great ship pursued her flying course over the raging sea. The waves rose mountains high, as if they would have overtopped the mast; but the ship dived like a swan between them, and then rose again on their lofty, foaming crests. To the little mermaid this appeared pleasant sport; not so to the sailors. At length the ship groaned and creaked; the thick planks gave way under the lashing of the sea as it broke over the deck; the mainmast snapped asunder like a reed; the ship lay over on her side; and the water rushed in. The little mermaid now perceived that the crew were in danger; even she herself was obliged to be careful to avoid the beams and planks of the wreck which lay scattered on the water. At one moment it was so pitch dark that she could not see a single object, but a flash of lightning revealed the whole scene; she could see every one who had been on board excepting the prince; when the ship parted, she had seen him sink into the deep waves, and she was glad, for she thought he would now be with her; and then she remembered that human beings could not live in the water, so that when he got down to her father's palace he would be quite dead. But he must not die. So she swam about among the beams and planks which strewed the surface of the sea, forgetting that they could crush her to pieces. Then she dived deeply under the dark waters, rising and falling with the waves, till at length she managed to reach the young prince, who was fast losing the power of swimming in that stormy sea. His limbs were failing him, his beautiful eyes were closed, and he would have died had not the little mermaid come to his assistance. She held his head above the water, and let the waves drift them where they wanted.

In the morning the storm had ceased; but of the ship not a single fragment could be seen. The sun rose up red and glowing from the water, and its beams brought back the hue of health to the prince's cheeks; but his eyes remained closed. The mermaid kissed his high, smooth forehead, and stroked back his wet hair; he seemed to her like the marble statue in her little garden, and she kissed him again, and wished that he might live. Presently they came in sight of land; she saw lofty blue mountains, on which the white snow rested as if a flock of swans were lying upon them. Near the coast were beautiful green forests, and close by stood a large building, whether a church or a convent she could not tell. Orange and citron trees grew in the garden, and before the door stood lofty palms. The sea here formed a little bay, in which the water was quite still, but very deep; so she swam with the handsome prince to the beach, which was covered with fine, white sand, and there she laid him in the warm sunshine, taking care to raise his head higher than his body. Then bells sounded in the large white building, and a number of young girls came into the garden. The little mermaid swam out farther from the shore and placed herself between some high rocks that rose out of the water; then she covered her head and neck with with the foam of the sea so that her little face might not be seen, and watched to see what would become of the poor prince. She did not wait long before she saw a young girl approach the spot where he lay. She seemed frightened at first, but only for a moment; then she fetched a number of people, and the mermaid saw that the prince came to life again, and smiled upon those who stood round him. But to her he sent no smile; he knew not that she had saved him. This made her very unhappy, and when he was led away into the great building, she dived down sorrowfully into the water, and returned to her father's castle. She had always been silent and thoughtful, and now she was more so than ever. Her sisters asked her what she had seen during her first visit to the surface of the water; but she would tell them nothing. Many an evening and morning did she rise to the place where she had left the prince. She saw the fruits in the garden ripen till they were gathered, the snow on the tops of the mountains melt away; but she never saw the prince, and therefore she returned home, always more sorrowful than before. It was her only comfort to sit in her own little garden, and fling her arm round the beautiful marble statue which was like the prince; but she gave up tending her flowers, and they grew in wild confusion over the paths, twining their long leaves and stems round the branches of the trees, so that the whole place became dark and gloomy. At length she could bear it no longer, and told one of her sisters all about it. Then the others heard the secret, and very soon it became known to two mermaids whose intimate friend happened to know who the prince was. She had also seen the festival on board ship, and she told them where the prince came from, and where his palace stood.

"Come, little sister," said the other princesses; then they entwined their arms and rose up in a long row to the surface of the water, close by the spot where they knew the prince's palace stood. It was built of bright yellow shining stone, with long flights of marble steps, one of which reached quite down to the sea. Splendid gilded cupolas rose over the roof, and between the pillars that surrounded the whole building stood life-like statues of marble. Through the clear crystal of the lofty windows could be seen noble rooms, with costly silk curtains and hangings of tapestry; while the walls were covered with beautiful paintings, which were a pleasure to look at. In the centre of the largest saloon a fountain threw its sparkling jets high up into the glass cupola of the ceiling, through which the sun shone down upon the water and upon the beautiful plants growing round the basin of the fountain. Now that she knew where he lived, she spent many an evening and many a night on the water near the palace. She would swim much nearer the shore than any of the others had ventured to do; indeed once she went quite up the narrow channel under the marble balcony, which threw a broad shadow on the water. Here she would sit and watch the young prince, who thought himself quite alone in the bright moonlight. She saw him many times of an evening sailing in a pleasant boat, with music playing and flags waving. She peeped out from among the green rushes, and if the wind caught her long silvery-white veil, those who saw it believed it to be a swan, spreading out its wings. On many a night, too, when the fishermen, with their torches, were out at sea, she heard them relate so many good things about the doings of the young prince, that she was glad she had saved his life when he had been tossed about half-dead on the waves. And she remembered that his head had rested on her bosom, and how heartily she had kissed him; but he knew nothing of all this, and could not even dream of her. She grew more and more fond of human beings, and wished more and more to be able to wander about with those whose world seemed to be so much larger than her own. They could fly over the sea in ships, and mount the high hills which were far above the clouds; and the lands they possessed, their woods and their fields, stretched far away beyond the reach of her sight. There was so much that she wished to know, and her sisters were unable to answer all her questions. Then she applied to her old grandmother, who knew all about the upper world, which she very rightly called the lands above the sea.

"If human beings are not drowned," asked the little mermaid, "can they live for ever? do they never die as we do here in the sea?"

"Yes," replied the old lady, "they must also die, and their term of life is even shorter than ours. We sometimes live to three hundred years, but when we cease to exist here we only become the foam on the surface of the water, and we have not even a grave down here of those we love. We have not immortal souls, we shall never live again; but, like the green sea-weed, when once it has been cut off, we can never flourish more. Human beings, on the contrary, have a soul which lives for ever, lives after the body has been turned to dust. It rises up through the clear, pure air beyond the glittering stars. As we rise out of the water, and behold all the land of the earth, so do they rise to unknown and glorious regions which we shall never see."

"Why have not we an immortal soul?" asked the little mermaid mournfully; "I would give gladly all the hundreds of years that I have to live, to be a human being only for one day, and to have the hope of knowing the happiness of that glorious world above the stars."

"You must not think of that," said the old woman; "we feel ourselves to be much happier and much better off than human beings."

"So I shall die," said the little mermaid, "and as the foam of the sea I shall be driven about never again to hear the music of the waves, or to see the pretty flowers nor the red sun. Is there anything I can do to win an immortal soul?"

"No," said the old woman, "unless a man were to love you so much that you were more to him than his father or mother; and if all his thoughts and all his love were fixed upon you, and the priest placed his right hand in yours, and he promised to be true to you here and hereafter, then his soul would glide into your body and you would obtain a share in the future happiness of mankind. He would give a soul to you and retain his own as well; but this can never happen. Your fish's tail, which amongst us is considered so beautiful, is thought on earth to be quite ugly; they do not know any better, and they think it necessary to have two stout props, which they call legs, in order to be handsome."

Then the little mermaid sighed, and looked sorrowfully at her fish's tail.

"Let us be happy," said the old lady, "and dart and spring about during the three hundred years that we have to live, which is really quite long enough; after that we can rest ourselves all the better. This evening we are going to have a court ball."

It was one of those splendid sights which we can never see on earth. The

walls and the ceiling of the large ball-room were of thick, but transparent crystal. Many hundreds of colossal shells, some of a deep red, others of a grass green, stood on each side in rows, with blue fire in them, which lighted up the whole saloon, and shone through the walls, so that the sea was also illuminated. Innumerable fishes, great and small, swam past the crystal walls; on some of them the scales glowed with a purple brilliancy, and on others they shone like silver and gold. Through the halls flowered a broad stream, and in it danced the mermen and the mermaids to the music of their own sweet singing. No one on earth has such a lovely voice as theirs. The little mermaid sang more sweetly than them all. The whole court applauded her with hands and tails; and for a moment her heart felt quite gay, for she knew she had the loveliest voice of any on earth or in the sea. But she soon thought again of the world above her, for she could not forget the charming prince, nor her sorrow that she had not an immortal soul like his; therefore she crept away silently out of her father's palace, and while everything within was gladness and song, she sat in her own little garden sorrowful and alone. Then she heard the bugle sounding through the water, and thought – "He is certainly sailing above, he on whom my wishes depend, and in whose hands I should like to place the happiness of my life. I will venture all for him, and to win an immortal soul; while my sisters are dancing in my father's palace, I will go to the sea witch, of whom I have always been so much afraid, but she can give me counsel and help."

And then the little mermaid went out from her garden, and took the road to the foaming whirlpools, behind which the sorceress lived. She had never been that way before: neither flowers nor grass grew there; nothing but bare, grey, sandy ground stretched out to the whirlpool, where the water, like foaming mill-wheels, whirled round everything that it seized, and cast it into the fathomless deep. Through the midst of these crushing whirlpools the little mermaid was obliged to pass, to reach the dominions of the sea witch; and also for a long distance the only road lay right across a quantity of warm, bubbling mire, called by the witch her turf-moor. Beyond this stood her house, in the centre of a strange forest, in which all the trees and flowers were polypi, half animals and half plants; they looked like serpents with a hundred heads growing out of the ground. The branches were long slimy arms, with fingers like flexible worms, moving limb after limb from the root to the top. All that could be reached in the sea they seized upon, and held fast, so that it never escaped from their clutches. The little mermaid was so alarmed at what she saw, that she stood still, and her heart beat with fear, and she was very nearly turning back; but she thought of the prince, and of the human soul for which she longed, and her courage returned. She fastened her long flowing hair round her head, so that the polypi might not seize hold of it. She laid her hands together across her bosom, and then she darted forward as a fish shoots through the water, between the supple arms and fingers of the ugly polypi, which were stretched out on each side of her. She saw that each held in its grasp something it had seized with its numerous little arms, as if they were iron bands. The white skeletons of human beings who had perished at sea, and had sunk down into the deep waters, skeletons of land animals, oars, rudders, and chests of ships were lying tightly grasped by their clinging arms; even a little mermaid, whom they had caught and strangled; and this seemed the most shocking of all to the little princess.

She now came to a space of marshy ground in the wood, where large, fat water-snakes were rolling in the mire, and showing their ugly, drab-coloured bodies. In the midst of this spot stood a house, built with the bones of shipwrecked human beings. There sat the sea witch, allowing a toad to eat from her mouth, just as people sometimes feed a canary with a piece of sugar. She called the ugly water-snakes her little chickens, and allowed them to crawl all over her bosom.

"I know what you want," said the sea witch; "it is very stupid of you, but you shall have your way, and it will bring you to sorrow, my pretty princess. You want to get rid of your fish's tail, and to have two supports instead of it, like human beings on earth, so that the young prince may fall in love with you, and that you may have an immortal soul." And then the witch laughed so loud and disgustingly, that the toad and the snakes fell to the ground, and lay there wriggling about. "You are just in time," said the witch; "for after sunrise to-morrow I should not be able to help you till the end of another year. I will prepare a draught for you, with which you must swim to land to-morrow before sunrise, and sit down on the shore and drink it. Your tail will then disappear, and shrink up into what mankind call legs; and you will feel great pain, as if a sword were passing through you. But all who see you will say that you are the prettiest little human being they ever saw. You will still have the same floating gracefulness of movement, and no dancer will ever tread so lightly; but at every step you take it will feel as if you were treading upon sharp knives, and that the blood must flow. If you will bear all this, I will help you."

"Yes, I will," said the little princess in a trembling voice, as she thought of the prince and the immortal soul.

"But think again," said the witch; "for when once your shape has become like a human being, you can no more be a mermaid. You will never return through the water to your sisters, or to your father's palace again; and if you do not win the love of the prince, so that he is willing to forget his father and mother for your sake, and to love you with his whole soul, and allow the priest to join your hands that you may be man and wife, then you will never have an immortal soul. The first morning after he marries another your heart will break, and you will become foam on the crest of the waves."

"I will do it," said the little mermaid, and she became pale as death.

"But I must be paid also," said the witch, "and it is not a trifle that I ask. You have the sweetest voice of any who dwell here in the depths of the sea, and you believe that you will be able to charm the prince with it also; but this voice you must give to me; the best thing you possess will I have for the price of my draught. My own blood must be mixed with it, that it may be as sharp as a two-edged sword."

"But if you take away my voice," said the little mermaid, "what is left for me?"

"Your beautiful form, your graceful walk, and your expressive eyes; surely with these you can enchain a man's heart. Well, have you lost your courage? Put out your little tongue that I may cut it off as my payment; then you shall have the powerful draught."

"It shall be," said the little mermaid.

Then the witch placed her cauldron on the fire, to prepare the magic draught. "Cleanliness is a good thing," said she, scouring the vessel with snakes, which she had tied together in a large knot; then she pricked herself in the breast, and let the black blood drop into it. The steam that rose formed itself into such horrible shapes that no one could look at them without fear. Every moment the witch threw something else into the vessel, and when it began to boil, the sound was like the weeping of a crocodile. When at last the magic draught was ready, it looked like the clearest water. "There it is for you," said the witch. Then she cut off the mermaid's tongue, so that she became dumb, and would never again speak or sing. "If the polypi should seize hold of you as you return through the wood," said the witch, "throw over them a few drops of the potion, and their fingers will be torn into a thousand pieces." But the little mermaid had no occasion to do this, for the polypi sprung back in terror when they caught sight of the glittering draught, which shone in her hand like a twinkling star.

So she passed quickly through the wood and the marsh, and between the rushing whirlpools. She saw that in her father's palace the torches in the ball-room were extinguished, and all within asleep; but she did not venture to go in to them, for, now she was dumb and going to leave them for ever, she felt as if her heart would break. She stole into the garden, took a flower from the flower-beds of each of her sisters, kissed her hand a thousand times towards the palace, and then rose up through the dark blue waters. The sun had not risen when she came in sight of the prince's palace, and

approached the beautiful marble steps, but the moon shone clear and bright. Then the little mermaid drank the magic draught, and it seemed as if a two-edged sword went through her delicate body: she into a swoon, and lay like one dead. When the sun arose and shone over the sea, she recovered, and felt a sharp pain; but just before her stood the handsome young prince. He fixed his coal-black eyes upon her so earnestly that she cast down her own, and then became aware that her fish's tail was gone, and that she had as pretty a pair of white legs and tiny feet as any little maiden could have; but she had no clothes, so she wrapped herself in her long, thick hair. The prince asked her who she was, and where she came from; and she looked at him mildly and sorrowfully with her deep blue eyes: but she could not speak. Then he took her by the hand, and led her to the palace. Every step she took was as the witch had said it would be, she felt as if treading upon the points of needles or sharp knives; but she bore it willingly, and stepped as lightly by the prince's side as a soap-bubble, so that he and all who saw her wondered at her graceful, swaying movements. She was very soon arrayed in costly robes of silk and muslin, and was the most beautiful creature in the palace; but she was dumb, and could neither speak nor sing. Beautiful female slaves, dressed in silk and gold, stepped forward and sang before the prince and his royal parents: one sang better than all the others, and the prince clapped his hands and smiled at her. This was a great sorrow to the little mermaid; she knew how much more sweetly she herself could sing once, and she thought, "Oh if he could only know that! The slaves next performed some pretty fairy-like dances, to the sound of beautiful music. Then the little mermaid raised her lovely white arms, stood on the tips of her toes, and glided over the floor, and danced as no one yet had been able to dance. At each moment her beauty became more revealed, and her expressive eyes appealed more directly to the heart than the songs of the slaves. Every one was enchanted, especially the prince, who called her his little foundling; and she danced again quite readily, to please him, though each time her foot touched the floor it seemed as if she trod on sharp knives.

The prince said she should remain with him always, and she received permission to sleep at his door, on a velvet cushion. He had a page's dress made for her, that she might accompany him on horseback. They rode together through the sweet-scented woods, where the green boughs touched their shoulders, and the little birds sang among the fresh leaves. She climbed with the prince to the tops of high mountains; and although her tender feet bled so that even her steps were marked, she only laughed, and followed him till they could see the clouds beneath them looking like a flock of birds travelling to distant lands. While at the prince's palace, and when all the household were asleep, she would go and sit on the broad marble steps; for it eased her burning feet to bathe them in the cold sea-water; and then she thought of all those below in the deep.

Once during the night her sisters came up arm-in-arm, singing sorrowfully, as they floated on the water. She beckoned to them, and then they recognised her, and told her how she had grieved them. After that, they came to the same place every night; and once she saw in the distance her old grandmother, who had not been to the surface of the sea for many years, and the old Sea King, her father, with his crown on his head. They stretched out their hands towards her, but they did not venture so near the land as her sisters did.

As the days passed, she loved the prince more fondly, and he loved her as he would love a little child; but it never came into his head to make her his wife: yet, unless he married her, she could not receive an immortal soul; and, on the morning after his marriage with another, she would dissolve into the foam of the sea.

"Do you not love me the best of them all?" the eyes of the little mermaid seemed to say, when he took her in his arms, and kissed her fair forehead.

"Yes, you are dear to me," said the prince; "for you have the best heart, and you are the most devoted to me; and you are like a young maiden whom I once saw, but whom I shall never meet again. I was in a ship that was wrecked, and the waves cast me ashore near a holy temple, where several young maidens performed the service. The youngest of them found me on the shore, and saved my life. I saw her but twice, and she is the only one in the world whom I could love; but you are like her, and you have almost driven her image out of my mind. She belongs to the holy temple, and my good fortune has sent you to me instead of her; and we will never part."

"Ah, he knows not that it was I who saved his life," thought the little mermaid. "I carried him over the sea to the wood where the temple stands; I sat beneath the foam, and watched till the human beings came to help him. I saw the pretty maiden that he loves better than he loves me;" and the mermaid sighed deeply, but she could not shed tears. "He says the maiden belongs to the holy temple, therefore she will never return to the world. They will meet no more; while I am by his side, and see him every day. I will take care of him, and love him, and give up my life for his sake."

Very soon it was said that the prince must marry, and that the beautiful daughter of a neighbouring king would be his wife, for a fine ship was being fitted out. Although the prince gave out that he merely intended to pay a visit to the king, it was generally supposed that he really went to see his daughter. A great company were to go with him. The little mermaid smiled, and shook her head. She knew the prince's thoughts better than any of the others.

"I must travel," he had said to her; "I must see this beautiful princess: my parents desire it; but they will not oblige me to bring her home as my bride. I cannot love her; she is not like the beautiful maiden in the temple, whom you resemble. If I were forced to choose a bride, I would rather choose you, my dumb foundling, with those expressive eyes." And then he kissed her rosy mouth, played with her long waving hair, and laid his head on her heart, while she dreamed of human happiness and an immortal soul. "You are not afraid of the sea, my dumb child," said he, as they stood on the deck of the noble ship which was to carry them to the country of the neighbouring king. And then he told her of storm and of calm, of strange fishes in the deep beneath them, and of what the divers had seen there; and she smiled at his descriptions, for she knew better than any one what wonders were at the bottom of the sea.

In the moonlight night, when all on board were asleep, excepting the man at the helm, who was steering, she sat on the deck, gazing down through the clear water. She thought she could distinguish her father's castle, and upon it her aged grandmother, with the silver crown on her head, looking through the rushing tide at the keel of the vessel. Then her sisters came up on the waves, and gazed at her mournfully, wringing their white hands. She beckoned to them, and smiled, and wanted to tell them how happy and well off she was; but the cabin-boy approached, and when her sisters dived down he thought it was only the foam of the sea which he saw.

The next morning the ship sailed into the harbour of a beautiful town belonging to the king whom the prince was going to visit. The church bells were ringing, and from the high towers sounded a flourish of trumpets; and soldiers, with flying colours and glittering bayonets, lined the roads through which they passed. Every day was a festival; balls and entertainments followed one another.

But the princess had not yet appeared. People said that she was being brought up and educated in a religious house, where she was learning every royal virtue. At last she came. Then the little mermaid, who was very anxious to see whether she was really beautiful, was obliged to acknowledge that she had never seen a more perfect vision of beauty. Her skin was delicately fair, and beneath her long dark eye-lashes her laughing blue eyes shone with truth and purity.

"It was you," said the prince, "who saved my life when I lay as if dead on the beach;" and he folded his blushing bride in his arms. "Oh, I am too happy," said he to the little mermaid; "my fondest hopes are all fulfilled.

You will rejoice at my happiness; for your devotion to me is great and sincere."

The little mermaid kissed his hand, and felt as if her heart were already broken. His wedding morning would bring death to her, and she would change into the foam of the sea. All the church bells rung, and the heralds rode about the town proclaiming the betrothal. Perfumed oil was burning in costly silver lamps on every altar. The priests waved the censers, while the bride and bridegroom joined their hands and received the blessing of the bishop. The little mermaid, dressed in silk and gold, held up the bride's train; but her ears heard nothing of the festive music, and her eyes saw not the holy ceremony: she thought of the night of death which was coming to her, and of all she had lost in the world. On the same evening the bride and bridegroom went on board ship; cannons were roaring, flags waving, and in the centre of the ship a costly tent of purple and gold had been erected. It contained elegant couches, for the reception of the bridal pair during the night. The ship, with swelling sails and a favourable wind, glided away smoothly and lightly over the calm sea. When it grew dark a number of coloured lamps were lit, and the sailors danced merrily on the deck. The little mermaid could not help thinking of her first rising out of the sea, when she had seen similar festivities and joy; and she joined in the dance, poised herself in the air as a swallow when he pursues his prey, and all present cheered her with wonder. She had never danced so elegantly before. Her tender feet felt as if cut with sharp knives, but she cared not for it; a sharper pang had pierced through her heart. She knew this was the last evening she should ever see the prince, for whom she had forsaken her kindred and her home; she had given up her beautiful voice, and suffered unheard-of pain daily for him, while he knew nothing of it. This was the last evening that she would breathe the same air with him, or gaze on the starry sky and the deep sea; an eternal night, without a thought or a dream, awaited her: she had no soul, and now she could never win one. All was joy and gaiety on board ship till long after midnight; she laughed and danced with the rest, while the thoughts of death were in her heart. The prince kissed his beautiful bride, while she played with his raven hair, till they went arm-in-arm to rest in the splendid tent. Then all became still on board the ship; the helmsman, alone awake, stood at the helm. The little mermaid leaned her white arms on the edge of the vessel, and looked towards the east for the first blush of morning, for that first ray of the dawn which was to be her death. She saw her sisters rising out of the flood: they were as pale as herself; but their long beautiful hair waved no more in the wind, it had been cut off.

"We have given our hair to the witch," said they, "to obtain help for you, that you may not die to-night. She has given us a knife: here it is, see it is very sharp. Before the sun rises you must plunge it into the heart of the prince; when the warm blood falls upon your feet they will grow together again, and form into a fish's tail, and you will be once more a mermaid, and return to us to live out your three hundred years before you die and change into the salt sea foam. Haste, then; he or you must die before sunrise. Our old grandmother mourns so for you, that her white hair is falling off from sorrow, as ours fell under the witch's scissors. Kill the prince, and come back; hasten: do you not see the first red streaks in the sky? In a few minutes the sun will rise, and you must die." And then they sighed deeply and mournfully, and sank down beneath the waves.

The little mermaid drew back the crimson curtain of the tent, and beheld the fair bride with her head resting on the prince's breast. She bent down and kissed his fair brow, then looked at the sky on which the rosy dawn grew brighter and brighter; then she glanced at the sharp knife, and again fixed her eyes on the prince, who whispered the name of his bride in his dreams. *She* was in his thoughts, and the knife trembled in the hand of the little mermaid: then she flug it far away from her into the waves; the water turned red where it fell, and the drops that spurted up looked like blood. She cast one more lingering, half-fainting glance at the prince, and then threw herself from the ship into the sea, and thought her body was dissolving into foam. The sun rose above the waves, and his warm rays fell on the cold foam of the little mermaid, who did not feel as if she were dying. She saw the bright sun, and all around her floated hundreds of transparent beautiful beings; she could see through them the white sails of the ships, and the red clouds in the sky; their speech was melodious, but too ethereal to be heard by mortal ears, as they were also unseen by mortal eyes. The little mermaid perceived that she had a body like theirs, and that she continued to rise higher and higher out of the foam. "Where am I?" asked she, and her voice sounded ethereal, as the voice of those who were with her; no earthly music could imitate it.

"Among the daughters of the air," answered one of them. "A mermaid has not an immortal soul, nor can she obtain one unless she wins the love of a human being. On the power of another hangs her eternal destiny. But the daughters of the air, although they do not possess an immortal soul, can, by their good deeds, procure one for themselves. We fly to warm countries, and cool the sultry air that destroys mankind with the pestilence. We carry the perfume of the flowers to spread health and restoration. After we have striven for three hundred years to do all the good in our power, we receive an immortal soul and take part in the happiness of mankind. You, poor little mermaid, have tried with your whole heart to do as we are doing;

you have suffered and endured and raised yourself to the spirit-world by your good deeds; and now, by striving for three hundred years in the same way, you may obtain an immortal soul."

The little mermaid lifted her glorified eyes towards the sun, and felt them, for the first time, filling with tears. On the ship, in which she had left the prince, there were life and noise; she saw him and his beautiful bride searching for her; sorrowfully they gazed at the pearly foam, as if they knew she had thrown herself into the waves. Unseen she kissed the forehead of the bride, and fanned the prince, and then mounted with the other children of the air to a rosy cloud that floated through the æther.

"After three hundred years, thus shall we float into the kingdom of heaven," said she. "And we may even get there sooner," whispered one of her companions. "Unseen we can enter the houses of men, where there are children, and for every day on which we find a good child, who is the joy of his parents and deserves their love, our time of probation is shortened. The child does not know, when we fly through the room, that we smile with joy at his good conduct, for we can count one year less of our three hundred years. But when we see a naughty or a wicked child, we shed tears of sorrow, and for every tear a day is added to our time of trial!"

The Garden of Paradise

There was once a king's son who had a larger and more beautiful collection of books than any one else in the world, all full of splendid copperplate engravings. He could read and obtain information respecting every people of every land; but not a word could he find to explain the situation of the garden of paradise, and this was just what he most wished to know. His grandmother had told him when he was quite a little boy, just old enough to go to school, that each flower in the garden of paradise was a sweet cake, that the pistils were full of rich wine, that on one flower history was written, on another geography or tables; so those who wished to learn their lessons had only to eat some of the cakes, and the more they ate, the more history, geography, or tables they knew. He believed it all then; but as he grew older, and learnt more and more, he became wise enough to understand that the splendour of the garden of paradise must be very different to all this. "Oh, why did Eve pluck the fruit from the tree of knowledge? why did Adam eat the forbidden fruit?" thought the king's son: "if I had been there it would never have happened, and there would have been no sin in the world." The garden of paradise occupied all his thoughts till he reached his seventeenth year.

One day he was walking alone in the wood, which was his greatest pleasure, when evening came on. The clouds gathered, and the rain poured down as if the sky had been a waterspout; and it was as dark as the bottom of a well at midnight; sometimes he slipped over the smooth grass, or fell over stones that projected out of the rocky ground. Everything was dripping with moisture, and the poor prince had not a dry thread about him. He was obliged at last to climb over great blocks of stone, with water spirting from the thick moss. He began to feel quite faint, when he heard a most singular rushing noise, and saw before him a large cave, from which came a blaze of light. In the middle of the cave an immense fire was burning, and a noble stag, with its branching horns, was placed on a spit between the trunks of two pine-trees. It was turning slowly before the fire, and an elderly woman, as large and strong as if she had been a man in disguise, sat by, throwing one piece of wood after another into the flames.

"Come in," she said to the prince; "sit down by the fire, and dry yourself."

"There is a great draught here," said the prince, as he seated himself on the ground.

"It will be worse when my sons come home," replied the woman; "you are now in the cavern of the Winds, and my sons are the four Winds of heaven: can you understand that?"

"Where are your sons?" asked the prince.

"It is difficult to answer stupid questions," said the woman. "My sons have plenty of business on hand; they are playing at shuttlecock with the clouds up yonder in the king's hall," and she pointed upwards.

"Oh, indeed," said the prince; "but you speak more roughtly and harshly and are not so gentle as the women I am used to."

"Yes, that is because they have nothing elso to do; but I am obliged to be harsh, to keep my boys in order, and I can do it, although they are so headstrong. Do you see those four sacks hanging on the wall? Well, they are just as much afraid of those sacks, as you used to be of the rat behind the looking-glass. I can bend the boys together, and put them in the sacks without any resistance on their parts, I can tell you. There they stay, and dare not attempt to come out until I allow them to do so. And here comes one of them."

It was the North Wind who came in, bringing with him a cold, piercing blast; large hailstones rattled on the floor, and snowflakes were scattered around in all directions. He wore a bearskin dress and cloak. His sealskin cap was drawn over this ears, long icicles hung from his beard, and one hailstone after another rolled from the collar of his jacket.

"Don't go too near the fire," said the prince, "or your hands and face will be frost-bitten."

"Frost-bitten!" said the North Wind, with a loud laugh; "why frost is my greatest delight. What sort of a little snip are you, and how did you find your way to the cavern of the Winds?"

"He is my guest," said the old woman, "and if you are not satisfied with that explanation you can go into the sack. Do you understand me?"

That settled the matter. So the North Wind began to relate his adventures, whence he came, and where he had been for a whole month. "I come from the polar seas," he said; I have been on the Bear's Island with the Russian walrus-hunters. I sat and slept at the helm of their ship, as they sailed away from North Cape. Sometimes when I woke, the storm-birds would fly about my legs. They are curious birds; they give one flap with their wings, and then on their outstretched pinions soar far away."

"Don't make such a long story of it," said the mother of the winds; "what sort of a place is Bear's Island?"

120

"A very beautiful place, with a floor for dancing as smooth and flat as a plate. Half-melted snow, partly covered with moss, sharp stones, and skeletons of walruses and polar-bears, lie all about, their gigantic limbs in a state of green decay. It would seem as if the sun never shone there. I blew gently, to clear away the mist, and then I saw a little hut, which had been built from the wood of a wreck, and was covered with the skins of the walrus, the fleshy side outwards; it looked green and red, and on the roof sat a growling bear. Then I went to the sea shore, to look after birds' nests, and saw the unfledged nestlings opening their mouths and screaming for food. I blew into the thousand little throats, and quickly stopped their screaming. Farther on were the walruses with pig-s heads, and teeth a yard long, rolling about like great worms."

"You relate your adventures very well, my son," said the mother, "it makes my mouth water to hear you."

"After that," continued the North Wind, "the hunting commenced. The harpoon was flung into the breast of the walrus, so that a smoking stream of blood spirted forth like a fountain, and besprinkled the ice. Then I thought of my own game; I began to blow, and set my own ships, the great icebergs sailing, so that they might crush the boats. Oh, how the sailors howled and cried out! but I howled louder than they. They were obliged to unload their cargo, and throw their chests and the dead walruses on the ice. Then I sprinkled snow over them, and left them in their curshed boats to drift southward, and to taste salt water. They will never return to Bear's Island."

"So you have done mischief," said the mother of the Winds.

121

"I shall leave others to tell the good I have done," he replied. "But here comes my brother from the West; I like him best of all, for he has the smell of the sea about him, and brings in a cold, fresh air as he enters."

"Is that the little Zephyr?" asked the prince.

"Yes, it is the Zephyr," said the old woman; "but he is not little now. In years gone by he was a beautiful boy; now that is all past."

He came in, looking like a wild man, and he wore a slouched hat to protect his head from injury. In his hand he carried a club, cut from a mahogany tree in the American forests; not a trifle to carry.

"Whence do you come?" asked the mother.

"I come from the wilds of the forests, where the thorny brambles form thick hedges between the trees; where the water-snake lies in the wet grass, and mankind seems to be unknown."

"What were you doing there?"

"I looked into the deep river, and saw it rushing down from the rocks. The water-drops mounted to the clouds and glittered in the rainbow. I saw the wild buffalo swimming in the river, but the strong tide carried him away amidst a flock of wild ducks, which flew into the air as the waters dashed onwards, leaving the buffalo to be hurled over the waterfall. This pleased me; so I raised a storm, which rooted up old trees, and sent them floating down the river."

"And what else have you done?" asked the old woman.

"I have rushed wildly across the savannahs; I have stroked the wild horses, and shaken the cocoa-nuts from the trees. Yes, I have many stories to relate; but I need not tell everything I know. You know it all very well, don't you old lady?" And he kissed his mother so roughly, that she nearly fell backwards. Oh, he was, indeed, a wild fellow.

Now in came the South Wind, with a turban and a flowing Bedouin cloak. "How cold it is here!" said he, throwing more wood on the fire. "It is easy to tell that the North Wind has arrived here before me."

"Why it is hot enough here to roast a bear," said the North Wind.

"You are a bear yourself," said the other.

"Do you want to be put in the sack, both of you?" said the old woman. "Sit down, now, on that stone, yonder, and tell me where you have been."

"In Africa, mother. I went out with the Hottentots, who were lion-hunting in the Kaffir land, where the plains are covered with grass the colour of a green olive; and here I ran races with the ostrich, but I soon outstripped him in swiftness. At last I came to the desert, in which lie the golden sands, looking like the bottom of the sea. Here I met a caravan, and the travellers had just killed their last camel, to obtain water; there was very little for them, and they continued their painful journey beneath the burning sun, and over the hot sands, which stretched before them a vast, boundless desert. Then I rolled myself in the loose sand, and whirled it in burning columns over their heads. The dromedarys stood still in terror, while the merchants drew their caftans over their heads, and threw themselves on the ground before me, as they do before Allah, their god. Then I buried them beneath a pyramid of sand, which covers them all. When I blow that away on my next visit, the sun will bleach their bones, and travellers will see that others have been there before them; otherwise, in such a wild desert, they might not believe it possible."

"So you have done nothing but evil," said the mother. "Into the sack with you;" and, before he was aware, she had seized the South Wind round the body, and popped him into the bag. He rolled about on the floor, till she sat herself upon him to keep him still.

"These boys of yours are very lively," said the prince.

"Yes," she replied, "but I know how to correct them, when necessary; and here comes the fourth." In came the East Wind, dressed like a Chinese.

"Oh, you come from that quarter, do you?" said she; "I thought you had been to the garden of paradise."

"I am going there to-morrow," he replied; "I have not been there for a hundred years. I have just come from China, where I danced round the porcelain tower till all the bells jingled again. In the streets an official flogging was taking place, and bamboo canes were being broken on the shoulders of men of very high position, from the first to the ninth grade. They cried, "Many thanks, my fatherly benefactor;" but I am sure the words did not come from their hearts, so I rang the bells till they sounded, 'ding, ding-dong.'"

"You are a wild boy," said the old woman; "it is well for you that you are going to-morrow to the garden of paradise; you always get improved in your education there. Drink deeply from the fountain of wisdom while you are there, and bring home a bottleful for me."

"That I will," said the East Wind; "but why have you put my brother South in a bag? Let him out; for I want him to tell me all about the phœnix bird. The princess always wants to hear of this bird when I pay her my visit every hundred years. If you will open the sack, sweetest mother, I will give you two pocketfuls of tea, green and fresh as when I gathered it from the spot where it grew."

"Well, for the sake or the tea, and because you are my own boy, I will open the bag."

She did so, and the South Wind crept out, looking quite cast down, because the prince had seen his disgrace.

"There is a palm-leaf for the princess," he said. "The old phœnix, the only one in the world, gave it to me himself. He has scratched on it with his beak the whole of his history during the hundred years he has lived. She can there read how the old phœnix set fire to his own nest, and sat upon it while it was burning, like a Hindoo widow. The dry twigs around the nest crackled and smoked till the flames burst forth and consumed the phœnix to ashes. Amidst the fire lay an egg, red hot, which presently burst with a loud report, and out flew a young bird. He is the only phœnix in the world, and the king over all the other birds. He has bitten a hole in the leaf which I give you, and that is his greeting to the princess."

"Now let us have something to eat," said the mother of the Winds. So they all sat down to feast on the roasted stag; and as the prince sat by the side of the East Wind, they soon became good friends.

"Pray tell me," said the prince, "who is that princess of whom you have been talking? and where lies the garden of paradise?"

"Ho! ho!" said the East Wind, "would you like to go there? Well, you can fly off with me to-morrow; but I must tell you one thing – no human being has been there since the time of Adam and Eve. I suppose you have read of them in your Bible."

"Of course I have," said the prince.

"Well," continued the East Wind, "when they were driven out of the garden of paradise, it sunk into the earth; but it retained its warm sunshine, its balmy air, and all its splendour. The fairy queen lives there, in the island of happiness, where death never comes, and all is beautiful. I can manage to take you there tomorrow, if you will sit on my back. But now don't talk any more, for I want to go to sleep;" and then they all slept.

When the prince awoke in the early morning, he was not a little surprised at finding himself high up above the clouds. He was seated on the back of the East Wind, who held him faithfully; and they were so high in the air that woods and fields, rivers and lakes, as they lay beneath them, looked like a painted map.

"Good morning," said the East Wind. "You might have slept on awhile; for there is very little to see in the flat country over which we are passing, unless you like to count the churches; they look like spots of chalk on a green board." The green board was the name he gave to the green fields and meadows.

"It was very rude of me not to say good-bye to your mother and your brothers," said the prince.

"They will excuse you, as you were asleep," said the East Wind; and then they flew on faster than ever.

The leaves and branches of the tress rustled as they passed. When they flew over seas and lakes, the waves rose higher, and the large ships dipped

into the water like diving swans. As darkness came on, towards evening, the great towns looked charming; lights were sparkling, now seen, now hidden, just as the sparks go out one after another on a piece of burnt paper. The prince clapped his hands with pleasure; but the East Wind advised him not to express his admiration in that manner, or he might fall down, and find himself hanging on a church steeple. The eagle in the dark forests flies swiftly; but faster than he flew the East Wind. The Cossack, on his small horse, rides lightly o'er the plains; but lighter still passed the prince on the wings of the wind.

"There are the Himalayas, the highest mountains in Asia," said the East Wind. "We shall soon reach the garden of paradise now."

Then they turned southward, and the air became fragrant with the perfume of spices and flowers. Here figs and pomegranates grew wild, and the vines were covered with clusters of blue and purple grapes. Here they both descended to the earth, and stretched themselves on the soft grass, while the flowers bowed to the breath of the wind as if to welcome it. "Are we now in the garden of paradise?" asked the prince.

"No indeed," replied the East Wind; "but we shall be there very soon. Do you see that wall of rocks, and the cavern beneath it, over which the grape vines hang like a green curtain? Through that cavern we must pass. Wrap your cloak round you; for while the sun scorches you here, a few steps farther it will be icy cold. The bird flying past the entrance to the cavern feels as if one wing were in the region of summer, and the other in the depths of winter."

"So this then is the way to the garden of paradise?" asked the prince, as they entered the cavern. It was indeed cold; but the cold soon passed, for the East Wind spread his wings, and they gleamed like the brightest fire. As they passed on through this wonderful cave, the prince could see great blocks of stone, from which water trickled, hanging over their heads in fantastic shapes. Sometimes it was so narrow that they had to creep on their hands and knees, while at other times it was lofty and wide, like the free air. It had the appearance of a chapel for the dead, with petrified organs and silent pipes. "We seem to be passing through the valley of death to the garden of paradise," said the prince.

But the East Wind answered not a word, only pointed forwards to a lovely blue light which gleamed in the distance. The blocks of stone assumed a misty appearance, till at last they looked like white clouds in moonlight. The air was fresh and balmy, like a breeze from the mountains perfumed with flowers from a valley of roses. A river, clear as the air itself, sparkled at their feet, while in its clear depths could be seen gold and silver fish sporting in the bright water, and purple eels emitting sparks of fire at every moment, while the broad leaves of the water-lilies, that floated on its surface, flickered with all the colours of the rainbow. The flower in its colour of flame seemed to recieve its nourishment from the water, as a lamp is sustained by oil. A marble bridge, of such exquisite workmanship that it appeared as if formed of lace and pearls, led to the island of happiness, in which bloomed the garden of paradise. The East Wind took the prince in his arms, and carried him over, while the flowers and the leaves sang the sweet songs of his childhood in tones so full and soft that no human voice could venture to imitate. Within the garden grew large trees, full of sap; but whether they were palm-trees or gigantic water-plants, the prince knew not. The climbing plants hung in garlands of green and gold, like the illuminations on the margins of old missals or twined among the initial letters. Birds, flowers, and festoons appeared intermingled in seeming confusion. Close by, on the grass, stood a group of peacocks, with radiant tails outspread to the sun. The prince touched them, and found, to his surprise, that they were not really birds, but the leaves of the burdock tree, which shone with the colours of a peacock's tail. The lion and the tiger, gentle and tame, were springing about like playful cats among the green bushes, whose perfume was like the fragrant blossom of the olive. The plumage of the wood-pigeon glistened like pearls as it struck the lion's mane with its wings; while the antelope, usually so shy, stood near, nodding its head as if it wished to join in the frolic. The fairy of paradise next made her appearance. Her raiment shone like the sun, and her serene countenance beamed with happiness like that of a mother rejoicing over her child. She was young and beautiful, and a train of lovely maidens followed her, each wearing a bright star in her hair. The East Wind gave her the palm-leaf, on which was written the history of the phœnix; and her eyes sparkled with joy. She then took the prince by the hand, and led him into her palace, the walls of which were richly coloured, like a tulip-leaf when it is turned to the sun. The roof had the appearance of an inverted flower, and the colours grew deeper and brighter to the gazer. The prince walked to a window, and saw what appeared to be the tree of knowledge of good and evil, with Adam and Eve standing by, and the serpent near them. "I thought they were banished from paradise," he said.

The princess smiled, and told him that time had engraved each event on a window-pane in the form of a picture; but, unlike other pictures, all that it represented lived and moved, – the leaves rustled, and the persons went and came, as in a looking-glass. He looked through another pane, and saw the ladder in Jacob's dream, on which the angels were ascending and descending with outspread wings. All that had ever happened in the world here lived and moved on the panes of glass, in pictures such as time alone could produce. The fairy now led the prince into a large, lofty room with transparent walls, through which the light shone. Here were portraits, each one appearing more beautiful than the other – millions of happy beings, whose laughter and song mingled in one sweet melody: some of these were in such an elevated position that they appeared smaller than the smallest rosebud, or like pencil dots on paper. In the centre of the hall stood a tree, with drooping branches, from which hung golden apples, both great and small, looking like oranges amid the green leaves. It was the tree of knowledge of good and evil, from which Adam and Eve had plucked and eaten the forbidden fruit, and from each leaf trickled a bright red dew-drop, as if the tree were weeping tears of blood for their sin. "Let us now take the boat," said the fairy; "a sail on the cool waters will refresh us. But we shall not move from the spot, although the boat may rock on the swelling water; the countries of the world will glide before us, but we shall remain still."

It was indeed wonderful to behold. First came the lofty Alps, snow-clad, and covered with clouds and dark pines. The horn resounded, and the shepherds sang merrily in the valleys. The banana-trees bent their drooping branches over the boat, black swans floated on the water, and singular animals and flowers appeared on the distant shore. *New Holland,* the fifth division of the world, now glided by, with mountains in the background, looking blue in the distance. They heard the song of the priests, and saw the wild dance of the savage to the sound of the drums and trumpets of bone; the pyramids of Egypt rising to the clouds; columns and sphinxes, overthrown and buried in the sand, followed in their turn; while the northern lights flashed out over the extinguished volcanoes of the north, in fireworks none could imitate.

The prince was delighted, and yet he saw hundreds of other wonderful things more than can be described. "Can I stay here for ever?" asked he.

"That depends upon yourself," replied the fairy. "If you do not, like Adam, long for what is forbidden, you can remain here always."

"I should not touch the fruit on the tree of knowledge," said the prince; "there is abundance of fruit equally beautiful."

"Examine your own heart," said the princess, "and if you do not feel sure of its strength, return with the East Wind who brought you. He is about to fly back, and will not return here for a hundred years. The time will not seem to you more than a hundred hours, yet even that is a long time for temptation and resistance. Every evening, when I leave you, I shall be obliged to say, 'Come with me,' and to beckon to you with my hand. But you must not listen, nor move from your place to follow me; for with every step you will find your power to resist weaker. If once you attempted to follow me, you would soon find yourself in the hall, where grows the

tree of knowledge, for I sleep beneath its perfumed branches. If you stooped over me, I should be forced to smile. If you then kissed my lips, the garden of paradise would sink into the earth, and to you it would be lost. A keen wind from the desert would howl around you; cold rain fall on your head, and sorrow and woe be your future lot." "I will remain," said the prince.

So the East Wind kissed him on the forehead, and said, "Be firm: then shall we meet again when a hundred years have passed. Farewell, farewell."

Then the East Wind spread his broad pinions, which shone like the lightning in harvest, or as the northern lights in a cold winter.

"Farewell, farewell," echoed the trees and the flowers.

Storks and pelicans flew after him in feathery bands, to accompany him to the boundaries of the garden.

"Now we will commence dancing," said the fairy; "and when it is nearly over at sunset, while I am dancing with you, I shall make a sign, and ask you to follow me: but do not obey. I shall be obliged to repeat the same thing for a hundred years; and each time, when the trial is past, if you resist, you will gain strength, till resistance becomes easy, and at last the temptation will be quite overcome. This evening, as it will be the first time, I have warned you."

After this the fairy led him into a large hall, filled with white transparent lilies. The yellow stamina of each flower formed a tiny golden harp, from which came forth strains of music like the mingled tones of flute and lyre. Beautiful maidens, slender and graceful in form, and robed in transparent gauze, floated through the dance, and sang of the happy life in the garden of paradise, where death never entered, and where all would bloom for ever in immortal youth. As the sun went down, the whole heavens became crimson and gold, and tinted the lilies with the hue of roses. Then the beautiful maidens offered to the prince sparkling wine; and when he had drank, he felt happiness greater than he had ever known before. Presently the background of the hall opened and the tree of knowledge appeared, surrounded by a halo of glory that almost blinded him. Voices, soft and lovely as his mother's, sounded in his ears, as if she were singing to him, "My child, my beloved child." Then the fairy beckoned to him, and said in sweet accents, "Come with me, come with me." Forgetting his promise, forgetting it even on the very first evening, he rushed towards her, while she continued to beckon to him and to smile. The fragrance around him overpowered his senses, the music from the harps sounded more entrancing, while around the tree appeared millions of smiling faces, nodding and singing, "Man should know everything; man is the lord of the earth." The tree of knowledge no longer wept tears of blood, for the dewdrops shone like glittering stars.

"Come, come," continued that thrilling voice, and the prince followed the call. At every step his cheeks glowed, and the blood rushed wildly through his veins. "I must follow," he cried; "it is not a sin, it cannot be, to follow beauty and joy. I only want to see her asleep, and nothing will happen unless I kiss her, and that I will not do, for I have strength to resist, and a determined will." The fairy threw off her dazzling attire, bent back the boughs, and in another moment was hidden among them.

"I have not sinned yet," said the prince, "and I will not;" and then he pushed aside the boughs to follow the princess. She was lying already asleep, beautiful as only a fairy in the garden of paradise could be. She smiled as he bent over her, and he saw tears trembling on her beautiful eyelashes. "Do you weep for me?" he whispered. "Oh weep not, thou loveliest of women. Now do I begin to understand the happiness of paradise; I feel it to my inmost soul, in every thought. A new life is born within me. One moment of such happiness is worth an eternity of darkness and woe." He stooped and kissed the tears from her eyes, and touched her lips with his.

A clap of thunder, loud and awful, resounded through the trembling air. All around him fell into ruin. The lovely fairy, the beautiful garden, sunk deeper and deeper. The prince saw it sinking down in the dark night till it shone only like a star in the distance beneath him. Then he felt a coldness, like death, creeping over him; his eyes closed, and he became insensible.

When he recovered, a chilling rain was beating upon him, and a sharp wind blew on his head. "Alas! what have I done?" he sighed; "I have sinned like Adam, and the garden of paradise has sunk into the earth." He opened his eyes, and saw the star in the distance, but it was the morning star in heaven which glittered in the darkness. Presently he stood up and found himself in the depths of the forest close to the cavern of the Winds, and the mother of the Winds sat by his side. She looked angry, and raised her arm in the air as she spoke. "The very first evening!" she said. "Well, I expected it! If you were my son, you should go into the sack."

"And there he will have to go at last," said a strong old man, with large black wings, and a scythe in his hand, whose name was Death. "He shall be laid in his coffin, but not yet. I will allow him to wander about the world for a while, to atone for his sin, and to give him time to become better. But I shall return when he least expects me. I shall lay him in a black coffin, place it on my head, and fly away with it beyond the stars. There also blooms a garden of paradise, and if he is good and pious he will be admitted; but if his thoughts are bad, and his hearts is full of sin, he will sink with his coffin deeper than the garden of paradise has sunk. Once in every thousand years I shall go and fetch him, when he will either be condemned to sink still deeper, or be raised to a happier life in the world beyond the stars."

131

The Storks

On the roof of a house situated at the extremity of a small town, a stork had built his nest. There sat the mother-stork, with her four young ones, who all stretched out their little black bills, which had not yet become red. Not far off, upon the parapet, erect and proud, stood the father-stork; he had drawn one of his legs under him, being weary of standing on two. You might have fancied him carved in wood, he stood so motionless. 'It looks so grand,' thought he, 'for my wife to have a sentinel to keep guard over her nest; people cannot know that I am her husband, they will certainly think that I am commanded to stand here – how well it looks!' and so he remained standing on one leg.

In the street below, a number of children were playing togehter. When they saw the storks, one of the liveliest amongst them began to sing as much as he could remember of some old rhymes about storks, in which he was soon joined by the others –

'Stork! stork! long-legged stork!
Into thy nest I prithee walk;
There sits thy mate,
With her four children so great.
The first we'll hang like a cat,
The second we'll burn,
The third on a spit we'll turn,
The fourth drown dead as a rat!'

'Only listen to what the boys are singing,' said the little storks; 'they say we shall be hanged and burnt!'

'Never mind,' said the mother, 'don't listen to them; they will do you no harm.'

But the boys went on singing, and pointed their fingers at the storks: only one little boy, called Peter, said 'it was a sin to mock and tease animals, and that he would have nothing to do with it.'

The mother-stork again tried to comfort her little ones. 'Never mind,' said she; 'see how composedly your father is standing there, and upon one leg only.'

'But we are so frightened!' said the young ones, drawing their heads down into the nest.

The next day, when the children were again assembled to play together, and saw the storks, they again began their song –

'The first we'll hang like a cat,
The second we'll burn!'

'And are we really to be hanged and burnt?' asked the young storks.

'No indeed!' said the mother. 'You shall learn to fly: I will teach you myself. Then we can fly over to the meadow, and pay a visit to the frogs. They will bow to us in the water, and say, "Croak, croak!" and then we shall eat them; will not that be nice?'

'And what then?' asked the little storks.

'Then all the storks in the country will gather together, and the autumnal exercise will begin. It is of the greatest consequence that you should fly well then; for every one who does not, the general will stab to death with his bill; so you must pay great attention when we begin to drill you, and learn very quickly.'

'Then we shall really be killed after all, as the boys said? Oh, listen! they are singing it again!'

'Attend to me, and not to them!' said the mother. 'After the grand exercise, we shall fly to warm countries, far, far away from here, over mountains and forests. We shall fly to Egypt, where are the three-cornered stone houses whose summits reach the clouds; they are called pyramids, and are older than it is possible for storks to imagine. There is a river too, which overflows its banks, so as to make the whole country like a marsh, and we shall go into the marsh and eat frogs.'

'Oh!' said the young ones.

'Yes, it is delightful! one does nothing but eat all the day long. And whilst we are so comfortable, in this country not a single green leaf is left on the trees, and it is so cold that the clouds are frozen, and fall down upon the earth in little white pieces.' – She meant snow, but she could not express herself more clearly.

'And will the naughty boys be frozen to pieces too?' asked the young storks.

'No, they will not be frozen to pieces; but they will be nearly as badly off as if they were; they will be obliged to crowd round the fire in their little dark rooms; while you, on the contrary, will be flying about in foreign lands, where there are beautiful flowers and warm sunshine.'

Well, time passed away, and the young storks grew so tall, that when they stood upright in the nest they could see the country around to a great

distance. The father-stork used to bring them every day the nicest little frogs, as well as snails, and all the other stork tit-bits he could find. Oh! It was so droll to see him show them his tricks; he would lay his head upon his tail, make a rattling noise with his bill, and then tell them such charming stories all about the moors.

'Now you must learn to fly!' said the mother one day; and accordingly, all the four young storks were obliged to come out upon the parapet. Oh, how they trembled! And though they balanced themselves on their wings, they were very near falling.

'Only look at me,' said the mother. 'This is the way you must hold your heads; and in this manner place your feet, – one two! one, two! this will help you to get on.' She flew a little way, and the young ones made an awkward spring after her, – bounce! down they fell; for their bodies were heavy.

'I will not fly,' said one of the young ones, as he crept back into the nest. 'I do not want to go into the warm countries!'

'Do you want to be frozen to death during the winter? Shall the boys come, and hang, burn, or roast you? Wait a little, I will call them!'

'Oh no!' said the little stork; and again he began to hop about on the roof like the others. By the third day they could fly pretty well, and so they thought they could also sit and take their ease in the air; but bounce! down they tumbled, and found themselves obliged to make use of their wings. The boys now came into the street, singing their favourite song –

'Stork! stork! long-legged stork!'

'Shall not we fly down and peck out their eyes?' said the young ones.

'No, leave them alone!' said the mother. 'Attend to me, that is of much more importance! – one, two, three, now to the right! one, two three, now to the left, round the chimneypot! That was very well; you managed your wings so neatly last time, that I will permit you to come with me to–morrow to the marsh: several first–rate stork families will be there with their children. Let it be said that mine are the prettiest and best behaved of all; and remember to stand very upright, and to throw out your chest; that looks well, and gives such an air of distinction!'

'But are we not to take revenge upon those rude boys?' asked the young ones.

'Let them screech as much as they please! You will fly among the clouds, you will go to the land of the pyramids, when they must shiver with cold, and have not a single green leaf to look at, nor a single sweet apple to eat!'

'Yes, we shall be revenged!' whispered they one to another. And then they were drilled again.

Of all the boys in the town, the forwardest in singing nonsensical verses was also the same one who had begun teasing the storks, a little urchin not more than six years old. The young storks indeed fancied him a hundred years old, because he was bigger than either their father or mother, and what should they know about the ages of children, or grown up human beings! All their schemes of revenge were aimed at this little boy; he had been the first to tease them, and continued to do so. The young storks were highly excited about it, and the older they grew, the less they were inclined to endure persecution. Their mother, in order to pacify them, at last promised that they should be revenged, but not until the last day of their stay in this place.

'We must first see how you behave yourselves at the grand exercise; if then you should fly badly, and the general should thrust his beak into your breast, the boys will, in some measure, be proved in the right. Let me see how well you will behave!'

'Yes, that you shall!' said the young ones. And now they really took great pains, practised every day, and at last flew so lightly and prettily, that it was a pleasure to see them.

Well, now came the autumn. All the storks assembled, in order to fly together to warm countries for the winter. What a practising there was! Away they went over woods and fields, towns and villages, merely to see how well they could fly, for they had a long journey before them. The young storks distinguished themselves so honourably that they were pronounced 'worthy of frogs and serpents.' This was the highest character they could obtain; now they were allowed to eat frogs and serpents, and accordingly they did eat them.

'Now we will have our revenge!' said they.

'Very well!' said the mother; 'I have been thinking what will be the best. I know where the pool is in which all the little human children lie until the storks come and take them to their parents: the pretty little things sleep and dream so pleasantly as they will never dream again. All parents like to have a little child, and all children like to have a little brother or sister. We will fly to the pool and fetch one for each of the boys who has not sung that wicked song, nor made a jest of the storks; and the other naughty children shall have none.'

'But he who first sung those naughty rhymes! that great ugly fellow! what shall we do to him?' cried the young storks.

'In the pool there lies a little child who has dreamed away his life; we will take it for him, and he will weep because he has only a little dead brother. But as the good boy who said it was a sin to mock and tease animals, surly you have not forgotten him? We will bring him two little ones, a brother and a sister. And as this little boy's name is Peter, you too shall for the future be called "Peter!"'

And it came to pass just as the mother said; and all the storks were called 'Peter,' and are still so called to this very day.

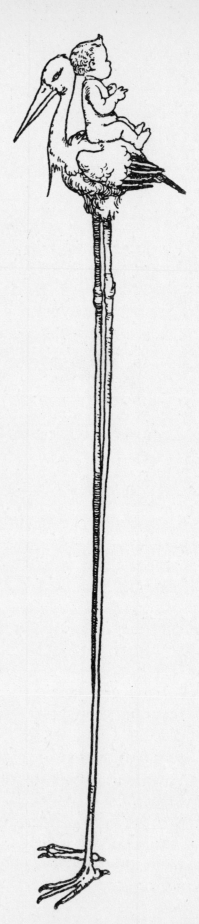

138

The Tinder-Box

A soldier came marching along the high road: "Left, right – left, right." He had his knapsack on his back, and a sword at his side; he had been to the wars, and was now returning home. As he walked on, he met a very frightful-looking old witch in the road. Her under-lip hung quite down on her breast, and she stopped and said, "Good evening, solider; you have a very fine sword, and a large knapsack, and you are a real soldier; so you shall have as much money as ever you like."

"Thank you, old witch," said the soldier.

"Do you see that large tree?" said the witch, pointing to a tree which stood beside them. "Well, it is quite hollow inside, and you must climb to the top, when you will see a hole, through which you can let yourself down into the tree to a great depth. I will tie a rope round your body, so that I can pull you up again when you call out to me."

"But what am I to do, down there in the tree?" asked the soldier.

"Get money," she replied; "for you must know that when you reach the ground under the tree, you will find yourself in a large hall, lighted up by three hundred lamps; you will then see three doors, which can be easily opened, for the keys are in all the locks. On entering the first of the chambers, to which these doors lead, you will see a large chest, standing in the middle of the floor, and upon it a dog seated, with a pair of eyes as large as teacups. But you need not be at all afraid of him; I will give you my blue checked apron, which you must spread upon the floor, and then boldly seize hold of the dog, and place him upon it. You can then open the chest, and take from it as many pence as you please, they are only copper pence; but if you would rather have silver money, you must go into the second chamber. Here you will find another dog, with eyes as big as mill-wheels; but do not let that trouble you. Place him upon my apron, and then take what money you please. If, however, you like gold best, enter the third chamber, where there is another chest full of it. The dog who sits on this chest is very dreadful; his eyes are as big as a tower, but do not mind him. If he also is placed upon my apron, he cannot hurt you, and you may take from the chest what gold you will."

"This is not a bad story," said the soldier; "but what am I to give you, you old witch? for, of course, you do not mean to tell me all this for nothing."

"No," said the witch; "but I do not ask for a single penny. Only promise to bring me an old tinder-box, which my grandmother left behind the last time she went down there."

"Very well; I promise. Now tie the rope round my body."

"Here it is," replied the witch; "and here is my blue checked apron."

As soon as the rope was tied, the soldier climbed up the tree, and let himself down through the hollow to the ground beneath; and here he found, as the witch had told him, a large hall, in which many hundred lamps were all burning. Then he opened the first door. "Ah!" there sat the dog, with the eyes as large as teacups, staring at him.

"You're a pretty fellow," said the soldier, seizing him, and placing him on the witch's apron, while he filled his pockets from the chest with as many pence as they would hold. Then he closed the lid, seated the dog upon it again, and walked into another chamber. And, sure enough, there sat the dog, with eyes as big as mill-wheels.

"You had better not look at me in that way," said the soldier; "you will make your eyes water;" and then he seated him also upon the apron, and opened the chest. But when he saw what a quantity of silver money it contained, he very quickly threw away all the coppers he had taken, and filled his pockets and his knapsack with nothing but silver.

Then he went into the third room, and there the dog was really hideous; his eyes were, truly, as big as towers, and they turned round and round in his head like wheels.

"Good morning," said the soldier, touching his cap, for he had never seen such a dog in his life. But after looking at him more closely, he thought he had been civil enough, so he placed him on the floor, and opened the chest. Good gracious, what a quantity of gold there was! enough to buy all the sugar-sticks of the sweetstuff women; all the tin-soldiers, whips, and rocking-horses in the world, or even the whole town itself. There was, indeed, an immense quantity. So the soldier now threw away all the silver money he had taken, and filled his pockets and his knapsack with gold instead; and not only his pockets and his knapsack, but even his cap and his boots, so that he could scarcely walk.

He was really rich now; so he replaced the dog on the chest, closed the door, and called up through the tree, "Now pull me out, you old witch."

"Have you got the tinder-box?" asked the witch.

"No; I declare I quite forgot it." So he went back and fetched the tinder-box, and then the witch drew him up out of the tree, and he stood again in the high road, with his pockets, his knapsack, his cap, and his boots full of gold.

"What are you going to do with the tinder-box?" asked the soldier.

"That is nothing to you," replied the witch; "you have the money, now give me the tinder-box."

"I tell you what," said the soldier, "if you don't tell me what you are going to do with it, I will draw my sword and cut off your head."

"No," said the witch.

The soldier immediately cut off her head, and there she lay on the ground. Then he tied up all his money in her apron, and slung it on his back like a bundle, put the tinder-box in his pocket, and walked off to the nearest town. It was a very nice town, and he put up at the best inn, and ordered a dinner of all his favourite dishes, for now he was rich and had plenty of money. The servant, who cleaned his boots, thought they certainly were a very shabby pair to be worn by such a rich gentleman, for he had not yet bought any new ones. The next day, however, he procured some good clothes and proper boots, so that our soldier soon became known as a fine gentleman, and the people visited him, and told him all the wonders that were to be seen in the town, and of the king's beautiful daughter, the princess.

"Where can I see her?" asked the soldier.

"She is not to be seen at all," they said; "she lives in a large copper castle, surrounded by walls and towers. No one but the king himself can pass in or out, for there has been a prophecy that she will marry a common soldier, and the king cannot bear to think of such a marriage."

"I should very much like to see her," thought the soldier; but he could not obtain permission to do so. However, he passed a very pleasant time; went to the theatre, drove in the king's garden, and gave a great deal of money to the poor, which was very good of him; he remembered what it had been in olden times to be without a shilling. Now he was rich, had fine clothes, and many friends, who all declared he was a fine fellow and a real gentleman, and all this gratified him exceedingly. But his money would not last for ever; and as he spent and gave away a great deal daily, and received none, he found himself at last with only two shillings left. So he was obliged to leave his elegant rooms, and live in a little garret under the roof, where he had to clean his own boots, and even mend them with a large needle. None of his friends came to see him, there were too many stairs to mount up. One dark evening, he had not even a penny to buy a candle; then all at once he remembered that there was a piece of candle stuck in the tinder-box, which he had brought from the old tree, into which the witch had helped him.

He found the tinder-box, but no sooner had he struck a few sparks from the flint and steel, than the door flew open, and the dog with eyes as big as teacups, whom he had seen while down in the tree, stood before him, and said, "What orders, master?"

"Hallo," said the soldier; "well this is a pleasant tinder-box, if it brings me all I wish for."

"Bring me some money," said he to the dog.

He was gone in a moment, and presently returned, carrying a large bag of coppers in his mouth. The soldier very soon discovered after this the value of the tinder-box. If he struck the fllint once, the dog who sat on the chest of copper money made his appearance; if twice, the dog came from the chest of silver; and if three times, the dog with eyes like towers, who watched over the gold. The soldier had now plenty of money; he returned to his elegant rooms, and re-appeared in his fine clothes, so that his friends knew him again directly, and made as much of him as before.

After a while he began to think it was very strange that no one could get a look at the princess. "Every one says she is very beautiful," he thought to himself; "but what is the use of that if she is to be shut up in a copper castle surrounded by so many towers. Can I by any means get to see her. Stop! where is my tinder-box?" Then he struck a light, and in a moment the dog, with eyes as big as teacups, stood before him.

"It is midnight," said the soldier, "yet I should very much like to see the princess, if only for a moment."

The dog disappeared instantly, and before the soldier could even look round, he returned with the princess. She was lying on the dog's back asleep, and looked so lovely, that every one who saw her would know she was a real princess. The soldier could not help kissing her, true soldier as he was. Then the dog ran back with the princess; but in the morning, while at breakfast with the king and queen, she told them what a singular dream she had had during the night, of a dog and a soldier, that she had ridden on the dog's back, and been kissed by the soldier.

"That is a very pretty story, indeed," said the queen. So the next night one of the old ladies of the court was set to watch by the princess's bed, to discover whether it really was a dream, or what else it might be.

The soldier longed very much to see the princess once more, so he sent for the dog again in the night to fetch her, and to run with her as fast as ever he could. But the old lady put on waterboots, and ran after him as quickly as he did, and found that he carried the princess into a large house. She thought it would help her to remember the place if she made a large cross on the door with a piece of chalk. Then she went home to bed, and the dog presently returned with the princess. But when he saw that a cross had been made on the door of the house, where the soldier lived, he took another piece of chalk and made crosses on all the doors in the town, so that the lady-in-waiting might not be able to find out the right door.

Eearly the next morning the king and queen accompanied the lady and all the officers of the household, to see where the princess had been.

"Here it is," said the king, when they came to the first door with a cross on it.

"No, my dear husband, it must be that one," said the queen pointing to a second door having a cross also.

"And here is one, and there is another!" they all exclaimed; for there were crosses on all the doors in every direction.

So they felt it would be useless to search any farther. But the queen was a very clever woman; she could do a great deal more then merely ride in a carriage. She took her large gold scissors, cut a piece of silk into squares, and made a neat little bag. This bag she filled with buckwheat flour, and tied it round the princess's neck; and then she cut a small hole in the bag, so that the flour might be scattered on the ground as the princess went along. During the night, the dog came again and carried the princess on his back, and ran with her to the soldier, who loved her very much, and wished that he had been a prince, so that he might have her for a wife. The dog did not observe how the flour ran out of the bag all the way from the castle wall to the soldier's house, and even up to the window, where he had climbed with the princess. Therefore in the morning the king and queen

144

found out where their daughter had been, and the soldier was taken up and put in prison. Oh, how dark and disagreeable it was as he sat there, and the people said to him, "To-morrow you will be hanged." It was not very pleasant news, and besides, he had left the tinder-box at the inn. In the morning he could see through the iron grating of the little window how the people were hastening out of the town to see him hanged; he heard the drums beating, and saw the soldiers marching. Every one ran out to look at them, and a shoemaker's boy, with a leather apron and slippers on, galloped by so fast, that one of his slippers flew off and struck against the wall where the soldier sat looking through the iron grating. "Hallo, you shoemaker's boy, you need not be in such a hurry," cried the soldier to him. "There will be nothing to see till I come; but if you will run to the house where I have been living, and bring me my tinder-box, you shall have four shillings, but you must put your best foot foremost."
The shoemaker's boy liked the idea of getting the four shillings, so he ran very fast and fetched the tinder-box, and gave it to the soldier. And now

we shall see what happened. Outside the town a large gibbet had been erected, round which stood the soldiers and several thousands of people. The king and the queen sat on splendid thrones opposite to the judges and the whole council. The soldier already stood on the ladder; but as they were about to place the rope round his neck, he said that an innocent request was often granted to a poor criminal before he suffered death. He wished very much to smoke a pipe, as it would be the last pipe he should ever smoke in the world. The king could not refuse this request, so the soldier took his tinder-box, and struck fire, once, twice, thrice, – and there in a moment stood all the dogs; – the one with eyes as big as teacups, the one with eyes as large as mill-wheels, and the third, whose eyes were like towers. "Help me now, that I may not be hanged," cried the soldier.

And the dogs fell upon the judges and all the councillors; seized one by the legs, and another by the nose, and tossed them many feet high in the air, so that they fell down and were dashed to pieces.

"I will not be touched," said the king. But the largest dog seized him, as well as the queen, and threw them after the others. Then the soldiers and all the people were afraid, and cried, "Good soldier, you shall be our king, and you shall marry the beautiful princess."

So they placed the soldier in the king's carriage, and the three dogs ran on in front and cried "Hurrah!" and the little boys whistled through their fingers, and the soldiers presented arms. The princess came out of the copper castle, and became queen, which was very pleasing to her. The wedding festivities lasted a whole week, and the dogs sat at the table, and stared with all their eyes.

A Story from the Sand-Hills

In sunny Spain, where the fiery blossoms of the pomegranate flourish among the dark laurels, and the orange groves pour forth fragrance, it is warm and beautiful, while from the mountains comes a cool and refreshing breeze. Brightly the golden cupolas of the Moorish halls, with their gorgeous ornaments and many-coloured walls, glitter in the sun. There is a sound of song and castanets; youths and maidens join in the dance under the blooming acacia; while even the beggar sits upon the marble stone, refreshing himself with a juicy melon, and dreamily enjoying life. At night there is a procession of children through the streets, with candles and waving flags, and over them all lofty and clear rises the sky, studded with sparkling stars. The whole is like a glorious dream.

In an open balcony sat a newly married couple, who completely gave themselves up to the charm, for they also possessed the good things of this life – health and cheerfulness, riches and honour. "We are as happy as it is possible to be," they said, from the depths of their hearts. They had, indeed, but one step more in the ladder of human happiness, and they were already happy in the hope that God would give them a child – a son, who should resemble them in form and spirit. The happy child would be welcomed with rejoicing, would be tended with every care and love, and enjoy all those advantages of wealth and luxury which riches and influence can procure. And so the days passed like a festival.

"Life is a gracious gift from God, a gift almost beyond our power to appreciate," said the young wife; "and yet they tell us that fulness of joy is only to be found in the future for ever and ever; I cannot compass the thought."

"Perhaps the thought arises from the arrogance of mankind," said the husband. "It seems like pride to believe that we shall live for ever, that we shall be as gods. Were not these the words of the serpent, the father of lies?"

"Surely you do not doubt the existence of a future life?" exclaimed the young wife, and it seemed like the first shadow of evil passing over the sunny region of her thoughts.

"Faith realizes it, and the priests tell us it is so," he replied; "but amidst all this happiness I feel as if it were presumptuous to expect it to continue for ever, in another life after this. So much has been given to us in this present state of existence, that we ought to be, we must be content with it."

"Yes," replied the young wife, "it has been certainly given to us, but to how many thousands this life is one continued scene of painful trial! How many have been sent into the world, as it appears, only to suffer poverty and shame, sickness and misfortune! If there were no life after this, things on earth would be too unequal, and we should feel inclined to accuse the Almighty of injustice."

"Not so," replied the husband; "yonder beggar has joys which appear great to him, and which delight him more than the splendours of his palace delight a king. And then do you not suppose that the dumb beast of burden, which endures hunger and blows, and works itself to death, does not equally feel its hard fate? Might it not therefore also expect a future life, and complain of the injustice that has not placed him higher in the scale of creation?"

"Christ has said," replied the wife, "'In my Father's house are many mansions;' heaven is as limitless as the love of our Creator. Even the dumb beast is His creature; and I firmly believe that no life will be lost, but that each will receive that amount of happiness which he is able to enjoy, and which is sufficient for him."

"The world is sufficient for me," said the husband, as he threw his arm round his beautiful, amiable wife. Then he sat by her side on the open balcony, and smoked his cigarette, while the cool air was filled with the fragrance of pinks and orange blossoms. Sounds of music, and the clatter of castanets came up from the road beneath; the stars glittered above them, and two eyes, full of affection, the eyes of his wife, looked on him with the undying glance of love. "Such a moment," said he, "surely makes it worth while to be born – to die – and to be annihilated."

The young wife raised her hand as a gentle reproof, but the shadow passed away from her world, and they were happy – quite happy. Everything seemed to work together for them. They advanced in honour and prosperity and joy. A change came, but it was only a change of place, not of enjoyment, either of life or happiness. The young man was chosen by his sovereign, the King of Spain, to proceed to the court of Russia as ambassador; for his high birth and attainments gave him a title to such an honour. He possessed also a large fortune of his own, as well as one equally large, brought him by his wife, who was the daughter of a rich and highly respected merchant. One of this merchant's largest and finest ships was about to sail during the year to Stockholm, and it was arranged that the young people, the merchant's daughter and son-in-law, should continue their voyage in

it from thence to St. Petersburg. All the arrangements made for them were princely; rich carpets for the feet, and silk and luxurious furniture suited for the voyage were put on board the vessel for their use.

In an old war song, entitled "The Son of England's King," it says, –

"He sailed in a gallant ship,
* And the anchor was gilded with gold,*
Each rope was woven with silk,
* With riches and pomp untold."*

These words rose to the mind of one who saw this ship leave the coasts of Spain. Here was the same pomp, the same luxury, and the same parting wish:

"God grant that all of us may meet
* Once more in peace and joy."*

149

It blew a fair wind when they left the Spanish coast, so that they hoped to arrive at their destination in a few weeks. But when they reached the broad ocean, the wind sank down, the sea became smooth, and the ship was becalmed. However, the stars of heaven shone brightly, and many festive evenings were spent in that sumptuous cabin. At length the voyagers began to wish for wind, for a favouring breeze. But they wished in vain, for not a breeze stirred; and when, after some weeks, the wind did arise, it was contrary, for it blew from the south-west, and after two months carried them into the North Sea, between Scotland and Jutland. Then the wind increased, till they were in the condition described in the old song, –

"'Mid the stormy sea and the pelting rain,
To seek for shelter was all in vain;
No hope of throwing, with eager hand,
Their anchor of gold near the Danish land."

At the time this happened, King Christian VII., who sat on the Danish throne, was still a young man. Much has changed or been changed since then. Lakes and marshes have been converted into green meadows, heath has become arable land, and in the shelter of the peasants' houses, on the West Jute, grow apple-trees and rose-bushes; but they require care, to protect them from the keen north-west wind.

While in West Jutland, the mind can easily go back to the old times, even long before the days of King Christian VII. The purple heath extends now, as it did then, for miles. There are the still "Huns' graves," the supernatural appearances in the sky, and the sandy, uneven roads crossing it in every direction. Westward, where large rivulets run into the bay, extend marshes and meadow land, girded with lofty sand-hills, which, like a row of Alps, raise their peaked summits, on the side nearest the sea, to a great height. Here and there are ridges of clay, from which the sea, year after year, bites out huge mouthfuls, causing the overhanging shores to fall as if by the shock of an earthquake. Thus it is even at this day, and thus it was many, many years ago, when the happy pair were sailing in the richly appointed ship. It was Sunday, and a bright sunny morning towards the latter end of September. The bells of the churches in the Bay of Nissum were chiming sweetly, and their music rolled through the air like a chain of sounds. The churches there are built almost entirely of hewn boulder stones, each like a piece of rock. The North Sea might foam over them, and they would remain unmoved. Most of them are without steeples, and the bells are hung between two beams in the open air. At the close of the service, the congregation passed out into the churchyard, where not a tree nor a bush

could be seen; not a flower had been planted, nor a wreath hung on the graves. Rough mounds marked the spots where the dead lay buried, and long, waving grass grew thickly over the whole churchyard. Here and there a grave had for a monument a half-decayed block of wood, rudely cut into the form of a coffin, and these blocks are often brought from the forest of West Jutland. This forest is like the shores of the wild sea: here the inhabitants find beams and planks and fragments from wrecks, which have been cast ashore by the breakers, and are soon discoloured by the wind and the sea-fogs. One of these blocks had been placed by loving hands on a child's grave; and a woman who came out of church stepped towards it. She stood still with her eyes resting on the weather beaten monument, and in a few moments her husband came and joined her. Neither of them spoke a word; but he took her hand, and led her away from the grave across the purple heath, over moor and meadow, towards the sand-hills. For a long time they walked thus silently, side by side.

"It was a good sermon to-day," said the man at length. "If we had not a living God, we should have nothing."

"Yes," replied the woman. "He sends joy and sorrow, and He has a right to send them. To-morrow our little boy would have been five years old, if we had been permitted to keep him."

"It is useless to continue fretting, wife," said the man. "The boy is well off now. He is where we hope and pray to go."

They said no more, but went on toward their house among the sand-hills. Suddenly, in front of one of the houses, where the seaweed did not bind the sand together with its twining roots, there arose what appeared a thick cloud of smoke. A gust of wind, rushing between the hills, hurled the particles of sand high into the air. Then came another gust, so violent that the strings of fish hung up to dry flapped and beat wildly against the walls of the house; and then all was still again, and the sun shone forth with renewed heat. Husband and wife stepped into the house; quickly they took off their Sunday clothes; and, coming forth again, hurried away over the hills which stood there like huge waves of sand suddenly arrested in their course, while the seaweeds and the bluish stems of the sand-grass covered them with ever-changing colours. A few neighbours joined them, and helped one another to draw the boats higher up on the sand. The wind now blew as strong as ever; it was cold and cutting; and as they returned over the sand-hills, sand and sharp stones blew in their faces. The waves, crested with white foam, rose high in the air, and the wind cut the crests off, and scattered the foam on every side.

Evening came on. In the air was a rushing sound, a moaning or complaining, like the voices of despairing spirits, that sounded in the fisherman's little hut, which was on the very margin of the hill, above the hoarse rolling of the sea. The sand rattled against the window-panes, and every now and then came a violent gust of wind that shook the house to its foundation. It was dark, but about midnight the moon would rise. By-and-by the air became clearer, but the storm still swept over the agitated sea in all its fury. The families of the fishermen were in bed, but in such weather there was no thought of closing an eye to sleep.

Presently there was a knocking at the window, the door opened, and a voice said, "There is a large ship aground on the outermost reef." In a moment the fisherman and his wife sprang from their lowly couch and hastily dressed. The moon had risen, so that it was light enough for those who could venture to open their eyes in a whirlwind of flying sand, to find their way to the seashore. The violence of the wind was so terrible that only by stooping low and creeping on between the gusts, was it possible to pass among the sand-hills. The salt spray flew up in the air like down, while the foaming ocean rolled like a roaring cataract towards the beach. It required a practised eye to descry the vessel in the offing. The vessel was a noble brig, and as the billows lifted it once again over the reef three or four cables' length towards the shore, it struck upon the second reef and remained fixed. To render assistance was impossible; the sea rolled over the deck of the vessel, making a clean breach each time. Those on shore fancied they heard cries for help from those on board, and could see plainly the anxious but useless efforts made by the stranded crew. A wave came rolling onward, falling like a rock upon the bowsprit and separating it from the vessel. The stern was raised high above the waters, and two people

standing upon it were seen to embrace and then plunge together into the sea. In a very short time, one of the large waves, rolling towards the sand-hills, threw a body on shore. It was a woman, a corpse as the sailors said; but the women thought they discerned signs of life in her, and the stranger was carried across the sand-hills to the fisherman's hut. How beautiful and fair she was, certainly they thought, she must be a great lady. They laid her upon a humble bed, on which not a yard of linen could be seen, but it had a thick woollen coverlet, which was very warm. Life returned to her, but she was delirious, and knew nothing of what had happened or where she was; it was better so, for everything she loved and valued lay buried in the sea. It was with her ship as with the vessel in the song of "The Son of England's King:"

"Alas! 'twas a terrible sight to see
The gallant ship sink rapidly."

All that remained of the wreck now and then drifted on shore, or was driven over the coast by the still roaring wind. After a short period of rest, which succeeded the delirium, the strange lady awoke in pain, while cries of anguish and fear issued from her lips. She opened her wonderfully beautiful eyes, and spoke a few words, but no one understood her. And behold, as a reward for the pain and sorrow she had suffered, she held in her arms a new-born child, the child that was to have rested upon an elegant cradle, adorned by silken curtains, in a home of magnificence; which was to have been welcomed with joy to a life enriched with all the good things of earth. And now Providence had ordained that its birth should take place in this humble dwelling, and that it should not even know the happiness of a mother's kiss; for when the fisherman's wife laid the child upon the mother's bosom, it rested on a heart that beat no more – the Spanish lady was dead. The child which should have been nursed amid wealth and luxury was cast alone upon the world, washed as it were by the sea among the sand-hills to partake of the fate and hardships of the poor. And here, again we are reminded of the old song about the king's son, in which mention is made of the customs prevalent at that time, when the inhabitants of the sea coasts plundered those who were wrecked and cast ashore. These hard and inhuman customs had disappeared from the shores of Jutland; the inhabitants had ceased from treating the shipwrecked with cruelty, and the ship which had struck on a rock, some little distance south of Nissum Bay, had foundered at the spot on which it struck. Affectionate sympathy existed then, as it does now in many a bright example. The dying mother and the unfortunate child would have found succour and help wherever they had been cast by the winds; nowhere would it have been more earnest than in the hut of the poor fisherman's wife. Only yesterday she had stood with a heavy heart beside the grave in which lay her child, who would have been five years old that day, had God permitted it to live. No one knew who the dead stranger was, nor could any one form the least conjecture.

The pieces of the wreck gave no clue to the matter. For a long time no tidings of the daughter or son-in-law reached the rich house of the Spanish merchant. They had evidently not reached their destination, and violent storms had been raging for many weeks. At last the news officially arrived – "Foundered at sea, and all lost." But in the sand-hills, near Hunsby, in the fisherman's hut, there still lived a little scion of that rich Spanish family. "Where heaven sends food for two, a third can manage to find a meal;" and in the depths of the sea is many a dish of fish for those who are hungry. And they called the boy Jurgen.

"It is certainly a Jewish child," said some; "it has such a dark complexion." "For the same reason, it might be Italian or Spanish," observed the clergyman.

But to the fisherman's wife these nations seemed all one, and she consoled herself with the thought that the child had been baptized a Christian. The boy throve; the noble blood in his veins was warm, and he became strong on the homely fare. He grew apace in the lowly hut, and the Danish dialect, spoken by the West Jutes, became his language. The strip of pomegranate, transplanted from Spanish soil, became a hardy plant on the coast of West Jutland. So may circumstances change the future of a man's life.

To this home he clung with a deep-rooted attachment that became part of his being. He was destined to experience cold and hunger, and to share the misfortunes and hardships that surround the poor; but he also tasted of their joys. Childhood has sunny spots for all conditions, which linger on the memory in after-life with radiant brightness. The boy had many sources of pleasure and enjoyment. The whole coast for miles and miles was full of playthings; it was a mosaic of pebbles, some red as coral or yellow as amber, and others again white and rounded and smoothed by the sea till they looked like birds' eggs. The bleached skeletons of fish, the water plants dried by the wind, sea-weed white and glittering like long linen bands, waving between the stones, – all seemed made to give pleasure and amusement to the eye and the thoughts of this boy, who had an intelligent mind, and possessed many great faculties. He formed picture-frames and ships of shells to decorate the room. His foster-mother used to say he could make a stick into something wonderful from his own ideas, though he was so young and small. He had a sweet voice; melody seemed to flow naturally from his lips. And in his heart were hidden chords, which might have sounded over the world had he been placed anywhere else than in the fisherman's hut by the North Sea.

One day, another ship was wrecked near the coast; and, among other things, a chest containing valuable bulbous flower-roots drifted on shore. Some were put into saucepans and cooked, for they were supposed to be good to eat; and others lay neglected on the sand till they became dry and shrivelled. They accomplished no purpose for which they had ben formed; they unfolded not the rich colours whose germ was within them. Would it be better with Jurgen? The flower-bulbs had soon played their part in life, but he had still years of discipline before him. Neither he nor his friends remarked how one day followed another in its course, for there was always plenty to do and see. The sea itself was a great lesson-book, unfolding each day a new leaf of calm or storm, – the crested wave or the smooth surface. Visits to the church were festive occasions; but, among other festal occasions in the fisherman's house, one was always welcomed with joy. It occurred twice in the year, and was, in fact, the visit of the brother of Jurgen's foster-mother, the eel-breeder of Zjaltring, in the nieghbourhood of the Bon Hill. He used to come in a cart filled with eels. The cart was covered, and looked like a box, and was painted all over with blue and white flowers. It was drawn by two dun oxen, and Jurgen was allowed to guide them. The eel-breeder was a witty fellow and a merry guest; he always brought a measure of brandy with him. Each one took a glassful or a cupful if there were not enough glasses; even Jurgen was allowed to have a thimbleful that he might digest the fat eel, so the eel-breeder said. He always told one story over and over again; and if his hearers laughed, he would repeat it to them.

As Jurgen, during his childhood, and even later, would refer to this story of the eel-breeder's and make use of it in various ways, it may be as well that we should hear it also.

"An eel and her daughters were in a creek, and the young eels wanted to go farther up. 'Don't go too far,' said their mother, 'or the ugly eel-spearer might come and snap you up.' But they went too far; and of eight daughters only three returned to the mother. They wept, and said, 'We only went a little way beyond the entrance, and the ugly eel-spearer came directly and stabbed five of our sisters to death.'

"'They'll come back again,' said the mother eel.

"'Oh no,' exlaimed the daughters, 'for he skinned them, cut them in two, and fried them.'

"'Oh, they'll come again,' the mother-eel persisted.

"'No,' replied the daughters, 'for he ate them up.'

"'They'll come again,' repeated the mother-eel.

"'But he drank brandy after them,' continued the daughters.

"'Ah, then they'll never come back,' said the mother, and she burst out crying, 'It's the brandy that buries the eels.'

"'And therefore,' said the eel-breeder in conclusion, 'it is always right to take brandy after eating eels.'"

And this story was the most humorous recollection, the tinsel thread, that wound itself through the story of Jurgen's life. He also wanted to go a little way outside the entrance, and up the bay, that is to say, out into the world in a ship; and his mother said like the eel-mother, "There are so many had people, eel-spearers, out there." But he did wish to go a little way beyond

156

the sand-hills – a little way into the dunes, and he got his wish at last. Four delightful days, the happiest of his childhood, fell to his lot. For the whole beauty and splendour of Jutland, all the joy and sunshine of his home seemed concentrated in these four days. He was to go on a visit, a festival to him, though it was certainly a burial ceremony. A wealthy relative of the fisherman died. His farm lay far inland, and a little towards the north-east. Jurgen's foster-parents were going, and he was to accompany them from the sand-hills, across heath and moor. They passed the green meadows, through which the river Skjäm rolls its course, a river that contains many eels – where mother-eels dwell with their daughters, who are caught and eaten up by wicked people. But men sometimes act quite as wickedly towards their own fellow-man; for had not the knight Sir Bugge been murdered by wicked people? and though he was well spoken of, did he not want to kill the architect, as the legend tells us, who had built the castle with its thick walls and towers, by which Jurgen's parents now stood, just where the river falls into the bay? The wall and the ramparts still remained, but the rest was in red, crumbling ruins. The story says that Sir Bugge, after the architect had left him, said to one of his men, "Go after him and say, 'Master, the tower shakes.' If he turns round, you are to kill him, and take from him the money I have just paid him; but if he does not turn round, let him depart in peace." The man obeyed, but the architect did not turn round; he called back to the man, "The tower does not shake in the least, but one day there will come a man from the west, in a blue cloak, who will cause it to shake in reality;" and indeed, so it happened, a hundred years after, for the North Sea broke in and cast down the tower. The man who then lived in the castle built a new one higher up at the end of the meadow, and that one is standing to this day, and is called Nürre Vosburg.

Past this castle went Jurgen and his foster-parents. They had told him the story during the long winter evenings, and now he saw the lordly castle, with its double moat and trees and shrubs. A wall, covered with ferns, rose close to the moat; but most beautiful of all were the lofty lime-trees, which grew up to the highest windows, and filled the air with sweet fragrance. In a north-west corner of the garden stood a large bush, covered with blossoms, that looked like winter's snows amid the green of summer. It was a juniper-tree, the first Jurgen had ever seen in such bloom. He never forgot it, nor the lime-trees. The *child* treasured these memories of beauty and fragrance to gladden the heart of the *old man*. From Närre Vosburg, where the juniper blossomed, the journey became more pleasant; for they were overtaken by others on their way to the funeral, who were riding in wagons. Our travellers had to sit all together on a little box at the back of the wagon; but even this they felt was better than walking. So they continued their journey across the rugged heath, while the oxen which drew the wagon stopped every now and then to taste some fresh grass which grew in patches among the heather. The sun was shining warmly when, in the distance there arose a strange appearance, something like smoke rising, and yet clearer than even the air; for it was transparent, and looked more like rays of light rolling and dancing afar over the heath.

"That is Lokeman driving his flocks of sheep," said some one. This was enough to excite the imagination of Jurgen. It seemed to him as if they were about to enter fairy-land, though everything around him was real. How quiet it was! Far and wide the heath extended, looking like beautiful tapestry in its varied colouring. The heather bloomed, the dark green of the juniper-bushes and the pale tints of the young oak-saplings mingling together, made them like nosegays rising from the earth. An inviting place for a picnic, were it not for the number of poisonous adders with which the place was infested. The travellers spoke of this, as well as of the time when the place was overrun with wolves; and, on that account, even now this region is called Wolfsburg. The old man who guided the oxen related that, in the lifetime of his father, the horses had to fight for their lives with these wild beasts, who were now extinct; and that one morning when he went out to bring in the horses, he found one of them standing with its fore-feet on a wolf it had killed, but the savage beast had torn the flesh of the poor horse's legs.

The journey over the deep sand and the wide heath came to an end too quickly. The stopped before the door of the house of mourning, where they found plenty of guests, both within and without. Wagon after wagon stood side by side, while the oxen and the horses had been turned out to graze on the barren pasture. Great sand-hills, like those at home by the North Sea, rose behind the house, and extended far and wide. How had they come here, to a spot inland, three miles from the sea? and they were as large and as high as those on the coast. They had been brought thither by the wind, and what a history would theirs be! Psalms were sung, and a few of the old people shed tears; but most of the guests were cheerful enough, as it appeared to Jurgen; and there was plenty to eat and drink. Eels there were of the fattest, requiring brandy to bury them, as the eel-breeder said; and certainly his words were not forgotten here. Jurgen went where he liked in the house, and by the third day he felt as much at home as in the fisherman's hut on the sand-hills, where he had passed his early days. Here, on the heath, were riches unknown to him before; for flowers and blackberries and wild strawberries, so large and sweet, were to be found in such profusion, that sometimes they were crushed beneath the step of the passers-by, and the heath would be coloured with their red juice. Here was a Hun's grave, yonder was another. Then columns of smoke rose in the still air, which they told him came from a heath-fire; how brightly it blazed in the dark evening! The fourth day arrived, on which the funeral festivities were to close, and they were to go back from the land sand-hills to the sand-hills by the sea.

"Ours are the right ones," said the old fisherman, Jurgen's foster-father; "these have no strength."

And on the way home they talked of the origin of these inland sand-hills, and related how they came there. Certainly it was a very clever way to account for them. This is the explanation they gave: —

"A corpse had been found on the coast, which the peasants buried in the churchyard. From that moment the sand began to fly about, and the sea broke in with violence. A wise man in the parish advised them to open the grave, and see if the buried man was not lying sucking his thumb; for if so, he must be a sailor, and the sea would not rest until it had got him back. So they opened the grave, and really found him with his thumb in his mouth. Then they laid him on a cart, and harnessed two oxen to it, and the oxen ran off with the cart as if they had been stung by an adder, and carried the seaman over heath and moorland to the ocean. Then the sand ceased to fly inland; but the hills still remained."

All this Jurgen treasured up in his memory of the happiest days of his childhood – the days of the burial feast. How delightful it must be to travel into strange places, and see strange people! And before he had reached his fourteenth year, he had to travel into distant lands. While still a child, he went out in a ship as a sailor-boy; and his experiences of the world were bad weather, raging seas, malicious and hard-hearted men. There were cold nights and bad living; but the hardest to endure were blows. He felt his noble Spanish blood boil within him, and angry words would rise to his lips; but he gulped them down; it was better, although he compared his feelings to those of the eel when it is flayed, cut up, and put into the frying-pan.

"I shall get over it," said a voice within him.

At one time he saw the Spanish coast, the native land of his parents, and even visited the town in which they had lived in happiness and prosperity; but he knew nothing of his origin or his relations, and they knew just as little about him. The poor sailorboy was not allowed to land; but on the last day that the ship remained in harbour he managed to get ashore. There were several purchases to be made, and he was sent to bring them on board. Jurgen, in his shabby clothes, which looked as if they had been washed in the ditch and dried in the chimney – he, an inhabitant of the sand-dunes, stood for the first time in a great city. How lofty the houses appeared, and how full the streets were of people, some pushing this way, and some that, – a perfect maelstrom of citizens and peasants, monks and soldiers! The jingling of the bells on the trappings of the asses; the chiming of the church bells; calling, shouting, hammering, and knocking, – all going on at once. Each trade was located on the basement of the houses, or on the pathway. The sun shone with great heat, and the air was so close that it seemed like being in an oven full of beetles and cockroaches, bees and flies, all humming and buzzing together. Jurgen hardly knew where he was, or which way he went, till he found himself in front of the mighty portal of a cathedral. Light streamed through the dark aisles, and a fragrance of incense was wafted towards him; yet the poorest beggar could venture up the steps into the temple. Jurgen followed the sailor who was with him into the church, and stood in the sacred edifice. Pictures in golden frames were before him; on the altar stood a figure of the Virgin, with the child Jesus, surrounded by lights and flowers; priests in festive robes were chanting, and choir-boys,

clothed in white, swung the silver censers. What splendour, what magnificence, was here! It streamed in upon his soul, and overpowered him. The church and the faith of his parents touched a chord in his heart, that caused his eyes to overflow with tears.

From the church they went to the market-place, where a quantity of provisions was given to him to carry. The way to the harbour was long, and tired and overcome with various emotions, he rested for a few moments before a splendid house, with marble pillars, statues, and broad steps. Here he rested his burden against the wall; then a porter in livery came out, lifted up a silver-headed cane, and drove him away – him! the grandson of that house! Ah, how little they thought that such was the case! They knew nothing about him, neither did he know about himself. And after this he returned on board, and again had to endure hard words, cuffs, much work, and little sleep; such were his experiences of the world. They say it is well to endure hardships in youth; and so it is, if age brings something good with it. When his time of service expired, and the vessel lay once more at Ringkjübing, in Jutland, he came on shore and went home to the sand-hills, by Hunsby, but his foster-mother had died while he had been away on his voyage. A hard winter followed this summer; snow-storms upon land and sea, and it was difficult to get far from home. How differently things are ordered in the world: here biting cold and snow-storms, while in the land of Spain there was burning sunshine and oppressive heat. Still here at home, when there came a clear frosty day, and Jurgen saw the swans flying in flocks, from the sea towards the land, and across to Vosburg, it appeared to him that people could breathe more freely in such a climate. The summer, too, in these regions was splendid, and, in imagination, he saw the heath bloom, and become purple with the rich, juicy berries, and the elder and the lime-trees at Vosburg in blossom. He decided to go there once more.

Spring came on, and the fishing began. Jurgen was an active assistant in this; he had grown much during the preceding year, and was now strong and quick at work. He was full of life; he knew how to swim and dive, and could turn over and tumble in the strong tide. They often warned him to beware of the sharks, who could easily seize the best swimmer, draw him down, and devour him; but such was not to be Jurgen's fate.

At a neighbour's house on the down was a boy named Martin, with whom Jurgen was very friendly; they had served together on board a ship sailing to Norway, and also on another to Holland, without even having quarrelled. But a person can be easily excited to quarrel, when he is naturally hot-tempered, for he often shows it in many ways; and this is just what Jurgen did one day, when they had fallen out about the merest trifle.

They were sitting behind the cabin door, eating out of a delf plate, which they had placed between them. Jurgen held his pocket-knife in his hand, and lifted it towards Martin, and at the same time became ashy pale, and there was an ugly look in his eyes.

Martin only said, "Ah! you are one of that sort, are you, accustomed to use a knife?"

The words were scarcely spoken, when Jurgen's hand sank down. He answered not a syllable, but went on eating, and afterwards returned to his work.

When they were resting again he stepped up to Martin, and said, "You may hit me in the face, I deserve it; but I feel sometimes as if something inside me was boiling over."

"There, let it pass," said Martin; and after that they were almost better friends than ever. And when they got back to the dunes, and began telling their adventures, this was told also. Martin said Jurgen was certainly very hasty, but a good fellow after all. They were both young and healthy, well grown and strong but Jurgen was the more clever of the two.

In Norway, the peasants, in spring, lead out their cattle to graze on the mountains. In Jutland, the fishermen live during the spring amid the sand-

162

hills, where huts have been erected for them. They are built of pieces of wrecks, and roofed with heather and turf; there are sleeping-places within, ranged against the walls, and here they live and sleep during the fishing season. Every fisherman has a female helper, or manager, as she is called, who baits his hooks, prepares warm beer for him when he comes on shore, and gets the dinner cooked and ready for him by the time he comes back to to the hut, tired and hungry. Besides this, the housekeepers bring up the fish from the boat, cut them open, and prepare them, and have generally a great deal to do. Jurgen, his father, and several other fishermen and their housekeepers, inhabited the same hut. Martin occupied the next one. One of the girls, named Elsie, had known Jurgen from childhood. They were glad to meet again, and in many things were of the same mind, but in outward appearance there was great contrast between them, for he was dark, and she was pale and fair, and had flaxen hair, and eyes as blue as the sea in sunshine.

One day as they were walking together, and Jurgen holding her hand very firmly in his, she said to him, "Jurgen, I have something on my mind which I want to tell you. Let me be your housekeeper, for you are like a brother to me. But Martin has engaged himself to me, and he and I are lovers, but you need not tell the rest." Then it seemed to Jurgen as if the sand were loose, and giving way beneath his feet. He spoke not a word, but merely nodded his head to signify "yes." More was not necessary, but suddenly there arose in his heart a feeling of hatred against Martin, and the more he thought, the more convinced he felt that Martin had stolen away from him the only being he ever loved, and that it was Elsie; he had never thought of Elsie in this way before, but now it became all plain to him.

When the sea is rather agitated, and the fishermen are coming home in their boat, it is a wonderful sight to see how they manage to cross the reef. One of the men stands upright in the bow of the boat, and the others watch him, sitting with the oars in their hands. Outside the reef it appears as if the boat were not approaching the land, but going back to sea. At last, the man standing up in the boat gives them the signal that the great wave is coming which is to lift them over the reef. A moment, and then the boat is raised so high in the air, that her keel may be seen from the shore; and at the next she is entirely hidden from the eye; neither mast, nor keel, nor men can be seen; it is as if they had been devoured by the sea. But presently they emerge from the deep, like a great sea animal sporting with the waves, and the oars move as if they were the creature's legs. The second and the third reef are passed in the same manner, and then the fishermen jump into the water, and the boat is pushed forward on the heaving waves, till it is at length drawn up safely on shore, beyond the reach of the breakers. A wrong order

163

given by the man in the bow in front of the reef, the slightest hesitation, and the boat would be lost. "Then it would be all over with me and Martin, too." This thought passed through the mind of Jurgen one day, when they were out at sea in the same boat together. His foster-father was on board, but he was taken suddenly ill when only a few oars' stroke from the reef, and Jurgen sprang from his seat to take his father's place in the bow.

"Father, let me come," he said; and his eye glanced towards Martin, and across the waves; but while every oar bent with the strong pull of the rowers, as the great wave rose before them, he looked in the pale face of his father, and dared not obey the evil suggestion of his heart. The boat crossed the reef safely and came to land, but the evil thought remained in his mind, and roused up those bitter feelings which had existed there since he and Martin had quarrelled. He could not crush down these feelings, nor did he endeavour to do so. He felt that Martin had robbed him of a treasure, and this he thought cause enough for his hatred of his former friend. Several of the fishermen noticed the change, but not Martin, who was as obliging and talkative as ever, perhaps too much of the latter. Jurgen's foster-father took to his bed, which became his death-bed, for during the following week he died, and Jurgen found himself heir of the little house behind the sand-hills. It was but small, certainly, but still it was something, at all events more than Martin could boast of.

"You will not go to sea again now, I suppose," observed one of the old fishermen; "you will always stay with us now." But this was not Jurgen's intention; he wanted to see a little more of the world.

The eel-breeder of Zjaltring had an uncle in Alt Skagen, who was a fisherman, but at the same time a prosperous merchant, who had ships of his own at sea. He was said to be a good old man, and service with him would not be amiss.

Alt Skagen lies to the extreme north of Jutland, with the whole length of the peninsula between it and Hunsby dunes. This was what pleased Jurgen, for he did not wish to remain to the wedding of Martin and Elsie, which was to be celebrated in a few weeks. The old fisherman thought it was a very foolish thing to leave this part of the country; for now that he had a home, perhaps Elsie would be inclined to take him instead of Martin. Jurgen answered so indifferently that it was not easy to understand his intentions. Then the old man brought Elsie to talk to him, and she said, "You have a home of your own now, and you should consider that." But Jurgen thought of other things besides his home. The sea has its dark billows, but in the human heart the waves of passion are fiercer in their roll. Many thoughts, many hopes and fears, rushed through the brain of Jurgen as he talked to Elsie.

"If Martin had a house like mine, which would you rather have for a lover?"

164

"But Martin has no house, and cannot get one."

"Well, let us suppose that he has one."

"Why then I should take Martin, certainly; that is what my heart tells me to do now, but we cannot live upon love."

Then Jurgen thought over it all night. Something was working within him he hardly knew what, but it was stronger even than his love for Elsie. So, after considering the matter carefully, he went to Martin, and offered to let the house to him on most reasonable terms, saying that he wished to go to sea again because he liked it. Elsie kissed him when she heard of it, for she loved Martin best. Jurgen proposed to start early in the morning; so the evening before his departure, when it was growing rather late, he felt a wish to visit Martin once more. As he went along, he met the old fisherman among the dunes, who was angry at his leaving the place. The old man joked about Martin, and declared it was not fair for all the girls to be so fond of him. Jurgen flung this speech to the winds, but he said farewell to the old man, and went on towards the house where Martin dwelt. He heard loud talking within – Martin was not alone, and this made Jurgen hesitate, for he did not wish to meet Elsie. So, on second thoughts, he felt it better not to hear any more thanks from Martin, and therefore turned back.

On the following morning, before break of day, he fastened on his knapsack, took his wooden provision-box in his hand, and went away over the sand-hills, towards the path by the coast. This road was more pleasant than the heavy sand-road; besides, it was shorter, and he intended first to go to Zjaltring, near Bowberg, where the eel-breeder lived, to whom he had promised a visit. The sea lay before him clear and blue; shells and pebbles, the playthings of his youth, crunched beneath his feet. While thus marching on, his nose suddenly began to bleed; it was a trifling occurrence, but little matters are sometimes of great importance. A few large drops fell upon one of his sleeves; he wiped them off, and stopped the bleeding, and it seemed to him that this had cleared and lightened his brain. The sea-ane-mone bloomed here and there in the sand as he passed. He broke off a stalk, and stuck it in his hat: he determined to be merry and light-hearted, for he was going out into the wide world, a little beyond the entrance of the bay, as the young eels had wished to do. "Beware of bad people, who will catch you, and flay you, and cut you in two, and put you in the frying-pan." He smiled to himself as he repeated this in his mind, for he thought he should easily find his way through the world: youthful courage is a good defence.

The sun was high in the heavens when he approached the narrow entrance to Nissum Bay. He looked back, and saw two horsemen galloping a long distance behind him, and they were accompanied by other people. But this did not trouble him: it was no concern of his. The ferry-boat was on the opposite side of the bay. Jurgen called to the ferryman, and the latter came over with the boat. Jurgen stepped in, but before they had reached half-way across, the men whom he had seen riding so hastily behind came up, hailed the ferryman, and commanded him to return in the name of the law. Jurgen knew not the meaning of all this, but he thought it best to turn, and therefore himself took an oar and rowed back. The moment the boat touched the shore, the men sprang on board, and before he was aware, they had bound his hands with a rope. "This wicked deed will cost thee thy life," said they; "it is well we have caught thee."

He was accused of no less than murder: Martin had been found dead, with a knife thrust into his throat. Late on the previous evening one of the fishermen had met Jurgen going towards Martin's house. Jurgen had been known to raise his knife against Martin before this, so every one felt sure he was the murderer. The prison was in a town at a great distance, and the wind was contrary for going there by sea; but in half an hour the bay could be crossed, and it was only a quarter of a mile from the opposite side to Nörre Vosburg, a great castle with ramparts and moat.

One of the horsemen was a brother of the head keeper of the castle, and he said it could easily be managed that Jurgen should for the present be placed in the dungeon at Vosburg, where "Long Martha," the gipsy, had been shut up till her execution.

No notice was taken of Jurgen's defence, although he spoke on his oath. The few drops of blood on his shirt sleeve were a witness against him. But he was conscious of his innocence, and, as there seemed no hope of immediately clearing himself, he submitted to his fate. The party landed just at the spot where Sir Bugge's castle had once stood, and where Jurgen had walked with his foster-parents, after the burial feast, during the four happiest days of his childhood. He was led along the old path over the meadow to Vosburg, and again the elders blossomed, and the lofty lime-trees perfumed the air: it seemed but yesterday that he had been here before. From the two wings of the castle, a staircase leads down to the entrance of a low, vaulted cellar. Here "Long Martha" had been imprisoned, and from thence she was led away to the scaffold. It is said that she took away the lives of five children, that she might devour their hearts, and was under the delusion that if she could obtain two more she would be able to fly and make herself invisible. In this dungeon there was no window, but a narrow loop-hole very near the ceiling admitted the air; no refreshing fragrance from the blooming lime-trees could reach that dwelling, where all was dark and mouldy. There was only a rough bench to lie upon; but a good conscience is a soft pillow, and therefore Jurgen could sleep well. The thick oaken door was locked and fastened outside by an iron bar, but the goblin Superstition can creep through a key-hole in the baron's castle, as easily as into a fisherman's hut; and what should prevent it from creeping in now, where poor Jurgen sat thinking of Martha and her terrible deeds?

Her last thought on the night before her execution was perhaps breathed aloud within these dungeon walls, and all the wickedness which tradition said had been practised within the castle in the olden times, when Sir Schwandwedel dwelt there, came into Jurgen's mind, and made him shudder for a moment. But a refreshing thought penetrated his heart even here, like a sunbeam; it was the remembrance of the blooming elders and the fragrant lime-trees.

He was not left long in the castle; they carried him off to the town of Ringkjöbing, where he was imprisoned with equal severity. Those times were not like ours. The common people were treated harshly. It was not long after these days when the farmer who owned a small farm, could become a knight; and common servants were often made magistrates, and had it in their power to condemn a poor man, for even a small offence, to lose his property, or to suffer corporal punishment. Judges of this kind were even then to be found; especially in Jutland, so far from the capital and from well-ordered and enlightened rulers.

Jurgen had no cause to hope that his case would be speedily settled. He felt cold and cheerless in his prison. When would this state of things end? It seemed his fate to suffer misfortune and sorrow innocently. He had leisure now to reflect on the different positions allotted to man on earth, and to wonder at his own. And yet he felt sure all would be made clear in the next life, in the existence that awaits us after death. His faith had been strengthened in the fisherman's hut; a faith, which had never brightened his father's mind amidst the wealth of sunny Spain, had been learnt by him in poverty, and was now a light of comfort in the hour of sorrow and distress, a sign of that mercy of God which never fails.

The storms of the spring equinox began to blow, and in the lull of the wind, the rolling and moaning of the North Sea could be heard for miles inland, like the rushing of a thousand wagons over undermined hollow ground. Jurgen, in his prison, heard these sounds, and they were a relief to him. No melody could have touched his heart as did these sounds from the sea; the rolling boundless ocean, on which a man can be borne before the wind through the world, carrying with him his home wherever he journeys, just as the snail carries his house with him, even into a strange country. How eagerly he listened to its deep moaning, and then the thought arose, "Free! free!" How happy to be free, even in rags and barefooted! Sometimes, when such thoughts crossed his mind, the fiery nature rose within him, and he struck the thick wall with his clenched first.

Weeks, months, a whole year went by, and then it was discovered how Jurgen had been wronged. Niels the thief, called also a horse-dealer, was arrested for the murder of Martin. On the afternoon before Jurgen's departure from home, and before the murder, Niels had met Martin at a beer-shop in the Ringkjöbing. A few glasses were drank; not sufficient to cloud the brain, but enough to loosen Martin's tongue. He began to boast, and to say he had got a house, and intended to marry; and when Niels asked him where he expected to get the money, Martin slapped his pocket proudly, and said, "The money is there where it ought to be." That boast cost him his life; for, when he left, Niels followed him, and stabbed him in the throat with a knife, intending to rob the murdered man of the gold he had boasted of, and which did not exist. All these circumstances came out in the evidence, but for us it is enough to know that Jurgen was set at liberty.

But what compensation did he get for having been imprisoned a whole year, and shut out from all communication with men? None. They told him it was good fortune enough to be proved innocent, and that he might go.

The mayor gave him two dollars for his travelling expenses, and many of the citizens offered him provisions and beer.

There were still some good people; they were not all hard and pitiless. But the best of all was that the merchant Bronne of Skjagen, into whose service Jurgen had been about to enter a year previous, was just at that time in Ringkjöbing on business. Bronne heard the whole story; he was a kind-hearted man, and understood what Jurgen must have felt and suffered. He therefore determined to make it up to him in some way, and show him him that there were still some kind people in the world. So Jurgen went forth from prison as if to paradise, to find freedom, affection, and trust.

"Let all be buried and forgotten," said Bronne the merchant. "Let us draw a thick line through last year, or we may as well burn the almanac. In two days we will start for dear, lively, peaceful little Skjagen."

They call Skjagen an out-of-the-way place in a corner, but it is a good, warm chimney-corner, with windows that open to all the world. What a journey that was! It was like taking fresh breath; out of the cold dungeon air into the warm sunshine. The heath was blooming in pride and beauty. The shepherd's boy sat on the Hun's grave, and blew a pipe, which he had carved for himself out of a sheep bone. The "Fata morgana," the beautiful aerial wonder of distant lands, represented hanging gardens and waving forests; and the wonderful cloud, called "Lokeman driving his flock," floated in the distance.

On, through the land of the Wendals, they went towards Skjagen, the place from whence emigrated the men with long beards (the Longobardi or Lombards). A story is told that in the days of King Snio, all the children and the old people were in danger of being killed, and a noble lady, named Gambaruk, advised the young people to emigrate. Jurgen had heard this story; and although he had never seen the land of the Lombards, he yet had an idea that it was somewhere beyond the Alps, not so very far from Spain, in the south, which he had visited in his boyhood. He thought of the piles of southern fruit; the red blossoms of the pomegranate; of the humming, murmuring, and toiling in the great beehive of a city which he had seen; but how beautiful is that land in which is home! And Jurgen's home was Denmark.

At length they arrived at Wendelskajn, as Skjagen is called in the old Norwegian and Icelandic writings. At that time, old Skjagen, including the eastern and western towns, extended for miles, with its sand-hills and arable land, as far as the lighthouse near the Skjagenzweigs. Then, as now, the houses were scattered about among the waving, shifting sand-hills, – a kind of desert, where the wind sported with the sand, and where the voices of the sea-gull and the cry of the wild swan strike harshly upon the ear. In the southwest, about a mile from the sea, lies old Skjagen; and here dwelt merchant Bronne, and here was Jurgen to live in future. The dwelling-house was tarred; the small outbuildings had each an overturned boat for a roof; even the pigsty had been put together with pieces of wreck. There was no fence; for here, indeed, was nothing to fence in but long rows of fishes, hung upon lines, one above the other, to dry in the wind. The coast was littered with stale herrings; for those fish were so plentiful that a net was scarcely thrown into the sea before it was filled. They were caught by cart-loads, and many of them were often thrown back into the sea, or left to lie on the shore. The old man's wife and daughter, and even the servants, came to meet him with great rejoicing. There was a great squeezing of hands, talking, and questioning. And the daughter, what a dear face, and what lovely eyes she had! The interior of the house was comfortable and roomy. Fritters that a king would have considered a dainty dish were placed on the table, and there was wine from the vintage of Skjagen; that is, the sea, which brought the grapes to its shores, ready pressed and prepared, in barrels and in bottles.

When the mother and daughter heard who Jurgen was, and how innocently he had suffered, they looked at him in a still more friendly manner; and the eyes of the charming Clara had a look of great interest, as she listened to his story. Jurgen found a happy home at Skjagen. It did his heart good, for it had been sorely tried. He had drunk the bitter dregs in the cup of affliction, which sometimes harden and sometimes soften the heart. Jurgen's heart was still soft; it was young, and had yet room in it. It was all the better for him, therefore, that in three weeks Miss Clara was going away in one of her father's ships to Christiansand, in Norway, to visit an aunt, and to stay the whole winter. On the Sunday before her departure, they all went to the church, which stood at a short distance from the town. It had been built centuries before, by Scotchmen and Dutchmen. At that time it was large and handsome, but was now in rather a ruinous condition. The sand had even heaped itself round the walls, but the graves were kept free from it. The road to it was heavy, through deep sand; but the people gladly overcame these difficulties to get to the house of God, to sing psalms, and to hear the sermon. This church was the largest north of the Limfjord. Upon the altar stood a lifelike figure of the Virgin Mary, with a golden crown on her head and the Child Jesus in her arms. There were also, in the choir, carved figures of the holy apostles, and on the wall hung portraits of the old mayors and magistrates of Skjagen; the pulpit was of carved work. The sun shone brightly into the church, and its rays fell on the polished brass chandelier and on the little ship hanging from the vaulted roof. Jurgen felt overpowered with a holy, childlike feeling, similar to that which he had felt when, as a boy, he stood in the splendid Spanish cathedral. But here the feeling was different; he had the consciousness of being one of the congregation. After the sermon followed the holy communion. He partook of the bread and wine, and it happened that he knelt beside Clara; but his thoughts were so entirely fixed upon God and the holy service, that he did not notice his neighbour until he rose from his knees, and then he saw tears rolling down her cheeks.

Two days after she left Skjagen and went to Norway. He remained, and made himself useful in the house, and in the business. He went out fishing, and at that time fish were more plentiful and larger than they are now. The shoals of mackerel shone in the water as darkness came on, and discovered themselves by their brightness. Every Sunday he went to church, and as he sat there, his eye resting on the statue of the Virgin Mary on the altar, he sometimes thought of Clara, and how kind and friendly she had been to him; and his glance for a moment fall on the spot where they had knelt side by side. Autumn came, and brought rain and snow; and when the snow thawed, the water remained on the roads; the sand could not absorb it. They were obliged to wade through it from house to house. Ships were lost on the destroying reefs; storms of snow and sand raged; the sand flew into the houses, so that to avoid it the owners had almost to creep up the chimney. But on the shores of the North Sea the weather was not so boisterous, and the merchant's house was well sheltered and warm; in the evenings merchant Bronne would read to them from an old book of the Danish Prince Hamlet, and of a great battle which had been fought not many miles from his house. He also told them of a churchyard in which was a grave supposed to be Hamlet's. Then Jurgen sang the song about the king's son, and his beautiful ship.

And so the autumn and winter passed away. There was wealth, comfort, and happiness, even among the domestic animals, who were all well fed and well treated. The kitchen looked bright with its coppers, and tins, and from the roof hung hams, and corned beef, and winter stores in profusion. All this is still to be seen in rich farms on the west coast of Jutland; plenty to eat and drink, clean and decorated rooms, clever heads, happy tempers, and hospitality such as is found in an Arab's tent. Never since the famous burial feast had Jurgen passed such a happy time, and yet Mistress Clara was absent, except in the thoughts and memory of all.

In April a ship was to start for Norway, in which Jurgen was to sail. He was full of life and spirits, and looked so stout and well that Dame Bronne said it was a pleasure to see him.

"And it's a pleasure to look at you, too, old wife," said the old merchant. "Jurgen has brought new life into our winter evenings, and into you, mother. You look younger than ever this year, and bonny, too; but then you were the prettiest girl in Wiborg, which is saying a great deal, for I have always found the girls of Wiborg much prettier than any others."

All this was nothing to Jurgen, but he thought of a certain Skjagen maiden, who was also pretty. He was about to visit that maiden; for the next morning the ship would set sail for Christiansand, in Norway, and as the wind was favourable, it was likely soon to arrive in port.

One morning, about a week after Jurgen had started to fetch Clara home, Bronne went out to the lighthouse, which stands not far from Old Skjagen. The light was out in the lantern, and the sun already high in the heavens when he mounted the tower. The sand-banks extend a whole mile from the shore, beneath the water. Outside these banks many ships could be seen that day, and with the help of his telescope the old man thought he could descry the "Karen Bronne," as his ship was calles. Yes! surely, there she was, sailing homewards with Jurgen and Clara on board. To them the church and the lighthouse appeared as a heron and a swan rising out of the blue waters.

Clara sat on deck, and saw the sand-hills gradually appearing in the

distance. If the wind held up, they might reach her home in about an hour. So near were they to home and all its joys – so near to death and all its terrors! A plank in the ship gave way, and the water rushed in. The crew flew to the pumps, and attempted to stop the leak. A signal of distress was hoisted, but they were still a full mile from the shore. Fishing boats were in sight, but far too distant to be of use. The wind blew towards the shore, the tide was in their favour, but all in vain – nothing could save the ship from sinking!

Jurgen threw his right arm round Clara and pressed her to him. With what a look she gazed in his face, as, with a prayer to God for help, he breasted the waves, which were rushing over the sinking ship! She uttered a cry, but she felt safe; certain that he would not leave her to sink. And in this hour of terror and danger Jurgen experienced the feelings of the king's son, as related in the song, –

"In the hour of danger the king's brave son
Embraced the bride he had nobly won."

How rejoiced he felt that he was a good swimmer. He struggled onward with his feet and one hand, while with the other he firmly held up the young girl. He rested on the waves, he trod the water, he practised all the arts he knew, so as to reserve strength enough to reach the shore. He heard Clara utter a sigh, and felt her shudder convulsively, and he pressed her more closely to him. Now and then a wave rolled over her, and at last one higher than the rest buried them in deep but clear water. He seemed for a moment confused, and heard sounds as of screaming birds, while shoals of fish passed before him. He had reached within a few cables' length of the land, when he saw clearly beneath the water a white figure gazing at him; a wave lifted him, and the form approached. He felt a shock, – it grew dark, and everything vanished from his gaze.

On the sand-reef, convered with water at high tide, lay part of one wreck of a vessel; the white figure-head resting against the anchor, the sharp, iron edge of which rose above the surface of the water. Jurgen had come in contact with this, and the tide had driven him against it with double force. He was sinking, fainting and stunned with the blow; but the next wave lifted him and the young girl towards the shore, and some fishermen approaching with a boat, grasped them and dragged them into it. The blood streamed down Jurgen's face; he seemed dead, yet he still held the young girl so closely that they were obliged to take her from him by force. They laid her pale and lifeless in the boat, and rowed hastily to shore. Every means were tried to restore Clara to life, but they were useless. For some distance Jurgen had been swimming to shore with a corpse in his arms, and exhausting his strength for one who was dead.

Jurgen still breathed, so the fishermen carried him to the nearest house upon the sand-hills, where a smith and general dealer live who knew something of surgery, and he bound up Jurgen's wounds in a temporary manner, till a surgeon could be obtained next day from the nearest town. The brain of the injured man was affected, and in his delirium he uttered wild cries; but on the third day he lay quiet and exhausted on his couch. His life seemed to hang on a thread, and the surgeon said it would be better for him that this thread should be snapped. "Let us pray," he said, "that God may take him to Himself, for he will never be the same man again." But life would not depart from him – the thread would not snap, but the thread of memory broke – the thread of his mental power had been cut through; and more terrible still, a body remained – a living, healthy body, that wandered about like a spectre.

Jurgen remained in the house of the merchant Bronne. "He injured himself in his endeavours to save our child," said the old man, "he is our son now." People called Jurgen imbecile: that was not the correct term. He was like an instrument in which the strings are loose, and will give no sound. At times, and for a few minutes, they would regain their power and sound as of old. He would sing snatches of songs or old melodies; pictures of the past would rise before him, and then disappear as in a mist; but generally he would sit staring into vacancy – his mind a blank. We may believe that he did not suffer, but his dark eyes lost their brillancy, and looked like clouded glass.

"Poor imbecile Jurgen," said the people. And this was the end of a life whose infancy would have been cradled in luxury, had his parents lived! He was like a rare plant torn from its native soil, and thrown upon the sand to wither there. And was this one of God's creatures, fashioned in His own image and after His likeness, to have no better destiny? Was he to be merely the sport of chance? No! the all-loving Creator would repay him in the life to come, for what he had suffered and lost in this. "The Lord is good to all, and His tender mercies are over all His works," says the psalmist; and these words of David were repeated in patience and hope by the old, pious wife of the merchant; and the prayer of her heart was that Jurgen might soon be summoned to enter into eternal life.

In the charchyard, where the walls are surrounded with sand, Clara lay buried. Jurgen appeared to have no idea of this; it did not enter his mind, which could only retain fragments of the past. Every Sunday he went to church with the old people, and sat silent, gazing on vacancy. One day, while the psalms were being sung, he uttered a deep sigh, and a light came

175

into his eyes, as he fixed them upon the place at the altar where he had often knelt during a year with his friend who was dead. He uttered her name, and then became pale as death, while the tears rolled down his checks. They led him out of the church; he told the bystanders he was quite well, and had never been ill. He had been so heavily afflicted – the waif cast forth upon the world – remembered nothing of his sufferings. "The Lord our Maker is wise, and full of loving kindness; who can doubt it?" In Spain, where the warm breezes blow over the Moorish cupola, and among the orange and myrtle groves, where the song and the castanets are ever heard where children march in procession through the streets with flags and lighted tapers, in a luxurious house sat the rich merchant, a childless old man. How much of his wealth would he not have given to be able once more to press his daughter to his heart, or her child, which had perhaps never seen the light of life. "Poor child!" "Yes, poor child; a child still, yet more than thirty years of age, for Jurgen had reached that age while living in Skjagen.

Drifting sands had covered the graves in the churchyard, quite up to the walls of the church; but the dead must be buried among the relations and the loved ones who had gone before them. Merchant Bronne and his wife were laid with their children in one of these graves neneath the white sand. It was spring time, the season of storms. The sand from the hills near Hunsby was whirled up in clouds; the sea ran high, and flocks of birds flew about in the storm, or ran shrieking across the sand-dunes. Shipwreck followed shipwreck, on the reefs of Skjagenzweig.

One evening Jurgen sat alone in his room; suddenly his mind seemed to become clearer, and a feeling of unrest came upon him, such as had often driven him forth, in his younger days, to wander on the heath and among the sand-dunes. "Home, home!" he exclaimed. No one heard him. He went out of the house, and turned his steps towards the dunes. Sand and stones blew in his face, and were whirled about. He continued his way on towards the church. The sand lay high round the walls, half covering the windows, but the heap had been shovelled away from before the door, and there was a clear and free pathway to enter, so Jurgen went into the church.

The storm continued to howl over the town of Skjagen; there had not been such a terrible tempest nor such a raging sea within the memory of man. But Jurgen was in the temple of God; and while a night of desolation reigned without, a light arose in his soul, which was never to be extinguished; the heavy weight which pressed on his brain seemed to burst and disperse. He thought he heard the sound of the organ, but it was the moaning of the sea in the storm. He sat down on one of the seats, and behold the candles were lighted one by one, and a brightness diffused around, which he had

never seen but in the cathedral in Spain. The pictures of the old citizens seemed endued with life; they stepped forth from the walls, against which they had hung for centuries, and seated themselves near the entrance of the church. The gates and doors flew open, and all the dead from the church-yard entered at the sound of the music, and filled the seats in the church. Then the music of the psalm pealed forth like the noise of waters, and Jurgen saw that his old foster-parents from the Hunsby dunes, and the old Merchant Bronne and his wife were there; and at their side, close to Jurgen, sat their lovely daughter Clara. She gave him her hand, and they both went to the altar, where they had once knelt together, and the priest joined their hands and united them for life. Then came the sound of wonderful music, like the voice of a child, full of joy and expectation, swelling like the tones of a full organ, at one time soft and sweet, then like the sounds of a tempest, full and strong enough to burst the stone tombs of the dead. Then the little ship, which hung down from the roof of the choir, descended, and appeared wonderfully large and beautiful, with its silken sails and golden rigging: "every rope with silk entwined," as the old song says.

The newly married pair went on board, and the whole congregation with them, for there was room and enjoyment for all. Then the walls and arches of the church appeared covered with the bloom of juniper and lime-trees, wafting coolness and freshness from their waving branches. They bent and parted, and the ship sailed between them, through the air and over the sea; and every taper in the church became a star, and the murmuring of the wind was a psalm, in which they all joined. "Through love to glory, no life

177

is lost; the future is full of happiness and joy. Hallelujah." These were the last words spoken by Jurgen in this world. The thread that bound his immortal soul to earth snapped asunder; nothing but a dead body lay in the dark church, while around it the storm raged, covering it with loose sand. The following day was Sunday, and the priests and the congregation proceeded to the church. The road had always been heavy, now the sand made it almost impassable; and when they at length reached the church, a great heap of sand lay piled up before them. The whole building was buried in sand. The priest offered a short prayer; he said that God had closed the door of His house here, and that the congregation must go and build a new one for Him elsewhere. So they sung a psalm under the open sky, and went back to their homes. Jurgen was nowhere to be found in the town of Skjagen, nor among the dunes, though they sought for him diligently. It was supposed that the waves which had rolled far upon the sand had swept him away; but his body lay buried in a great sepulchre, the sand-covered church. The Lord had thrown from His hand in the storm a covering for his grave, a heavy heap of sand, which rests upon it to this day. The vaulted roof of the church, the arched cloisters, and the stone aisles were entirely covered with the whirling sand. The white thorn and the wild roses now grow above the spot where the church lies buried; but the tower, like a gigantic tombstone over a grave, can be seen for miles round. No king has a more splendid tombstone. No one disturbs the rest of the dead, no one knows of this; we are the first to hear of it. For the storm sung the tale to me among the sand-hills.

Elfin-Mount

Several large lizards were running nimbly in and out among the clefts of an old tree; they could understand each other perfectly well, for they all spoke the lizards' language. 'Only hear what a rumbling and grumbling there is in the old Elfin-mount yonder!' observed one lizard. 'I have not been able to close my eyes for the last two nights; I might as well have had the toothache, for the sleep I have had!'

'There is something in the wind, most certainly!' rejoined the second lizard. 'They raise the Mount upon four red pillars till cock-crowing; there is a regular cleaning and dusting going on, and the Elfin-maidens are learning new dances – such a stamping they make in them! There is certainly something in the wind!'

'Yes; I have been talking it over with an earth-worm of my acquaintance,' said a third lizard. 'The earth-worm has just come from the Mount; he has been grubbing in the ground there for days and nights together, and has overheard a good deal; he can't see at all, poor wretch! but no one can be quicker than he is at feeling and hearing. They are expecting strangers at the Elfin-mount – distinguished strangers; but who they are, the earth-worm would not say; most likely he did not know. All the wills-o'-the-wisp are engaged to form a procession of torches – so they call it; and all the silver and gold, of which there is such a store in the Elfin-mount, is being fresh rubbed up, and set out to shine in the moonlight.'

'But who can these strangers be?' exclaimed all the lizards with one voice. 'What can be in the wind? Only listen! – what buzzing and humming!'

Just then the Elfin-mount parted asunder; and an elderly Elfin damsel came tripping out – she was the old Elfin-King's housekeeper, and distantly related to his family, on which account she wore an amber heart on her forehead, but was otherwise plainly dressed. Like all other elves, she was hollow in the back. She was very quick and light-footed; trip – trip – trip, away she ran, straight into the marsh, to the night-raven. 'You are invited to Elfin-mount, for this very evening,' said she; 'but will you not first do us a very great kindness, and be the bearer of the other invitations? You do not keep house, yourself, you know; so you can easily oblige us. We are ex-

179

pecting some very distinguished strangers, Trolds in fact; and his Elfin Majesty intends to welcome them in person.'

'Who are to be invited?' inquired the night-raven.

Why, to the grand ball all the world may come; even men, if they could but talk in their sleep, or do a little bit of anything in our way. But the first banquet must be very select; none but guests of the very highest rank must be present. To say the truth, I and the King have been having a little dispute; for I insist, that not even ghosts may be admitted to-night. The Mer-King and his daughters must be invited first; they don't much like coming on land, but I'll promise they shall each have a wet stone, or, pehaps, something better still, to sit on; and then, I think, they cannot possibly refuse us this time. All old Trolds of the first rank we must have; also, the River-Spirit and the Nisses; and, I fancy, we cannot pass over the Death-Horse and Kirkegrim; true, they do not belong to our set, they are too solemn for us; but they are connected with the family, and pay us regular visits.'

'Caw!' said the night-raven; and alway he flew to bear the invitations.

The Elfin-maidens were still dancing in the Elfin-mount; they danced with long scarfs woven from mist and moonlight, and for those who like that sort of thing it looks pretty enough. The large state-room in the Mount had been regularly cleaned and cleared out; the floor had been washed with moonshine, and the walls rubbed with witches' fat till they shone as tulips do when held up to the light. In the kitchen, frogs were roasting on the spit; while divers other choice dishes, such as mushroom seed, hemlock soup, etc., were prepared or preparing. These were to supply the first courses; rusty nails, bits of coloured glass, and such like dainties, were to come in for the dessert; there was also bright saltpetre wine, and ale brewed in the brewery of the Wise Witch of the Moor.

The old Elfin-King's gold crown had been fresh rubbed with powdered slate-pencil; new curtains had been hung up in all the sleeping-rooms, – yes, there was indeed a rare bustle and commotion.

'Now, we must have the rooms scented with cows' hairs and swine's bristles; and then, I think, I shall have done my part!' said the Elfin-King's housekeeper.

'Dear papa,' said the youngest of the daughters, 'won't you tell me now who these grand visitors are?'

'Well!' replied His Majesty, 'I suppose there's no use in keeping it a secret. Let two of my daughters get themselves ready for their wedding-day, that's all! Two of them most certainly will be married. The Chief of the Norwegian Trolds, he who dwels in old Dofrefield, and has so many castles of freestone among these rocky fastnesses, beside a gold-mine, – which is a capital thing, let me tell you, – he is coming down here with his two

boys, who are both to choose themselves a bride. Such an honest, straight-forward, true old Norseman is this mountain chief! so merry and jovial! he and I are old comrades; he came down here years ago to fetch his wife; she is dead now; she was the daughter of the Rock-King at Möen. Oh, how I long to see the old Norseman again! His sons, they say, are rough un-mannerly cubs, but perhaps report may have done them injustice, and at any rate they are sure to improve in a year or two, when they have sown their wild oats. Let me see how you will polish them up!'

'And how soon are they to be here?' inquired his youngest daughter again.

'That depends on wind and weather!' returned the Elfin-King. 'They travel economically; they come at the ship's convenience. I wanted them to pass over by Sweden, but the old man would not hear of that. He does not keep pace with the times, that's the only fault I can find with him.'

Just then two wills-o'-the-wisp were seen dancing up in a vast hurry, each trying to get before the other, and to be the first to bring the news.

'They come, they come!' cried both with one voice.

'Give me my crown, and let me stand in the moonlight!' said the Elfin-King.

And his seven daughters lifted their long scarfs and bowed low to the earth. There stood the Trold Chief from the Dofrefield, wearing a crown composed of icicles and polished pine cones; for the rest, he was equipped in a bear-skin cloak and sledge-boots; his sons were clad more slightly, and kept their throats uncovered, by way of showing that they cared nothing about the cold.

'Is that a mount?' asked the youngest of them, pointing to it. 'Why, up in Norway we should call it a cave!'

'You foolish boy!' replied his father; 'a cave you go into, a mount you go up! Where are your eyes, not to see the difference?'

The only thing that surprised them in this country, they said, was that the people should speak and understand their language.

'Behave yourselves now!' said the old man; 'don't let your host fancy you never went into decent company before!'

And now they all entered the Elfin-mount, into the grand saloon, where a really very select party was assembled, although at such short notice that it seemed almost as though some fortunate gust of wind had blown them together. And every possible arrangement had been made for the comfort of each of the guests; the Mer-King's family, for instance, sat at table in large tubs of water, and they declared they felt quite as if they were at home. All behaved with strict good-breeding except the two young northern Trolds, who at last so far forgot themselves as to put their legs on the table.

'Take your legs away from the plates!' said their father, and they obeyed, but not so readily as they might have done. Presently they took some pine cones out their pockets and began pelting the lady who sat between them, and then, finding their boots incommode them, they took them off, and coolly gave them to this lady to hold. But their father, the old mountain Chief, conducted himself very differently; he talked so delightfully about the proud Norse mountains, and the torrents, white with dancing spray, that dashed foaming down their rocky steeps with a noise loud and hoarse as thunder, yet musical as the full burst of an organ, touched by a master hand; he told of the salmon leaping up from the wild waters while the Neck was playing on his golden harp; he told of the star-light winter nights when the sledge bells tinkled so merrily, and the youths ran with lighted torches over the icy crust, so glassy and transparent that through it they could see the fishes whirling to and fro in deadly terror beneath their feet; he told of the gallant northern youths and pretty maidens singing songs of old time, and dancing the Hallinge dance, – yes, so charmingly he described all this, that you could not but fancy you heard and saw it all. Oh fie, for shame: all of a sudden the mountain Chief turned round upon the elderly

Elfin maiden, and gave her a cousinly salute, and he was not yet connected ever so remotely with the family.

The young Elfin-maidens were now called upon to dance. First they danced simple dances, then stamping dances, and they did both remarkably well. Last came the most difficult of all, the 'Dance out of the dance,' as it was called. Bravo! how long their legs seemed to grow, and how they whirled and spun about! You could hardly distinguish legs from arms, or arms from legs. Round and round they went, such whirling and twirling, such whirring and whizzing there was that it made the death-horse feel quite dizzy, and at last he grew so unwell that he was obliged to leave the table. 'Hurrah!' cried the mountain Chief, 'they know how to use their limbs with a vengeance! but can they do nothing else than dance, stretch out their feet, and spin round like a whirlwind?'

'You shall judge for yourself,' replied the Elfin-King, and here he called the eldest of his daughters to him. She was transparent and fair as moonlight; she was, in fact, the most delicate of all the sisters; she put a white wand between her lips and vanished: that was her accomplishment.

But the mountain Chief said he should not at all like his wife to possess such an accomplishment as this, and he did not think his sons would like it either.

The second could walk by the side of herself, just though she had a shadow, which elves and trolds never have.

The accomplishment of the third sister was of quite another kind: she had learned how to brew good ale from the Wise Witch of the Moor, and she also knew how to lard alder-wood with glow-worms.

'She will make a capital housewife,' remarked the old mountain Cief.

And now advanced the fourth Elfin damsel; she carried a large gold harp and no sooner had she struck the first chord than all the company lifted their left feet – for elves are leftsided – and when she struck the second chord, they were all compelled to do whatever she wished.

'A dangerous lady, indeed!' said the old Trold Chief. Both of his sons now got up and strode out of the mount; they were heartily weary of these accomplishments.

'And what can the next daughter do?' asked the mountain Chief.

'I have learned to love the north,' replied she, 'and I have resolved never to marry unless I may go to Norway.'

But the youngest of the sisters whispered to the old man, 'That is only because she has heard an old Norse rhyme, which says that when the end of the world shall come, the Norwegian rocks shall stand firm amid the ruins; she is very much afraid of death, and therefore she wants to go to Norway.'

'Ho, ho!' cried the mountain Chief, 'sits the wind in that quarter? But what can the seventh and last do?'

'The sixth comes before the seventh,' said the Elfin-King; for he could count better than to make such a mistake. How-ever, the sixth seemed in no hurry to come forward.

'I can only tell people the truth,' said she. 'Let no one trouble himself about me; I have enough to do to sew my shroud!'

And now came the seventh and last, and what could she do? Why, she could tell fairy tales, as many as any one could wish to hear.

'Here are my five fingers,' said the mountain Chief; 'tell me a story for each finger.'

And the Elfin-maiden took hold of his wrist, and told her stories, and he laughed till his sides ached, and when she came to the finger that wore a gold ring, as though it knew it might be wanted, the mountain Chief suddenly exclaimed, 'Hold fast what thou hast; the hand is thine! I will have thee myself to wife!' But the Elfin-maiden said that she had still two more stories to tell, one for the ring-finger, and another for the little finger.

'Keep them for next winter, we'll hear them then,' replied the mountain Chief. 'And we'll hear about the "Loves of the Fir-Tree and the Birch," about the Valkyria's gifts too, for we all love fairy legends in Norway, and no one there can tell them so charmingly as thou dost. And then we will sit in our rocky halls, whilst the fir-logs are blazing and crackling in the stove, and drink mead out of the golden horns of the old Norse kings; the Neck has thaught me a few of his rare old ditties, besides the Garbo will often come and pay us a visit, and he will sing thee all the sweet songs that the mountain maidens sang in days of yore; – that will be most delightful! The salmon in the torrent will spring up and beat himself against the rock walls, but in vain, he will not be able to get in. Oh, thou canst not imagine what a happy, glorious life we lead in that dear old Norway! But where are the boys?'

Where were the boys? Why, they were racing about in the fields and blowing out the poor wills-o'-the-wisp, who were just ranging themselves in the proper order to make a procession of torches.

'What do you mean by making all this riot?' inquired the mountain Chief. 'I have been choosing you a mother; now you come and choose yourselves wives from among your aunts.'

But his sons said they would rather make speeches and drink toasts; they had not the slightest wish to marry. And accordingly they made speeches, tossed off their glasses and turned them topsy-turvy on the table, to show that they were quite empty; after this they took off their coats, and most unceremoniously lay down on the table and went to sleep. But the old mountain Chief, the while, danced round the hall with his young bride, and exchanged boots with her, because that is not so vulgar as exchanging rings.

'Listen, the cock is crowing!' exclaimed the lady-housekeeper. 'We must make haste and shut the window-shutters close, or the sun will scorch our complexions.'

And herewith Elfin-mount closed.

But outside, in the cloven trunk, the lizards kept running up and down, and one and all declared, 'What a capital fellow that old Norwegian Trold is!' 'For my part, I prefer the boys,' said the earth-worm; – but he, poor wretch, could see nothing either of them or of their father, so his opinion was not worth much.

The Princess and the Pea

Once upon a time there was a prince and he wanted to marry a princess, only she had to be a *real* princess. So he went all over the world looking for one. But every time there was something the matter: princesses there were in plenty, but whether they were real princesses or not, he could never really make out, there was always something not quite right about them. So he came home again and was so very sad, because he did so want a real princess.

Now, one night there was a terrible storm. It thundered and lightened and the rain poured down – it was frightful! All at once there was a knock at the city gate, and the old king went out to open it.

There, standing outside, was a princess. But dear me, what a sight she looked, in the wind and the rain! The water was running down her hair and her clothes, and it was running in at the toes of her shoes and out again at the heels. And then she said she was a real princess.

'We'll see about that!' thought the old queen. But she didn't say anything; she went into the bedroom, took off all the bedclothes, and put a pea in the bottom of the bed. Then she took twenty mattresses and put them on top of the pea, and then again twenty featherbeds on top of the mattresses.

That was to be the princesses's bed for the night.

In the morning they asked her how she had slept.

'Dreadfully!' said the princess. 'I hardly got a wink of sleep all night! Goodness knows what can have been in the bed! There was something hard in it, and now I'm just black and blue all over! It's really dreadful!'

So now they were able to see that she was a real princess, because she had felt the pea right through the twenty mattresses and the twenty feather-beds. Only a real princess could be so tender as that.

So the prince took her for his wife, now he knew he had a real princess. And the pea was placed in the museum, where it may still be seen – if nobody has taken it.

There, now that was a real story!

The Ugly Duckling

It was lovely summer weather in the country, and the golden corn, the green oats, and the haystacks piled up in the meadows looked beautiful. The stork walking about on his long red legs chattered in the Egyptian language, which he had learnt from his mother. The corn-fields and meadows were surrounded by large forests, in the midst of which were deep pools. It was, indeed, delightful to walk about in the country. In a sunny spot stood a pleasant old farm-house close by a deep river, and from the house down to the water side grew great burdock leaves, so high, that under the tallest of them a little child could stand upright. The spot was as wild as the centre of a thick wood. In this snug retreat sat a duck on her nest, watching for her young brood to hatch; she was beginning to get tired of her task, for the little ones were a long time coming out of their shells, and she seldom had any visitors. The other ducks liked much better to swim about in the river than to climb the slippery banks, and sit under a burdock leaf, to have a gossip with her. At length one shell cracked, and then another, and from

each egg came a living creature that lifted its head and cried, "Peep, peep."
"Quack, quack," said the mother, and then they all quacked as well as
they could, and looked about them on every side at the large green leaves.
Their mother allowed them to look as much as they liked, because green is
good for the eyes. "How large the world is," said the young ducks, when
they found how much more room they now had than while they were inside
the egg-shell. "Do you imagine this is the whole world?" asked the mother;
"Wait till you have seen the garden; it stretches far beyond that to the parson's field, but I have never ventured to such a distance. Are you all out?"
she continued, rising; "No, I declare, the largest egg lies there still. I wonder
how long this is to last, I am quite tired of it;" and she seated herself again
on the nest.

"Well, how are you getting on?" asked an old duck, who paid her a visit.

"One egg is not hatched yet," said the duck, "it will not break. But just look
at all the others, are they not the prettiest little ducklings you ever saw?
They are the image of their father, who is so unkind, he never comes to see
me."

"Let me see the egg that will not break," said the old duck; "I have no doubt it is a turkey's egg. I was persuaded to hatch some once, and after all my care and trouble with the young ones, they were afraid of the water. I quacked and clucked, but all to no purpose. I could not get them to venture in. Let me look at the egg. Yes, that is a turkey's egg; take my advice, leave it where it is, and teach the other children to swim."

"I think I will sit on it a little while longer," said the duck; "as I have sat so long already, a few days will be nothing."

"Please yourself," said the old duck, and she went away.

At last the large egg broke, and a young one crept forth, crying, "Peep, peep." It was very large and ugly. The duck stared at it, and exclaimed, "It is very large, and not at all like the others. I wonder if it really is a turkey. We shall soon find out, however, when we go to the water. It must go in, if I have to push it in myself."

On the next day the weather was delightful, and the sun shone brightly on the green burdock leaves, so the mother duck took her young brood down to the water, and jumped in with a splash. "Quack, quack," cried she, and one after another the little ducklings jumped in. The water closed over their heads, but they came up again in an instant, and swam about quite prettily with their legs paddling under them as easily as possible, and the ugly duckling was also in the water swimming with them.

"Oh," said the mother, "that is not a turkey; how well he uses his legs, and how upright he holds himself! He is my own child, and he is not so very ugly after all if you look at him properly. Quack, quack! come with me now, I will take you into grand society, and introduce you to the farmyard, but you must keep close to me or you may be trodden upon; and, above all, beware of the cat."

When they reached the farmyard, there was a great disturbance, two families were fighting for an eel's head, which, after all, was carried off by the cat. "See, children, that is the way of the world," said the mother duck,

whetting her beak, for she would have liked the eel's head herself. "Come, now, use your legs, and let me see how well you can behave. You must bow your heads prettily to that old duck yonder; she is the highest born of them all, and has Spanish blood, therefore she is well off. Don't you see she has a red rag tied to her leg, which is something very grand, and a great honour for a duck; it shows that every one is anxious not to lose her, as she can be recognised both by man and beast. Come, now, don't turn in your toes, a well-bred duckling spreads his feet wide apart, just like his father and mother, in this way; now bend your neck, and say 'quack.'"

The ducklings did as they were bid, but the other ducks stared, and said, "Look, here comes another brood, as if there were not enough of us already! and what a queer-looking object one of them is; we don't want him here," and then one flew out and bit him in the neck.

"Let him alone," said the mother; "he is not doing any harm."

"Yes, but he is so big and ugly," said the spiteful duck, "and therefore he must be turned out."

"The others are very pretty children," said the old duck with the rag on her leg, "all but that one; I wish his mother could improve him a little."

"That is impossible, your grace," replied the mother; "he is not pretty; but he has a very good disposition, and swims as well or even better than the others. I think he will grow up pretty, and perhaps be smaller; he has remained too long in the egg, and therefore his figure is not properly formed;" and then she stroked his neck and smoothed the feathers, saying, "It is a drake, and therefore not of so much consequence. I think he will grow up strong, and able to take care of himself."

"The other ducklings are graceful enough," said the old duck. "Now make yourself at home, and if you find an eel's head, you can bring it to me."

And so they made themselves comfortable; but the poor duckling, who had crept out of his shell last of all, and looked so ugly, was bitten and pushed and made fun of, not only by the ducks, but by all the poultry. "He is too big," they all said, and the turkey cock, who had been born into the world with spurs, and fancied himself really an emperor, puffed himself out like a vessel in full sail, and flew at the duckling, and became quite red in the head with passion, so that the poor little thing did not know where to go, and was quite miserable because he was so ugly and laughed at by the whole farmyard. So it went on from day to day till it got worse and worse. The poor duckling was driven about by every one; even his brothers and sisters were unkind to him, and would say, "Ah, you ugly creature, I wish the cat would get you," and his mother said she wished he had never been born. The ducks pecked him, the chickens beat him, and the girl who fed the poultry kicked him with her feet. So at last he ran away, frightening the little birds in the hedge as he flew over the palings.

"They are afraid of me, because I am so ugly," he said. So he closed his eyes, and flew still farther, until he came out on a large moor, inhabited by wild ducks. Here he remained the whole night, feeling very tired and sorrowful.

In the morning, when the wild ducks rose in the air, they stared at their new comrade. "What sort of a duck are you?" they all said, coming round him.

He bowed to them, and was as polite as he could be, but he did not reply to their question. "You are exceedingly ugly," said the wild ducks, "but that will not matter if you do not want to marry one of our family."

Poor thing! he had no thoughts of marriage; all he wanted was permission to lie among the rushes, and drink some of the water on the moor. After he had been on the moor two days, there came two wild geese, or rather goslings, for they had not been out of the egg long, and were very saucy. "Listen, friend," said one of them to the duckling, "you are so ugly, that we like you very well. Will you go with us, and become a bird of passage? Not far from here is another moor, in which there are some pretty wild geese, all unmarried. It is a chance for you to get a wife; you may be lucky, ugly as you are."

"Pop, pop," sounded in the air, and the two wild geese fell dead among the rushes, and the water was tinged with blood. "Pop, pop," echoed far and wide in the distance, and whole flocks of wild geese rose up from the rushes. The sound continued from every direction, for the sportsmen surrounded

the moor, and some were even seated on branches of trees, overlooking the
rushes. The blue smoke from the guns rose like clouds over the dark trees,
and as it floated away across the water, a number of sporting dogs bounded
in among the rushes, which bent beneath them wherever they went. How
they terrified the poor duckling! He turned away his head to hide it under
his wing, and at the same moment a large terrible dog passed quite near him.
His jaws were open, his tongue hung from his mouth, and his eyes glared
fearfully. He thrust his nose close to the duckling, showing his sharp
teeth, and then "splash, splash," he went into the water without touching
him. "Oh," sighed the duckling, "how thankful I am for being so ugly;
even a dog will not bite me." And so he lay quite still, while the shot rattled
through the rushes, and gun after gun was fired over him. It was late in the
day before all became quiet, but even then the poor young thing did not
dare to move. He waited quietly for several hours, and then, after looking

carefully around him, hastened away from the moor as fast as he could. He ran over field and meadow till a storm arose, and he could hardly struggle against it. Towards evening, he reached a poor little cottage that seemed ready to fall, and only remained standing because it could not decide on which side to fall first. The storm continued so violently, that the duckling could go no farther; he sat down by the cottage, and then he noticed that the door was not quite closed in consequence of one of the hinges having given way. There was therefore a narrow opening near the bottom large enough for him to slip through, which he did very quietly, and got shelter for the night. A woman, a tom cat, and a hen lived in this cottage. The tom cat, whom his mistress called, "My little son," was a great favourite; he could raise his back, and purr, and could even throw out sparks from his fur if it were stroked the wrong way. The hen had very short legs, so she was called "Chickie short legs." She laid good eggs, and her mistress loved her as if she had been her own child. In the morning, the strange visitor was discovered, and the tom cat began to purr, and the hen to cluck.

"What is that noise about?" said the old woman, looking round the room, but her sight was not very good; therefore, when she saw the duckling she thought it must be a fat duck, that had strayed from home. "Oh what a prize!" she exclaimed, "I hope it is not a drake, for then I shall have some duck's eggs. I must wait and see." So the duckling was allowed to remain on trial for three weeks, but there were no eggs. Now the tom cat was the master of the house, and the hen was mistress, and they always said, "We and the world," for they believed themselves to be half the world, and the better half too. The duckling thought that others might hold a different opinion on the subject, but the hen would not listen to such doubts. "Can you lay eggs?" she asked, "No." "Then have the goodness to hold your tongue. "Can you raise your back, or purr, or throw out sparks?" said the tom cat, "No." "Then you have no right to express an opinion when sensible people are speaking." So the duckling sat in a corner, feeling very low-spirited, till the sunshine and the fresh air came into the room through the open door, and then he began to feel such a great longing for a swim on the water, that he could not help telling the hen.

"What an absurd idea," said the hen. "You have nothing else to do, therefore you have foolish fancies. If you could purr or lay eggs, they would pass away."

"But it is so delightful to swim about on the water," said the duckling, "and so refreshing to feel it close over your head, while you dive down to the bottom."

"Delightful indeed!" said the hen, "why, you must be crazy! Ask the cat, he is the cleverest animal I know, ask him how he would like to swim about

on the water, or to dive under it, for I will not speak of my own opinion;
ask our mistress, the old woman – there is no one in the world more clever
than she is. Do you think she would like to swim, or to let the water close
over her head?"

"You don't understand me," said the duckling.

"We don't understand you? Who can understand you, I wonder? Do you
consider yourself more clever than the cat, or the old woman? I will say

197

nothing of myself. Don't imagine such nonsense, child, and thank your good fortune that you have been received here. Are you not in a warm room, and in society from which you may learn something. But you are a chatterer, and your company is not very agreeable. Believe me, I speak only for your good. I may tell you unpleasant truths, but that is a proof of my friendship. I advise you, therefore, to lay eggs, and learn to purr as quickly as possible."

"I believe I must go out into the world again," said the duckling.

"Yes, do," said the hen. So the duckling left the cottage, and soon found water on which it could swim and dive, but was avoided by all other animals, because of its ugly appearance. Autumn came, and the leaves in the forest turned to orange and gold; then, as winter approached, the wind caught them as they fell and whirled them in the cold air. The clouds, heavy with hail and snow-flakes, hung low in the sky, and the raven stood on the ferns crying, "Croak, croak." It made one shiver with cold to look at him. All this was very sad for the poor little duckling. One evening, just as the sun set amid radiant clouds, there came a large flock of beautiful birds out of the bushes. The duckling had never seen any like them before. They were swans, and they curved their graceful necks, while their soft plumage shone with dazzling whiteness. They uttered a singular cry as they spread their glorious wings and flew away from those cold regions to warmer countries across the sea. As they mounted higher and higher in the air, the ugly little duckling felt quite a strange sensation as he watched them. He whirled himself in the water like a wheel, stretched out his neck towards them, and uttered a cry so strange that it frightened himself. Could he ever forget those beautiful, happy birds; and when at last they were out of his sight, he dived under the water, and rose again almost beside himself with excitement. He knew not the names of these birds, nor where they had flown, but he felt towards them as he had never felt for any other bird in the world. He was not envious of these beautiful creatures, but wished to be as lovely as they. Poor ugly creature, how gladly he would have lived even with the ducks had they only given him encouragement. The winter grew colder and colder; he was obliged to swim about on the water to keep him from freezing, but every night the space on which he swam became smaller and smaller. At length it froze so hard that the ice in the water crackled as he moved, and the duckling had to paddle with his legs as well as he could, to keep the space from closing up. He became exhausted at last, and lay still and helpless, frozen fast in the ice.

Early in the morning, a peasant, who was passing by, saw what had happened. He broke the ice in pieces with his wooden shoe, and carried the duckling home to his wife. The warmth revived the poor little creature; but when the children wanted to play with him, the duckling thought they would do him

some harm; so he started up in terror, fluttered into the milk-pan, and splashed the milk about the room. Then the woman clapped her hands, which frightened him still more. He flew first into the buttercask, then into the meal-tub, and out again. What a condition he was in! The woman screamed, and struck at him with the tongs; the children laughed and screamed, and tumbled over each other, in their efforts to catch him; but luckily he escaped. The door stood open; the poor creature could just manage to slip out among the bushes, and lie down quite exhausted in the newly fallen snow.

It would be very sad, were I to relate all the misery and privations which the poor little duckling endured during the hard winter; but when it had passed, he found himself lying one morning in a moor amongst the rushes. He felt the warm sun shining, and heard the lark singing, and saw that all around was beautiful spring. Then the young bird felt that his wings were strong, as

he flapped them against his sides, and rose high into the air. They bore him onwards, until he found himself in a large garden, before he knew how it had happened. The apple-trees were in full blossom, and the fragrant elders bent their long green branches down to the stream which wound round a smooth lawn. Everything looked beautiful, in the freshness of early spring. From a thicket close by came three beautiful white swans, rustling their feathers, and swimming lightly over the smooth water. The duckling remembered the lovely birds, and felt more strangely unhappy than ever.

"I will fly to these royal birds," he exclaimed, "and they will kill me, because I am so ugly, and dare to approach them; but it does not matter: better be killed by them than pecked by the ducks, beaten by the hens, pushed about by the maiden who feeds the poultry, or starved with hunger in the winter."

Then he flew to the water, and swam towards the beautiful swans. The moment they espied the stranger, they rushed to meet him with outstretched wings.

"Kill me," said the poor bird; and he bent his head down to the surface of the water, and awaited death.

But what did he see in the clear stream below? His own image; no longer a dark, grey bird, ugly and disagreeable to look at, but a graceful and beautiful swan. To be born in a duck's nest, in a farmyard, is of no consequence to a bird, if it is hatched from a swan's egg. He now felt glad at having suffered sorrow and trouble, because it enabled him to enjoy so much better all the pleasure and happiness around him; for the great swans swam round the new-comer, and stroked his neck with their beaks, as a welcome.

Into the garden presently came some little children, and threw bread and cake into the water.

"See," cried the youngest, "there is a new one;" and the rest were delighted, and ran to their father and mother, dancing and clapping their hands, and shouting joyously, "There is another swan come; a new one has arrived." Then they threw more bread and cake into the water, and said, "The new one is the most beautiful of all; he is so young and pretty." And the old swans bowed their heads before him.

Then he felt quite ashamed, and hid his head under his wing; for he did not know what to do, he was so happy, and yet not at all proud. He had been as persecuted and despised for his ugliness, and now he heard them say he was the most beautiful of all the birds. Even the elder-tree bent down its boughs into the water before him, and the sun shone warm and bright. Then he rustled his feathers, curved his slender neck, and cried joyfully, from the depths of his heart, "I never dreamed of such happiness as this, while I was an ugly duckling."

The Emperor's New Clothes

Many years ago there lived an Emperor, who cared so much for new clothes that he spent all his money upon them, that he might be very fine. He did not care about his soldiers or the theatre, and only liked to drive out to show his new clothes to his people.

One day two cheats came to the city where he lived. They gave themselves out as weavers, and declared that they could weave the finest stuff any one could imagine. Not only were their colours and patterns, they said, uncommonly beautiful, but the clothes made of the stuff possessed the wonder-

ful quality that they became invisible to any one who was unfit for the office he held or who was incorrigibly stupid.

"Those would be capital clothes!" thought the Emperor. "If I wore those, I should be able to find out what men in my empire are not fit for the positions they hold; I could distinguish the clever from the stupid. Yes, the stuff must be woven for me directly!"

And he gave the two cheats a lot of money that they might begin their work at once.

As for them, they put up two looms, and pretended to be working; but they had nothing at all on their looms. They at once demanded the finest silk and the costliest gold; this they put into their own pockets, and worked at the empty looms till far into the night.

"I should like to know how far they have got on with the stuff," thought the Emperor. But he felt quite uncomfortable when he thought that those who were not fit for their offices could not see it. He believed, indeed, that he had nothing to fear for himself, but yet he preferred first to send some one else to see how matters stood. All the people in the whole city knew what peculiar power the stuff possessed, and all were anxious to see how bad or how stupid their neighbours were.

"I will send my honest old Minister to the weavers," thought the Emperor. "He can judge best how the stuff looks, for he has sense, and no one understands his office better than he."

Now the good old Minister went out into the hall where the two cheats sat working at the empty looms.

"Mercy preserve us!" thought the old Minister, and he opened his eyes wide. "I cannot see anything at all!" But he did not say this.

"Mercy!" thought he, "can I indeed be so stupid? I never thought that, not a soul must know it. Am I not fit for my office? – No, it will never do for me to tell that I could not see the stuff."

"Do you say nothing to it?" said one of the weavers.

"Oh, it is charming – quite charming!" answered the old Minister, as he peered through his spectacles. "What a fine pattern, and what colours! Yes, I shall tell the Emperor that I am very much pleased with it."

"Well, we are glad of that," said both the weavers; and then they named the colours, and explained the strange pattern. The old Minister listened attentively, that he might be able to repeat it when the Emperor came. And he did so.

The Emperor soon sent again, dispatching another honest statesman, to see how the weaving was going on, and if the stuff would soon be ready. He fared just like the first: he looked and looked, but, as there was nothing to be seen but the empty looms, he could see nothing.

"Is not that a pretty piece of stuff?" asked the two cheats, and they displayed and explained the handsome pattern which was not there at all.

"I am not stupid!" thought the man; "it must be my good office, for which I am not fit. It is odd enough, but I must not let it be noticed." And so he praised the stuff which he did not see, and expressed his pleasure at the beautiful colours and the charming pattern. "Yes, it is enchanting," he said to the Emperor.

All the people in the town were talking of the gorgeous stuff. The Emperor wished to see it himself while it was still upon the loom. With a whole crowd of chosen men, among whom were also the two honest statesmen who had already been there, he went to the two cunning cheats, who were now weaving with might and main without fibre or thread.

"Is that not splendid?" said the two old statesmen, who had already been there once. "Does not your Majesty remark the pattern and the colours?" And then they pointed to the empty loom, for they thought that others could see the stuff.

"What's this?" thought the Emperor. "I can see nothing at all! That is terrible. Am I stupid? Am I not fit to be Emperor? That would be the most dreadful thing that could happen to me. – Oh, it is *very* pretty!" he said aloud. "It has our exalted approbation." And he nodded in a contented way, and gazed at the empty loom, for he would not say that he saw nothing. The whole suite whom he had with him looked and looked, and saw nothing, any more than the rest; but, like the Emperor, they said, "That *is* pretty!" and counselled him to wear these splendid new clothes for the first time at the great procession that was presently to take place. "It is splendid, tasteful, excellent!" went from mouth to mouth. On all sides there seemed to be general rejoicing, and the Emperor gave the cheats the title of Imperial Court Weavers.

The whole night before the morning on which the procession was to take place the cheats were up, and had lighted more than sixteen candles. The people could see that they were hard at work, completing the Emperor's new clothes. They pretended to take the stuff down from the loom; they made cuts in the air with great scissors; they sewed with needles without thread; and at last they said, "Now the clothes are ready!"

The Emperor came himself with his noblest cavaliers; and the two cheats lifted up one arm as if they were holding something, and said, "See, here are the trousers! Here is the coat! Here is the cloak!" and so on. "It is as light as a spider's web: one would think one had nothing on; but that is just the beauty of it."

"Yes," said all the cavaliers; but they could not see anything, for nothing was there.

"Does your Imperial Majesty please to condescend to undress?" said the cheats; "then we will put on you the new clothes here in front of the great mirror."

The Emperor took off his clothes, and the cheats pretended to put on him each new garment as it was ready; and the Emperor turned round and round before the mirror. "Oh, how well they look! How capitally they fit!" said all. "What a pattern! What colours! That *is* a splendid dress!"

"They are standing outside with the canopy which is to be borne above your Majesty in the procession!" announced the head master of the ceremonies.

"Well, I am ready," replied the Emperor. "Does it not suit me well?" And then he turned again to the mirror, for he wanted it to appear as if he contemplated his adornment with great interest.

The chamberlains, who were to carry the train, stooped down with their hands toward the floor, just as if they were picking up the mantle; then they pretended to be holding something up in the air. They did not dare to let it be noticed that they saw nothing.

So the Emperor went in procession under the rich canopy, and every one in the streets said, "How incomparable are the Emperor's new clothes! What a train he has to his mantle! How it fits him!" No one would let it be perceived that he could see nothing, for that would have shown that he was not fit for his office, or was very stupid. No clothes of the Emperor's had ever had such a success as these.

"But he has nothing on!" a little child cried out at last.

"Just hear what that innocent says!" said the father; and one whispered to another what the child had said.

"But he has nothing on!" said the whole people at length. That touched the Emperor, for it seemed to him that they were right; but he thought within himself, "I must go through with the procession." And the chamberlains held on tighter than ever, and carried the train which did not exist at all.

Holger Danske

In Denmark there stands an old castle named Kronenburg, close by the Sound of Elsinore, where large ships, both English, Russian, and Prussian, pass by hundreds every day. And they salute the old castle with cannons, "Boom, boom," which is as if they said, "Good-day." And the cannons of the old castle answer "Boom," which means "Many thanks." In winter no ships sail by, for the whole Sound is covered with ice as far as the Swedish coast, and has quite the appearance of a high-road. The Danish and the Swedish flags wave, and Danes and Swedes say, "Good-day," and "Thank you" to each other, not with cannons, but with a friendly shake of the hand; and they exchange white bread and biscuits with each other, because foreign articles taste the best.

But the most beautiful sight of all is the old castle of Kronenburg, where Holger Danske sits in the deep, dark cellar, into which no one goes. He is clad in iron and steel, and rests his head on his strong arm; his long beard hangs down upon the marble table, into which it has become firmly rooted; he sleeps and dreams, but in his dreams he sees everything that happens in Denmark. On each Christmas-eve an angel comes to him and tells him that all he has dreamed is true, and that he may go to sleep again in peace, as Denmark is not yet in any real danger; but should danger ever come, then Holger Danske will rouse himself, and the table will burst asunder as he draws out his beard. Then he will come forth in his strength, and strike a blow that shall sound in all the countries of the world.

An old grandfather sat and told his little grandson all this about Holger Danske, and the boy knew that what his grandfather told him must be true. As the old man related this story, he was carving an image in wood to represent Holger Danske, to be fastened to the prow of a ship; for the old grandfather was a carver in wood, that is, one who carved figures for the heads of ships, according to the names given to them. And now he had carved Holger Danske, who stood there erect and proud, with his long beard, holding in one hand his broad battle-axe, while with the other he leaned on the Danish arms. The old grandfather told the little boy a great deal about Danish men and women who had distinguished themselves in olden times, so that he fancied he knew as much even as Holger Danske himself, who, after all, could only dream; and when the little fellow went to bed, he thought so much about it that he actually pressed his chin against the counterpane, and imagined that he had a long beard which had become rooted to it. But the old grandfather remained sitting at his work and carving away at the last part of it, which was the Danish arms. And when he had finished he looked at the whole figure, and thought of all he had heard and read, and what he had that evening related to his little grandson. Then he nodded his head, wiped his spectacles and put them on, and said, "Ah, yes; Holger Danske will not appear in my lifetime, but the boy who is in bed there may very likely live to see him when the event really comes to pass." And the old grandfather nodded again; and the more he looked at Holger Danske, the more satisfied he felt that he had carved a good image of him. It seemed to glow with the colour of life; the armour glittered like iron and steel. The hearts in the Danish arms grew more and more red; while the lions, with gold crowns on their heads, were leaping up.* "That is the most beautiful coat of arms in the world," said the old man. "The lions represent strength; and the hearts, gentleness and love." And as he gazed on the uppermost lion, he thought of King Canute, who chained great England to Denmark's throne; and he looked at the second lion, and thought of Waldemar, who united Denmark and conquered the Vandals. The third lion reminded him of Margaret, who united Denmark, Sweden, and Norway. But when he gazed at the red hearts, their colours glowed more deeply, even as flames, and his memory followed each in turn. The first led him to a dark, narrow prison, in which sat a prisoner, a beautiful woman, daughter of Christian the Fourth, Eleanor Ulfeld;** and the flame became a rose on her bosom, and its blossoms were not more pure than the heart of this noblest and best of all Danish women. "Ah, yes; that is indeed a noble heart in the Danish arms," said the grandfather. And his spirit followed the second flame, which carried him out to sea,*** where cannons roared and the ships lay shrouded in smoke, and the flaming heart attached itself to the breast of Hvitfeldt in the form of the ribbon of an order, as he blew himself

* The Danish arms consists of three lions between nine hearts.

**This highly-gifted princess was the wife of Corfitz Ulfeld; he was accused of high treason, and Eleanor, whose only fault was the truest love to her unhappy husband, was compelled to remain for twenty-two years in a miserable dungeon, till the death of her persecutor, Queen Sophia Amelia.

***In the naval battle, which took place in Kjöge Bay in 1710, between the Danes and the Swedes, Hvitfeldt's ship, the Danebrog, took fire. To save the town of Kjöge, and the Danish fleet which were being driven by the wind towards his burning ship, he blew up his vessel, with himself and his whole crew.

and his ship into the air in order to save the fleet. And the third flame led him to Greenland's wretched huts, where the preacher, Hans Egede,* ruled with love in every word and action. The flame was as a star on his breast, and added another heart to the Danish arms. And as the old grandfather's spirit followed the next hovering flame, he knew whither it would lead him. In a peasant woman's humble room stood Frederick the Sixth,** writing his name with chalk on the beam. The flame trembled on his breast and in his heart, and it was in the peasant's room that his heart became one for the Danish arms. The old grandfather wiped his eyes, for he had known King Frederick, with his silvery locks and his honest blue eyes, and lived for him, and he folded his hands and remained for some time silent. Then his daughter came to him and said it was getting late, that he ought to rest for a while, and that the supper was on the table.

"What you have been carving is very beautiful, grandfather," said she. "Holger Danske and the old coat of arms; it seems to me as if I have seen the face somewhere."

"No, that is impossible," replied the old grandfather; "but *I* have seen it, and I have tried to carve it in wood, as I have retained it in my memory. It was a long time ago, while the English fleet lay in the roads, on the second

* Hans Egede went to Greenland in 1821, and worked there for fifteen long years amid incredible privations and difficulties. He not only spread the Christian religion, but was himself the pattern of a noble Christian.

** Once, while on a journey to the western coast of Jutland, the king came to the cottage of an old woman. As he was leaving, she ran after him, and asked him to write his name on a beam as a remembrance of his visit. The king turned back and complied with her request. Through his whole life he interested himself for the peasantry, and on that account it was that the Danish peasants begged to be allowed to carry the coffin to the royal vault at Roeskilde, four Danish miles from Copenhagen.

of April,* when we showed that we were true, ancient Danes. I was on board the *Denmark*, in Steene Bille's squadron; I had a man by my side whom even the cannon balls seemed to fear. He sung old songs in a merry voice, and fired and fought as if he were something more than a man. I still remember his face, but from whence he came, or whither he went, I know not; no one knows. I have often thought it might have been Holger Danske himself, who had swam down to us from Kronenburg to help us in the hour of danger. That was my idea, and there stands his likeness.''

The wooden figure threw a gigantic shadow on the wall, and even on part of the ceiling; it seemed as if the real Holger Danske stood behind it, for the shadow moved; but this was no doubt caused by the flame of the lamp not burning steadily. Then the daughter-in-law kissed the old grandfather, and led him to a large arm-chair by the table; and she, and her husband, who was the son of the old man and the father of the little boy who lay in bed, sat down to supper with him. And the old grandfather talked of the Danish lions and the Danish hearts, emblems of strength and gentleness, and explained quite clearly that there is another strength than that which lies in a sword, and he pointed to a shelf where lay a number of old books, and

* On the second of April, 1801, occurred the sanguinary naval engagement between the Danes and the English, under Sir Hyde Parker and Nelson.

amongst them a collection of Holberg's plays, which are much read and are so clever and amusing that it is easy to fancy we have known the people of those days, who are described in them.

"He knew how to fight also," said the old man; "for he lashed the follies and prejudices of people during his whole life."

Then the grandfather nodded to a place above the looking-glass, where hung an almanac, with a representation of the Round Tower* upon it, and said "Tycho Brahe was another of those who used a sword, but not one to cut into the flesh and bone, but to make the way of the stars of heaven clear, and plain to be understood. And then *he* whose father belonged to my calling, – yes, he, the son of the old image-carver, he whom we ourselves have seen, with his silvery locks and his broad shoulders, whose name is known in all lands; – yes, he was a sculptor, while I am only a carver. Holger Danske can appear in marble, so that people in all countries of the world may hear of the strength of Denmark. Now let us drink the health of Bertel."**

But the little boy in bed saw plainly the old castle of Kronenburg, and the Sound of Elsinore, and Holger Danske, far down in the cellar, with his beard rooted to the table, and dreaming of everything that was passing above him.

And Holger Danske did dream of the little humble room in which the image-carver sat; he heard all that had been said, and he nodded in his dream, saying, "Ah, yes, remember me, you Danish people, keep me in your memory, I will come to you in the hour of need."

The bright morning light shone over Kronenburg, and the wind brought the sound of the hunting-horn across from the neighbouring shores. The ships sailed by and saluted the castle with the boom of the cannon, and Kronenburg returned the salute, "Boom, boom." But the roaring cannons did not awake Holger Danske, for they meant only "Good morning," and "Thank you." They must fire in another fashion before he awakes; but wake he will, for there is energy yet in Holger Danske.

* The Astronomical Observatory at Copenhagen.

** Bertel Thorwaldsen.

The Darning-Needle

There was once a darning-needle who thought herself so fine that she fancied she must be fit for embroidery. "Hold me tight," she would say to the fingers, when they took her up, "don't let me fall; if you do, I shall never be found again, I am so very fine."

"That is your opinion, is it?" said the fingers, as they seized her round the body.

"See, I am coming with a train," said the darning-needle, drawing a long thread after her; but there was no knot in the thread.

The fingers then placed the point of the needle against the cook's slipper. There was a crack in the upper leather, which had to be sewn together.

"What coarse work!" said the darning-needle, "I shall never get through. I shall break! – I am breaking!" and sure enough she broke. "Did I not say so?" said the darning-needle, "I know I am too fine for such work as that."

"This needle is quite useless for sewing now," said the fingers; but they still held it fast, and the cook dropped some sealing-wax on the needle, and fastened her handkerchief with it in front.

"So now I am a breast-pin," said the darning-needle; "I knew very well I should come to honour some day; merit is sure to rise;" and she laughed, quietly to herself, for of course no one ever saw a darning-needle laugh. And there she sat as proudly as if she were in a state coach, and looked all around her. "May I be allowed to ask if you are made of gold?" she inquired of her neighbour, a pin; "you have a very pretty appearance, and a curious head, although you are rather small. You must take pains to grow, for it is not every one who has sealing-wax dropped upon him;" and as she spoke, the darning-needle drew herself up so proudly that she fell out of the hand-kerchief right into the sink, which the cook was cleaning. "Now I am going on a journey," said the needle, as she floated away with the dirty water, "I do hope I shall not be lost." But she really was lost in a gutter. "I am too fine for this world," said the darning-needle, as she lay in the gutter; "but I know who I am, and that is always some comfort." So the darning-needle kept up her proud behaviour, and did not lose her good humour. Then there floated over her all sorts of things, – chips and straws, and pieces of old newspaper. "See how they sail," said the darning-needle; "they do not know what is under them. I am here, and here I shall stick. See, there goes a chip, thinking of nothing in the world but himself – only a chip. There's a straw going by now; how he turns and twists about! Don't be thinking too much of yourself, or you may chance to run against a stone. There swims a piece of newspaper; what is written upon it has been forgotten long ago, and yet it gives itself airs. I sit here patiently and quietly. I know who I am, so I shall not move."

One day something lying close to the darning-needle glittered so splendidly that she thought it was a diamond; yet it was only a piece of broken bottle. The darning-needle spoke to it, because it sparkled, and represented herself as a breast-pin. "I suppose you are really a diamond?" she said.

"Why yes, something of the kind," he replied; and so each believed the other to be very valuable, and then they began to talk about the world, and the conceited people in it.

"I have been in a lady's work-box," said the darning-needle, "and this lady was the cook. She had on each hand five fingers, and anything so conceited as these five fingers I have never seen; and yet they were only employed to take me out of the box and to put me back again."

"Were they not high-born?"

"High-born!" said the darning-needle, "no indeed, but so haughty. They were five brothers, all born fingers; they kept very proudly together, though they were of different lengths. The one who stood first in the rank was named the thumb, he was short and thick, and had only one joint in his back, and could therefore make but one bow; but he said that if he were cut off from a man's hand, that man would be unfit for a soldier. Sweet-tooth, his neighbour, dipped himself into sweet or sour, pointed to the sun and moon, and formed the letters when the fingers wrote. Longman, the middle finger, looked over the heads of all the others. Gold-band, the next finger, wore a golden circle round his waist. And little Playman did nothing at all, and seemed proud of it. They were boasters, and boasters they will remain; and therefore I left them."

"And now we sit here and glitter," said the piece of broken bottle.

At the same moment more water streamed into the gutter, so that it overflowed, and the piece of bottle was carried away.

"So he is promoted," said the darning-needle, "while I remain here; I am too fine, but that is my pride, and what do I care?" And so she sat there in her pride, and had many such thoughts as these, – "I could almost fancy that I came from a sunbeam, I am so fine. It seems as if the sunbeams were always looking for me under the water. Ah! I am so fine that even my

mother cannot find me. Had I still my old eye, which was broken off, I believe I should weep; but no, I would not do that, it is not genteel to cry."

One day a couple of street boys were paddling in the gutter, for they sometimes found old nails, farthings, and other treasures. It was dirty work, but they took great pleasure in it. "Hallo!" cried one, as he pricked himself with the darning-needle, "here's a fellow for you."

"I am not a fellow, I am a young lady," said the darning-needle; but no one heard her.

The sealing-wax had come off, and she was quite black; but black makes a person look slender, so she thought herself even finer than before.

"Here comes an egg-shell sailing along," said one of the boys; so they stuck the darning-needle into the egg-shell.

"White walls, and I am black myself," said the darning-needle, "that looks well; now I can be seen, but I hope I shall not be sea-sick, or I shall break again." She was not sea-sick, and she did not break. "It is a good thing against sea-sickness to have a steel stomach, and not to forget one's own importance. Now my sea-sickness has past: delicate people can bear a great deal."

Crack went the egg-shell, as a waggon passed over it. "Good heavens, how it crushes!" said the darning-needle. "I shall be sick now. I am breaking!" but she did not break, though the waggon went over her as she lay at full length; and there let her lie.

The Snow Queen

Story the first

Which describes a looking-glass and the broken fragments.

You must attend to the commencement of this story, for when we get to the end we shall know more than we do now about a very wicked hobgoblin; he was one of the very worst, for he was a real demon. One day, when he was in a merry mood, he made a looking-glass which had the power of making everything good or beautiful that was reflected in it almost shrink to nothing, while everything that was worthless and bad looked increased in size and worse than ever. The most lovely landscapes appeared like boiled spinach, and the people became hideous, and looked as if they stood on their heads and had no bodies. Their countenances were so distorted that no one could recognise them, and even one freckle on the face appeared to spread over the whole of the nose and mouth. The demon said this was very amusing. When a good or pious thought passed through the mind of any one it was misrepresented in the glass; and then how the demon laughed at his cunning invention. All who went to the demon's school – for he kept a school – talked everywhere of the wonders they had seen, and declared that people could now, for the first time, see what the world and mankind were really like. They carried the glass about everywhere, till at last there was not a land nor a people who had not been looked at through this distorted mirror. They wanted even to fly with it up to heaven to see the angels, but the higher they flew the more slippery the glass became, and they could scarcely hold it, till at last it slipped from their hands, fell to the earth, and was broken into millions of pieces. But now the looking-glass caused more unhappiness than ever, for some of the fragments were not so large as a grain of sand, and they flew about the world into every country. When one of these tiny atoms flew into a person's eye, it stuck there unknown to him, and from that moment he saw everything through a distorted medium, or could see only the worst side of what he looked at, for even the smallest fragment retained the same power which had belonged to the whole mirror. Some few persons even got a fragment of the looking-glass in their hearts, and this was very terrible, for their hearts became cold like a lump of ice. A few of the pieces were so large that they could be used as window-panes; it would have been a sad thing to look at our friends through them. Other pieces were made into spectacles; this was dreadful for those who wore them, for they could see nothing either rightly or justly. At all this the wicked demon laughed till his sides shook – it tickled him so to see the mischief he had done. There were still a number of these little fragments of glass floating about in the air, and now you shall hear what happened with one of them.

Second Story.

A LITTLE BOY AND A LITTLE GIRL

In a large town, full of houses and people, there is not room for everybody to have even a little garden, therefore they are obliged to be satisfied with a few flowers in flower-pots. In one of these large towns lived two poor children who had a garden something larger and better than a few flower-pots. They were not brother and sister, but they loved each other almost as much as if they had been. Their parents lived opposite to each other in two garrets, where the roofs of neighbouring houses projected out towards each other, and the water-pipe ran between them. In each house was a little window, so that any one could step across the gutter from one window to the other. The parents of these children had each a large wooden box in which they cultivated kitchen herbs for their own use, and a little rose-bush in each box, which grew splendidly. Now after a while, the parents decided to place these two boxes across the waterpipe, so that they reached from one window to the other and looked like two banks of flowers. Sweet-peas drooped over the boxes, and the rose-bushes shot forth long branches, which were trained round the windows and clustered together almost like a triumphal arch of leaves and flowers. The boxes were very high, and the children knew they must not climb upon them, without permission, but they were often, however, allowed to step out together and sit upon their little stools under the rosebushes, or play quietly. In winter all this pleasure came to an end, for the windows were sometimes quite frozen over. But then they would warm copper pennies on the stove, and hold the warm pennies against the frozen pane; there would be very soon a little round hole through which they could peep, and the soft bright eyes of the little boy and girl would beam through the hole at each window as they looked at each other. Their names were Kay and Gerda. In summer they could be together with one jump from the window, but in winter they had to go up and down the long stair-case and out through the snow before they could meet.

"See there are the white bees swarming," said Kay's old grandmother one day when it was snowing.

"Have they a queen bee?" asked the little boy, for he knew that the real bees always had a queen.

"To be sure they have," said the grandmother. "She is flying there where the swarm is thickest. She is the largest of them all, and never remains on the earth, but flies up to the dark clouds. Often at midnight she flies through the streets of the town, and looks in at the windows, then the ice freezes on the panes into wonderful shapes, that look like flowers and castles."

"Yes, I have seen them," said both the children, and they knew it must be true.

"Can the Snow Queen come in here?" asked the little girl.

"Only let her come," said the boy, "I'll set her on the stove and then she'll melt."

Then the grandmother smoothed his hair and told him some more tales. One evening, when little Kay was at home, half undressed, he climbed on a chair by the window and peeped out through the little hole. A few flakes of snow were falling, and one of them, rather larger than the rest, alighted on the edge of one of the flower boxes. This snow-flake grew larger and larger till at last it became the figure of a woman, dressed in garments of white gauze, which looked like millions of starry snow-flakes linked together. She was fair and beautiful, but made of ice – shining and glittering ice. Still she was alive and her eyes sparkled like bright stars, but there was neither peace nor rest in their glance. She nodded towards the window, and waved

221

her hand. The little boy was frightened and sprang from the chair; at the same moment it seemed as if a large bird flew by the window. On the following day there was a clear frost, and very soon came the spring. The sun shone; the young green leaves burst forth; the swallows built their nests; windows were opened, and the children sat once more in the garden on the roof, high above all the other rooms. How beautifully the roses blossomed this summer. The little girl had learnt a hymn in which roses were spoken of, and then she thought of their own roses, and she sang the hymn to the little boy, and he sang too: –

"Roses bloom and cease to be,
But we shall the Christ-child see."

Then the little ones held each other by the hand, and kissed the roses, and looked at the bright sunshine, and spoke to it as if the Christ-child were there. Those were splendid summer days. How beautiful and fresh it was out among the rose-bushes, which seemed as if they would never leave off blooming. One day Kay and Gerda sat looking at a book full of pictures of animals and birds, and then just as the clock in the church tower struck twelve, Kay said, "Oh, something has struck my heart!" and soon after, "There is something in my eye."
The little girl put her arm round his neck, and looked into his eye, but she could see nothing.
"I think it is gone," he said. But it was not gone; it was one of those bits of the looking-glass – that magic mirror, of which we have spoken – the ugly glass which made everything great and good appear small and ugly, while all that was wicked and bad became more visible, and every little fault could be plainly seen. Poor little Kay had also received a small grain in his heart, which very quickly turned to a lump of ice. He felt no more pain, but the glass was there still. "Why do you cry?" said he at last; "it makes you look ugly. There is nothing the matter with me now. Oh, see!" he cried suddenly, "that rose is worm-eaten, and this one is quite crooked. After all, they are ugly roses, just like the box in which they stand." And then he kicked the boxes with his foot, and pulled off the two roses.
"Kay, what are you doing?" cried the little girl; and then, when he saw how frightened she was, he tore off another rose, and jumped through his own window away from sweet little Gerda.
When she afterwards brought out the picture book, he said, "It was only fit for babies in long clothes," and when grandmother told any stories, he would interrupt her with "but;" or, when he could manage it, he would get

behind her chair, put on a pair of spectacles, and imitate her very cleverly, to make people laugh. By-and-by he began to mimic the speech and gait of persons in the street. All that was peculiar or disagreeable in a person he would imitate directly, and people said, "That boy will be very clever; he has a remarkable genius." But it was the piece of glass in his eye, and the coldness in his heart, that made him act like this. He would even tease little Gerda, who loved him with all her heart. His games, too, were quite different; they were not so childish. One winter's day, when it snowed, he brought out a burning-glass, then he held out the tail of his blue coat, and let the snowflakes fall upon it. "Look in this glass, Gerda," said he; and she saw how every flake of snow was magnified, and looked like a beautiful flower or a glittering star. "Is it not clever?" said Kay, "and much more interesting than looking at real flowers. There is not a single fault in it, and the snow flakes are quite perfect till they begin to melt."

Soon after, Kay made his appearance in large thick gloves, and with his sledge at his back. He called upstairs to Gerda, "I've got leave to go into the great square, where the other boys play and ride." And away he went.

In the great square, the boldest among the boys would often tie their sledges to country people's carts, and go with them a good way. This was capital. But while they were all amusing themselves, and Kay with them, a great sledge came by; it was painted white, and in it sat some one wrapped in a rough white fur, and wearing a white cap. The sledge drove twice round the square, and Kay fastened his own little sledge to it, so that when it went away, he followed with it. It went faster and faster right through the next street, and then the person who drove turned round and nodded pleasantly to Kay, just as if they were acquainted with each other, but whenever Kay wished to loosen his little sledge the driver nodded again, so Kay sat still, and they drove out through the town gate. Then the snow began to fall so heavily that the little boy could not see a hand's breadth before him, but still they drove on; then he suddenly loosened the cord so that the large sledge might go on without him, but it was of no use, his little carriage held fast, and away they went like the wind. Then he called out loudly, but nobody heard him, while the snow beat upon him, and the sledge flew onwards. Every now and then it gave a jump as if they were going over hedges and ditches. The boy was frightened, and tried to say a prayer, but he could re-member nothing but the multiplication table.

The snow-flakes became larger and larger till they appeared like great white chickens. All at once they sprang on one side, the great sledge stopped, and the person who had driven it rose up. The fur and the cap, which were made entirely of snow, fell off, and he saw a lady, tall and white: it was the Snow Queen.

223

"We have driven well," said she, "but why do you tremble? here, creep into my warm fur." Then she seated him beside her in the sledge, and as she wrapped the fur round him he felt as if he were sinking into a snow drift. "Are you still cold," she asked, as she kissed him on the forehead. The kiss was colder than ice; it went quite through to his heart, which was already almost a lump of ice; he felt as if he were going to die, but only for a moment; he soon seemed quite well again, and did not notice the cold all around him. "My sledge! don't forget my sledge," was his first thought, and then he looked and saw that it was bound fast to one of the white chickens, which flew behind him with the sledge at its back. The Snow Queen kissed little Kay again, and by this time he had forgotten little Gerda, his grandmother, and all at home.

"Now you must have no more kisses," she said, "or I should kiss you to death."

Kay looked at her, and saw that she was so beautiful, he could not imagine a more intelligent and lovely face; she did not now seem to be made of ice, as when he had seen her through his window, and she had nodded to him. In his eyes she was perfect, and he did not feel at all afraid. He told her he could do mental arithmetic, as far as fractions, and that he knew the number of square miles and the number of inhabitants in the country. And she always smiled so that he thought he did not know enough yet, and looked round the vast expanse as she flew higher and higher with him upon a black cloud, while the storm blew and howled as if it were singing old songs. They flew over woods and lakes, over sea and land; below them roared the wild wind; the wolves howled and the snow crackled; over them flew the black screaming crows, and above all shone the moon, clear and bright, – and so Kay passed through the long winter's night, and by day he slept at the feet of the Snow Queen.

Third Story

The Flower Garden of the Woman who could Conjure

But how fared little Gerda during Kay's absence? What had become of him, no one knew, nor could any one give the slightest information, excepting the boys, who said that he had tied his sledge to another very large one, which had driven through the street, and out at the town gate. Nobody knew where it went; many tears were shed for him, and little Gerda wept bitterly for a long time. She said she knew he must be dead, that he was drowned in the river which flowed close by the school. Oh, indeed, those long winter days were very dreary. But at last spring came, with warm sunshine. "Kay is dead and gone," said little Gerda.

"I don't believe it," said the sunshine.

"He is dead and gone," she said to the sparrows.

"We don't believe it," they replied; and at last little Gerda began to doubt it herself. "I will put on my new red shoes," she said one morning, "those that Kay has never seen, and then I will go down to the river, and ask for him." It was quite early when she kissed her old grandmother, who was still asleep; then she put on her red shoes, and went quite alone out of the town gates towards the river. "Is it true that you have taken my little playmate away from me?" she said to the river. "I will give you my red shoes if you will give him back to me." And it seemed as if the waves nodded to her in a strange manner. Then she took off her red shoes, which she liked better than anything else, and threw them both into the river, but they fell near the the bank, and the little waves carried them back to land, just as if the river would not take from her what she loved best, because they could not give her back little Kay, But she thought the shoes had not been thrown out far enough. Then she crept into a boat that lay among the reeds, and threw the shoes again from the farther end of the boat into the water, but it was not fastened, and her movement sent it gliding away from the land. When she saw this, she hastened to reach the end of the boat, but before she could do so, it was more than a yard from the bank, and drifting away faster than ever. Then little Gerda was very much frightened, and began to cry, but no one heard her except the sparrows, and they could not carry her to land, but they flew along by the shore, and sang, as if to comfort her, "Here we are! Here we are!" The boat floated with the stream; little Gerda sat quite still with only her stockings on her feet; the red shoes floated after her, but she could not reach them because the boat kept so much in advance. The banks on each side of the river were very pretty. There were beautiful flowers, old trees, sloping fields, in which cows and sheep were grazing, but not a man to be seen. Perhaps the river will carry me to little Kay, thought Gerda, and the she became more cheerful, and raised her head, and looked at the beautiful green banks; and so the boat sailed on for hours. At length she came to a large cherry orchard, in which stood a small house with strange red and blue windows. It had also a thatched roof, and outside, were two wooden soldiers, that presented arms to her as she sailed past. Gerda called out to them, for she though they were alive, but of course they did not answer; and as the boat drifted nearer to the shore, she saw what they really were. Then Gerda called still louder, and there came a very old woman out of the house, leaning on a crutch. She wore a large hat to shade

225

her from the sun, and on it were painted all sorts of pretty flowers. "You poor little child," said the old woman, "how did you manage to come all this distance into the wide world on such a rapid rolling stream?" And then the old woman walked into the water, seized the boat with her crutch, drew it to land, and lifted little Gerda out. And Gerda was glad to feel herself again on dry ground, although she was rather afraid of the strange old woman. "Come and tell me who you are," said she, "and how you came here."

Then Gerda told her everything, while the old woman shook her head, and said, "Hem-hem;" and when she had finished, Gerda asked if she had not seen little Kay, and the old woman told her he had not passed by that way, but he very likely would come. So she told Gerda not to be sorrowful, but to taste the cherries and look at the flowers; they were better than any picture-book, for each of them could tell a story. Then she took Gerda by the hand, and let her into the little house, and the old woman closed the door. The windows were very high, and as the panes were red, blue, and yellow, the daylight shone through them in all sorts of singular colours. On the table stood some beautiful cherries, and Gerda had permission to eat as many as she would. While she was eating them, the old woman combed out her long flaxen ringlets with a golden comb, and the glossy curls hung down on each side of the little round pleasant face, which looked fresh and blooming as a rose. "I have long been wishing for a dear little maiden like you," said the old woman, "and now you must stay with me, and see how happily we shall live together." And while she went on combing little Gerda's hair, she thought less and less about her adopted brother Kay, for the old woman could conjure, although she was not a wicked witch; she conjured only a little for her own amusement, and now, because she wanted to keep Gerda. Therefore she went into the garden, and stretched out her crutch towards all the rose-trees, beautiful though they were, and they immediately sunk into the dark earth, so that no one could tell where they had once stood. The old woman was afraid that if little Gerda saw roses, she would think of those at home, and then remember little Kay, and run away. Then she took Gerda into the flower-garden. How fragrant and beautiful it was! Every flower that could be thought of for every season of the year was here in full bloom; no picture-book could have more beautiful colours. Gerda jumped for joy, and played till the sun went down behind the tall cherry-trees; then she slept in an elegant bed with red silk pillows, embroidered with coloured violets; and then she dreamed as pleasantly as a queen on her wedding-day. The next day, and for many days after, Gerda played with the flowers in the warm sunshine. She knew every flower, and yet, although there were so many of them, it seemed as if one were missing, but which it was she could

226

227

not tell. One day, however, as she sat looking at the old woman's hat with the painted flowers on it, she saw that the prettiest of them all was a rose. The old woman had forgotten to take it from her hat when she made all the roses sink into the earth. But it is difficult to keep the thoughts together in everything; one little mistake upsets all our arrangements.

"What, are there no roses here?" cried Gerda; and she ran out into the garden, and examined all the beds, and searched and searched. There was not one to be found. Then she sat down and wept, and her tears fell just on the place where one of the rose-trees had sunk down. The warm tears moistened the earth, and the rose-tree sprouted up at once, as blooming as when it had sunk; and Gerda embraced it, and kissed the roses, and thought of the beautiful roses at home, and, with them, of little Kay.

"Oh, how I have been detained!" said the little maiden. "I wanted to seek for little Kay. Do you know where he is?" she asked the roses; "do you think he is dead?"

And the roses answered, "No, he is not dead. We have been in the ground where all the dead lie; but Kay is not there."

"Thank you," said little Gerda, and then she went to the other flowers, and looked into their little cups, and asked, "Do you know where little Kay is?" But each flower, as it stood in the sunshine, dreamed only of its own little fairy tale or history. Not one knew anything of Kay. Gerda heard many stories from the flowers, as she asked them one after another about him.

And what said the tiger-lily? "Hark, do you hear the drum? – 'tum, tum', – there are only two notes always, 'tum, tum.' Listen to the women's song of mourning! Hear the cry of the priest! In her long red robe stands the Hindoo widow by the funeral pile. The flames rise around her as she places herself on the dead body of her husband; but the Hindoo woman is thinking of the living one in that circle; of him, her son, who lighted those flames. Those shining eyes trouble her heart more painfully than the flames which will soon consume her body to ashes. Can the fire of the heart be extinguished in the flames of a funeral pile?"

"I don't understand that at all," said little Gerda.

"That is my story," said the tiger-lily.

What says the convolvulus? "Near yonder narrow road stands an old knight's castle; thick ivy creeps over the old ruined walls, leaf over leaf, even to the balcony, in which stands a beautiful maiden. She bends over the balustrades, and looks up the road. No rose on its stem is fresher than she; no apple-blossom, wafted by the wind, floats more lightly than she moves. Her rich silk rustles as she bends over and exclaims, 'Will he not come?'"

"Is it Kay you mean?" asked Gerda.

"I am only speaking of a story of my dream," replied the flower.

228

What said the little snowdrop? "Between two trees a rope is hanging; there is a piece of board upon it; it is a swing. Two pretty little girls, in dresses white as snow, and with long green ribbons fluttering from their hats, are sitting upon it, swinging. Their brother, who is taller than they are, stands in the swing; he has one arm round the rope, to steady himself; in one hand he holds a little bowl, and in the other a clay pipe; he is blowing bubbles. As the swing goes on, the bubbles fly upward, reflecting the most beautiful varying colours. The last still hangs from the bowl of the pipe, and sways in the wind. On goes the swing; and then a little black dog comes running up. He is almost as light as the bubble, and he raises himself on his hind legs, and wants to be taken into the swing; but it does not stop, and the dog falls; then he barks, and gets angry. The children stoop towards him, and the bubble bursts. A swinging plank, a light sparkling foam picture, – that is my story."

"It may be all very pretty what you are telling me," said little Gerda; "but you speak so mournfully, and you do not mention little Kay at all."

What do the hyacinths say? "There were three beautiful sisters, fair and delicate. The dress of one was red, of the second blue, and of the third pure white. Hand in hand, they danced in the bright moonlight, by the calm lake; but they were human beings, not fairy elves. The sweet fragrance attracted them, and they disappeared in the wood; here the fragrance became stronger. Three coffins, in which lay the three beautiful maidens, glided from the thickest part of the forest across the lake. The fire-flies flew lightly over them, like little floating torches. Do the dancing maidens sleep, or are they dead? The scent of the flowers says that they are corpses. The evening bell tolls their knell."

"You make me quite sorrowful," said little Gerda; "your perfume is so strong, you make me think of the dead maidens. Ah! is little Kay really dead then? The roses have been in the earth, and they say no."

"Cling, clang," tolled the hyacinth bells. "We are not tolling for little Kay; we do not know him. We sing our song, the only one we know."

Then Gerda went to the buttercups that were glittering amongst the bright green leaves.

"You are little bright suns," said Gerda; "tell me if you know where I can find my playfellow."

And the buttercups sparkled gaily, and looked again at Gerda. What song could the buttercups sing? It was not about Kay.

"The bright warm sun shone on a little court, on the first warm day of spring. His bright beams rested on the white walls of the neighbouring house; and close by bloomed the first yellow flower of the season, glittering like gold in the sun's warm ray. An old woman sat in her arm-chair at the

230

house-door, and her granddaughter, a poor and pretty servant-maid came to see her for a short visit. When she kissed her grandmother, there was gold everywhere: the gold of the heart in that holy kiss; it was a golden morning; there was gold in the beaming sunlight, gold in the leaves of the lowly flower, and on the lips of the maiden. There, that is my story," said the buttercup.

"My poor old grandmother!" sighed Gerda; "she is longing to see me, and grieving for me as she did for little Kay; but I shall soon go home now, and take little Kay with me. It is no use asking the flowers; they know only their own songs, and can give me no information."

And then she tucked up her little dress, that she might run faster; but the narcissus caught her by the leg as she was jumping over it; so she stopped and looked at the tall yellow flower, and said, "Perhaps you may know something."

Then she stooped down quite close to the flower, and listened; and what did it say?

"I can see myself, I can see myself," said the narcissus. "Oh, how sweet is my perfume! Up in a little room with a bow-window, stands a little dancing girl, half undressed; she stands sometimes on one leg, and sometimes on both, and looks as if she would tread the whole world under her feet. She is nothing but a delusion. She is pouring water out of a tea-pot on a piece of stuff which she holds in her hand; it is her boddice. 'Cleanliness is a good thing,' she says. Her white dress hangs on a peg; it has also been washed in the tea-pot, and dried on the roof. She puts it on, and ties a saffron-coloured handkerchief round her neck, which makes the dress look whiter. See how she stretches out her legs, as if she were showing off on a stem. I can see myself, I can see myself."

"What do I care for all that," said Gerda, "you need not tell me such stuff." And then she ran to the other end of the garden. The door was fastened, but she pressed against the rusty latch, and it gave way. The door sprang open, and little Gerda ran out with bare feet into the wide world. She looked back three times, but no one seemed to be following her. At last she could run no longer, so she sat down to rest on a great stone, and when she looked round she saw that the summer was over, and autumn very far advanced. She had known nothing of this in the beautiful garden, where the sun shone and the flowers grew all the year round.

"Oh, how I have wasted my time!" said little Gerda; "it is autumn. I must not rest any longer," and she rose up to go on. But her little feet were wounded and sore, and everything around her looked so cold and bleak. The long willow-leaves were quite yellow. The dew-drops fell like water, leaf after leaf dropped from the trees, the sloe-thorn alone still bore fruit, but the sloes were sour, and set the teeth on edge. Oh, how dark and weary the whole world appeared!

Fourth Story

The Prince and Princess

Gerda was obliged to rest again, and just opposite the place where she sat, she saw a great crow come hopping across the snow towards her. He stood looking at her for some time, and then he wagged his head and said, "Caw, caw; good-day, good-day." He pronounced the words as plainly as he could, because he meant to be kind to the little girl; and then he asked her where she was going all alone in the wide world.

The word *alone* Gerda understood very well, and knew how much it expressed. So then she told the crow the whole story of her life and adventures, and asked him if he had seen little Kay.

The crow nodded his head very gravely, and said, "Perhaps I have – it may be."

"No! Do you think you have?" cried little Gerda, and she kissed the crow, and hugged him almost to death with joy.

"Gently, gently," said the crow. "I believe I know. I think it may be little Kay; but he has certainly forgotten you by this time for the princess."

"Does he live with a princess?" asked Gerda.

"Yes, listen," replied the crow; "but it is so difficult to speak your language. If you understand the crows' language then I can explain it better. Do you?"

"No, I have never learnt it," said Gerda, but my grandmother understands it, and used to speak it to me. I wish I had learnt it."

"It does not matter," answered the crow; "I will explain as well as I can, although it will be very badly done;" and he told her what he had heard. "In this kingdom where we now are," said he, "there lives a princess, who is so wonderfully clever that she has read all the newspapers in the world, and forgotten them too, although she is so clever. A short time ago, as she was sitting on her throne, which people say is not such an agreeable seat as is often supposed, she began to sing a song which commences in the words:

'Why should I not be married?'

'Why not indeed?' said she, and so she determined to marry if she could find a husband who knew what to say when he was spoken to, and not one who could only look grand, for that was so tiresome. Then she assembled all her court ladies together at the beat of the drum, and when they heard of her intentions they were very much pleased. 'We are so glad to hear it,' said they, 'we were talking about it ourselves the other day.' You may believe that every word I tell you is true," said the crow, "for I have a tame sweetheart who goes freely about the palace, and she told me all this."

Of course his sweetheart was a crow, for "birds of a feather flock together," and one crow always chooses another crow.

"Newspapers were published immediately, with a border of hearts, and the initials of the princess among them. They gave notice that every young man who was handsome was free to visit the castle and speak with the princess; and those who could reply loud enough to be heard when spoken to, were to make themselves quite at home at the palace; but the one who spoke best would be chosen as a husband for the princess. Yes, yes, you may believe me, it is all as true as I sit here," said the crow. "The people came in crowds. There was a great deal of crushing and running about, but no one succeeded either on the first or the second day. They could all speak very well while they were outside in the streets, but when they entered the palace gates, and saw the guards in silver uniforms, and the footmen in their golden livery on the staircase, and the great halls lighted up, they became quite confused. And when they stood before the throne on which the princess sat, they could do nothing but repeat the last words she had said; and she had no particular wish to hear her own words over again. It was just as if they had all taken something to make them sleepy while they were in the palace, for they did not recover themselves nor speak till they got back again into the street. There was quite a long line of them reaching from the town-gate to the palace. I went myself to see them," said the crow. "They were hungry and

234

thirsty, for at the palace they did not get even a glass of water. Some of the wisest had taken a few slices of bread and butter with them, but they did not share it with their neighbours; they thought if they went in to the princess looking hungry, there would be a better chance for themselves."

"But Kay! tell me about little Kay!" said Gerda, "was he amongst the crowd?"

"Stop a bit, we are just coming to him. It was on the third day, there came marching cheerfully along to the palace a little personage, without horses or carriage, his eyes sparkling like yours; he had beautiful long hair, but his clothes were very poor."

"That was Kay!" said Gerda joyfully. "Oh, then I have found him;" and she clapped her hands.

"He had a little knapsack on his back," added the crow.

"No, it must have been his sledge," said Gerda; "for he went away with it."

"It may have been so," said the crow; "I did not look at it very closely. But I know from my tame sweetheart that he passed through the palace gates, saw the guards in their silver uniform, and the servants in their liveries of gold on the stairs, but he was not in the least embarrassed. 'It must be very

tiresome to stand on the stairs,' he said. 'I prefer to go in.' The rooms were blazing with light. Councillors and ambassadors walked about with bare feet, carrying golden vessels; it was enough to make any one feel serious. His boots creaked loudly as he walked, and yet he was not at all uneasy."

"It must be Kay," said Gerda, "I know he had new boots on, I have heard them creak in grandmother's room."

"They really did creak," said the crow, "yet he went boldly up to the princess herself, who was sitting on a pearl as large as a spinning wheel, and all the ladies of the court were present with their maids, and all the cavaliers with their servants; and each of the maids had another maid to wait upon her, and the cavaliers' servants had their own servants as well as a page each. They all stood in circles round the princess, and the nearer they stood to the door, the prouder they looked. The servants' pages, who always wore slippers, could hardly be looked at, they held themselves up so proudly by the door."

"It must be quite awful," said little Gerda, "but did Kay win the princess?"

"If I had not been a crow," said he, "I would have married her myself, although I am engaged. He spoke just as well as I do, when I speak the

crows' language, so I heard from my tame sweetheart. He was quite free and agreeable, and said he had not come to woo the princess, but to hear her wisdom; and he was as pleased with her as she was with him."

"Oh certainly that was Kay," said Gerda, "he was so clever; he could work mental arithmetic and fractions. Oh, will you take me to the place?"

"It is very easy to ask that," replied the crow, "but how are we to manage it? However, I will speak about it to my tame sweetheart, and ask her advice; for I must tell you it will be very difficult to gain permission for a little girl like you to enter the palace."

"Oh, yes; but I shall gain permission easily," said Gerda, "for when Kay hears that I am here, he will come out and fetch me in immediately."

"Wait for me here by the palings," said the crow, wagging his head as he flew away.

It was late in the evening before the crow returned. "Caw, caw," he said, "she sends you greeting, and here is a little roll which she took from the kitchen for you; there is plenty of bread there, and she thinks you must be hungry. It is not possible for you to enter the palace by the front entrance. The guards in silver uniform and the servants in gold livery would not allow it. But do not cry, we will manage to get you in; my sweetheart knows a little back-staircase that leads to the sleeping apartments, and she knows where to find the key."

Then they went into the garden through the great avenue, where the leaves were falling one after another, and they could see the lights in the palace being put out in the same manner. And the crow led little Gerda to a back door, which stood ajar. Oh! how little Gerda's heart beat with anxiety and longing; it was just as if she were going to do something wrong, and yet she only wanted to know where little Kay was. "It must be he," she thought, "with those clear eyes, and that long hair." She could fancy she saw him smiling at her, as he used to at home, when they sat among the roses. He would certainly be glad to see her, and to hear what a long distance she had come for his sake, and to know how sorry they had all been at home because he did not come back. Oh what joy and yet fear she felt! They were now on the stairs, and in a small closet at the top a lamp was burning. In the middle of the floor stood the tame crow, turning her head from side to side, and gazing at Gerda, who curtsied as her grandmother had taught her to do.

"My betrothed has spoken so very highly of you, my little lady," said the tame crow, "your life-history, *Vita,* as it may be called, is very touching. If you will take the lamp, I will walk before you. We will go straight along this way, then we shall meet no one."

"It seems to me as if somebody were behind us," said Gerda, as something rushed by her like a shadow on the wall, and then horses with flying manes and thin legs, hunters, ladies and gentlemen on horseback, glided by her, like shadows on the wall.

"They are only dreams," said the crow, "they are coming to fetch the thoughts of the great people out hunting."

"All the better, for we shall be able to look at them in their beds more safely. I hope that when you rise to honour and favour, you will show a grateful heart."

"You may be quite sure of that," said the crow from the forest.

They now came into the first hall, the walls of which were hung with rose-coloured satin, embroidered with artificial flowers. Here the dreams again flitted by them, but so quickly that Gerda could not distinguish the royal persons. Each hall appeared more splendid than the last, it was enough to bewilder any one. At length they reached a bedroom. The ceiling was like a great palm-tree, with glass leaves of the most costly crystal, and over the centre of the floor two beds, each resembling a lily, hung from a stem of gold. One, in which the princess lay, was white, the other was red; and in this Gerda had to seek for little Kay. She pushed one of the red leaves aside, and saw a little brown neck. Oh, that must be Kay! She called his name out quite loud, and held the lamp over him. The dreams rushed back into the room on horseback. He woke, and turned his head round, it was not little Kay! The prince was only like him in the neck, still he was young and pretty. Then the princess peeped out of her white-lily bed, and asked what was the matter. Then little Gerda wept and told her story, and all that the crows had done to help her.

"You poor child," said the prince and princess; then they praised the crows, and said they were not angry with them for what they had done, but that it must not happen again, and this time they should be rewarded.

"Would you like to have your freedom?" asked the princess, "or would you prefer to be raised to the position of court crows, with all that is left in the kitchen for yourselves?"

Then both the crows bowed, and begged to have a fixed appointment, for they thought of their old age, and said it would be so comfortable to feel that they had provision for their old days, as they called it. And then the prince got out of his bed, and gave it up to Gerda, – he could not do more; and she lay down. She folded her little hands, and thought, "How good everybody is to me, men and animals too;" then she closed her eyes and fell into a sweet sleep. All the dreams came flying back again to her, and they looked like angels, and one of them drew a little sledge, on which sat Kay, and nodded to her. But all this was only a dream, and vanished as soon as she awoke.

The following day she was dressed from head to foot in silk and velvet, and they invited her to stay at the palace for a few days, and enjoy herself; but she begged for a pair of boots, and a little carriage, and a horse to draw it, so that she might go out into the wide world to seek for Kay. And she obtained, not only boots, but also a muff, and she was neatly dressed; and when she was ready to go, there, at the door, she found a coach, made of pure gold, with the coat-of-arms of the prince and princess shining upon it like a star, and the coachman, footman, and outriders all wearing golden crowns on their heads. The prince and princess themselves helped her into the coach, and wished her success. The forest crow, who was now married, accompanied her for the first three miles; he sat by Gerda's side, as he could not bear riding backwards. The tame crow stood in the doorway flapping her wings. She could not go with them, because she had been suffering from headache ever since the new appointment, no doubt from eating too much. The coach was well stored with sweet cakes, and under the seat were fruit and gingerbread nuts. "Farewell, farewell," cried the prince and princess, and little Gerda wept, and the crow wept; and then, after a few miles, the crow also said "Farewell," and this was the saddest parting. However, he flew to a tree, and stood flapping his black wings as long as he could see the coach, which glittered in the bright sunshine.

Fifth story

The Little Robber-Girl

The coach drove on through a thick forest, where it lighted up the way like a torch, and dazzled the eyes of some robbers, who could not bear to let it pass them unmolested.

"It is gold! it is gold!" cried they, rushing forward, and seizing the horses. Then they struck the little jockeys, the coachman, and the footman dead, and pulled little Gerda out of the carriage.

"She is fat and pretty, and she has been fed with the kernels of nuts," said the old robber-woman, who had a long beard and eyebrows that hung over her eyes. "She is as good as a little lamb; how nice she will taste!" and as she said this, she drew forth a shining knife, that glittered horribly. "Oh!" screamed the old woman at the same moment; for her own daughter, who held her back, had bitten her in the ear. She was a wild and naughty girl, and the mother called her an ugly thing, and had not time to kill Gerda.

"She shall play with me," said the little robber-girl; "she shall give me her

muff and her pretty dress, and sleep with me in my bed." And then she bit her mother again, and made her spring in the air, and jump about; and all the robbers laughed, and said, "See how she is dancing with her young cub."

"I will have a ride in the coach," said the little robber-girl; and she would have her own way; for she was so self-willed and obstinate.

She and Gerda seated themselves in the coach, and drove away, over stumps and stones, into the depths of the forest. The little robber-girl was about the same size as Gerda, but stronger; she had broader shoulders and a darker skin; her eyes were quite black, and she had a mournful look. She clasped little Gerda round the waist, and said, –

"They shall not kill you as long as you don't make me vexed with you. I suppose you are a princess."

"No," said Gerda; and then she told her all her history, and how fond she was of little Kay.

The robber-girl looked earnestly at her, nodded her head slightly, and said, "They shan't kill you, even if I do get angry with you; for I will do it myself." And then she wiped Gerda's eyes, and stuck her own hands in the beautiful muff which was so soft and warm.

The coach stopped in the courtyard of a robber's castle, the walls of which were cracked from top to bottom. Ravens and crows flew in and out of the and crevices, while great bulldogs, either of which looked as if it could swallow a man, were jumping about; but they were not allowed to bark. In the large old smoky hall a bright fire was burning on the stone floor. There was no chimney; so the smoke went up to the ceiling, and found a way out for itself. Soup was boiling in a large cauldron, and hares and rabbits were roasting on the spit.

"You shall sleep with me and all my little animals to-night," said the robber-girl, after they had had something to eat and drink. So she took Gerda to a corner of the hall, where some straw and carpets were laid down. Above them, on laths and perches, were more than a hundred pigeons, who all seemed to be asleep, although they moved slightly when the two little girls came near them. "These all belong to me," said the robber-girl; and she seized the nearest to her, held it by the feet, and shook it till it flapped its wings. "Kiss it," cried she, flapping it in Gerda's face. "There sit the wood-pigeons," continued she, pointing to a number of laths and a cage which had been fixed into the walls, near one of the openings. "Both rascals would fly away directly, if they were not closely locked up. And here is my old sweetheart 'Ba;' and she dragged out a reindeer by the horn; he wore a bright copper ring round his neck, and was tied up. "We are obliged to hold him tight too, or else he would run away from us also. I tickle his neck every evening with my sharp knife, which frightens him very much." And

then the robber-girl drew a long knife from a chink in the wall, and let it slide gently over the reindeer's neck. The poor animal began to kick, and the little robber-girl laughed, and pulled down Gerda into bed with her.

"Will you have that knife with you while you are asleep?" asked Gerda, looking at it in great fright.

"I always sleep with the knife by me," said the robber-girl. "No one knows what may happen. But now tell me again all about little Kay, and why you went out into the world."

Then Gerda repeated her story over again, while the woodpigeons in the cage over her cooed, and the other pigeons slept. The little robber-girl put one arm across Gerda's neck, and held the knife in the other, and was soon fast asleep and snoring. But Gerda could not close her eyes at all; she knew not whether she was to live or die. The robbers sat round the fire, singing and drinking, and the old woman stumbled about. It was a terrible sight for a little girl to witness.

Then the wood-pigeons said, "Coo, coo; we have seen little Kay. A white fowl carried his sledge, and he sat in the carriage of the Snow Queen, which drove through the wood while we were lying in our nest. She blew upon us, and all the young ones died excepting us two. Coo, coo."

"What are you saying up there?" cried Gerda. "Where was the Snow Queen going? Do you know anything about it?"

"She was most likely travelling to Lapland, where there is always snow and ice. Ask the reindeer that is fastened up there with a rope."

"Yes, there is always snow and ice," said the reindeer; "and it is a glorious place; you can leap and run about freely on the sparkling icy plains. The Snow Queen has her summer tent there, but her strong castle is at the North Pole, on an island called Spitzbergen."

"Oh, Kay, little Kay!" sighed Gerda.

"Lie still," said the robber-girl, "or I shall run my knife into your body."

In the morning Gerda told her all that the wood-pigeons had said; and the little robber-girl looked quite serious, and nodded her head, and said, "That is all talk, that is all talk. Do you know where Lapland is?" she asked the reindeer.

"Who should know better than I do?" said the animal, while his eyes sparkled. "I was born and brought up there, and used to run about the snow-covered plains."

"Now listen," said the robber-girl; "all our men are gone away, – only mother is here, and here she will stay; but at noon she always drinks out of a great bottle, and afterwards sleeps for a little while; and then I'll do something for you." Then she jumped out of bed, clasped her mother round the neck, and pulled her by the beard, crying, "My own little nanny goat,

good morning." Then her mother filliped her nose till it was quite red; yet she did it all for love.

When the mother had drunk out of the bottle, and was gone to sleep, the little robber-maiden went to the reindeer, and said, "I should like very much to tickle your neck a few times more with my knife, for it makes you look so funny; but never mind, – I will untie your cord, and set you free, so that you may run away to Lapland; but you must make good use of your legs, and carry this little maiden to the castle of the Snow Queen, where her play-fellow is. You have heard what she told me, for she spoke loud enough, and you were listening,"

Then the reindeer jumped for joy; and the little robber-girl lifted Gerda on his back, and had the forethought to tie her on, and even to give her her own little cushion to sit on.

"Here are your fur boots for you," said she; "for it will be very cold; but I must keep the muff; it is so pretty. However, you shall not be frozen for the want of it; here are my mother's large warm mittens; they will reach up to your elbows. Let me put them on. There, now your hands look just like my mother's."

But Gerda wept for joy.

"I don't like to see you fret," said the little robber-girl; "you ought to look quite happy now; and here are two loaves and a ham, so that you need not starve." These were fastened on the reindeer, and then the little robber-maiden opened the door, coaxed in all the great dogs, and then cut the string with which the reindeer was fastened, with her sharp knife, and said, "Now run, but mind you take good care of the little girl." And then Gerda stretched out her hand, with the great mitten on it, towards the little robber-girl, and said, "Farewell," and away flew the reindeer, over stumps and stones, through the great forest, over marshes and plains, as quickly as he could. The wolves howled, and the ravens screamed; while up in the sky quivered red lights like flames of fire. "There are my old northern lights," said the reindeer; "see how they flash." And he ran on day and night still faster and faster, but the loaves and the ham were all eaten by the time they reached Lapland.

Sixth Story

The Lapland Woman and the Finland Woman

They stopped at a little hut; it was very mean looking; the roof sloped nearly down to the ground, and the door was so low that the family had to creep on their hands and knees, when they went in and out. There was no one at home, but an old Lapland woman, who was cooking fish by the light of a train-oil lamp. The reindeer told her all about Gerda's story, after having first told his own, which seemed to him the most important, but Gerda was so pinched with the cold that she could not speak. "Oh, you poor things," said the Lapland woman, "you have a long way to go yet. You must travel more than a hundred miles farther, to Finland. The Snow Queen lives there now, and she burns Bengal lights every evening. I will write a few words on a dried stock-fish, for I have no paper, and you can take it from me to the Finland woman who lives there; she can give you better information than I can." So when Gerda was warmed, and had taken something to eat and drink, the woman wrote a few words on the dried fish, and told Gerda to take great care of it. Then she tied her again on the reindeer, and he set off at full speed. Flash, flash, went the beautiful blue northern lights in the air the whole night long. And at length they reached Finland, and knocked

246

at the chimney of the Finland woman's hut, for it had no door above the ground. They crept in, but it was so terribly hot inside that the woman wore scarcely any clothes; she was small and very dirty looking. She loosened little Gerda's dress, and took off the fur boots and the mittens, or Gerda would have been unable to bear the heat; and then she placed a piece of ice on the reindeer's head, and read what was written on the dried fish. After she had read it three times, she knew it by heart, so she popped the fish into the soup saucepan, as she knew it was good to eat, and she never wasted anything. The reindeer told his own story first, and then little Gerda's, and the Finlander twinkled with her clever eyes, but she said nothing. "You are so clever," said the reindeer; "I know you can tie all the winds of the world with a piece of twine. If a sailor unties one knot, he has a fair wind; when he unties the second, it blows hard; but if the third and fourth are loosened, then comes a storm, which will root up whole forests. Can you not give this little maiden something which will make her as strong as twelve men, to overcome the Snow Queen?"

"The power of twelve men!" said the Finland woman; "that would be of very little use." But she went to a shelf and took down and unrolled a large skin, on which were inscribed wonderful characters, and she read till the persiration ran down from her forehead. But the reindeer begged so hard for little Gerda, and Gerda looked at the Finland woman with such beseeching tearful eyes, that her own eyes began to twinkle again; so she drew the reindeer into a corner, and whispered to him while she laid a fresh piece of ice on his head, "Little Kay is really with the Snow Queen, but he finds everything there so much to his taste and his liking, that he believes it is the finest place in the world; but this is because he has a piece of broken glass in his heart, and a little piece of glass in his eye. These must be taken out, or he will never be a human being again, and the Snow Queen will retain her power over him."

"But can you not give little Gerda something to help her to conquer this power?"

"I can give her no greater power than she has already," said the woman; "don't you see how strong that is? How men and animals are obliged to serve her, and how well she has got through the world, barefooted as she is. She cannot receive any power from me greater than she now has, which consists in her own purity and innocence of heart. If she cannot herself obtain access to the Snow Queen, and remove the glass fragments from little Kay, we can do nothing to help her. Two miles from here the Snow Queen's garden begins; you can carry the little girl so far, and set her down by the large bush which stands in the snow, covered with red berries. Do not stay gossiping, but come back here as quickly as you can." Then the Finland

woman lifted little Gerda upon the reindeer, and he ran away with her as quickly as he could.

"Oh, I have forgotten my boots and my mittens," cried little Gerda, as soon as she felt the cutting cold, but the reindeer dared not stop, so he ran on till he reached the bush with the red berries; here he set Gerda down, and he kissed her, and the great bright tears trickled over the animal's cheeks; then he left her and ran back as fast as he could.

There stood poor Gerda, without shoes, without gloves, in the midst of cold, dreary, ice-bound Finland. She ran forwards as quickly as she could, when a whole regiment of snow-flakes came round her; they did not however, fall from the sky, which was quite clear and glittering with the northern lights. The snow-flakes ran along the ground, and the nearer they came to her, the larger they appeared. Gerda remembered how large and beautiful they looked through the burning-glass. But these were really larger, and much more terrible, for they were alive, and were the guards of the Snow Queen, and had the strangest shapes. Some were like great porcupines, others like twisted serpents with their heads stretching out, and some few were like little fat bears with their hair bristled; but all were dazzlingly white, and all were living snow-flakes. Then little Gerda repeated the Lord's Prayer, and the cold was so great that she could see her own breath come out of her mouth like steam as she uttered the words. The steam appeared to increase, as she continued her prayer, till it took the shape of little angels, who grew larger the moment they touched the earth. They all wore helmets on their heads, and carried spears and shields. Their number continued to increase more and more; and by the time Gerda had finished her prayers, a whole legion stood round her. They thrust their spears into the terrible snowflakes, so that they shivered into a hundred pieces, and little Gerda could go forward with courage and safety. The angels stroked her hands and feet, so that she felt the cold less, and she hastened on to the Snow Queen's castle.

But now we must see what Kay is doing. In truth he thought not of little Gerda, and never supposed she could be standing in the front of the palace.

Seventh story

Of the Palace of the Snow Queen, and what Happened there at Last

The walls of the palace were formed of drifted snow, and the windows and doors of the cutting winds. There were more than a hundred rooms in it, all as if they had been formed with snow blown together. The largest of them extended for several miles; they were all lighted up by the vivid light of the aurora, and they were so large and empty, so icy cold and glittering! There were no amusements here, not even a little bear's ball, when the storm might have been the music, and the bears could have danced on their hind legs, and shown their good manners. There were no pleasant games of snap-dragon, or touch, or even a gossip over the teatable, for the young-lady foxes. Empty, vast, and cold were the halls of the Snow Queen. The flickering flame of the northern lights could be plainly seen, whether they rose high or low in the heavens, from every part of the castle. In the midst of this empty, endless hall of snow was a frozen lake, broken on its surface into a thousand forms; each piece resembled another, from being in itself perfect as a work of art, and in the centre of this lake sat the Snow Queen, when she was at home. She called the lake "The Mirror of Reason," and said that it was the best, and indeed the only one in the world.

Little Kay was quite blue with cold, indeed almost black, but he did not feel it; for the Snow Queen had kissed away the icy shiverings, and his heart was already a lump of ice. He dragged some sharp, flat pieces of ice to and fro, and placed them together in all kinds of positions, as if he wished to make something out of them; just as we try to form various figures with little tablets of wood which we call "a Chinese puzzle." Kay's figures were very artistic; it was the icy game of reason at which he played, and in his eyes the figures were very remarkable, and of the highest importance; this opinion was owing to the piece of glass still sticking in his eye. He composed many complete figures, forming different words, but there was one word he never could manage to form, although he wished it very much. It was the word "Eternity." The Snow Queen had said to him, "When you can find out this, you shall be your own master, and I will give you the whole world and a new pair of skates." But he could not accomplish it.

"Now I must hasten away to warmer countries," said the Snow Queen. "I will go and look into the black craters of the tops of the burning mountains, Etna and Vesuvius, as they are called, – I shall make them look white, which will be good for them, and for the lemons and the grapes." And away flew the Snow Queen, leaving little Kay quite alone in the great hall which was so many miles in length; so he sat and looked at his pieces of ice, and was thinking so deeply, and sat so still, that any one might have supposed he was frozen.

Just at this moment it happened that little Gerda came through the great door of the castle. Cutting winds were raging around her, but she offered up a prayer and the winds sank down as if they were going to sleep; and she went on till she came to the large empty hall, and caught sight of Kay; she knew him directly; she flew to him and threw her arms round his neck, and held him fast, while she exclaimed, "Kay, dear little Kay, I have found you at last."

But he sat quite still, stiff and cold.

Then little Gerda wept hot tears, which fell on his breast, and penetrated into his heart, and thawed the lump of ice, and washed away the little piece of glass which had stuck there. Then he looked at her, and she sang –

"Roses bloom and cease to be,
But we shall the Christ-child see."

Then Kay burst into tears, and he wept so that the splinter of glass swam out of his eye. Then he recognised Gerda, and said, joyfully, "Gerda, dear little Gerda, where have you been all this time, and where have I been?" And he looked all around him, and said, "How cold it is, and how large and

empty it all looks," and he clung to Gerda, and she laughed and wept for joy. It was so pleasing to see them that the pieces of ice even danced about; and when they were tired and went to lie down, they formed themselves into the letters of the world which the Snow Queen had said he must find out before he could be his own master, and have the whole world and a pair of new skates. Then Gerda kissed his cheeks, and they became blooming; and she kissed his eyes, and they shone like her own; she kissed his hands and his feet, and then he became quite healthy and cheerful. The Snow Queen might come home now when she pleased, for there stood his certainty of freedom, in the word she wanted, written in shining letters of ice.

Then they took each other by the hand, and went forth from the great palace of ice. They spoke of the grandmother, and of the roses on the roof, and as they went on the winds were at rest, and the sun burst forth. When they arrived at the bush with red berries, there stood the reindeer waiting for them, and he had brought another young reindeer with him, whose udders were full, and the children drank her warm milk and kissed her on the mouth. Then they carried Kay and Gerda first to the Finland woman, where they warmed themselves thoroughly in the hot room, and she gave them directions about their journey home. Next they went to the Lapland woman, who had made some new clothes for them, and put their sleighs in order. Both the reindeer ran by their side, and followed them as far as the boundaries of the country, where the first green leaves were budding. And here they took leave of the two reindeer and the Lapland woman, and all said – Farewell. Then the birds began to twitter, and the forest too was full of green young leaves; and out of it came a beautiful horse, which Gerda remembered, for it was one which had drawn the golden coach. A young girl was riding upon it, with a shining red cap on her head, and pistols in her belt. It was the little robber-maiden, who had got tired of staying at home; she was going first to the north, and if that did not suit her, she meant to try some other part of the world. She knew Gerda directly, and Gerda remembered her: it was a joyful meeting.

"You are a fine fellow to go gadding about in this way," said she to little Kay, "I should like to know whether you deserve that any one should go to the end of the world to find you."

But Gerda patted her cheeks, and asked after the prince and princess.

"They have gone to foreign countries," said the robber-girl.

"And the crow?" asked Gerda.

"Oh, the crow is dead," she replied; "his tame sweetheart is now a widow, and wears a bit of black worsted round her leg. She mourns very pitifully, but it is all stuff. But now tell me how you managed to get him back."

Then Gerda and Kay told her all about it.

"Snip, snap, snare! it's all right at last," said the robber-girl.

Then she took both their hands, and promised that if ever she should pass through the town, she would call and pay them a visit. And then she rode away into the wide world. But Gerda and Kay went hand-in-hand towards home; and as they advanced, spring appeared more lovely with its green verdure and its beautiful flowers. Very soon they recognised the large town where they lived, and the tall steeples of the churches, in which the sweet bells were ringing a merry peal as they entered it, and found their way to their grandmother's door. They went upstairs into the little room, where all looked just as it used to do. The old clock was going "tick, tick," and the hands pointed to the time of day, but as they passed through the door into the room, they perceived that they were both grown up, and become a man and woman. The roses out on the roof were in full bloom, and peeped in at the window; and there stood the little chairs, on which they had sat when children; and Kay and Gerda seated themselves each on their own chair, and held each other by the hand, while the cold empty grandeur of the Snow Queen's palace vanished from their memories like a painful dream. The grandmother sat in God's bright sunshine, and she read aloud from the Bible, "Except ye become as little children, ye shall in no wise enter into the kingdom of God." And Kay and Gerda looked into each other's eyes, and all at once understood the words of the old song,

"Roses bloom and cease to be,
But we shall the Christ-child see."

And they both sat there, grown up, yet children at heart; and it was summer, – warm, beautiful summer.

The Angel

"Whenever a good child dies, an angel of God comes down from heaven, takes the dead child in his arms, spreads out his great white wings, and flies with him over all the places which the child has loved during his life. Then he gathers a large handful of flowers, which he carries up to the Almighty, that they may bloom more brightly in heaven than they do on earth. And the Almighty presses the flowers to His heart, but He kisses the flower that pleases Him best, and it receives a voice, and is able to join the song of the chorus of bliss."

These words were spoken by an angel of God, as he carried a dead child up to heaven, and the child listened as if in a dream. Then they passed over well-known spots, where the little one had often played, and through beautiful gardens full of lovely flowers.

"Which of these shall we take with us to heaven to be transplanted there?" asked the angel.

Close by grew a slender, beautiful, rose-bush, but some wicked hand had broken the stem, and the half-opened rose-buds hung faded and withered on the trailing branches.

"Poor rose-bush!" said the child, "let us take it with us to heaven, that it may bloom above in God's garden."

The angel took up the rose-bush; then he kissed the child, and the little one half-opened his eyes. The angel gathered also some beautiful flowers, as well as a few humble buttercups and heart's-ease.

"Now we have flowers enough," said the child; but the angel only nodded, he did not fly upward to heaven.

It was night, and quite still in the great town. Here they remained, and the angel hovered over a small, narrow street, in which lay a large heap of straw, ashes, and sweepings from the houses of people who had moved. There lay fragments of plates, pieces of plaster, rags, old hats, and other rubbish not pleasant to see. Amidst all this confusion, the angel pointed to the pieces of a broken flower-pot, and to a lump of earth which had fallen out of it. The earth had been kept from falling to pieces by the roots of a withered field-flower, which had been thrown amongst the rubbish.

"We will take this with us," said the angel, "I will tell you why as we
fly along."

And as they flew the angel related the history.

"Down in that narrow lane, in a low cellar, lived a poor sick boy; he had
been afflicted from his childhood, and even in his best days he could just
manage to walk up and down the room on crutches once or twice, but no
more. During some days in summer, the sunbeams would lie on the floor of
the cellar for about half an hour. In this spot the poor sick boy would sit
warming himself in the sunshine, and watching the red blood through his
delicate fingers as he held them before his face. Then he would say he had
been out, yet he knew nothing of the green forest in its spring verdure, till a
neighbour's son brought him a green bough from a beech-tree. This he
would place over his head, and fancy that he was in the beech-wood while
the sun shone, and the birds carolled gaily. One spring day the neighbour's
boy brought him some field-flowers, and among them was one to which the
root still adhered. This he carefully planted in a flower-pot, and placed in
a widow-seat near his bed. And the flower had been planted by a fortunate

hand, for it grew, put forth fresh shoots, and blossomed every year. It became a splendid flower-garden to the sick boy, and his little treasure upon earth. He watered it, and cherished it, and took care that it should have the benefit of every sunbeam that found its way into the cellar, from the earliest morning ray to the evening sunset. The flower entwined itself even in his dreams – for him it bloomed, for him spread its perfume. And it gladdened his eyes, and to the flower he turned, even in death, when the Lord called him. He has been one year with God. During that time the flower has stood in the window, withered and forgotten, till at length cast out among the sweepings into the street, on the day of the lodgers' removal. And this poor flower, withered and faded as it is, we have added to our nosegay, because it gave more real joy than the most beautiful flower in the garden of a queen.

"But how do you know all this?" asked the child whom the angel was carrying to heaven.

"I know it," said the angel, "because I myself was the poor sick boy who walked upon crutches, and I know my own flower well."

Then the child opened his eyes and looked into the glorious happy face of the angel, and at the same moment they found themselves in that heavenly home where all is happiness and joy. And God pressed the dead child to His heart, and wings were given him so that he could fly with the angel, hand in hand. Then the Almighty pressed all the flowers to His heart; but He kissed the withered field-flower, and it received a voice. Then it joined in the song of the angels, who surrounded the throne, some near, and others in a distant circle, but all equally happy. They all joined in the chorus of praise, both great and small, – the good, happy child, and the poor field-flower, that once lay withered and cast away on a heap of rubbish in a narrow, dark street.

A Great Sorrow

This story has two parts. The first part might be left out; but is explains a few particulars, we will relate it.

I was staying once for a few days at a gentleman's house in the country while the master was absent. In the meantime, a lady called from the next town to see him, as she wished, she said, to dispose of shares in her tan-yard. She had her papers with her, and I advised her to put them in an envelope, and address them to the "General Commissary of War, Knight, etc." She listened attentively, and then seized the pen; hesitated, and then begged me to repeat the address more slowly. I did so, and she began to write, but when she got half through the words, she stopped and sighed deeply, and said, "I am only a woman." She had a pug dog with her, and while she wrote Puggie seated himself on the ground and growled. She had brought him for his health and amusement, and it was not quite polite to offer a visitor only the bare floor to sit upon. Puggie had a snub nose, and he was very fat. "He doesn't bite," said the lady; "he has no teeth; he is like one of the family, very faithful, but sometimes grumpy. That is the fault of my grandchildren, they tease him so; when they play at having a wedding, they want to make him the bride's-maid, and he does not like it, poor old fellow." Then she finished the writing, gave up her papers, and went away, taking Puggie on her arm. And this ends the first part of the story.

PUGGIE DIED. And that begins the second part.

I arrived at the town about a week afterwards, and put up at an inn. The windows of the inn looked into a courtyard, which was divided into two parts by a wooden partition; in one half hung a quantity of skins and hides, both raw and tanned. It was evidently a tan-yard, containing all the materials required for tanning, and it belonged to the widow lady, Puggie's mistress. Puggie had died the morning I arrived there, and was to be buried in the yard. The grandchildren of the widow, that is to say, the tanner's widow, for Puggie had never been married, filled up the grave. It was a beautiful grave, and must have been quite pleasant to lie in. They bordered the grave with pieces of flower-pots, and strewed it over with sand. In the centre they stuck half a beer bottle, with the neck uppermost, which certainly was not allegorical. Then the children danced round the

259

grave, and the eldest of the boys among them, a practical youngster of seven years, proposed that there should be an exhibition of Puggie's burial place, for all who lived in the lane. The price of admission was to be a trouser button, which every boy was sure to have, as well as one to spare for a little girl. This proposal was agreed to with great exclamations of pleasure. All the children from the street, and even from the narrow lane at the back, came flocking to the place and each gave a button, and many were seen during the afternoon going about with their trousers held up by only one brace, but then they had seen Puggie's grave, and that was a sight worth much more. But in front of the tan-yard, close to the entrance, stood a very pretty little girl clothed in rags, with curly hair, and eyes so blue and clear it was a pleasure to look into them. The child spoke not a word, nor did she cry; but each time the little door opened, she gave a long, lingering look into the yard. She had not a button, she knew that too well, and therefore she remained standing sorrowfully outside, till all the other children had seen the grave, and were gone away; then she sat down, covered her eyes with her little brown hands, and burst into tears. She was the only one who had not seen Puggie's grave. It was as great a grief to her as any grown person could experience. I saw this from above; and how many a grief of our own and others can smake us smile, if looked at from above?

This is the story: and whoever does not understand it may go and purchase a share in the widow's tan-yard.

The Flax

The flax was in full bloom. It had the loveliest blue flowers, as soft as the wings on a moth, and even more delicate. The sun shone down on the flax and the rain-cloud watered it; and this was just as good for the flax as it is for little children to be washed and then have a kiss from mother. They are much nicer after that, aren't they? And so, too, was the flax. "They say that I hold myself remarkably well," said the flax, "and that I'm growing lovely and long – they'll get a fine piece of linen from me. My word, how lucky I am! I must be the very luckiest of the lot. I'm so well off – I shall go far. How the sun does cheer me up, and how I do enjoy the freshness of the rain! Yes, I'm wonderfully lucky. I'm the very luckiest of them all."

"Well, well," said the hedge-stakes. "You don't know the world, but we do. We've got knots in us." And they creaked out miserably:

"Snip, snap, snorum,

basselorum,

the song is over."

"No, it isn't!" said the flax. "The sun will shine tomorrow; the rain is so refreshing. I can hear myself growing; I can feel that I'm flowering. Yes, I'm the luckiest of them all."

But one day people came and seized the flax by its top and plucked it up, root and all – it did hurt. Then it was laid in water as though it was to be drowned, and after that it was put over the fire as if it was to be cooked. It was terrible.

"One can't always be on velvet," said the flax; "things have to be tried out before you can know them."

All the same things were as bad as could be. The flax was bruised and broken, scutched and hackled, and goodness knows what else besides. It was put on the spinning-wheel, where it whirred and purred – it was impossible to collect your thoughts.

"I've been amazingly lucky," thought the flax in the midst of its pain. "One must be thankful for the good one has enjoyed. Thankful, ay, thankful" – and it was still saying this when it came on the loom – and then it was turned into a splendid great piece of linen. The whole flax, every single bit that was growing on it, was turned into the one piece. "Oh, but this is

quite wonderful – I could never have believed it. Yes, yes, fortune is certainly on my side. A lot they knew about it, those hedge-stakes, with their "Snip, snap snorum,
basselorum!"
The song is by no means over. Why, it's only just beginning. How wonderful! True, I've had a hard time, but I've got something to show for it: I'm the luckiest of them all. I'm so strong and so smooth, so white and so tall. It's something very different to just being a plant, even if one has a flower. As a plant, there's no one to look after you, and you only get watered when it rains. Now I have someone to wait on me. The maid turns me round when it rains. Now I have someone to wait on me. The maid turns me round every morning, and the water-jug gives me a shower-bath every evening. Why, even the parson's wife has made a speech about me, saying I was the best bit of linen in the parish. I cannot be better off than I am."
And now the linen was brought into the house and came under the scissors. What clipping and cutting and pricking with needles – my word, there was! It was no fun at all. But the linen was made into twelve pairs of – things which are seldom mentioned, but must be worn by everyone; yes, a whole dozen of them.
"There now, look at that! At last I've come to something. So that's what I was marked out for. Oh, dear, it's too wonderful. Now I'll be some use in the world, and that's as it should be, that's enjoyment of the right kind. We've been turned into twelve garments; and yet we are all one and the same, we are a dozen. What marvellous luck."
Years passed – and at last they could hold together no longer.
"Some day there's got to be an end," said each of them. "I should like to have held out a little longer, but it's no good asking the impossible." And then they were torn into rags and remnants; they imagined they were clean done with, for they were combed and crushed and boiled and goodness knows what – and there they were, turned into the most delicate white paper!
"Why, this is a surprise – a most delightful surprise," said the paper. "Now I'm finer than ever, now I shall be written on. There's no end to what they can write. It really is astonishing luck." And the most delightful stories were written on it, stories that people read, good stories of the right kind that made men wiser and better. The words given to the paper were a blessing to many.
"This is more than ever I dreamed of, when I was a little blue flower in the field. How could I imagine that I should one day bring joy and knowledge to mankind. I still can't understand it. And yet, look! it has actually come to pass. Heaven knows I myself have done nothing but what in a small way

I was forced to do in order to exist. And yet I am borne on like this from one joy and honour to another. Every time I think "the song is over," it simply passes on to something much higher and better. I'm sure to be sent travelling now, sent right round the world, so that all mankind may read me. That's the most likely thing to happen. Previously, I had blue flowers; now, in place of those flowers, I have the most wonderful thoughts. I am the luckiest of all!"

But the paper didn't go travelling. It was sent to the printer; and all that was written on it was set up in type for a book; in fact, for hundreds and hundreds of books, because in that way many more people could get benefit and joy from it than if the single paper it was written on had gone chasing round the world and got worn out by the time it was half-way. "Yes," thought the paper with writing on it. "This, after all, is much the nicest way – one that never occurred to me. I shall stay at home and be respected like an old grandfather. It was on me that they wrote, into me that the words flowed straight from the pen. I stay here, while the books go chasing around. Now there is a real chance to get something done. Oh, how pleased, how lucky I am!"

The paper was then tied up in a bundle and laid on a shelf. "Repose is sweet, when your work is done," said the paper. "It's very right that we

should take ourselves in hand, and think seriously about what is in us. It's only now that I really understand what is in me. 'Know thyself' – that is the real step forward. What will happen next, I wonder? A going forward of some kind – always going forward!"

One day all the paper was put in the fireplace to be burnt, for it mustn't be sold to the grocer for wrapping up butter and sifted sugar, and all children in the house stood round to see it flare up; they wanted to see the ashes give out all those red sparks that seemed to turn away and go out, one after another, so quickly; those are the children running out of school, and the last spark of all is the schoolmaster. Sometimes you think he must have gone already; but there he comes, a bit after all the others.

All the paper lay in a bundle, on the fire. Ooh! how it went flaring up! "Ooh!" it sighed, and the next moment it was a sheet of flame. It blazed higher into the air than ever the flax had been able to lift its little blue flowers, and shone brighter than ever the white linen had been able to shine; all the letters written on it turned quite red in an instant, and all the words and thoughts went up in a blaze.

"Now I'm going right up into the sun," was the cry from the flame; and it was as though a thousand voices all said it at once, and the flame shot up through the chimney right out at the top. And, more delicate even than the flame, quite invisible to the human eye, there hovered tiny little beings, just as many as there had been blossoms on the flax. They were even lighter than the flame from which they had come, and when it went out and all that was left of the paper was the dusky ash, they danced away over it once more and wherever they touched it you could see their footprints; they were the red sparks: "The children ran out of school, and last of all came the schoolmaster". It was great fun to look at, and the children of the house stood singing over the dead ashes –

"Snip, snap, snorum,

basselorum,

the song is over."

But the little invisible beings each of them said: "No, no, the song is never over. That's what is so lovely about the whole thing. I know this, and that's why I'm the luckiest of them all."

But the children couldn't follow that, nor even hear it, and they were not meant to either; for children mustn't know everything.

The Travelling Companion

Poor John was very sad; for his father was so ill, he had no hope of his recovery. John sat alone with the sick man in the little room, and the lamp had nearly burnt out; for it was late in the night.

"You have been a good son, John," said the sick father," and God will help you on in the world." He looked at him, as he spoke, with mild, earnest eyes, drew a deep sigh, and died; yet it appeared as if he still slept.

John wept bitterly. He had no one in the wide world now; neither father, mother, brother, nor sister. Poor John! he knelt down by the bed, kissed his dead father's hand, and wept many, many bitter tears. But at last his eyes closed, and he fell asleep with his head resting against the hard bed-post. Then he dreamed a strange dream; he thought he saw the sun shining upon him, and his father alive and well, and even heard him laughing as he used to do when he was very happy. A beautiful girl, with a golden crown on her head, and long, shining hair, gave him her hand; and his father said, "See what a bride you have won. She is the loveliest maiden on the whole earth." Then he awoke, and all the beautiful things vanished before his eyes, his father lay dead on the bed, and he was all alone. Poor John!

During the following week the dead man was buried. The son walked behind the coffin which contained his father, whom he so dearly loved, and would never again behold. He heard the earth fall on the coffin-lid, and watched it till only a corner remained in sight, and at last that also disappeared. He felt as if his heart would break with its weight of sorrow, till those who stood round the grave sang a psalm, and the sweet, holy tones brought tears into his eyes, which relieved him. The sun shone brightly down on the green trees, as if it would say, "You must not be so sorrowful, John. Do you see the beautiful blue sky above you? You father is up there, and he prays to the loving Father of all, that you may do well in the future."

"I will always be good," said John, "and then I shall go to be with my father in heaven. What joy it will be when we see each other again! How much I shall have to relate to him, and how many things he will be able to explain to me of the delights of heaven, and teach me as he once did on earth. Oh, what joy it will be!"

He pictured it all so plainly to himself, that he smiled even while the tears ran down his cheeks.

The little birds in the chestnut-trees twittered, "Tweet, tweet;" they were so happy, although they had seen the funeral; but they seemed as if they knew that the dead man was now in heaven, and that he had wings much larger and more beautiful than their own; that he was happy now, because he had been good here on earth, and they were glad of it. John saw them fly away out of the green trees into the wide world, and he longed to fly with them; but first he cut out a large wooden cross, to place on his father's grave; and when he brought it there in the evening, he found the grave decked out with gravel and flowers. Strangers had done this; they who had known the good old father who was now dead, and who had loved him very much.

Early the next morning, John packed up his little bundle of clothes, and placed all his money, which consisted of fifty dollars and a few shillings, in his girdle; with this he determined to try his fortune in the world. But first he went into the churchyard; and, by his father's grave, he offered up a prayer, and said, "Farewell."

As he passed through the fields, all the flowers looked fresh and beautiful in the warm sunshine, and nodded in the wind, as if they wished to say, "Welcome to the green wood, where all is fresh and bright."

Then John turned to have one more look at the old church, in which he had been christened in his infancy, and where his father had taken him every Sunday to hear the service and join in singing the psalms. As he looked at the old tower, he espied the ringer standing at one of the narrow openings, with his little pointed red cap on his head, and shading his eyes from the sun with his bent arm. John nodded farewell to him, and the little ringer waved his red cap, laid his hand on his heart, and kissed his hand to him a great many times, to show that he felt kindly towards him, and wished him a prosperous journey.

John continued his journey, and thought of all the wonderful things he should see in the large, beautiful world, till he found himself further away from home than ever he had been before. He did not even know the names of the places he passed through, and could scarcely understand the language of the people he met, for he was far away, in a strange land. The first night he slept on a haystack, out in the fields, for there was no other bed for him; but it seemed to him so nice and comfortable that even a king need not wish for a better. The field, the brook, the haystack, with the blue sky above, formed a beautiful sleeping-room. The green grass, with the little red and white flowers, was the carpet; the elder-bushes and the hedges of wild roses looked like garlands on the walls; and for a bath he could have the clear,

fresh water of the brook; while the rushes bowed their heads to him, to wish him good morning and good evening. The moon, like a large lamp, hung high up in the blue ceiling, and he had no fear of its setting fire to his curtains. John slept here quite safely all night; and when he awoke, the sun was up, and all the little birds were singing round him, "Good morning, good morning. Are you not up yet?"

Outside the church door stood an old beggar, leaning on his crutch. John gave him his silver shillings, and then he continued his journey, feeling lighter and happier than ever. Towards evening, the weather became very stormy, and he hastened on as quickly as he could, to get shelter; but it was quite dark by the time he reached a little lonely church which stood on a hill. "I will go in here," he said, "and sit down in a corner; for I am quite tired, and want rest."

So he went in, and seated himself; then he folded his hands, and offered up his evening prayer, and was soon fast asleep and dreaming, while the thunder rolled and the lightning flashed without. When he awoke, it was still night;

but the storm had ceased, and the moon shone in upon him through the windows. Then he saw an open coffin standing in the centre of the church, which contained a dead man, waiting for burial. John was not at all timid; he had a good conscience, and he knew also that the dead can never injure any one. It is living wicked men who do harm to others. Two such wicked persons stood now by the dead man, who had been brought to the church to be buried. Their evil intentions were to throw the poor dead body outside the church door, and not leave him to rest in his coffin.

"Why do you do this?" asked John, when he saw what they were going to do; "it is very wicked. Leave him to rest in peace, in Christ's name."

"Nonsense," replied the two dreadful men. "He has cheated us; he owed us money which he could not pay, and now he is dead we shall not get a penny; so we mean to have our revenge, and let him lie like a dog outside the church door."

"I have only fifty dollars," said John, "it is all I possess in the world, but I will give it to you if you will promise me faithfully to leave the dead man in peace. I shall be able to get on without the money; I have strong and healthy limbs, and God will always help me."

"Why, of course," said the horrid men, "if you will pay his debt we will both promise not to touch him. You may depend upon that;" and then they took the money he offered them, laughed at him for his good nature, and went their way. Then he laid the dead body back in the coffin, folded the hands, and took leave of it; and went away contentedly through the great forest. All around him he could see the prettiest little elves dancing in the moonlight, which shone through the trees. They were not disturbed by his appearance, for they knew he was good and harmless among men. They are wicked people only who can never obtain a glimpse of fairies. Some of them were not taller than the breadth of a finger, and they wore golden combs in their long, yellow hair. They were rocking themselves together on the large dew-drops with which the leaves and the high grass were sprinkled. Sometimes the dew-drops would roll away, and then they fell down between the stems of the long grass, and caused a great deal of laughing and noise among the other little people. It was quite charming to watch them at play. Then they sang songs, and John remembered that he had learnt those pretty songs when he was a little boy. Large speckled spiders, with silver crowns on their heads, were employed to spin suspension bridges and palaces from one hedge to another, and when the tiny drops fell upon them, they glittered in the moonlight like shining glass. This continued till sunrise. Then the little elves crept into the flower-buds, and the wind seized the bridges and palaces, and fluttered them in the air like cobwebs.

270

As John left the wood, a strong man's voice called after him, "Hallo, comrade, where are you travelling?"

"Into the wide world," he replied; "I am only a poor lad, I have neither father nor mother, but God will help me."

"I am going into the wide world also," replied the stranger; "shall we keep each other company?"

"With all my heart," said he, and so they went on together. Soon they began to like each other very much, for they were both good; but John found out that the stranger was much more clever than himself. He had travelled all over the world, and could describe almost everything. The sun was high in the heavens when they seated themselves under a large tree to eat their breakfast, and at the same moment an old woman came towards them. She was very old and almost bent double. She leaned upon a stick and carried on her back a bundle of firewood, which she had collected in the forest; her apron was tied round it, and John saw three great stems of fern and some willow twings peeping out. Just as she came close up to them, her foot slipped and she fell to the ground screaming loudly: poor old woman, she had broken her leg! John proposed directly that they should carry the old woman home to her cottage; but the stranger opened his knapsack and took out a box, in which he said he had a salve that would quickly make her leg well and strong again, so that she would be able to walk home herself, as if her leg had never been broken. And all that he would ask in return was the three fern stems which she carried in her apron.

"That is rather too high a price," said the old woman, nodding her head quite strangely. She did not seem at all inclined to part with the fern stems. However, it was not very agreeable to lie there with a broken leg, so she gave them to him; and such was the power of the ointment, that no sooner had he rubbed her leg with it than the old mother rose up and walked even better than she had done before. But then this wonderful ointment could not be bought at a chemist's.

"What can you want with those three fern rods?" asked John of his fellow-traveller.

"Oh, they will make capital brooms," said he; "and I like them because I have strange whims sometimes." Then they walked on together for a long distance.

"How dark the sky is becoming," said John; "and look at those thick, heavy clouds."

"Those are not clouds," replied his fellow-traveller; "they are mountains – large lofty mountains – on the tops of which we should be above the clouds, in the pure, free air. Believe me, it is delightful to ascend so high, to-morrow we shall be there." But the mountains were not so near as they appeared;

271

they had to travel a whole day before they reached them, and pass through black forests and piles of rock as large as a town. The journey had been so fatiguing that John and his fellow-traveller stopped to rest at a roadside inn, so that they might gain strength for their journey on the morrow. In the large public room of the inn a great many persons were assembled to see a comedy performed by dolls. The showman had just erected his little theatre, and the people were sitting round the room to witness the performance. Right in front, in the very best place, sat a stout butcher, with a great bull-dog by his side who seemed very much inclined to bite. He sat staring with all his eyes, and so indeed did every one else in the room. And then the play began. It was a pretty piece, with a king and queen in it, who sat on a beautiful throne, and had gold crowns on their heads. The trains to their dresses were very long, according to the fashion; while the prettiest of wooden dolls, with glass eyes and large moustaches, stood at the doors, and opened and shut them, that the fresh air might come into the room. It was a very pleasant play, not at all mournful; but just as the queen stood up and walked across the stage, the great bulldog, who should have been held back by his master, made a spring forward, and caught the queen in his teeth by the slender waist, so that it snapped in two. This was a very dreadful disaster. The poor man, who was exhibiting the dolls, was much annoyed, and quite sad about his queen; she was the prettiest doll he had, and the bull-dog had broken her head and shoulders off. But after all the people were gone away, the stranger, who came with John, said that he could soon set her to rights. And then he brought out his box and rubbed the doll with some of the salve with which he had cured the old woman when she broke her leg. As soon as this was done the doll's back became quite right again; her head and shoulders were fixed on, and she could even move her limbs herself: there was now no occasion to pull the wires, for the doll acted just like a living creature, excepting that she could not speak. The man to whom the show belonged was quite delighted at having a doll who could dance of herself without being pulled by the wires; none of the other dolls could do this.

During the night, when all the people at the inn were gone to bed, some one was heard to sigh so deeply and painfully, and the sighing continued for so long a time, that every one got up to see what could be the matter. The showman went at once to his little theatre and found that it proceeded from the dolls, who all lay on the floor sighing piteously, and staring with their glass eyes; they all wanted to be rubbed with the ointment, so that, like the queen, they might be able to move of themselves. The queen threw herself on her knees, took off her beautiful crown, and, holding it in her hand, cried, "Take this from me, but do rub my husband and his courtiers."

The poor man who owned the theatre could scarcely refrain from weeping; he was so sorry that he could not help them. Then he immediately spoke to John's comrade, and promised him all the money he might receive at the next evening's performance, if he would only rub the ointment on four or five of his dolls. But the fellow-traveller said he did not require anything in return, excepting the sword which the showman wore by his side. As soon as he received the sword he anointed six of the dolls with the ointment, and they were able immediately to dance so gracefully that all the living girls in the room could not help joining in the dance. The coachman danced with the cook, and the waiters with the chambermaids, and all the strangers joined; even the tongs and the fire-shovel made an attempt, but they fell down after the first jump. So after all it was a very merry night. The next morning John and his companion left the inn to continue their journey through the great pine-forests and over the high mountains. They arrived at last at such a great height that towns and villages lay beneath them, and the church steeples looked like little specks between the green trees. They could see for miles round, far away to places they had never visited, and John saw more of the beautiful world than he had ever known before. The sun shone brightly in the blue firmament above, and through the clear mountain air came the sound of the huntsman's horn, and the soft, sweet notes brought tears into his eyes, and he could not help exclaiming. "How good and loving God is to give us all this beauty and loveliness in the world to make us happy!"

His fellow-traveller stood by with folded hands, gazing on the dark woods and the towns bathed in the warm sunshine. At this moment there sounded over their heads sweet music. They looked up, and discovered a large white swan hovering in the air, and singing as never bird sang before. But the song soon became weaker and weaker, the bird's head drooped, and he sunk slowly down, and lay dead at their feet.

"It is a beautiful bird," sais the traveller, "and these large white wings are worth a great deal of money. I will take them with me. You see now that a sword will be very useful."

So he cut off the wings of the dead swan with one blow, and carried them away with him.

They now continued their journey over the mountains for many miles, till they at length reached a large city, containing hundreds of towers, that shone in the sunshine like silver. In the midst of the city stood a splendid marble palace, roofed with pure red gold, in which dwelt the king. John and his companion would not go into the town immediately; so they stopped at an inn outside the town, to change their clothes; for they wished to appear respectable as they walked through the streets. The landlord told them

that the king was a very good man, who never injured any one; but as to his daughter, "Heaven defend us!"

She was indeed a wicked princess. She possessed beauty enough – nobody could be more elegant or prettier than she was; but what of that? for she was a wicked witch; and in consequence of her conduct many noble young princes had lost their lives. Any one was at liberty to make her an offer; were he a prince or a beggar, it mattered not to her. She would ask him to guess three things which she had just thought of, and if he succeeded, he was to marry her, and be king over all the land when her father died; but if he could not guess these three things, then she ordered him to be hanged or to have his head cut off. The old king, her father, was very much grieved at her conduct, but he could not prevent her from being so wicked, because he once said he would have nothing more to do with her lovers; she might do as she pleased. Each prince who came and tried the three guesses, so that he might marry the princess, had been unable to find them out, and had been hanged or beheaded. They had all been warned in time, and might have left her alone, if they would. The old king became at last so distressed at all these dreadful circumstances, that for a whole day every year he and his soldiers knelt and prayed that the princess might become good; but she continued as wicked as ever. The old women who drank brandy would colour it quite black before they drank it, to show how they mourned; and what more could they do?

"What a horrible princess!" said John; "she ought to be well flogged. If I were the old king, I would have her punished in some way."

Just then they heard the people outside shouting, "Hurrah!" and, looking out, they saw the princess passing by; and she was really so beautiful that everybody forgot her wickedness, and shouted, "Hurrah!" Twelve lovely maidens in white silk dresses, holding golden tulips in their hands, rode by her side on coal-black horses. The princess herself had a snow-white steed, decked with diamonds and rubies. Her dress was of cloth of gold, and the whip she held in her hand looked like a sunbeam. The golden crown on her head glittered like the stars of heaven, and her mantle was formed of thousands of butterflies' wings sewn together. Yet she herself was more beautiful than all.

When John saw her, his face became as red as a drop of blood, and he could scarcely utter a word. The princess looked exactly like the beautiful lady with the golden crown, of whom he had dreamed on the night his father died. She appeared to him so lovely that he could not help loving her.

"It could not be true," he thought, "that she was really a wicked witch, who ordered people to be hanged or beheaded, if they could not guess her thoughts. Every one has permission to go and ask her hand, even the poorest begger. I shall pay a visit to the palace," he said; "I must go, for I cannot help myself."

Then they all advised him not to attempt it; for he would be sure to share the same fate as the rest. His fellow-traveller also tried to persuade him against it; but John seemed quite sure of success. He brushed his shoes and his coat, washed his face and his hands, combed his soft flaxen hair, and then went out alone into the town, and walked to the palace.

"Come in," said the king, as John knocked at the door. John opened it, and the old king, in a dressing-gown and embroidered slippers came towards him. He had the crown on his head, carried his sceptre in one hand, and the orb in the other. "Wait a bit," said he, and he placed the orb under his arm, so that he could offer the other hand to John; but when he found that John was another suitor, he began to weep so violently, that both the sceptre and the orb fell to the floor, and he was obliged to wipe his eyes with his dressing-gown. Poor old king! "Let her alone," he said; "you will fare as badly as all the others. Come, I will show you." Then he led him out into the princess's pleasure gardens, and there he saw a frightful sight. On every tree hung three or four king's sons who had wooed the princess, but had not been able to guess the riddles she gave them. Their skeletons rattled in every breeze, so that the terrified birds never dared to venture into the garden. All the flowers were supported by human bones instead of sticks, and human skulls in the flowerpots grinned horribly. It was really a doleful garden for a princess. "Do you see all this?" said the old king; "your fate will be the same as those who are here, therefore do not attempt it. You really make me very unhappy, – I take these things to heart so very much." John kissed the good old king's hand, and said he was sure it would be all right, for he was quite enchanted with the beautiful princess. Then the princess herself came riding into the palace yard with all her ladies, and he wished her "Good morning." She looked wonderfully fair and lovely when she offered her hand to John, and he loved her more than ever. How could she be a wicked witch, as all the people asserted? He accompanied her into the hall, and the little pages offered them gingerbread nuts and sweetmeats, but the old king was so unhappy he could eat nothing, and besides, gingerbread nuts were too hard for him. It was decided that John should come to the palace the next day, when the judges and the whole of the counsellors would be present, to try if he could guess the first riddle. If he succeeded, he would have to come a second time; but if not, he would lose his life, – and no one had ever been able to guess even one. However, John was not at all anxious about the result of his trial; on the contrary, he was very merry. He thought only of the beautiful princess, and believed that in some way he should have help, but how he knew not, and did not like to think about it; so he danced along the high-road as he went back to the inn, where he had left his fellow-traveller waiting for him. John could not refrain from telling him how gracious the princess had been, and how beautiful she looked. He longed for the next day so much, that he might go to the palace and try his luck at guessing the riddles. But his comrade shook his head, and looked very mournful. "I do so wish you to do well," said he; "we might have continued together much longer, and now I am likely to lose you; you poor dear John! I could shed tears, but I will not make you unhappy on the last night we may be together. We will be merry, really merry this evening; to-morrow, after you are gone, I shall be able to weep undisturbed."

It was very quickly known among the inhabitants of the town that another suitor had arrived for the princess, and there was great sorrow in consequence. The theatre remained closed, the women who sold sweetmeats tied crape round the sugar-sticks, and the king and the priests were on their knees in the church. There was a great lamentation, for no one expected John to succeed better than those who had been suitors before.

In the evening John's comrade prepared a large bowl of punch, and said, "Now let us be merry, and drink to the health of the princess." But after drinking two glasses. John became so sleepy, that he could not possibly keep his eyes open, and fell fast asleep. Then his fellow-traveller lifted him gently out of his chair, and laid him on the bed; and as soon as it was quite dark, he took the two large wings which he had cut from the dead swan, and tied them firmly to his own shoulders. Then he put into his pocket the largest of the three rods which he had obtained from the old woman who had fallen and broken her leg. After this he opened the window, and flew away over the town, straight towards the palace, and seated himself in a corner, under the window which looked into the bedroom of the princess.

The town was perfectly still when the clocks struck a quarter to twelve. Presently the window opened, and the princess, who had large black wings to her shoulders, and a long white mantle, flew away over the city towards a high mountain. The fellow-traveller, who had made himself invisible, so that she could not possibly see him, flew after her through the air, and whipped the princess with his rod, so that the blood came whenever he struck her. Ah, it was a strange flight through the air! The wind caught her mantle, so that it spread out on all sides, like the large sail of a ship, and the moon shone through it. "How it hails, to be sure!" said the princess, at each blow she received from the rod; and it served her right to be whipped.

At last she reached the side of the mountain, and knocked. The mountain opened with a noise like the roll of thunder, and the princess went in. The traveller followed her; no one could see him, as he had made himself invisible. They went through a long, wide passage. A thousand gleaming spiders ran here and there on the walls, causing them to glitter as if they were illuminated with fire. They next entered a large hall built of silver and gold. Large red and blue flowers shone on the walls, looking like sunflowers in size, but no one could dare to pluck them, for the stems were hideous poisonous snakes, and the flowers were flames of fire, darting out of their jaws. Shining glow-worms covered the ceiling, and sky-blue bats flapped their transparent wings. Altogether the place had a frightful appearance. In the middle of the floor stood a throne supported by four skeleton horses, whose harness had been made by fiery-red spiders. The throne itself was made of milk-white glass, and the cushions were little black mice, each biting the other's tail. Over it hung a canopy of rose-coloured spider's webs, spotted with the prettiest little green flies, which sparkled like precious stones. On the throne sat an old magician with a crown on his ugly head, and a sceptre in his hand. He kissed the princess on the forehead, seated her by his side on the splendid throne, and then the music commenced. Great black grasshoppers played the mouth organ, and the owl struck herself on

278

the body instead of a drum. It was altogether a ridiculous concert. Little black goblins with false lights in their caps danced about the hall; but no one could see the traveller, and he had placed himself just behind the throne where he could see and hear everything. The courtiers who came in afterwards looked noble and grand; but any one with common sense could see what they really were, only broomsticks, with cabbages for heads. The magician had given them life, and dressed them in embroidered robes. It answered very well, as they were only wanted for show. After there had been a little dancing, the princess told the magician that she had a new suitor, and asked him what she should think of for the suitor to guess when he came to the castle the next morning.

"Listen to what I say," said the magician, "you must choose something very easy, he is less likely to guess it then. Think of one of your shoes, he will never imagine it is that. Then cut his head off; and mind you do not forget to bring his eyes with you to-morrow night, that I may eat them."

The princess curtsied low, and said she would not forget the eyes.

The magician then opened the mountain and she flew home again, but the traveller followed and flogged her so much with the rod, that she sighed quite deeply about the heavy hail-storm, and made as much haste as she could to get back to her bedroom through the window. The traveller then returned to the inn where John still slept, took off his wings and laid down on the bed, for he was very tired. Early in the morning John awoke, and when his fellow-traveller got up, he said that he had had a very wonderful dream about the princess and her shoe, he therefore advised John to ask her if she had not thought of her shoe. Of course the traveller knew this from what the magician in the mountain had said.

"I may as well say that as anything else," said John. "Perhaps your dream may come true; still I will say farewell, for if I guess wrong I shall never see you again."

Then they embraced each other, and John went into the town and walked to the palace. The great hall was full of people, and the judges sat in armchairs, with eider-down cushions to rest their heads upon, because they had so much to think of. The old king stood near, wiping his eyes with his white pocket-handkerchief. When the princess entered, she looked even more beautiful than she had appeared the day before, and greeted every one present most gracefully; but to John she gave her hand, and said, "Good morning to you."

Now came the time for John to guess what she was thinking of; and oh, how kindly she looked at him as she spoke. But when he uttered the single word shoe, she turned as pale as a ghost; all her wisdom cauld not help her, for he had guessed rightly. Oh, how pleased the old king was! It was quite

amusing to see how he capered about. All the people clapped their hands, both on his account and John's, who had guessed rightly the first time. His fellow-traveller was glad also, when he heard how successful John had been. But John folded his hands, and thanked God, who, he felt quite sure, would help him again; and he knew he had to guess twice more. The evening passed pleasantly like the one preceding. While John slept, his companion flew behind the princess to the mountain, and flogged her even harder than before; this time he had taken two rods with him. No one saw him go in with her, and he heard all that was said. The princess this time was to think of a glove, and he told John as if he had again heard it in a dream. The next day, therefore, he was able to guess correctly the second time, and it caused great rejoicing at the palace. The whole court jumped about as they had seen the king do the day before, but the princess lay on the sofa, and would not say a single word. All now depended upon John. If he only guessed rightly the third time, he would marry the princess, and reign over the kingdom after the death of the old king; but if he failed, he would lose his life, and the magician would have his beautiful blue eyes. That evening John said his prayers and went to bed very early, and soon fell asleep calmly. But his companion tied on his wings to his shoulders, took three rods, and, with his sword at his side, flew to the palace. It was a very dark night, and so stormy that the tiles flew from the roofs of the houses, and the trees in the garden upon which the skeletons hung bent themselves like reeds before the wind. The lightning flashed, and the thunder rolled in one long-continued peal all night. The window of the castle opened, and the princess flew out. She was pale as death, but she laughed at the storm as if it were not bad enough. Her white mantle fluttered in the wind like a large sail, and the traveller flogged her with the three rods till the blood trickled down, and at last she could scarcely fly; she contrived, however, to reach the mountain. "What a hail-storm!" she said, as she entered; "I have never been out in such weather as this."

"Yes, there may be too much of a good thing sometimes," said the magician. Then the princess told him that John had guessed rightly the second time, and if he succeeded the next morning, he would win, and she could never come to the mountain again, or practise magic as she had done, and therefore she was quite unhappy. "I will find out something for you to think of which he will never guess, unless he is a greater conjuror than myself. But now let us be merry."

Then he took the princess by both hands, and they danced with all the little goblins and Jack o' lanterns in the room. The red spiders sprang here and there on the walls quite as merrily, and the flowers of fire appeared as if they were throwing out sparks. The owl beat the drum, the crickets whistled, and the grasshoppers played the mouth organ. It was a very ridiculous ball. After they had danced enough, the princess was obliged to go home, for fear she should be missed at the palace. The magician offered to go with her, that they might be company to each other on the way. Then they flew away through the bad weather, and the traveller followed them, and broke his three rods across their shoulders. The magician had never been out in such a hailstorm as this. Just by the palace the magician stopped to wish the princess farewell, and to whisper in her ear, "To-morrow think of my head." But the traveller heard it, and just as the princess slipped through the window into her bedroom, and the magician turned round to fly back to the mountain, he seized him by the long black beard, and with his sabre cut off the wicked conjuror's head just behind his shoulders, so that he could not even see who it was. He threw the body into the sea to the fishes, and after dipping the head into the water, he tied it up in a silk handkerchief, took it with him to the inn, and then went to bed. The next morning he gave

283

John the handkerchief, and told him not to untie it till the princess asked him what she was thinking of. There were so many people in the great hall of the palace that they stood as thick as radishes tied together in a bundle. The council sat in their arm-chairs with the white cushions. The old king wore new robes, and the golden crown and sceptre had been polished up so that he looked quite smart. But the princess was very pale, and wore a black dress as if she were going to a funeral.

"What have I thought of?" asked the princess, of John. He immediately untied the handkerchief, and was himself quite frightened when he saw the head of the ugly magician. Every one shuddered, for it was terrible to look at; but the princess sat like a statue, and could not utter a single word. At length she rose and gave John her hand, for he had guessed rightly.

She looked at no one, but sighed deeply, and said, "You are my master now; this evening our marriage must take place."

"I am very pleased to hear it," said the old king. "It is just what I wish."

Then all the people shouted "Hurrah." The band played music in the street, the bells rang, and the cake-women took the black crape off the sugar-sticks. There was universal joy. Three oxen, stuffed with ducks and chickens, were roasted whole in the market-place, where every one might help himself to a slice. The fountains spouted forth the most delicious wine, and whoever bought a penny loaf at the baker's received six large buns, full of raisins, as a present. In the evening the whole town was illuminated. The soldiers fired off cannons, and the boys let off crackers. There was eating and drinking, dancing and jumping everywhere. In the palace, the high-born gentlemen and the beautiful ladies danced with each other, and they could be heard at a great distance singing the following song:

"Here are maidens, young and fair,
Dancing in the summer air;
Like to spinning-wheels at play,
Pretty maidens dance away –
Dance the spring and summer through
Till the sole falls from your shoe."

But the princess was still a witch, and she could not love John. His fellow-traveller had thought of that, so he gave John three feathers out of the swan's wings, and a little bottle with a few drops in it. He told him to place a large bath full of water by the princess's bed, and put the feathers and the drops into it. Then, at the moment she was about to get into bed, he must give her a little push, so that she might fall into the water, and then dip her three times. This would destroy the power of the magician, and she would

284

love him very much. John did all that his companion told him to do. The princess shrieked aloud when he dipped her under the water the first time, and struggled under his hands in the form of a great black swan with fiery eyes. As she rose the second time from the water, the swan had become white, with a black ring round its neck. John allowed the water to close once more over the bird, and at the same time it changed into a most beautiful princess. She was more lovely even than before, and thanked him, while her eyes sparkled with tears, for having broken the spell of the magician. The next day, the king came with the whole court to offer their congratulations, and stayed till quite late. Last of all came the travelling companion; he had his staff in his hand and his knapsack on his back. John kissed him many times and told him he must not go, he must remain with him, for he was the cause of all his good fortune. But the traveller shook his head, and said gently and kindly, "No: my time is up now; I have only paid my debt to you. Do you remember the dead man whom the bad people wished to throw out of his coffin? You gave all you possessed that he might rest in his grave; I am that man." As he said this, he vanished.

The wedding festivities lasted a whole month. John and his princess loved each other dearly, and the old king lived to see many a happy day, when he took their little children on his knees and let them play with his sceptre. And John became king over the whole country.

The Swineherd

There was once a poor Prince, who had a kingdom: his kingdom was very small, but still quite large enough to marry upon; and he wished to marry. It was certainly rather cool of him to say to the Emperor's daughter, "Will you have me?" But so he did; for his name was renowned far and wide; and there were a hundred Princesses who would have answered "Yes!" and "Thank you kindly."

We shall see what this Princess said. Listen!

It happened, that where the Prince's father lay buried there grew a rose-tree — a most beautiful rose-tree, which blossomed only once in every five years, and even then bore only one flower, but that *was* a rose! It smelt so sweet, that all cares and sorrows were forgotten by him who inhaled its fragrance.

And furthermore, the Prince had a nightingale, who could sing in such a manner that it seemed as though all sweet melodies dwelt in her little throat. So the Princess was to have the rose, and the nightingale; and they were accordingly put into large silver caskets, and sent to her.

The Emperor had them brought into a large hall, where the Princess was playing at "Visiting," with the ladies of the court; and when she saw the caskets with the presents, she clapped her hands for joy.

"Ah, if it were but a little pussy-cat!" exclaimed she, but the rose-tree, with its beautiful rose, came to view.

"Oh, how prettily it is made!" said all the courtladies.

"It is more than pretty," said the Emperor; "it is charming!"

But the Princess touched it, and was almost ready to cry.

"Fie, papa!" said she, "it is not made at all, it is natural!"

"Fie!" cried all the courtiers, "it is natural!"

"Let us see what is in the other casket, before we get into a bad humour," proposed the Emperor. So the nightingale came forth, and sang so delightfully that at first no one could say anything ill-humoured of her.

"*Superbe! charmant!*" exclaimed the ladies; for they all used to chatter French, each one worse than her neighbour.

"How much the bird reminds me of the musical box, that belonged to our blessed Empress!" remarked an old Knight. "Oh yes! these are the same tones, the same execution."

"Yes! yes!" said the Emperor, and he wept like a child at the remembrance.

"I will still hope that it is not a real bird," said the Princess.

"Yet it is a real bird," said those who had brought it. "Well, then, let the bird fly," returned the Princess; and she positively refused to see the Prince. However, he was not to be discouraged; he daubed his face over brown and black; pulled his cap over his ears, and knocked at the door.

"Good day to my lord the Emperor!" said he. "Can I have employment at the palace?"

"Why, yes," said the Emperor; "I want someone to take care of the pigs, for we have a great many of them."

So the Prince was appointed "Imperial Swineherd." He had a dirty little room close by the pigsty; and there he sat the whole day, and worked. By the evening, he had made a pretty little saucepan. Little bells were hung all round it; and when the pot was boiling, these bells tinkled in the most charming manner, and played the old melody: –

Ach! du lieber Augustin,
Alles ist weg, weg, weg!
Ah! dear Augustine!
All is lost, lost, lost!

But what was still more curious, whoever held his finger in the smoke of this saucepan, immediately smelt all the dishes that were cooking on every hearth in the city: this, you see, was something quite different from the rose. Now the Princess happened to walk that way; and when she heard the tune, she stood quite still, and seemed pleased; for she could play "Lieber Augustin;" it was the only piece she knew, and she played it with one finger.

"Why, there is my piece!" said the Princess; "that swineherd must certainly have been well educated! Go in and ask him the price of the instrument."

So one of the court-ladies must run in; however, she drew on wooden slippers first.

"What will you take for the saucepan?" inquired the lady.

"I will have ten kisses from the Princess," said the swineherd.

"Yes, indeed!" said the lady.

"I cannot sell it for less," rejoined the swineherd.

"Well, what does he say?" asked the Princess.

"I cannot tell you, really," replied the lady; "it is too bad!"

"Then you can whisper it!" So the lady whispered it.

"He is an impudent fellow!" said the Princess, and she walked on; but when she had gone a little way, the bells tinkled so prettily,

Ach! du lieber Augustin,
Alles ist weg, weg, weg!

"Stay," said the Princess. Ask him if he will have ten kisses from the ladies of my court."

"No, thank you!" answered the swineherd: "ten kisses from the Princess, or I keep the saucepan myself."

"That must not be either!" said the Princess; "but do you all stand before me, that no one may see us."

And the court-ladies placed themselves in front of her, and spread out their dresses; the swinehard got ten kisses, and the Princess – the saucepan.

That was delightful! the saucepan was kept boiling all the evening, and the whole of the following day. They knew perfectly well what was cooking at every fire throughout the city, from the chamberlain's to the cobbler's; the court-ladies danced, and clapped their hands.

"We know who has soup and who has pancakes for dinner to-day, who has cutlets, and who has eggs. How interesting!"

"Yes, but keep my secret, for I am an Emperor's daughter."

The swineherd – that is to say the Prince, for no one knew that he was other than an ill-favoured swineherd, – let not a day pass without working at something; he at last constructed a rattle, which, when it swung round, played all the waltzes and jigtunes which have ever been heard since the creation of the world.

"Ah, that is *superbe!*" said the Princess when she passed by; "I have never heard prettier compositions! Go in and ask him the price of the instrument; but mind, he shall have no more kisses!"

"He will have a hundred kisses from the Princess!" said the lady who had been to ask.

"I think he is not in his right senses!" replied the Princess, and walked on; but when she had gone a little way, she stopped again. "One must encourage art," said she; "I am the Emperor's daughter. Tell him, he shall, as on yesterday, have ten kisses from me, and may take the rest from the ladies of the court."

"Oh! – but we should not like that at all!" said they. "What are you muttering?" asked the Princess; "if I can kiss him, surely you can! Remember that you owe everything to me." So the ladies were obliged to go to him again.

"A hundred kisses from the Princess!" said he, "or else let every one keep his own."

"Stand round!" said she; and all the ladies stood round her whilst the kissing was going on.

"What can be the reason for such a crowd close by the pigsty?" said the Emperor, who happened just then to step out on the balcony; he rubbed his eyes and put on his spectacles. "They are the ladies of the court; I must go down and see what they are about!" So he pulled up his slippers at the heel, for he had trodden them down.

As soon as he had got into the court-yard, he moved very softly, and the ladies were so much engrossed with counting the kisses, that all might go on fairly, that they did not perceive the Emperor. He rose on his tip-toes.

"What is all this?" said he, when he saw what was going on, and he boxed the Princess's ears with his slipper, just as the swineherd was taking the eighty-sixth kiss.

"March out!" cried the Emperor, for he was very angry; and both Princess and swineherd were thrust out of the city.

The Princess now stood and wept, the swineherd scolded, and the rain poured down.

"Alas! unhappy creature that I am!" said the Princess. "If I had but married the handsome young Prince! Ah! how unfortunate I am!"

And the swineherd went behind a tree, washed the black-and-brown colour from his face, threw off his dirty clothes, and stepped forth in his princely robes; he looked so noble that the Princess could not help bowing before him.

"I am come to despise thee," said he. "Thou wouldst not have an honourable prince! thou couldst not prize the rose and the nightingale, but thou wast ready to kiss the swineherd for the sake of a trumpery plaything. Thou art rightly served."

He then went back to his own little kingdom, and shut the door of his palace in her face. Now she might well sing

"Ach! du lieber Augustin,
Alles ist weg, weg, weg!"

The Old House

A very old house stood once in a street with several that were quite new and clean. The date of its erection had been carved on one of the beams, and surrounded by scrolls formed of tulips and hop-tendrils; by this date it could be seen that the old house was nearly three hundred years old. Verses too were written over the windows in old-fashioned letters, and grotesque faces, curiously carved, grinned at you from under the cornices. One storey projected a long way over the other, and under the roof ran a leaden gutter, with a dragon's head at the end. The rain was intended to pour out at the dragon's mouth, but it ran out of his body instead, for there was a hole in the gutter. The other houses in the street were new and well built, with large window panes and smooth walls. Any one could see they had nothing to do

295

with the old house. Perhaps they thought, "How long will that heap of rubbish remain here to be a disgrace to the whole street. The parapet projects so far forward that no one can see out of our windows what is going on in that direction. The stairs are as broad as the staircase of a castle, and as steep as if they led to a church-tower. The iron railing looks like the gate of a cemetery, and there are brass knobs upon it. It is really too ridiculous." Opposite the old house were more nice new houses, which had just the same opinion as their neighbours.

At the window of one of them sat a little boy with fresh rosy cheeks, and clear sparkling eyes, who was very fond of the old house, in sunshine or in moonlight. He would sit and look at the wall from which the plaster had in some places fallen off, and fancy all sorts of scenes which had been in former times. How the street must have looked when the houses had all gable roofs, open staircases, and gutters with dragons at the spout. He could even see soldiers walking about with halberds. Certainly it was a very good house to look at for amusement.

And old man lived in it, who wore knee-breeches, a coat with large brass buttons, and a wig, which any one could see was a real wig. Every morning an old man came to clean the rooms, and to wait upon him, otherwise the old man in the knee-breeches would have been quite alone in the house. Sometimes he came to one of the windows and looked out; then the little boy nodded to him, and the old man nodded back again, till they became acquainted, and were friends, although they had never spoken to each other; but that was of no consequence.

The little boy one day heard his parents say, "The old man opposite is very well off, but he is terribly lonely." The next Sunday morning the little boy wrapped something in a piece of paper and took it to the door of the old house, and said to the attendant who waited upon the old man, "Will you please to give this from me to the gentleman who lives here; I have two tin soldiers, and this is one of them, and he shall have it, because I know he is terribly lonely."

And the old attendant nodded and looked very pleased, and then he carried the tin soldier into the house.

Afterwards he was sent over to ask the little boy if he would not like to pay a visit himself. His parents gave him permission, and so it was that he gained admission to the old house.

The brass knobs on the railings shone more brightly than ever, as if they had been polished on account of his visit; and on the doors were carved trumpeters standing in tulips, and it seemed as if they were blowing with all their might, their cheeks were so puffed out, "Tanta-ra-ra, the little boy is coming; Tanta-ra-ra, the little boy is coming."

Then the door opened. All round the hall hung old portraits of knights in armour, and ladies in silk gowns; and the armour rattled, and the silk dresses rustled. Then came a staircase which went up a long way, and then came down a little way and led to a balcony, which was in a very ruinous state. There were large holes and long cracks, out of which grew grass and leaves, indeed the whole balcony, the courtyard, and the walls were so overgrown with green that they looked like a garden. In the balcony stood flower-pots, on which were heads having asses' ears, but the flowers in them grew just as they pleased. In one pot pinks were growing all over the sides, at least the green leaves were shooting forth stalk and stem, and saying as plainly as they could speak, "The air has fanned me, the sun has kissed me, and I am promised a little flower for next Sunday – really for next Sunday."

Then they entered a room in which the walls were covered with leather, and the leather had golden flowers stamped upon it.

"Gilding will fade in damp weather,
To endure, there is nothing like leather,"

said the walls. Chairs handsomely carved, with elbows on each side, and with very high backs, stood in the room, and as they creaked they seemed to say, "Sit down. Oh dear, how I am creaking. I shall certainly have the gout like the old cupboard. Gout in my back, ugh."

And then the little boy entered the room where the old man sat.

"Thank you for the tin soldier my little friend," said the old man, "and thank you also for coming to see me."

"Thanks, thanks," or "Creak, creak," said all the furniture.

There was so much that the pieces of furniture stood in each other's way to get a sight of the little boy.

On the wall near the centre of the room hung the picture of a beautiful lady, young and gay, dressed in the fashion of the olden times, with powdered hair, and a full, stiff skirt. She said neither "thanks" nor "creak," but she looked down upon the little boy with her mild eyes; and then he said to the old man,

"Where did you get that picture?"

"From the shop opposite," he replied. "Many portraits hang there that none seem to trouble themselves about. The persons they represent have been dead and buried long since. But I knew this lady many years ago, and she has been dead nearly half a century."

Under a glass beneath the picture hang a nosegay of withered flowers, which were no doubt half a century old too, as least they appeared so.

297

And the pendulum of the old clock went to and fro, and the hands turned round; and as time passed on, everything in the room grew older, but no one seemed to notice it.

"They say at home," said the little boy, "that you are very lonely."

"Oh," replied the old man, "I have pleasant thoughts of all that is passed, recalled by memory; and now you are come to visit me, and that is very pleasant."

Then he took from the book-case, a book full of pictures representing long processions of wonderful coaches, such as are never seen at the present time. Soldiers like the knave of clubs, and citizens with waving banners. The tailors had a flag with a pair of scissors supported by two lions, and on the shoemakers' flag there were not boots, but an eagle with two heads, for the shoemakers must have everything arranged so that they can say, "This is a pair." What a picture-book it was; and then the old man went into another room to fetch apples and nuts. It was very pleasant, certainly, to be in that old house.

"I cannot endure it," said the tin soldier, who stood on a shelf, "it is so lonely and dull here. I have been accustomed to live in a family, and I cannot get used to this life. I cannot bear it. The whole day is long enough, but the evening is longer. It is not here like it was in your house opposite, when your father and mother talked so cheerfully together, while you and all the dear children made such a delightful noise. No, it is all lonely in the old man's house. Do you think he gets any kisses? Do you think he ever has friendly looks, or a Christmas tree? He will have nothing now but the grave. Oh, I cannot bear it."

"You must not look only on the sorrowful side," said the little boy; "I think everything in this house is beautiful, and all the old pleasant thoughts come back here to pay visits."

"Ah, but I never see any, and I don't know them," said the tin soldier, "and I cannot bear it."

"You must bear it," said the little boy. Then the old man came back with a pleasant face, and brought with him beautiful preserved fruits, as well as apples and nuts; and the little boy thought no more of the tin soldier. How happy and delighted the little boy was; and after he returned home, and while days and weeks passed a great deal of nodding took place from one house to the other, and then the little boy went to pay another visit. The carved trumpeters blew "Tanta-ra-ra. There is the little boy. Tanta-ra-ra." The swords and amour on the old knight's pictures rattled. The silk dresses rustled, the leather repeated its rhyme, and the old chairs had the gout in their backs, and cried, "Creak;" it was all exactly like the first time; for in that house, one day and one hour were just like another. "I cannot bear it any

longer," said the tin soldier; "I have wept tears of tin, it is so melancholy here. Let me go to the wars, and lose an arm or a leg, that would be some change; I cannot bear it. Now I know what it is to have visits from one's old recollections, and all they bring with them. I have had visits from mine, and you may believe me it is not altogether pleasant. I was very nearly jumping from the shelf. I saw you all in your house opposite, as if you were really present. It was Sunday morning, and you children stood round the table, singing the hymn that you sing every morning. You were standing quietly, with your hands folded, and your father and mother were looking just as serious, when the door opened, and your little sister Maria, who is not two years old, was brought into the room. You know she always dances when she hears music and singing of any sort; so she began to dance immediately, although she ought not to have done so, but she could not get into the right time because the tune was so slow; so she stood first on one leg and then on the other, and bent her head very low, but it would not suit the music. You all stood looking grave, although it was very difficult to do so, but I laughed so to myself that I fell down from the table, and got a bruise, which is there still; I know it was not right to laugh. So all this, and everything else that I have seen, keeps running in my head, and these must be the old recollections that bring so many thoughts with them. Tell me whether you still sing on Sundays, and tell me about your little sister Maria, and how my old comrade is, the other tin soldier. Ah, really he must be very happy; I cannot endure this life."

"You are given away," said the little boy; "you must stay. Don't you see that." Then the old man came in, with a box containing many curious things to show him. Rouge-pots, scent-boxes, and old cards, so large and so richly gilded, that none are ever seen like them in these days. And there were smaller boxes to look at, and the piano was opened, and inside the lid were painted landscapes. But when the old man played, the piano sounded quite out of tune. Then he looked at the picture he had bought at the broker's, and his eyes sparkled brightly as he nodded at it, and said, "Ah, she could sing that tune."

"I will go to the wars! I will go to the wars!" cried the tin soldier as loud as he could, and threw himself down on the floor. Where could he have fallen? The old man searched, and the little boy searched, but he was gone, and could not be found. "I shall find him again," said the old man, but he did not find him. The boards of the floor were open and full of holes. The tin soldier had fallen through a crack between the boards, and lay there now in an open grave. The day went by, and the little boy returned home; the week passed, and many more weeks. It was winter, and the windows were quite frozen, so the little boy was obliged to breathe on the panes, and rub a hole to peep through at the old house. Snow drifts were lying in all the scrolls and on the inscriptions, and the steps were covered with snow as if no one were at home. And indeed nobody was at home, for the old man was dead. In the evening, a hearse stopped at the door, and the old man in his coffin was placed in it. He was to be taken to the country to be buried there in his own grave; so they carried him away; no one followed him, for all his friends were dead; and the little boy kissed his hand to the coffin as the hearse moved away with it. A few days after, there was an auction at the old house, and from his window the little boy saw the people carrying away the pictures of old knights and ladies, the flower-pots with the long ears, the old chairs, and the cupboards. Some were taken one way, some another. *Her* portrait, which had been bought at the picture dealer's, went back again to his shop, and there it remained, for no one seemed to know her, or to care for the old picture. In the spring, they began to pull the house itself down; people called it complete rubbish. From the street could be seen the room in which the walls were covered with leather, ragged and torn, and the green in the balcony hung straggling over the beams; they pulled it down quickly, for it looked ready to fall, and at last it was cleared away altogether. "What a good riddance," said the neighbours' houses. Very shortly, a fine new house was built farther back from the road; it had lofty windows and smooth walls, but in front, on the spot where the old house really stood, a little garden was planted, and wild vines grew up over the neighbouring walls; in front of the garden were large iron railings and a great gate, which looked very stately. People used to stop and peep through the railings. The sparrows assembled in dozens upon the wild vines, and chattered all together as loud as they could, but not about the old house; none of them could remember it, for many years had passed by, so many indeed, that the little boy was now a man, and a really good man too, and his parents were very proud of him. He was just married, and had come, with his young wife, to reside in the new house with the garden in front of it, and now he stood there by her side while she planted a field flower that she thought very pretty. She was planting it herself with her little hands, and pressing down the earth with her fingers. "Oh dear, what was that?" she exclaimed, as something pricked her. Out of the soft earth something was sticking up. It was – only think! – it was really the tin soldier, the very same which had been lost up in the old man's room, and had been hidden among old wood and rubbish for a long time, till it sunk into the earth, where it must have been for many years. And the young wife wiped the soldier, first with a green leaf, and then with her fine pocket-handkerchief, that smelt of such beautiful perfume. And the tin soldier felt as if he was recovering from a fainting fit. "Let me see him," said the young

man, and then he smiled and shook his head, and said, "It can scarcely be the same, but it reminds me of something that happened to one of my tin soldiers when I was a little boy." And then he told his wife about the old house and the old man, and of the tin soldier which he had sent across, because he thought the old man was lonely; and he related the story so clearly that tears came into the eyes of the young wife for the old house and the old man. "It is very likely that this is really the same soldier," said she, "and I will take care of him, and always remember what you have told me; but some day you must show me the old man's grave."

"I don't know where it is," he replied; "no one knows. All his friends are dead; no one took care of him, and I was only a little boy."

"Oh, how dreadfully lonely he must have been," said she.

"Yes, terribly lonely," cried the tin soldier; "still it is delightful not to be forgotten."

"Delightful indeed," cried a voice quite near to them; no one but the tin soldier saw that it came from a rag of the leather which hung in tatters; it had lost all its gilding, and looked like wet earth, but it had an opinion, and it spoke it thus: –

"Gilding will fade in damp weather,
To endure there is nothing like leather."

But the tin soldier did not believe any such thing.

The Toad

The well was deep, and so the rope was long; the windlass had scarcely room to go round when a bucket of water was to be hauled up over the edge of the well. The sun could never reach down far enough to be reflected in the water, however clear that was; but as far as it did manage to shine, there was green of some sort growing between the stones.

It was there that a family of toads were living. They had immigrated; actually they plunged headlong down into the well after old Mother Toad, who was still living. The green frogs, who had settled there much earlier and used to swim about in the water, recognized that they were cousins and called them "our well-guests". But these quite intended to stay there; they thoroughly enjoyed living on dry land, as they called the wet stones.

Mother Frog had gone travelling once. She had been in the bucket when it was drawn up, but the light proved too strong for her and she had trouble with her eyes. Luckily she managed to get out of the bucket and tumbled with a fearful splash into the water and lay for three days afterwards with a pain in the back. She hadn't much to tell about the world up above, though she did know – in fact they all knew – that the well was not the whole world. Mother Toad should have been able to tell them a thing or two, but she never answered when she was asked, and so they never asked her.

"She's fat, ugly and loathsome," said the young green frogs. "Her brats will be just as loathsome."

"Quite possibly," said Mother Toad, "but one of them has a jewel in its head, or else I have."

The green frogs glared when they heard this and, as they didn't like it, they made faces and dived to the bottom. But the young toads stretched their hind-legs in sheer pride; each one thought he had the jewel. Then they squatted with their heads quite still, though finally they began asking what they were proud of and what this jewel thing really was.

"It's something so fine and precious," said Mother Toad, "that I can't describe it. It's a thing you wear to please yourself, and that the others go and get annoyed about. But no more questions! I shan't answer."

"Well, I haven't got the jewel," said the smallest toad, which was as ugly as could be. "Why should I have anything so fine? And if it annoys others,

then it can't give me any pleasure. No, all I want is just to be allowed to go
up to the edge of the well and look out. That must be grand."

"Much better stay where you are," said Mother Toad. "You're at home
here; you know your way about. Mind the bucket, or it'll squash you.
And, remember, if you do find your way into it, you may tumble out. Not
everyone falls as luckily as I did, with no damage done to legs or eggs."

"Ko-eks!" said the little toad, as though it were trying to talk.

It did so want to go up to the edge of the well and look out. It felt such a
longing for the green things growing up there; and when the next morning
it happened that the bucket, filled with water, was being hauled up and
stopped for a moment in front of the stone where the toad was squatting,
the little creature quivered all over, jumped into the full bucket and sank
to the bottom of the water, which was then drawn up and emptied.

"Ugh!« said the fellow who saw it. "That's as ugly as ever I see'd, that is.«
And he gave a kick with his clog at the toad, which came near to being

304

badly hurt, though it just managed to get away in among some tall stinging nettles. It saw masses of stalks. It also looked overhead and saw the sun shining on the leaves, which were quite transparent. It was the same for the little toad as it is for us when we suddenly go into a big wood where the sun comes shining through between boughs and foliage.

"It's far nicer here than down in the well," said the little toad. "I should like to stay here all my life." It stopped there for an hour; it stopped for two. "I wonder what there is outside," it said. "Having come so far, I may as well go a bit further." Then it hopped along as quickly as it could and came out on to the road, where it had the sun on its back and was sprinkled with dust as it marched across the highway.

"This really *is* dry land," said the toad. "For me, it's almost too much of a good thing; it tickles."

Now it reached the ditch. Here grew forget-me-not and meadow-sweet and, close by, a quickset hedge with bushes of may and alder; here, too, was convolvulus, growing as bindweed; masses of colour, and a fluttering butterfly. The toad thought this was a flower that had broken loose in order to have a better look at the world, which was of course so likely.

"If only I could speed along like that," said the toad. "Ko-eks, ko-eks! What fun!"

It stayed on for eight nights and days in this ditch and never went short of food. On the ninth day it thought: "Time to be moving!" ... And yet what ever could be more delightful? Possibly a little toad or some green frogs. There had been sounds on the wind last night as if there were "cousins" not far away.

"It's wonderful to be alive, to come up out of the well, to lie among stinging nettles, to crawl across the dusty road, to have a good rest in the wet ditch! But on we go! Look out for frogs or a little toad – they're a thing no one can do without. Nature is not enough." So it continued to ramble.

Going through the field, it came to a large pond with rushes round it and made straight for them.

"This is rather too damp for you, isn't it?" said the frogs, "though you are very welcome. Are you a 'he' or a 'she'? Not that it makes any difference. You will be just as welcome."

Then the toad was invited to a concert in the evening, a family concert: lots of enthusiasm, but thin voices – we've met that before. No refreshments; only free drinks – the whole pond if they liked.

"Now I must be getting on," said the little toad. It still felt a desire for something better.

It saw the stars twinkling, so far and so clear; it saw the new moon shining; it saw the sun rising higher and higher.

"I see I'm still in the well, in a large well. I must go up higher; I'm so restless and full of longing." And when the moon was full and round, the poor creature thought, "I wonder if that's the bucket being trundled down for me to jump into, in order to go up higher. Or is the sun the great bucket? How huge, how gorgeous it is! It has room for us all. I must look out for a chance. Oh, how my head's shining! I don't believe the jewel can shine brighter. Still, I haven't got that, and I'm not sorry. No, higher up into splendour and joy! I feel confident, and yet anxious. It's a difficult step to take, but it's got to be done. Forward! Straight on towards the main road!"

And it stepped out – as far as a crawling animal like that can step out – and soon found itself on a public highway where people lived; there were both flower-gardens and kitchen-gardens. It came and rested by a cabbage-patch.

"Good heavens!" it said; "what a lot of different creatures there are whom I've never known! And how lovely and big the world is! But I must have a

look round it and not stay squatting in one place.'' With that, the toad hopped into the cabbage-garden. "How green it is here, how beautiful!"

"Yes, of course," said the caterpillar on its leaf. "My leaf is the biggest of the lot. It covers up half the world, but that's the part I can do without."

"Cluck, cluck!" was heard, and some chickens came tripping into the garden. The leading hen had very quick eyesight; she spied the caterpillar on the curly leaf and pecked at it, so that it fell twisting and turning to the ground. The hen peered first with one eye, then with the other, not knowing what might come of all this wriggling.

"It's not doing that because it wants to," thought the hen and drew back its head to strike. The toad became so frightened that it crawled straight towards the hen.

"So it has troops in support," said the hen. "Filthy vermin!" And it turned away. "I don't want that tiny green morsel; it only makes my throat tickle." The other hens thought the same, and off they went.

"I wriggled away from it," said the caterpillar. "It's a great thing to have presence of mind, though the hardest job is still left, namely, to get up on my cabbage-leaf again. Where is it?"

The little toad came along to show his sympathy and say how glad it was that its ugliness had frightened the hens away.

"What ever do you mean by that?" asked the caterpillar. "Why, I wriggled away from them myself. You're a hideous sight. Kindly allow me to go back to where I was … I smell cabbage! Here's my leaf! There's no place like home. But I must go higher up."

"That's it – higher up," said the little toad, "higher up. It feels just as I do, but today it's not in the mood because of the fright it had. We all want to go higher up," and it looked up as high as it could.

The stork was in its nest on the farmer's roof. He was clacking his beak, and Mother Stork was clacking too.

"Fancy living so high up," thought the toad. "If only I could come up there!"

In the farmhouse lived two young students. One was a poet, the other a naturalist. The first sang and took delight in writing about all that God had created and how it was mirrored in his heart; he sang it out, short, clear and rich in melodious verse. The other student tackled the problem itself and split it right up if need be. He considered the works of God as a big sum of subraction and multiplication; he was determined to get to know it all, inside and out, and to talk intelligently about it. It was all intelligence, and joy and wisdom were in his talk. They were kindly, gay young fellows, both of them.

"I say – there's a good specimen of a toad," said the naturalist. "I must have it to keep in spirits."

"But you've already got two others," said the poet. "Leave it in peace to enjoy itself." "Yes, but it's so beautifully ugly," said the other.

"Of course, if we could find the jewel in its head!" said the poet, "then I'd take a hand myself in cutting it open."

"Jewel!" said the other. "You must be good at natural history."

"Well, isn't there something rather nice in the popular belief that the toad, the ugliest of all creatures, often has the most precious jewel hidden in its head? Isn't it the same with human beings? Think of the jewel that AEsop had – yes, and Socrates."

The toad heard no more and didn't understand half of what it did hear. The two friends went away, and the toad escaped being put into spirits.

"They spoke about the jewel, too," said the toad. "Good thing I haven't got it, or it might have been very awkward for me."

There was clacking of beaks on the farmer's roof. Father Stork was giving his family a lecture, and they were casting sidelong glances at the two young men in the garden.

"Man is the most conceited of creatures," said the stork. "Listen what a clatter they make. But their rattle can't compare with ours. They plume themselves on their ready speech and on their language. A fine language, indeed, that slops over into gibberish every day's journey we go; they just can't understand each other. We can speak our language all over the world, both in Denmark and in Egypt. Men can't fly either. They get speed with a discovery they call 'the railway', but they often break their necks doing

308

that. It gives my beak the shivers whenever I think of it. The world can do without mankind; we don't need them. If only we may keep frogs and earthworms!"

"That was a top-hole speech," thought the little toad. "He's a great man, that stork, and what a lofty perch he's got – I've never seen anything like it – and how he can swim!" it exclaimed, as the stork went speeding through the air with outstretched wings.

Meanwhile, Mother Stork was chattering in her nest all about the land of Egypt, the waters of the Nile and the glorious mud to be found in foreign parts; it sounded so novel and attractive to the little toad.

"I must go to Egypt," it said. "If only the stork would take me with him – or one of the young ones might. I'd pay him back with a good turn on his wedding-day. That's it; I shall go to Egypt, for I'm so lucky. All this endless longing of mine, it's far better, isn't it, than having a jewel in my head."

And yet it *had* got the jewel – that endless longing to go up, always up! It gleamed inside it, gleamed with joy, gleamed with yearning.

At that very moment up came the stork. He had seen the toad in the grass, and he swooped down and grabbed the little creature not too gently. The beak squeezed, the wind whistled; it was far from pleasant, yet up it went, up to Egypt, it felt sure – and so its eyes shone, just as though a spark were flying out of them: "Ko-eks, ko-eks!"

The body was dead, the toad killed. But the spark from its eyes, what became of that?

The sunbeam took it. The sunbeam carried off the jewel from the toad's head. Where to?

It's no good asking the naturalist; much better ask the poet. You'll hear it all from him like a fairy tale, bringing in the caterpillar and the stork family, too. Just imagine – the caterpillar is transformed and turned into a pretty butterfly. The stork family flies over the mountains and away across the sea to far-off Africa, and yet finds the shortest way home again to Denmark – to the same spot, the same roof. Yes, it's almost too fantastic, isn't it? and yet it's true. You can ask the naturalist if you like; he'll have to admit it. And you know it yourself, too, because you've seen it.

"But what about the jewel in the toad's head?"

"Have a look for it in the sun. Try if you can find it there."

The light up there is too dazzling. We haven't yet got eyes that can gaze into all the splendour that God has created, but we shall get them one day; and that will be the finest fairy tale of all, for we shall be in it ourselves.

310

Little Claus and Great Claus

In a village there once lived two men who had the same name. They were both called Claus. One of them had four horses, but the other had only one; so to distinguish them, people called the owner of the four horses, "Great Claus," and him who had only one, "Little Claus." Now we shall hear what happened to them, for this is a true story.

Through the whole week, Little Claus was obliged to plough for Great Claus, and lend him his one horse; and once a week, on a Sunday, Great Claus lent him all his four horses. Then how Little Claus would smack his whip over all five horses, they were as good as his own on that one day. The sun shone brightly, and the church bells were ringing merrily as the people passed by, dressed in their best clothes, with their prayer-books under their arms. They were going to hear the clergyman preach. They looked at Little Claus ploughing with his five horses, and he was so proud that he smacked his whip, and said, "Gee-up, my five horses."

"You must not say that," said Great Claus; "for only one of them belongs to you." But Little Claus soon forgot what he ought to say, and when any one passed he would call out, "Gee-up, my five horses!"

"Now I must beg you not to say that again," said Great Claus; "for if you do, I shall hit your horse on the head, so that he will drop dead on the spot, and there will be an end of him."

"I promise you I will not say it any more," said the other; but as soon as people came by, nodding to him, and wishing him "Good day," he became so pleased, and thought how grand it looked to have five horses ploughing in his field, that he cried out again, "Gee-up, all my horses!"

"I'll gee-up your horses for you," said Great Claus; and, seizing a hammer, he struck the one horse of Little Claus on the head, and he fell dead instantly.

"Oh, now I have no horse at all," said Little Claus, weeping. But after a while he took off the dead horse's skin, and hung the hide to dry in the wind. Then he put the dry skin into a bag, and, placing it over his shoulder, went out into the next town to sell the horse's skin. He had a very long way to go, and had to pass through a dark, gloomy forest. Presently a storm arose, and he lost his way, and before he discovered the right path, evening came on, and it was still a long way to the town, and too far to return home before night. Near the road stood a large farmhouse. The shutters outside the windows were closed, but lights shone through the crevices and at the top. "I might get permission to stay here for the night," thought Little Claus; so he went up to the door and knocked. The farmer's wife opened the door; but when she heard what he wanted, she told him to go away, as her husband would not allow her to admit strangers. "Then I shall be obliged to lie out here," said Little Claus to himself, as the farmer's wife shut the door in his face. Near to the farmhouse stood a large haystack, and between it and the house was a small shed, with a thatched roof. "I can lie up there," said Little Claus, as he saw the roof; "it will make a famous bed, but I hope the stork will not fly down and bite my legs;" for on it stood a living stork, whose nest was in the roof. So Little Claus climbed to the roof of the shed, and while he turned himself to get comfortable, he discovered that the wooden shutters, which were closed, did not reach to the tops of the windows of the farmhouse, so that he could see into a room, in which a large table was laid out with wine, roast meat, and a splendid fish. The farmer's wife and the sexton were sitting at the table together; and she filled his glass, and helped him plenteously to fish, which appeared to be his favourite dish. "If I could only get some, too," thought Little Claus; and then, as he stretched his neck towards the window he spied a large, beautiful pie, – indeed they had a glorious feast before them.

At this moment he heard some one riding down the road, towards the farmhouse. It was the farmer returning home. He was a good man, but still he had a very strange prejudice, – he could not bear the sight of a sexton. If one appeared before him, he would put himself in a terrible rage. In consequence of this dislike, the sexton had gone to visit the farmer's wife during her husband's absence from home, and the good woman had placed before him the best she had in the house to eat. When she heard the farmer coming she was frightened, and begged the sexton to hide himself in a large empty chest that stood in the room. He did so, for he knew her husband could not endure the sight of a sexton. The woman then quickly put away the wine, and hid all the rest of the nice things in the oven; for if her husband had seen them he would have asked what they were brought out for.

"Oh, dear," sighed Little Claus from the top of the shed, as he saw all the good things disappear.

"Is any one up there?" asked the farmer, looking up and discovering Little Claus. "Why are you lying up there? Come down, and come into the house with me." So Little Claus came down and told the farmer how he had lost his way, and begged for a night's lodging.

"All right," said the farmer; "but we must have something to eat first." The woman received them both very kindly, laid the cloth on a large table,

CARBONNEAU. SC.

313

and placed before them a dish of porridge. The farmer was very hungry, and ate his porridge with a good appetite, but Little Claus could not help thinking of the nice roast meat, fish, and pies, which he knew were in the oven. Under the table, at his feet, lay the sack containing the horse's skin, which he intended to sell at the next town. Now Little Claus did not relish the porridge at all, so he trod with his foot on the sack under the table, and the dry skin squeaked quite loud. "Hush!" said Little Claus to his sack, at the same time treading upon it again, till it squeaked louder than before. "Hallo! what have you got in your sack?" asked the farmer.

"Oh, it is a conjuror," said Little Claus; "and he says we need not eat porridge, for he has conjured the oven full of roast meat, fish, and pie."

"Wonderful!" cried the farmer, starting up and opening the oven door; and there lay all the nice things hidden by the farmer's wife, but which he supposed had been conjured there by the wizard under the table. The woman dared not say anything; so she placed the things before them, and they both ate of the fish, the meat, and the pastry.

Then Little Claus trod again upon his sack, and it squeaked as before. "What does he say now?" asked the farmer.

"He says," replied Little Claus, "that there are three bottles of wine for us, standing in the corner, by the oven."

So the woman was obliged to bring out the wine also, which she had hidden, and the farmer drank it till he became quite merry. He would have liked such a conjuror as Little Claus carried in his sack. "Could he conjure up the evil one?" asked the farmer. "I should like to see him now, while I am so merry."

"Oh, yes!" replied Little Claus, "my conjuror can do anything I ask him, – can you not?" he asked, treading at the same time on the sack till it squeaked. "Do you hear? he answers 'Yes,' but he fears that we shall not like to look at him."

"Oh, I am not afraid. What will he be like?"

"Well, he is very much like a sexton."

"Ha!" said the farmer, "then he must be ugly. Do you know I cannot endure the sight of a sexton. However, that doesn't matter, I shall know who it is; so I shall not mind. Now then, I have got up my courage, but don't let him come too near me."

"Stop, I must ask the conjuror," said Little Claus; so he trod on the bag, and stooped his ear down to listen.

"What does he say?"

"That you must go and open that large chest which stands in the corner, and you will see the evil one crouching down inside; but you must hold the lid firmly, that he may not slip out."

314

"Will you come and help me hold it?" said the farmer, going towards the chest in which his wife had hidden the sexton, who now lay inside, very much frightened. The farmer opened the lid a very little way, and peeped in.

"Oh," cried he, springing backwards, "I saw him, and he is exactly like our sexton. How dreadful it is!" So after that he was obliged to drink again, and they sat and drank till far into the night.

"You must sell your conjuror to me," said the farmer; "ask as much as you like, I will pay it; indeed I would give you directly a whole bushel of gold."

"No, indeed, I cannot," said Little Claus; "only think how much profit I could make out of this conjuror."

"But I should like to have him," said the farmer, still continuing his entreaties.

"Well," said Little Claus at length, "you have been so good as to give me a night's lodging, I will not refuse you; you shall have the conjuror for a bushel of money, but I will have quite full measure."

"So you shall," said the farmer; "but you must take away the chest as well. I would not have it in the house another hour; there is no knowing if *he* may not be still there."

So Little Claus gave the farmer the sack containing the dried horse's skin, and received in exchange a bushel of money – full measure. The farmer also gave him a wheelbarrow on which to carry away the chest and the gold.

"Farewell," said Little Claus, as he went off with his money and the great chest, in which the sexton lay still concealed. On one side of the forest was a broad, deep river, the water flowed so rapidly that very few were able to swim against the stream. A new bridge had lately been built across it, and in the middle of this bridge Little Claus stopped, and said, loud enough to be heard by the sexton, "Now, what shall I do with this stupid chest; it is heavy as if it were full of stones: I shall be tired if I roll it any farther, so I may as well throw it into the river; if it swims after me to my house, well and good, and if not, it will not much matter."

So he seized the chest in his hand and lifted it up a little, as if he were going to throw it into the water.

"No, leave it alone," cried the sexton from within the chest; "let me out first."

"Oh," exclaimed Little Claus, pretending to be frightened, "he is in there still, is he? I must throw him into the river, that he may be drowned."

"Oh, no; oh, no," cried the sexton; "I will give you a whole bushel full of money if you will let me go."

"Why, that is another matter," said Little Claus, opening the chest. The

315

sexton crept out, pushed the empty chest into the water, and went to his house, then he measured out a whole bushel full of gold for Little Claus, who had already received one from the farmer, so that now he had a barrow full.

"I have been well paid for my horse," said he to himself when he reached home, entered his own room, and emptied all his money into a heap on the floor. "How vexed Great Claus will be when he finds how rich I have become all through my one horse; but I shall not tell him exactly how it all happened." Then he sent a boy to Great Claus to borrow a bushel measure. "What can he want it for?" thought Great Claus; so he smeared the bottom of the measure with tar, that some of whatever was put into it might stick there and remain. And so it happened; for when the measure returned, three new silver florins were sticking to it.

"What does this mean?" said Great Claus; so he ran off directly to Little Claus and asked, "Where did you get so much money?"

"Oh, for my horse's skin, I sold it yesterday."

"It was certainly well paid for then," said Great Claus; and he ran home to his house, seized a hatchet, and knocked all his four horses on the head, flayed off their skins, and took them to the town to sell. "Skins, skins, who'll buy skins?" he cried, as he went through the streets. All the shoemakers and tanners came running, and asked how much he wanted for them.

"A bushel of money, for each," replied Great Claus.

"Are you mad?" they all cried; "do you think we have money to spend by the bushel?"

"Skins, skins," he cried again, "who'll buy skins?" But to all who inquired the price, his answer was, "A bushel of money."

"He is making fools of us," said they all; then the shoemakers took their straps, and the tanners their leather aprons, and began to beat Great Claus.

"Skins, skins!" they cried, mocking him; "yes, we'll mark your skin for you, till it is black and blue."

"Out of the town with him," said they. And Great Claus was obliged to run as fast as he could, he had never before been so throughly beaten.

"Ah," said he, as he came to his house: "Little Claus shall pay me for this; I will beat him to death."

Meanwhile the old grandmother of Little Claus died. She had been cross, unkind, and really spiteful to him; but he was very sorry, and took the dead woman and laid her in his warm bed to see if he could bring her to life again. There he determined that she should lie the whole night, while he seated himself in a chair in a corner of the room as he had often done be-

316

fore. During the night, as he sat there, the door opened, and in came Great Claus with a hatchet. He knew well where Little Claus's bed stood; so he went right up to it, and struck the old grandmother on the head, thinking it must be Little Claus.

"There," cried he, "now you cannot make a fool of me again;" and then he went home.

"That is a very wicked man," thought Little Claus; "he meant to kill me. It is a good thing for my old grandmother that she was already dead, or he would have taken her life." Then he dressed his old grandmother in her best clothes, borrowed a horse of his neighbour, and harnessed it to a cart. Then he placed the old woman on the back seat, so that she might not fall out as he drove, and rode away through the wood. By sunrise they reached a large inn, where Little Claus stopped and went to get something to eat. The landlord was a rich man, and a good man too; but as passionate as if he had been made of pepper and snuff.

"Good morning," said he to Little Claus; "you are come betimes to-day."

"Yes," said Little Claus; "I am going to the town with my old grandmother; she is sitting at the back of the wagon, but I cannot bring her into the room. Will you take her a glass of mead? But you must speak very loud, for she cannot hear well."

"Yes, certainly I will," replied the landlord; and, pouring out a glass of mead, he carried it out to the dead grandmother, who sat upright in the cart. "Here is a glass of mead from your grandson," said the landlord. The dead woman did not answer a word, but sat quite still. "Do you not hear?" cried the landlord as loud as he could; "here is a glass of mead from your grandson."

Again and again he bawled it out, but as she did not stir he flew into a passion, and threw the glass of mead in her face; it struck her on the nose, and she fell backwards out of the cart, for she was only seated there, not tied in.

"Hallo!" cried Little Claus, rushing out of the door, and seizing hold of the landlord by the throat; "you have killed my grandmother; see, here is a great hole in her forehead."

"Oh how unfortunate," said the landlord, wringing his hands. "This all comes of my fiery temper. Dear Little Claus, I will give you a bushel of money; I will bury your grandmother as if she were my own; only keep silent, or else they will cut off my head, and that would be disagreeable."

So it happened that Little Claus received another bushel of money, and the landlord buried his old grandmother as if she had been his own. When Little Claus reached home again, he immediately sent a boy to Great Claus, requesting him to lend him a bushel measure. "How is this?" thought Great Claus; "did I not kill him? I must go and see for myself." So he went to Little Claus, and took the bushel measure with him. "How did you get all this money?" asked Great Claus, staring with wide open eyes at his neighbour's treasures.

"You killed my grandmother instead of me," said Little Claus; "so I have sold her for a bushel of money."

"That is a good price at all events," said Great Claus. So he went home, took a hatchet, and killed his old grandmother with one blow. Then he placed her on a cart, and drove into the town to the apothecary, and asked him if he would buy a dead body.

"Whose is it, and where did you get it?" asked the apothecary.

"It is my grandmother," he replied; "I killed her with a blow, that I might get a bushel of money for her."

"Heaven preserve us!" cried the apothecary, "you are out of your mind. Don't say such things, or you will lose your head." And then he talked to him seriously about the wicked deed he had done, and told him that such a wicked man would surely be punished. Great Claus got so frightened that he rushed out of the surgery, jumped into the cart, whipped up his horses, and drove home quickly. The apothecary and all the people thought him mad, and let him drive where he liked.

"You shall pay for this," said Great Claus, as soon as he got into the high-road, "that you shall, Little Claus." So as soon as he reached home he took the largest sack he could find and went over to Little Claus. "You have played me another trick," said he. "First, I killed all my horses, and then my old grandmother, and it is all your fault; but you shall not make a fool of me any more." So he laid hold of Little Claus round the body, and pushed him into the sack, which he took on his shoulders, saying, "Now I'm going to drown you in the river."

He had a long way to go before he reached the river, and Little Claus was not a very light weight to carry. The road led by the church, and as they passed he could hear the organ playing and the people singing beautifully. Great Claus put down the sack close to the church-door, and thought he might as well go in and hear a psalm before he went any farther. Little Claus could not possibly get out of the sack, and all the people were in church; so in he went.

"Oh dear, oh dear," sighed Little Claus in the sack, as he turned and twisted about; but he found he could not loosen the string with which it was tied. Presently an old cattle driver, with snowy hair, passed by, carrying a large staff in his hand, with which he drove a large herd of cows and oxen before him. They stumbled against the sack in which lay Little Claus, and

318

turned it over. "Oh dear," sighed Little Claus, "I am very young, yet I am soon going to heaven."

"And I, poor fellow," said the drover, "I, who am so old already, cannot get there."

"Open the sack," cried Little Claus; "creep into it instead of me, and you will soon be there."

"With all my heart," replied the drover, opening the sack, from which sprung Little Claus as quickly as possible. "Will you take care of my cattle?" said the old man, as he crept into the bag.

"Yes," said Little Claus, and he tied up the sack, and then walked off with all the cows and oxen.

When Great Claus came out of church, he took up the sack, and placed it on his shoulders. It appeared to have become lighter, for the old drover was not half so heavy as Little Claus.

"How light he seems now," said he. "Ah, it is because I have been to a church." So he walked on to the river, which was deep and broad, and threw the sack containing the old drover into the water, believing it to be Little Claus. "There you may lie!" he exclaimed; "you will play me no more tricks now." Then he turned to go home, but when he came to a place where two roads crossed, there was Little Claus driving the cattle. "How is this?" said Great Claus. "Did I not drown you just now?"

"Yes," said Little Claus; "you threw me into the river about half an hour ago."

"But wherever did you get all these fine beasts?" asked Great Claus.

"These beasts are sea-cattle," replied Little Claus. "I'll tell you the whole story, and thank you for drowing me; I am above you now, I am really very rich. I was frightened, to be sure, while I lay tied up in the sack, and the wind whistled in my ears when you threw me into the river from the bridge, and I sank to the bottom immediately; but I did not hurt myself, for I fell upon beautifully soft grass which grows down there; and, in a moment, the sack opened, and the sweetest little maiden came towards me. She had snow-white robes, and a wreath of green leaves on her wet hair. She took me by the hand, and said, 'So you are come, Little Claus, and here are some cattle for you to begin with. About a mile farther on the road, there is another herd for you.' Then I saw that the river formed a great highway for the people who live in the sea. They were walking and driving here and there from the sea to the land at the spot where the river terminates. The bed of the river was covered with the loveliest flowers and sweet fresh grass. The fish swam past me as rapidly as the birds do here in the air. How handsome all the people were, and what fine cattle were grazing on the hills and in the valleys!"

"But why did you come up again," said Great Claus, "if it was all so beautiful down there? I should not have done so."

"Well," said Little Claus, "it was good policy on my part; you heard me say just now that I was told by the sea-maiden to go a mile farther on the road, and I should find a whole herd of cattle. By the road she meant the river, for she could not travel any other way; but I knew the winding of the river, and how it bends, sometimes to the right and sometimes to the left, and it seemed a long way, so I chose a shorter one; and, by coming up to the land, and then driving across the fields back again to the river, I shall save half a mile, and get all my cattle more quickly."

"What a lucky fellow you are!" exclaimed Great Claus. "Do you think I should get any sea-cattle if I went down to the bottom of the river?"

"Yes, I think so," said Little Claus; "but I cannot carry you there in a sack, you are too heavy. However, if you will go there first, and then creep into a sack, I will throw you in with the greatest pleasure."

"Thank you," said Great Claus; "but remember, if I do not get any sea-cattle down there I shall come up again and give you a good thrashing."

"No, now, don't be too fierce about it!" said Little Claus, as they walked on towards the river. When they approached it, the cattle, who were very thirsty, saw the stream, and ran down to drink.

"See what a hurry they are in," said Little Claus, "they are longing to get down again."

"Come, help me, make haste," said Great Claus; "or you'll get beaten." So he crept into a large sack, which had been lying across the back of one of the oxen.

"Put in a stone," said Great Claus, "or I may not sink."

"Oh, there's not much fear of that," he replied; still he put a large stone into the bag, and then tied it tightly, and gave it a push.

"Plump!" In went Great Claus, and immediately sank to the bottom of the river.

"I'm afraid he will not find any cattle," said Little Claus, and then he drove his own beasts homewards.

The Daisy

Now listen. In the country, close by the roadside, stood a pleasant house; you have seen one like it, no doubt, very often. In front, lay a little garden enclosed in palings, and full of blooming flowers. Near the hedge, in the soft green grass, grew a little daisy. The sun shone as brightly and warmly upon her as upon the large and beautiful garden flowers, so the daisy grew from hour to hour. Every morning she unfolded her little white petals, like shining rays round the little golden sun in the centre of the flower. She never thought of being unseen down in the grass, or that she was only a poor, insignificant flower. She felt too happy to care for that, so she turned towards the warm sun, looked up to the blue sky, and listened to the lark singing high in the air. One day, the little flower was as joyful as if it had been a great holiday, and yet it was only Monday. All the children were at school, and while they sat on their forms learning their lessons, she, on her little stem, learnt also from the warm sun and from everything around her, how good God is, and she was glad to hear the lark in his pleasant song express exactly her own feelings. And the daisy admired the happy bird who could warble so sweetly and fly so high; but she was not sorrowful from regret at her own inability to do the same. "I can see and hear," thought she; "the sun shines upon me, and the wind kisses me: what else do I need to make me happy?" Within the palings grew a number of garden flowers, who appeared more proud and conceited in proportion as they were scentless. The peonies considered it a grand thing to be so large, and puffed themselves out to be larger than the roses. The tulips knew that they were marked with beautiful colours, and held themselves bolt upright, that they might be seen more plainly. They did not notice the little daisy outside, but she looked at them and thought, "How rich and beautiful they are! No wonder the pretty bird flies down to visit them. How glad I am that I grow so near them, that I may admire their beautiful appearance." Just at this moment, the lark flew down, crying "Tweet," but he did not go near the peonies and tulips; he hopped into the grass near the lowly daisy. She trembled for joy, and hardly knew what to think. The little bird hopped round the daisy, singing, "Oh what sweet soft grass, and what a lovely little flower, with gold in its heart, silver on its dress." For the yellow centre in the daisy looked like gold, and the leaves around were glittering white, like silver. How happy the little daisy felt, no one can describe – the bird kissed it with his beak, sang to it, and then flew up again into the blue air above. It was, at least, a quarter of an hour before the daisy could recover herself. Half ashamed, yet happy in herself, she glanced at the other flowers; they must have seen the honour she had received, and would understand her delight and pleasure. But the tulips looked prouder than ever, indeed, they were evidently quite vexed about it. And the peonies were quite disgusted, and could they have spoken, the poor little daisy would have no doubt received a good scolding. She could see they were all out of temper, and it made her very sorry.

At this moment there came into the garden a girl, with a large sharp knife, which glittered in her hand. She went straight up to the tulips and cut down several of them, one after another.

"Oh dear," sighed the daisy, "how shocking! It is all over with them now." The girl carried the tulips away, and the daisy felt very glad to grow outside in the grass, and to be only a poor little flower. When the sun set, she folded up her leaves and went to sleep, and dreamt the whole night long of the warm sun and the pretty little bird. The next morning, when the flower joyfully stretched out its white leaves once more to the warm air and the light, she recognised the voice of the bird, but his song sounded mournful and sad. Alas! he had good reason to be sad – he had been caught and made a prisoner in a cage that hung close by the open window. He sung of the happy time when he could fly in the air joyous and free; of the young green corn in the fields from which he would spring higher and higher to sing his glorious song, and now he was a prisoner in a cage. The little daisy wished very much that she could help him. But what could she do? In her anxiety she forgot all the beautiful things around her, the warm sunshine and her own pretty shining white leaves. Alas! she could think of nothing but the captive bird, and her own inability to help him. Two boys came into the garden; one of them carried a large sharp knife in his hand like the one with which the girl had cut down the tulips. They went straight up to the little daisy who could not think what they were going to do. "We can cut out a nice piece of turf for the lark here," said one of the boys, and he began to cut a square piece round the daisy so that she stood just in the centre. "Pull up the flower," said the other boy, and the daisy trembled with fear, for to pluck it up would destroy its life, and it wished so much to live and to be taken to the captive lark, in his cage, on the piece of turf. "No, let it stay," said the boy, "it looks so pretty." So the daisy remained, and was put with the turf in the lark's cage. The poor bird was complaining loudly about his lost freedom, and beat his wings against the iron bars of his cage. The little daisy could not speak nor utter one word to console him, and she would gladly have done so. The whole morning passed in this manner.

"Here is no water," said the captive lark; "they are all gone out and have forgotten to give me a drop of water to drink. My throat is hot and dry; I feel as if I had fire and ice within me, and the air is so heavy. Alas! I must die; I must bid farewell to the warm sunshine, the fresh green, and all the beautiful things which God has created." And then he thrust his beak into the cool turf to refresh himself a little with the fresh grass, and his eye fell on the daisy; then the bird nodded to it and kissed it with his beak, and said, "You also will wither here, you poor little flower! They have given you to me with the little patch of green grass on which you grow, in exchange for the whole world which was mine out there. Each little blade of grass was to me as a great tree, and each of your white leaves a flower. Alas! you only show me how much I have lost." "Oh if I could only comfort him," thought the daisy, but she could not move a leaf; yet the perfume from her leaves was stronger than is usual in these flowers, and the bird noticed it, and though he was fainting with thirst, and in his pain pulled up the green blades of grass, he did not touch the flower. The evening came, and yet no one appeared to bring the bird a drop of water; then he stretched out his pretty wings and shook convulsively, he could only sing, "Tweet, tweet," in a weak, mournful tone. His little head bent down towards the flower; the bird's heart was broken with want and pining. Then the flower could not fold its leaves as it had done the evening before, to sleep, but it drooped sick and sorrowful towards the earth. Not till morning did the boys come, and when they found the bird dead, they wept many and bitter tears; they dug a pretty grave for him, and adorned it with leaves of flowers. The bird's lifeless body was placed in a smart red box, and he was buried with great honour. Poor bird! while he was alive and could sing, they forgot him and allowed him to sit in his cage and suffer want, but now he was dead, they mourned for him with many tears, and buried him in royal state. But the turf with the daisy on it was thrown out into the dusty road. No one thought of the little flower which had felt more for the poor bird than any one else, and would have been so glad to help and console him, if she had been able to do so.

The Marsh King's Daughter

The storks tell their young ones ever so many fairy tales, all of them from the fen and the moss. Generally the tales are suited to the youngsters' age and understanding. The baby birds are pleased if they are told just 'kribly, krably, plurry-murry!' which they think wonderful; but the older ones will have something with more sense in it, or, at the least, a tale about themselves. Of the two oldest and longest tales which have been told among the storks, one we all know – that about Moses, who was placed by this mother in an ark on the waters of the Nile, was found by the king's daughter, and then was taught all learning, and became a great man, and no one knows where he was buried. Everybody has heard that tale.

But the other story is not known at all even now; perhaps because it is really a chimney-corner tale. It has been handed down by mother-stork to mother-stork for hundreds of years, and each in turn has told it better, till now we are telling it best of all.

The first pair of storks who knew it had their summer quarters on a Viking's log-house by the moor in Wendsyssel, which is in the county of Hjörring, near Skagen in Jutland, if we want to be accurate. To this day there is still an enormous great moss there. You can read all about it in your geography book. The moss lies where was once the bottom of the sea, before the great upheaval of the land; and now it stretches for miles, surrounded on all sides by watery meadows and quivering bog, with turf-moss cloudberries and stunted trees growing. A fog hangs over it almost continually, and till about seventy years ago wolves were still found there. It may certainly be called a wild moor, and you can imagine what lack of paths and what abundance of swamp and sea was there thousands of years ago. In that waste man saw ages back just what he sees to-day. The reeds were just as high, with the same kind of long leaves and purplish-brown, feathery flowers as they have now; the birches stood with white bark and fine, loose-hung leaves just as they now stand; and for the living creatures that came there, why, the fly wore its gauze suit of just the same cut as now, and the colour of the stork's dress was white and black, with red stockings. On the other hand, the men of that time wore different clothes from those we wear. But whoever it was, poor peasant or free hunter, that trod on the quagmire, it happened thousands of years ago just as it does to-day – in he went and down he sank, down to the Marsh King, as they called him, who reigned beneath in the great Moss Kingdom. He was called also the Mire King, but we will call him by the stork's name for him – Marsh King. People know very little about how he governed, but perhaps that is just as well.

Near to the moss, and right in the Liim Fjord, stood the Viking's log-house, with paved cellar and tower two storeys high. On the roof the storks had built their nest. Mother-stork sat on her eggs, and was positive they would turn out well.

One evening father-stork had been out for a long time, and when he came home he seemed excited and flurried.

'I've dreadful news for you!' he said to mother-stork.

'Don't get excited,' said she. 'Remember I'm sitting on my eggs, and I might be upset by it, and then the eggs would suffer.'

'You must know it!' he answered. 'She has come here, our landlord's daughter in Egypt! She has ventured on the journey here, and she is lost!'

'Why, she is of fairy descent! Tell me all about it; you know I can't bear to wait at this time, when I'm sitting.'

'Listen, mother. It's as you told me. She has believed what the doctor said, that the moor-flowers here could do her sick father good, and so she has flown here in a feather-dress with the other winged princesses, who have to come to the north every year to bathe and renew their youth. She has come, and she is lost!'

'You're getting too long-winded!' said mother-stork. 'The eggs may be chilled! I can't bear to be excited!'

'I have watched,' said father-stork, 'and in the evening, when I went into the reeds, where the quagmire is able to bear me, there came three swans. Something in the way they flew told me, "Watch; that isn't a real swan; it's only swan feathers." You know the feeling, mother, as well as I do; you can tell if it is right.'

'Yes, certainly,' said she; 'but tell me about the princess. I'm tired of hearing about the swan's feathers.'

'Here, in the middle of the moor, you know,' said father-stork, 'is a kind of lake; you can see a part of it if you stand up. There, by the reeds and the green quagmire, lies a great elder-stump. The three swans lighted on it, flapped their wings, and looked round them. Then one of them threw off her swan's plumage, and I saw it was our own princess, of our house in Egypt. Then she sat down, and she had no other covering than her own long, black hair. I heard her ask the two others to take great care of her swan-skin while she plunged under the water to gather a flower which she thought

she saw. They nodded, and lifted up the loose feather-dress. "I wonder what they mean to do with it," said I to myself; and no doubt she asked them the same. And she got an answer, something she could see for herself. They flew aloft with her feather-dress! "Sink down," they cried; "you shall

329

never fly in the swan-skin again; never see Egypt again! Stay in the moss!"
And so they tore her feather-dress into a hundred pieces, till the feathers
flew about as if it was snowing, and off flew the two good-for-nothing
princesses.'

'Oh, how dreadful!' said mother-stork. 'I can't bear to hear it. But, tell me,
what else happened?'

'Our princess moaned and wept. Her tears fell on the elder-stump, and it was
quite moved, for it was the Marsh King himself, who lives in the quagmire.
I saw the stump turn itself, so it wasn't only a trunk, for it put out long, muddy
boughs like arms. Then the unhappy girl was frightened, and sprang aside
into the quivering marsh, which will not bear me, much less her. In at once
she sank, and down with her went the elder-stump – it was he who pulled
her down. Then a few big black bubbles, and no trace of her left. She is
engulfed in the marsh, and will never return to Egypt with her flower. You
couldn't have borne to see it, mother!'

'You shouldn't have told me anything of the sort just now; it may affect the
eggs. The princess can take good care of herself. She'll get help easily enough.
Had it been you or I, there would have been an end of us.'

'However, I'll go day by day to see about it,' said father-stork; and so he
did.

The days and months went by. He saw at last one day that right from the
bottom of the marsh a green stalk pushed up till it reached the surface of
the water. Out of it grew a leaf, that grew wider and wider, and close to it
a bud put out. Then one morning, as the stork was flying over it, it opened,
with the sun's warmth, into a full-blown flower, in the middle of which lay
a beautiful child, a little girl, as if she were fresh from the bath. So like was
the child to the princess from Egypt, that at first the stork believed it to be
herself turned a child again. But when he thought it over, he decided that it
more likely to be the child of the princess and the Marsh King, and that
was why she was lying in a water lily.

'She mustn't be left lying there,' thought father-stork, 'and there are too
many already in my nest. But I have it! The Viking's wife has no children,
and she has often wished for a little one. Yes, I get the name for bringing the
babies; I will do it in sober truth for once! I'll fly to the Viking's wife with
the child. They'll be delighted!'

So the stork took the little girl, flew to the log-house, made a hole with his
beak in the window, with panes made of bladder, laid the child on the bosom
of the Viking's wife, and flew away to mother-stork to tell her all about it.
Her young ones heard it too, for they were now old enough.

'Listen; the princess is not dead. She has sent her little one up, and the child
has a home found for her.'

'Yes so I said from the first, said mother-stork 'Now think a little about your own children. It's almost time for our journey. I begin to feel a tingling under my wings. The cuckoo and the nightingale are off already, and I hear the quails chattering about it, and saying that we shall soon have a favourable wind. Our young ones are quite fit for training, I'm sure.'

Glad indeed was the Viking's wife when she woke in the morning to find the beautiful little child near her side. She kissed and fondled it, but it screamed with passion, and threw out its arms and legs, and seemed utterly miserable. At last it cried itself to sleep, and there it lay, one of the prettiest babies you could set eyes on.

The Viking's wife was so happy, so gay, so well, that she could not but hope that her husband and his men would return as suddenly as the little one had come, and so she and all her household busied themselves to get everything into order. The long coloured tapestries, which she and her maidens had woven with figures of their gods – Odin, Thor, Freya, as they were called – were hung up; the slaves were set to polish the old shields used for decoration; cushions were arranged on the benches and dry wood placed on the hearth in the middle of the hall, so that the fire could be lit in a moment. The Viking's wife took her share in the work, so that by the evening she was very tired, and slept soundly.

When she woke towards daybreak she was terribly frightened. The little child had vanished! She sprang up, lighted a brand, and looked everywhere around. There, just at the foot of the bed where she had lain, was, not a baby, but a great ugly toad! In utter disgust at it she took a heavy stick to kill it, but the creature looked at her with such wonderfully sad eyes that she could not destroy it. Once more she gazed round; the toad uttered a faint, mournful croak. She started, and sprang from the bedside to the window, and opened it. At that moment the sun rose, and cast its rays upon the bed and upon the great toad. All at once it seemed that the creature's wide mouth shrank, and became small and rosy; the limbs filled out into the most charming shape. It was her own beautiful babe that lay there, not the hideous reptile!

'What is this?' cried the dame. 'Was it an ill dream? Yes, there is my own sweet elfin child lying there!' She kissed it, and pressed it to her heart; but it fought and bit like a wild kitten!

The Viking, however, did not come that day, nor the next; for though he was one his way, the wind was against him as it blew to the south for the storks. Fair wind for one is foul for the other.

In those two days and nights the Viking's wife saw clearly how it was with her little child. And dreadful indeed was the spell that lay on it. By day it was as beautiful as an angel of light, but it had a bad, evil disposition. By

331

night, on the other hand, it was a hideous toad, quiet, sad, with sorrowful eyes. It had two natures, which changed with its outward form. And so it was that the baby, brought by the stork, had by daylight its mother's own rightful shape, but its father's temper; while again, night made the kinship with him evident in the bodily form, in which, however, dwelt the mother's mind and heart. Who could loose the spell cast by the power of witchcraft? The Viking's wife was worn and distressed about it, and her heart was heavy for the unhappy being, of whose condition she did not think that she dared tell her husband if he came home then, for he would certainly follow the custom and practice of the time, and expose the poor child on the high-road for any one that liked to take away. The good dame had not the heart to do this: her husband should see the child only by daylight.

One morning the wings of storks were heard above the roof. More than a hundred pairs of the birds had rested themselves for the night after their heavy exercise, and they now flew up, preparatory to starting southwards. 'All ready, and the wives and children?' was their cry.

'Oh, I'm so light,' said the young storks. 'My bones feel all kribly-krably, as if I was filled with live frogs! How splendid it is to have to go abroad!'

'Keep up in the flight,' said father and mother, 'and don't chatter so much; it tires the chest.'

And they flew.

At the same moment a horn sounded over the moor. The Viking had landed with all his men, returning laden with booty from the coasts of Gaul, where the people, like those of Britain, used to chant in their terror: 'From the rage of the Northmen, Lord, deliver us!' Guess what stir and festival now came to the Viking's stronghold near the moor! A barrel of mead was brought into hall; a huge fire was lighted; horses were slaughtered; everything went duly. The heathen priest sprinkled the slaves with warm blood, to begin their new life; the fire crackled; the smoke curled under the roof; the soot fell down from the beams – but they were used to that. Guests were invited, and received valuable gifts. Plots and treachery were forgotten; they drank deep and threw the picked bones in each other's faces in good-humoured horse-play. The bard – a kind of musician, but a warrior as well, who went with them, saw their exploits, and sang about them – gave them a song in which they heard all their warrior-deeds and feats of prowess. Each verse ended with the refrain:

'Wealth, kindred, life cannot endure,
But the warrior's glory standeth sure.'

And they all clashed upon their shields, and beat upon the table with knives and fists, and made great clamour.

333

The Viking's wife sat on the cross-bench in the open banqueting-hall. She wore a robe of silk, with bracelets of gold and beads of amber. She had put on her dress of state, and the bard sang of her, and told of the golden treasure she had brought to her wealthy lord, while he was delighted with the beautiful child, for he could see it by day in all its loveliness. He was well pleased with the baby's wildness, and said she would become a right warrior-maid, and fight as his champion. She did not even blink her eyes when a skilful hand cut her eyelashes with a sharp sword as a rough joke.

The barrel of mead was drained, and a second brought in, and all got well drunk, for they were folk who loved to drink their fill. They had a proverb: 'The kine know when to go to stall from pasture, but the fool never knows when he has had enough.' They knew it well enough, but know and do are different things. They had another proverb, too: 'The dearest friend grows wearisome when he outstays his welcome.' But on they stayed. Meat and mead are good: it was glorious! – and the slaves slept in the warm ashes, and dipped their fingers in the fat and licked them. Oh, it was a great time!

Once again that year the Viking went on a raid, though the autumn gales were rising. He led his men to the coast of Britain – 'just over the water,' he said; and his wife remained with the little girl. And truth to tell, the foster-mother soon grew fonder of the unhappy toad with the gentle eyes and deep sigh than of the beautiful child that fought and bit all about her.

The raw, dank autumn mist, 'Mouthless,' which devours the leaves lay over forest and moor; 'Bird Featherless,' as they called the snow, flew closely all around; winter was nigh at hand. The sparrows took the storks' nests for themselves, and criticised the ways of the late owners during their absence. And where were mother- and father-stork and their young ones all the time? Down in the land of Egypt, where the sun shone warm, as it does on a fine summer's day with us. Tamarinds and acacias bloomed round them; the crescent of Mahomet gleamed bright from the cupolas of the mosques; pairs and pairs of storks sat on the slender turrets, and rested after their long journey. Great flocks of them had built nest by nest on the huge pillars and broken arches of temples and forgotten cities. The date-palm raised its foliage on high, as if to keep off the glare of the sun. Grey-white pyramids stood out against the clear sky across the desert, where the ostrich raced at speed, and the lion crouched with great, wise eyes, and saw the marble sphinx that lay half-buried in the sand. The Nile flood had retired; the whole bed of the river was swarming with frogs, and to the stork family that was quite the best thing to be seen in the country. The young ones thought their eyes must be playing them tricks, it all seemed so wonderful.

'We always have it just like this in our warm country,' said mother-stork; and the young ones felt their appetites grow.

'Will there be anything more to see?' said they. 'Shall we go much farther into the country?'

'There is nothing better to see,' said mother-stork. 'At that green border is only a wild wood, where the trees crowd one upon another, and are entangled together with thorny creepers. Only an elephant with his clumsy legs can make a way there. The snakes are too large for us, and the lizards too lively. If you try to go into the desert you get your eyes full of sand in fair weather, and if there is much wind, you find yourself buried under a sand-heap. No, this is the best place. Here are frogs and locusts. I shall stop here, and you must stay with me.' And they stayed.

The old ones sat in their nest on the slender minaret and rested themselves, while yet they were busy preening their feathers and rubbing their beaks on their red-stockinged legs. They would raise their necks, bow gravely, and hold up their heads with their high foreheads, fine, smooth feathers, and brown eyes glancing sharply. The young hen-storks walked gravely about among the coarse reeds, stealing glances at the other young storks, and devouring a frog at every third step, or else a small snake, which they found so good for their health, and so tasty. The young males began to quarrel, beat each other with their wings, pecked, yes, stabbed till the blood flowed! And so one and another got betrothed, for that was the whole purpose of life. They built nests, and from that sprang new quarrels, for in hot countries tempers are so quick! Nevertheless, it was all delightful, especially to the old ones. Everything that one's own youngsters do becomes them. Every day there was sunshine; every day was so much taken up with eating that there was hardly time to think of amusement.

But inside the rich palace of their Egyptian landlord, as they called him, joy was unkown. Rich and mighty lord, there he lay on a couch, his limbs rigid, stretched out like a mummy, in the midst of the great hall with its many-coloured walls; it looked just as if he was lying in a tulip. His kinsmen and servants stood around him; he was not dead; you could not call him alive; he existed. The healing moss-flower from the northern land, which should have been searched for and gathered by her who loved him most dearly, would never be brought. His young and beautiful daughter, who flew in swan's-plumage over sea and land, far towards the north, would never return. 'She is dead and gone!' the two swan-maidens had told him on their return. They had invented a whole history of it. Said they: –

'We all three flew high in the air: a hunter saw us and shot an arrow; it struck our friend, and singing her farewell, like a dying swan, she slowly sank, in the midst of a forest lake. There we buried her, near the shore of the lake, under a fragrant weeping-birch. But we took our revenge! We bound fire under the wings of a swallow which had built under the hunter's thatched roof! The thatch caught; the house blazed up! He was burned in it, and the light shone over the lake as far as the drooping birch tree under which she is buried. She will never come back to the land of Egypt.'

And so they both wept; and the father-stork, when he heard it, chattered with his beak till it rattled again.

'Lies and make-up!' said he. 'I have a great mind to drive my beak into their hearts.'

'And break it off!' said mother-stork. 'And what good would that do? Think first of yourself and your own family; everything else is of no consequence!'

'However, I will seat myself on the edge of the open court in the morning, when all the learned doctors are met to talk about the illness. Perhaps they will come a little nearer the truth.'

And the learned doctors came together, and talked and talked all about, so that the stork could not make head or tail of it – nor did anything come of it for the sickness, or for the daughter in the moor; but, nevertheless, we shall be glad to hear something about it, for we are obliged to listen to a great deal.

But now it will be a very good thing to learn what had gone before this meeting, in order to understand the story better, for at least we know as much as father-stork.

'Love brings life! The highest love supports the highest life! Only through love will he be able to secure the preservation of his life!' was what they said; and very wisely and well said it was, according to the learned.

'That's a pretty thought!' said father-stork.

'I don't rightly understand it!' said mother-stork, 'and it isn't my fault, but the expressions! However, be that as it may, I've something else to think about!'

Then the learned men had spoken of love for one thing to another, of the difference there is between the affection of lovers and that of parent and child; of the love of plant and sunbeam, where the rays of the sun touch the bud and the young shoot thus comes forth – all this was expounded at such great length and in so learned a way that it was impossible for father-stork to follow it, much less to repeat it. He was quite thoughtful about it, and half closed his eyes and stood on one leg a whole day afterwards; such learning was too heavy for him to bear.

However, he understood one thing. He had heard both the common folk and those of the highest rank say the same thing from the bottom of their hearts – that it was a great misfortune for thousands of people, for the

336

country at large, that this man should be ill and not recover; it would be a joy and blessing if he were restored to health. 'But where does the flower of health grow for him?' that was what they had all inquired. They sought it from the scrolls of wisdom, from the twinkling stars, and from the winds; they had asked in all byways where they might find it, and at last the learned and wise announced, as we have said: 'Love brings forth life, the life of a father,' and so they said more than they themselves understood. They repeated it, and wrote it as a prescription: 'Love brings forth life'; but how was the thing to be done from this prescription? There lay the difficulty. At length they came to an agreement about it; the help must come from the princess, who was attached to her father with her whole soul and heart. And then they decided how it was to be brought about (all this was more than a year and a day before): she must go by night, at the new moon, to the marble sphinx near the desert, must clear away the sand from the door with her feet, and then go through the long passage that led into the middle of one of the great pyramids, where in his mummy-case lay one of the mighty kings of old, surrounded by splendour and magnificence. Here she was to hold her ear to the lips of the dead, and then it would be revealed to her how she was to gain life and health for her father.

All this she had done, and had learned in vision that, from the deep marsh in the land of Denmark, a spot most clearly indicated, she might bring home the marsh-flower, which there in the depth of the water had touched her breast. Then he would be healed. So she flew in swan's plumage from the land of Egypt to the moor.

You see, father-stork and mother-stork were aware of all this, and now we know the story more fully than before. We remember that the Marsh King dragged her down to him; we know that for those at home she is dead and gone; only the wisest of them all said still, with mother-stork: 'She takes good care of herself!' and they were obliged to wait, for that was all they knew about it.

'I believe I can steal the swans' plumage from the two good-for-nothing princesses!' said father-stork, 'then they will not be able to go to the moor to work mischief. I will hide the swans' skins themselves till they are wanted.'

'Where will you hide them?' asked mother-stork.

'In our nest on the moor!' said he. 'I and the youngest of our brood can be helped along with them, and if they are troublesome to us, there are plenty of places on the way where we can hide them till next time of moving. One swan's dress would be enough for her, but two are better; it is well to have plenty of luggage in a northern climate!'

'You will get no thanks for it!' said mother-stork. 'However, you are the master. I have nothing to say, except when I am sitting.'

In the Viking's stronghold near the moor, whither the storks flew at the spring, the little girl had received her name. They had called her Helga, but that was far too sweet for such a disposition as the one possessed by this most beautiful child. Month after month it became more evident, and as years went by – whilst the storks pursued the same journey, in autumn towards the Nile, in spring towards the moor – the little child became a grown girl, and before people thought of it, she was in her sixteenth year, and the most beautiful of maidens. But the fruit was a beautiful shell, the kernel hard and rough. She was wilder than most people even in that hard gloomy age.

It was a delight to her to splash with her white hands in the hot blood of the horse which had been slaughtered as a sacrifice; in her wildness she bit off the neck of the black cock which should have been slain by the heathen priest; and she said in sober earnest to her foster-father: –

'If thine enemy came and tied a rope to the beams of the roof, and lifted it over thy chamber, whilst thou wast asleep, I should not wake thee, even if I could! I would not hear it, my blood still so hums in my ears where thou didst slap me years ago! Thou! I remember!'

But the Viking did not believe what she said; he was, like the others, infatuated with her beauty; and he did not know how disposition and appearance changed in little Helga. She would sit without a saddle, as if she had grown to the horse, when it galloped at full speed; and she would not leap off, even when it fought with other vicious horses. In all her clothes she would often cast herself from the bank into the strong current of the fjord and swim to meet the Viking when his boat was steering towards the land. She cut off the longest lock from her beautiful long hair, and made it into a string for her bow. 'Self-made is well made!' she said.

The Viking's wife, according to the age and custom, was strong in will and in disposition, but towards the daughter she seemed a mild, anxious woman, for she knew that the dreadful child was bewitched.

When her mother stood on the balcony, or walked out into the courtyard, it seemed as if Helga took an evil delight in placing herself on the edge of the well, extending her arms and legs, and then leaping plump into the narrow, deep hole, where she, with her frog-nature, dived, and rose again, crawled out, just as if she was a cat, and came, dripping with water, into the lofty hall, so that the green leaves which were scattered on the floor floated about in the watery stream.

But there was one bond that restrained little Helga, and that was the dusk of the evening. Then she became quiet and pensive, and would allow herself to be called and led. She seemed to be drawn by some internal feeling to her mother, and when the sun went down and the transformation without and within her took place, she sat there quiet and melancholy, shrunken together into the figure of a toad. Her body, indeed, was now far larger than that creature's, but it was only so much the more disgusting. She looked like a miserable dwarf with frog's head, and web between the fingers. There was something of the deepest melancholy in the expression of her eyes; she had no voice but a hollow moan, just like a child that sobs in its dreams. The Viking's wife could then take her on her knees: she forgot the ugly form, and looked only at the sorrowful eyes, and more than once she said: –

'I could wish almost that thou wast always my dumb frog-child! Thou art more frightful to look at when thy beauty returns to thee.'

And she wrote runes against witchcraft and disease, and cast them over the wretched girl, but she saw no change.

'Now that she is a full-grown woman, and so like the Egyptian mother,' said father-stork, 'one could not believe that she was once so little that she lay in a water-lily. We have never seen her mother since! She did not take care of herself, as you and the learned men thought. Year out, year in, I have flown now in all directions over the moor, but she has never made any sign. Yes, let me tell you that every year when I have come up here some

339

days ahead of you, to mend the nest and put one thing and another straight, I have flown for a whole night, like an owl or a bat, to and fro over the open water, but it was no use! Nor have the two swan-dresses been any use which the young ones and I dragged hither from the land of the Nile. Toilsome work it was, and it took us three journeys to do it. They have now lain for many years at the bottom of the nest, and if such a disaster as a fire should happen at any time, and the log-house be burnt, they would be lost!'

'And our good nest would be lost also!' said mother-stork. 'You think too little of that, and too much of the feather-dress, and your moss-princess! You had better take it to her and stay in the bog! You are a useless father to your own family; I have said that ever since I sat on an egg for the first time! I only hope that we or our young ones may not get an arrow in the wing from that mad Viking girl! She does not know what she is doing. We have lived here a little longer than she, she should remember! We never forget our obligations; we pay our taxes yearly, a feather, an egg, and a young one, as is right. Do you think, when she is outside, I feel inclined to go down there, as in the old days, and as I do in Egypt, where I am half a companion with them, without their forgetting me, and peep into tub and pot? No, I sit up here worrying myself about her – the hussy ! – and about you too! You ought to have let her lie in the water-lily, and there would have been an end of her!'

'You are kinder than your words!' said father-stork. 'I know you better than you know yourself.'

And so he gave a jump, two heavy strokes of his wings, stretched his legs behind him, and off he flew. He sailed away, without moving his wings. At a good distance off he gave a powerful stroke; the sun shone on his white feathers; he stretched his neck and head forward! That was speed and flight!

'But he is still the handsomest of them all!' said the mother-stork, 'only I don't tell him that.'

Early that autumn the Viking came home with spoil and captives. Among these was a young Christian priest, one of those men who preached against the idols of the northern countries. Often at that period did the talk in the hall and in the bower of the women refer to the new faith, which had made its way into all the countries of the south, and by the holy Anskarius had brought even to Haddeby on the Schlei. Helga herself had heard of the faith in the White Christ, who out of love to men had given Himself to save them; but for her, as they say, it had gone in at one ear and out at the other. She seemed to have only a perception of that word 'love' when she crouched in that closed room in her miserable frogform. But the Viking's wife had listened to it, and felt herself wonderfully affected by the story and tradi-

340

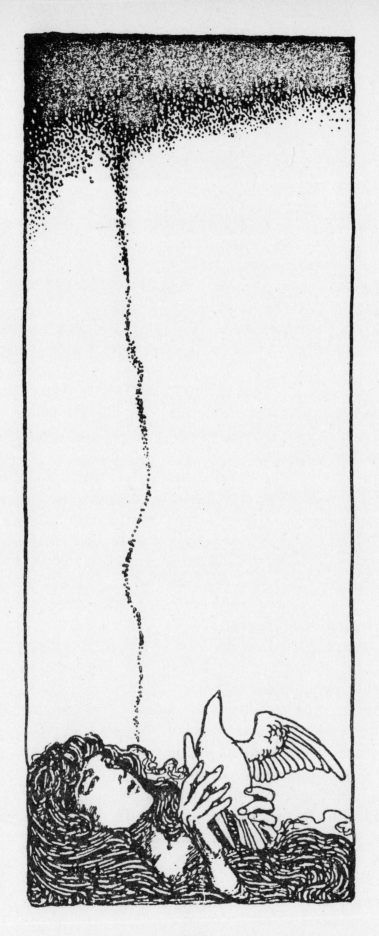

tions of the Son of the only true God. The men, on coming home from their expedition, had told of the splendid temples of costly hewn stone, erected for Him whose message was love; and they brought home with them a pair of heavy golden vessels, elaborately pierced, and with a fragrant odour about them, for they were censers, which the Christian priests used to swing before the altar where no blood was ever shed, but wine and consecrated bread changed into His body and blood who had given Himself for generations yet unborn.

In the deep paved cellar of the log house the young captive Christian priest was confined, his feet and hands securely bound. The Viking's wife said that he was 'as fair as Baldur,' and she was touched by his distress; but young Helga wished that a rope should be drawn through his legs, and that he should be tied to the tails of wild oxen.

'Then I would set the dogs loose. Halloo! away over bog and fen, out to the moor! That would be jolly to see! jollier still to be able to follow him on his course!'

But the Viking did not choose that he should be put to death that way, but, as a denier and opposer of the high gods, he should be offered the next morning on the blood-stone in the grove – the first time that a human sacrifice had been offered there.

Young Helga asked that she might sprinkle the images of the gods and the people with his blood. She sharpened her gleaming knife, and when one of the great, ferocious dogs, of which there were a good many in the court-yard, ran across her feet, she drove the knife into its side. 'That is to test it,' said she; and the Viking's wife looked sadly at the wild, ill-tempered girl, and, when the night came, and the beautiful bodily form of her daughter was changed for the beauty of soul, she spoke glowing words of sorrow to her from her own afflicted spirit.

The hideous toad with the goblin's body stood before her, and fixed its brown, sorrowful eyes on her; listening and seeming to understand with the intelligence of a human being.

'Never, even to my husband, has a word fallen from my tongue about the twofold nature I endure in thee,' said the Viking's wife. 'There is more pity in my heart for thee than I could have believed! Great is the love of a mother; but affection never comes into thy mind! Thy heart is like the cold clod! Whence didst thou then come into my house?'

At that the hideous form trembled and shook. It seemed as if the word touched some connexion between body and soul; great tears came into its eyes.

'Thy bitter trial will come some time!' said the Viking's wife; 'and terrible will it be for me! Better hadst thou been abandoned on the highway as a child, and the night-frost had lulled thee into death!' And the Viking's wife wept bitter tears, and, wrathful and sad, passed behind the loose curtains which hung over the beam and divided the room.

The shrunken toad sat alone in the corner. There was silence, but after a short interval there came from her breast a half-smothered sigh. It was as if, painfully, a soul awoke to life in a corner of her heart. She took one step forward, listened, took another step, and then with her awkward hands she seized the heavy bar that was placed before the door. Gently she put it back, and quietly she drew out the peg that was stuck in over the latch. She took the lighted lamp that stood in front of the rooms; it seemed as if a strong will gave her power. She drew the iron pin out of the bolted shutter, and moved gently towards the prisoner. He was asleep. She touched him with her cold, damp hand, and when he awoke and saw that hideous form, he shuddered, as if at an evil vision. She drew her knife, severed his bonds, and made signs to him to follow her.

He called upon the holy Name, made the sign of the cross, and as the figure stood unchanged, he repeated the words of the Bible: –

'"The Lord will preseve him and keep him alive: the Lord will deliver him in time of trouble." Who art thou? Whence is this reptile shape that yet is so full of deeds of compassion?'

The toad-figure beckoned and guided him behind sheltering curtains by a solitary way out to the stable, pointed at a horse; he mounted it, and she seated herself before him and held on by the mane of the animal. The prisoner understood her, and they rode away at a quick trot, by a path he would never have discovered, out to the open heath.

He forgot her hideous form, for the favour and mercy of the Lord were acting through this hobgoblin. He offered up pious prayers, and began to sing holy songs; and she trembled; was it the power of the prayers and hymns that acted upon her? or was it the coldness of the morning which was so quickly coming? What was it that she felt? She raised herself up in the breeze, and wished to stop the horse and spring off; but the Christian priest held her fast with all his strength, and sang aloud a Psalm, as if that would have power to loose the spell that held her in that hideous frog shape, and the horse galloped forward yet more wildly. The heaven became red; the first ray of the sun shot through the cloud, and with that clear spring of light came the change of form – she was the beautiful young girl with the demoniac, evil temper! In his arms he held a peerless maiden, and in utter terror he sprang from the horse and stopped it, for he thought he was encountering a new and deadly witchcraft. But young Helga at the same time leapt to the ground; the short child's frock reached only to her knees; she drew the sharp knife from her belt, and rushed at the startled man.

'Let me get at you!' she cried; 'let me get at you, and you shall feel the knife. Yes, you are as pale as hay! Slave! Beardless boy!'

She pressed him hard; they were engaged in a severe conflict, but it was as if an unseen power gave strength to the Christian. He held her fast, and the old oak tree hard by came to his help, for its roots, half loosened from the earth, caught her feet as they slipped under them. A spring gushed forth quite close to them; he sprinkled her with the fresh water on breast and face, and charged the unclean spirit to come out of her, signing her with the cross, according to the Christian rite. But the water of baptism had no power there, where the spring of faith had not yet arisen within.

Yet herein also was he strong; more than a man's strength against the rival power of evil lay in his act, and as if it overwhelmed her, she dropped her arms, looked with a surprised glance and pale cheeks at him, who seemed a powerful sorcerer, strong in wizardry and secret lore. They were dark runes which he spoke, mystic signs which he was making in the air! She would not have blinked if he had swung an axe or a sharp knife before her eyes, but she did when he made the sign of the cross on her forehead and breast; she now sat like a tame bird, her head bowed down on her bosom.

Gently he told her of the work of love she had done for him in the night, that she had come in the hideous skin of a frog, and had loosed his bonds, and brought him out to light and life. He said that she also was bound – bound in a closer bondage than he had been, but she, too, with him should come to light and life. He would bring her to Haddeby, to the holy Anskarius. There, in the Christian city, the enchantment would be broken. But he would not dare to carry her in front of him on the horse, although she herself was willing to sit there.

'You must sit behind me on the horse, not in front of me! Thy witch-beauty has a power that is from the evil one. I dread it – and yet there is victory for me in Christ!'

He bent his knees and prayed gently and earnestly. It was as if the silent glades of the forest were consecrated thereby into a holy church. The birds began to sing as if they belonged to a new brotherhood; the mint poured forth its fragrance as if it would take the place of incense. The priest proclaimed aloud the words of Holy Writ: –

'" The Dayspring from on high hath visited us, to give light to them that sit in darkness and in the shadow of death, and to guide our feet into the way of peace!"'

And he spoke about the longing of the whole Creation, and whilst he spoke the horse, which had carried them in its wild race, stood quiet, and shook the great brambles, so that the ripe, juicy berries fell on little Helga's hand, offering themselves for her refreshment.

Patiently she let herself be lifted on to the back of the horse, and sat there like one who walks in his sleep, who is not awake, but yet is not moving in his dream. The Christian fastened two boughs together with a strip of bark to form a cross, and held it aloft in his hands. So they rode through the forest, which became denser as the way grew deeper, or rather, there was no way at all. Sloes grew across the path; one was obliged to ride around them. The spring did not become a running brook, but a standing bog, and one had to ride around that. There was strength and refreshment in the fresh forest air; there was not less power in the word of gentleness which sounded in faith and Christian love, in the heartfelt desire to bring the possessed to light and life.

They say that the drops of rain can hollow the hard stone, the billows of the sea can in time wear smooth the broken, sharp-edged pieces of rock. The dew of Grace, which had descended upon little Helga, pierced the hardness and rounded the ruggedness of her nature, although it was not yet evident, and she was not yet aware of it herself. But what does the germ in the earth know of the refreshing moisture and the warm rays of the sun, while yet it is hiding within itself plant and flower?

As a mother's song for her child imperceptibly fastens itself into its mind, and it babbles single words after her, without understanding them, although they afterwards collect themselves in its thoughts, and become clear in the course of time, so in her the Word worked which is able to create.

They rode out of the forest, away over the heath, again through pathless forest, and towards evening they met some robbers.

'Where have you stolen that fair maiden?' they shouted; they stopped the horse, and snatched the two riders from it, for they were strong men. The priest had no other weapon than the knife which he had taken from little Helga to defend himself with; one of the robbers swung his axe, but the young Christian avoided it, and lightly sprang aside, or he would have been struck; but the edge of the axe sank deep into the horse's neck, so that the blood streamed out, and the animal fell to the earth. Then little Helga started, as if awakened out of a long, deep meditation, and threw herself down on the expiring animal. The Christian priest placed himself before her in order to defend her, but one of the robbers dashed a ponderous iron mace against his forehead, crushing it. The blood and brains spurted around, and he fell dead to the earth.

The robbers seized little Helga by her white arm. At that moment the sun went down, and as the last ray faded, she was changed to a hideous toad. Her greenish mouth opened across half her face; her arms became thin and slimy, and her hands grew broad an covered with webbing. Terror seized the robbers at the sight. She stood among them, a hideous monster; then, frog-like, hopped away, with bounds higher than she was herself, and vanished in the thicket. The robbers knew it for an evil trick of Loge, or secret magic art, and hurried away in affright.

The full moon was already rising, and soon shone forth in splendour, and little Helga crept forth from the thicket in the skin of a wretched toad. She stood by the bodies of the Christian priest and of the horse, and she looked at them with eyes that seemed to weep. Her frog's head uttered a moan like a child beginning to cry. She threw herself now upon one, now upon the other; she took water in her hand, which the webbed skin had made larger and more hollow, and poured it over them. They were dead, and would remain dead; she understood that. Wild animals would soon come and devour their bodies; but that must not be! So she dug in the earth as deep as she could. To open a grave for them was her wish, but she had nothing to dig it with except a strong bough of a tree and her weak hands; but on them there was webbing stretched between her fingers. She tore it, and the blood flowed. These means would be of no use, she could see. Then she took water and washed the dead man's face, covered it with fresh green leaves, fetched great boughs and laid them over him, shook leaves between them, then took the heaviest stones she was able to lift, laid them over the dead bodies, and filled up the openings with moss. Then the mound seemed strong and protected, but this arduous task had occupied the entire night – the sun now burst forth, and little Helga stood in all her beauty, with bleeding hands, and, for the first time, with tears on her flushed maiden cheeks.

In this transformation, it seemed as if the two natures struggled within her. She trembled, and gazed around her as if she had awoke from a frightful dream. Running to a slender beech, she held fast to it for support, then climbed to the top of the tree, as lithely as a cat, and clung fast to it. There she sat like a frightened squirrel, sat there all through the long day in the deep solitude of the forest, where all is still and deathlike as they say. Yet a pair of butterflies fluttered about at play or in quarrel; there were ant-hills close by with many hundreds of busy little creatures that crowded backwards and forwards. Countless gnats danced in the air, swarm upon swarm; hosts of buzzing flies chased each other about; birds, dragon-flies, and other small winged creatures filled the air. The earth-worm crept out from the moist soil, the mole raised itself above the ground. In all else it was still and death-like around, or what one calls death-like indeed! Nothing took any notice of little Helga, except the jays, which flew screaming around the top of the tree where she was sitting. They jumped along the branches near her in daring inquisitiveness. One glance of her eye was enough to chase them away again; but they could not quite make her out, neither could she understand herself.

When evening was near, and the sun began to go down, her approaching change called her to movement again. She let herself slide down from the tree, and when the last ray of the sun disappeared, she sat there in the toad's shrunken form, with the webbed skin of her hands lacerated, but her eyes now sparkled with a brilliancy of beauty which they had scarcely possessed before, even in her beautiful human shape. They were now the gentle eyes of a pious maiden that looked from behind the reptile's outward shape, and told of a deepened mind, of a true human heart. The beautiful eyes swam with tears, heavy tears that relieved her heart.

The cross of boughs bound together with a strip of bark, the last work of him who now lay dead and buried, was still lying on the grave she had made. Little Helga now took it, at some unprompted impulse, and planted it amongst the stones, over him and the slain horse. The sadness of the recollection brought tears to her eyes, and with the grief in her heart she traced the same sign in the earth around the grave that so honourably enclosed the dead. As with both hands she traced the sign of the cross, the webbing fell off like a torn glove! She washed herself in the water of the spring, and looked with astonishment at her fine white hands. Again she made the sign of the cross in the air between herself and the grave; her lips quivered, her tongue moved, and that Name, which she had heard pronounced most frequently on her ride through the forest, came audibly from her mouth – she said, 'Jesus Christ!'

The toad's skin fell off: she was a beautiful young maiden; but her head drooped wearily, her limbs needed repose – she slept.

Her slumber was short; at midnight she awoke. The dead horse was standing before her, shining, and full of life, that gleamed in light from its eyes and from its wounded neck. Close by she saw the murdered Christian priest, 'more beautiful than Baldur!' as the Viking's wife would have said; and he appeared surrounded with a glory of fire.

There was an earnest look in his large, gentle eyes, just and searching, so penetrating a gaze that it seemed to shine into the inmost recesses of her heart. Little Helga trembled before it, and her memory was awakened with a power as if it was the Day of Judgment. Every kind action that had been done for her, every kindly word that had been spoken to her, seemed endued with life; she understood that it was mercy which had taken care of her during her days of trial, in which the child of spirit and clay works and strives. She owned that she had only followed the bent of her own desire, and had done nothing on her own part. Everything had been given to her, everything had been allowed, so to speak. She bowed herself humbly,

ashamed before Him who alone can read the hidden things of the heart; and in that instant there seemed to come to her a firy touch of purifying flame – the flame of the Holy Spirit.

'Thou daughter of the mire,' said the Christian priest, 'from the mire, from the earth thou art sprung; from earth thou shalt again arise. The fire within thee returns in personality to its source; the ray is not from the sun, but from God. No soul shall perish, but far distant is the time when life shall be merged in eternity. I come from the land of the dead; so shalt thou at some time travel through the deep valley to the shining hill-country, where grace and fulness dwell. I may not lead thee to Hadde for Christian baptism. First thou must burst the water-shield over the deep moorland, and draw up the living root that gave thee life and cradled thee. Thou must do thy work before the consecration may come to thee.'

And he lifted her on to the horse, handed her a golden censer, like that which she had seen in the Viking's castle, from which there came a sweet, strong fragrance. The open wound on the forehead of the slain shone like a radiant diadem. He took the cross from the grave, raised it on high; and now they went off through the air, over the rustling forest, then over the mounds where the warriors were buried, sitting on their dead steeds; and these majestic forms arose, and rode out to the tops of the hills. A broad golden hoop with a gold knob gleamed on their foreheads in the moonlight, and their cloaks fluttered in the wind. The dragon that sits and broods over treasure raised its head, and looked after them. Dwarfs peered forth from the hills, and the furrows swarmed with red, blue, and green lights, like a cluster of sparks in a burnt piece of paper.

Away over wood and heath, stream and pool, they flew to the moor, and floated over that in great circles. The Christian priest raised the cross on high; it shone like gold, and from his lips came the eucharistic chant. Little Helga sang with him, as a child joins in the song of its mother. She swung the censer, and there came a fragrance as if from an altar, so powerful, so subtly operating, that the rushes and reeds of the moor put forth their flowers. All the germs sprang up from the deep soil; everything that had life arose. A veil of water-lilies spread itself like an embroidered carpet of flowers, and on it lay a sleeping woman, young and beautiful. Little Helga thought she saw herself mirrored in the still water; but it was her mother that she saw, the Marsh King's wife, the princess from the waters of the Nile.

The dead Christian priest bade the sleeper be lifted on to the horse; but that sank under the burden as if its body was only a winding-sheet flying in the breeze; but the sign of the cross made the airy phantom strong, and all three rode to the firm ground.

A cock crowed in the Viking's stronghold. The phantoms rose up in the mist, and were dispersed in the wind, but mother and daughter stood there together.

'Is that myself that I see in the deep water?' said the mother.

'Is that myself that I see in the bright shield?' exclaimed the daughter; and they came close together, breast to breast in each other's arms. The mother's heart beat strongest, and she understood it all.

'My child! My own heart's flower! My lotus from the deep waters!'

And she embraced her child, and wept over her; and the tears were as a baptism of new life and affection for little Helga.

'I came hither in a swan's skin, and I took it off,' said the mother. 'I sank through the quivering swamp, deep into the mire of the bog, that enclosed me as with a wall. But soon I found a fresher current about me; a power seemed to draw me ever deeper and deeper. I felt a pressure of sleep on my eyelids; I slept, I dreamt – I seemed to lie again in the pyramids of Egypt; but there still stood before me the moving elder-stump, which had frightened me on the surface of the moor. I looked at the crevices in the bark, and they shone forth in colours and became hieroglyphics – it was the case of a mummy which I was looking at. That burst, and out of it stepped a lord a thousand years old, a mummy form, black as pitch, shining black like a wood-snail or the slimy black mud – the Marsh King, or the mummy of the pyramid, I did not know which. He flug his arms about me, and I felt that I should die. When I first returned to life again, and my breast became warm, there was a little bird which beat its wings, and twittered and sang. It flew up from my breast towards the dark, heavy roof, but a long green band still fastened it to me. I heard and understood its longing notes: "Liberty! sunshine! to my father!" Then I thought of my father in the sunlit land of my home, my life, my affection! and I loosed the band and let him flutter away – home to his father. Since that hour I have not dreamed; I slept a long and heavy sleep till the moment when the sounds and fragrance arose and raised me.'

That green band from the mother's heart to the bird's wings, whither had it passed now? where was it lying cast away? Only the stork had seen it. The band was that green stalk; the knot was that shining flower which served as a cradle for the child who now had grown in beauty, and again reposed near the mother's heart.

And whilst they stood there in close embrace, the father-stork flew in circles about them, made speed to his nest, fetched from thence the feather-dresses kept for so many years and threw one over each of them; and they flew, and raised themselves from the earth like two white swans.

'Let us talk,' said father-stork, 'now that we can understand each other's speech, although the beak is cut differently on one bird and on the other! It is the most lucky thing possible that you came to-night. In the morning we should have been off, mother, and I, and the young ones! We are flying to the South! Yes, look at me! I am an old friend from the land of the Nile, and that is the mother; she has more in her heart than in her chatter. She always believed that the princess was only taken care of herself. I and the young ones have brought the swan-skins here. Well, how glad I am! And what a fortunate thing it is that I am here still! At daybreak we shall set off, a large party of storks. We fly in front; you can fly behind, and then you will not mistake the way. I and the young ones will then be able to keep an eye upon you!'

'And the lotus flower, that I ought to bring,' said the Egyptian princess, 'it flies in swan's plumage by my side! I have the flower of my heart with me; thus it has released itself. Homeward! homeward!'

But Helga said that she could not leave the land of Denmark till she had once more seen her foster-mother, the kind wife of the Viking. In Helga's thoughts came up every beautiful remembrance, every affectionate word, every tear which her foster-mother had shed, and it almost seemed at that instant as if she clung closest to that mother.

'Yes, we will go to the Viking's house,' said the stork-father. 'There I expect mother and the young ones. How they will open their eyes and chatter about it! Yes, mother doesn't say so very much; what she does is short and pithy, and so she thinks the best! I will sound the rattle directly, so that she will hear we are coming.'

And so father-stork chattered his beak, and flew with the swans to the Viking's stronghold.

Every one there was lying deep in slumber. The Viking's wife had not gone to rest till late that night; she was still in fear for little Helga, who had disappeared three days ago with the Christian priest. She must have helped him to escape, for it was her horse that was missing from the stable. By what power had all this been brought about? The Viking's wife thought about the wonderful works which she had heard were performed by the White Christ, and by those who believed in Him and followed Him. Her changing thoughts shaped themselves into a dream. It appeared to her that she was still sitting on her bed, awake, and meditating, and that darkness shrouded everything outside. A storm arose; she heard the rolling of the sea in the west and the east, from the North Sea and the waters of the Cattegat. That huge serpent which encircles the earth in the depths of the ocean shook convulsively; it was Ragnarök, the twilight of the gods, as the heathen called the last hour, when everything should pass away, even the high gods themselves. The trumpet sounded, and the gods rode forth over

the rainbow, arrayed in steel, to take part in the last contest. Before them flew the winged warrior-maidens, and behind them in array marched the forms of dead warriors. The whole sky was illuminated by the northern lights, but the darkness again prevailed. It was an appalling hour.

And close by the frightened Viking's wife little Helga sat on the floor in the hideous from of a toad, trembling and nestling herself up against her foster-mother, who took her on her lap and affectionately held her fast, although she seemed more hideous than a toad. The air was full of the sound of sword-strokes and the blows of maces, of arrows whizzing, as if a furious hail-storm was raging above them. The hour had come when earth and heaven should fail, the stars should fall, and everything be burned up in the fire of Surtr; but the dreamer knew that a new earth and heaven would come, and the corn wave where the sea now rolled over the barren sand bottom; that the God who cannot be named rules, and up to Him rose Valdur, the gentle and kind, loosed from the realm of death. He came – the Viking's wife saw him, and knew his face. It was the captive Christian priest. 'White Christ!' she cried aloud; and as she mentioned that Name she pressed a kiss on the hideous forehead of her frog-child; the toad's skin fell off, and little Helga stood there in all her beauty, gentle as she had never been before, and with beaming eyes. She kissed her foster-mother's hands, blessed her for all her care and affection with which she had surrounded her in the days of her distress and trial; thanked her for the thoughts to which she had given birth in her; thanked her for mentioning the Name which she repeated, 'White Christ!' and then little Helga rose up as a noble swan, her wings expanded themselves wide, wide, with a rustling as when a flock of birds of passage flies away!

With that the Viking's wife awoke, and still heard outside the same strong sound of wings. She knew that it was time for the storks to depart, and no doubt that was what she heard. Still, she wished to see them once before their journey, and to bid them farewell. She stood up, went out on to the balcony, and there she saw on the ridge of the out-house rows of storks, and round the courtyard and over the lofty trees crowds of others were flying in great circles. But straight in front of her, on the edge of the well, where little Helga had so often sat and frightened her with her wildness, two swans now sat and looked at her with intelligent eyes. Her dream came to her mind; it still quite filled her as if it had been reality. She thought of little Helga in the form of a swan, she thought of the Christian priest, and she felt a strange joy in her heart.

The swans beat their wings, and bent their necks, as if they wished so to salute her; and the Viking's wife stretched out her arms towards them as if she understood, and smiled at them through her tears.

Then, with a noise of wings and chattering, all the storks arose to start on their journey to the south.

'We cannot wait for the swans!' said mother-stork. 'If they wish to come with us they may; but we can't wait here till the plovers start! It is a very good thing to travel in family parties; not like the chaffinches and ruffs, where the males fly by themselves and the females by themselves; that is certainly not proper! And what are those swans flapping their wings for?'

'Every one flies in his own way!' said father-stork. 'The swans go in slanting line, the cranes in a triangle, and the plovers in a wavy, snake-like line.'

'Don't mention serpents when we are flying up here!' said mother-stork; 'it only excites the appetites of our young ones when they can't be satisfied.'

'Are those the high mountains down there which I have heard of?' asked Helga in the swan's skin.

'Those are thunder-clouds which drive below us,' said the mother.

'What are those white clouds which lift themselves so high?' asked Helga.

'Those are the everlasting snow-clad hills which you see,' said the mother; and they flew over the Alps, down towards the blue Mediterranean.

'Land of Africa! Coast of Egypt!' jubilantly sang the daughter of the Nile in her swan form, when, high in the air, she descried her native land, like a yellowish white, undulating streak.

And as the birds saw it, they hastened their flight.

'I smell the mud of the Nile and the wet frogs!' said mother-stork. 'It quite excites me! Yes, now you shall taste them; now you shall see the adjutant bird, the ibis, and the cranes! They all belong to our family, but they are not nearly so handsome as we are. They stick themselves up, especially the ibis; he is now quite pampered by the Egyptians – they make a mummy of him, and stuff him with aromatic herbs. I would rather be stuffed with live frogs, and so would you, and so you shall be. It is better to have something inside you while you live than to be in state when you are dead! That is my opinion, and that is always right!'

'Now the storks are come!' they said in the rich house on the bank of the Nile, where, in the open hall on soft cushions covered with a leopard's skin, the royal master lay outstretched, neither living nor dead, hoping for the lotus flower from the deep marsh in the north. Kinsmen and servants stood around him.

And into the hall flew two beautiful white swans, which had come with the storks! They threw off their dazzling feather-dress, and there stood two beautiful women, as much alike as two drops of dew! They bent down over the pale, withered old man; they put back their long hair, and when little Helga stooped over her grandfather, the colour returned to his cheeks, his eyes sparkled, and life came into his stiffened limbs. The old man raised himself healthy and vigorous; daughter and granddaughter held him in their arms as if they were giving him a morning salutation in their joy after a long, heavy dream.

And there was joy over all the house and in the storks' nest, but there it was chiefly over the good food, and the swarming hosts of frogs; and whilst the learned men made haste to note down in brief the history of the two princesses and the flower of health, which was such a great event and a blessing for house and country, the parent storks related it in their fashion to their own family, but not till they had all satisfied their hunger, or else they would have had something else to do than to listen to stories.

'Now you will become somebody!' whispered mother-stork; 'that is certain!' 'Well! what should I become?' said father-stork; 'and what have I done? A mere nothing!'

'You have done more than all the others! But for you and the young ones the two princesses would never have seen Egypt again, and made the old man well. You will become somebody! You will certainly receive a doctor's degree, and our young ones will bear it afterwards, and their young ones will have it in turn. You look already like an Egyptian doctor – in my eyes!'

The wise and learned expounded the fundamental idea, as they called it, that ran through the whole history: 'Love brings forth life!' – they gave that explanation in different ways – 'the warm sunbeam was the Egyptian princess, she descended to the Marsh King, and in their meeting the flower sprang forth –'

'I can't repeat the words quite right,' said father-stork, who had heard it from the roof, and was expected to tell them all about it in his nest. 'What they said was so involved, it was so clever, that they immediately received honours and gifts. Even the head cook obtained a high mark of distinction – that was for the soup!'

'And what did you receive?' inquired mother-stork; 'they ought not to forget the most important, and that is yourself. The learned have only chattered about it all, but your turn will come!'

Late that night, while peaceful slumber enwrapped the now prosperous house, there was one who was still awake; and that was not the father-sork, though he stood on one leg in the nest and slept like a sentinel. No, little Helga was awake. She leaned out over the balcony and gazed at the clear sky, with the great, bright stars, larger and purer in their lustre than she had seen them in the north, and yet the same. She thought of the Viking's wife by the moor, of her foster-mother's gentle eyes, and the tears she had shed over her poor toad-child, who now stood in the light and splendour of the stars by the waters of the Nile in the soft air of spring. She thought of the love in that heathen woman's breast, that love which she

356

had shown to a miserable creature who, in human form, was an evil brute, and in the form of an animal, loathsome to look at and to touch. She looked at the shining stars, and called to mind the splendour on the forehead of the dead man, when they flew away over forest and moor; tones resounded in her recollection, words she had heard pronounced when they rode away, and she sat as if paralysed – words about the great Author of Love, the highest Love, embracing all generations.

Yes, how much had been given, gained, obtained! Little Helga's thoughts were occupied, night and day, with all her good fortune, and she stood in contemplation of it like a child which turns quickly from the giver to all the beautiful presents that have been given; so she rose up in her increasing happiness, which could come and would come. She was indeed borne in mysterious ways to even higher joy and happiness, and in this she lost herself one day so entirely that she thought no more of the Giver. It was the strength of youthful courage that inspired her bold venture. Her eyes shone, but suddenly she was called back by a great clamour in the courtyard beneath. There she saw two powerful ostriches running hurriedly about in narrow circles. She had never before seen that creature, so great a bird, so clumsy and heavy. Its wings looked as if they were clipped, the bird itself as if it had been injured, and she inquired what had been done to it, and for the first time heard the tradition which the Egyptians relate about the ostrich.

The race had at one time been beautiful, its wings large and powerful; then, one evening, a mighty forest bird said to it: 'Brother, shall we fly to the river in the morning, if God will, and drink?' And the ostrich replied: 'I will.' When day broke they flew off, at first high up towards the sun – the eye of God – ever higher and higher, the ostrich far before all the others; it flew in its pride towards the light; it relied on its own strength, and not on the Giver; it did not say, 'If God will!' Then the avenging angel drew back the veil from the burning flame, and in that instant the bird's wings were burnt; it sank miserably to the earth. Its descendants are no longer able to raise themselves; they fly in terror, rush about in circles in that narrow space. It is a reminder to us men, in all our thoughts, in all our actions, to say: 'If·God will!'

And Helga thoughtfully bowed her head, looked at the hurrying ostrich, saw its fear, saw its silly delight at the sight of its own great shadow on the white sunlit wall. And deep seriousness fixed itself into her mind and thoughts. So rich a life, so full of prosperity, was given, was obtained – what would happen? What was yet to come?

The best thing: 'If God will!'

In the early spring, when the storks again started for the north, little Helga took her gold bracelet, scratched her name on it, beckoned to the stork-father, placed the golden circlet about his neck, and asked him to bear it to the Viking's wife, by which she would understand that her foster-daughter was alive, and that she was happy, and thought of her.

'That is heavy to carry!' thought the father-stork when it was placed around his neck; 'but one does not throw gold and honour on the high-road. They will find it true up there that the stork brings fortune!'

'You lay gold, and I lay eggs!' said the mother-stork; 'but you only lay once, and I lay every year! But it vexes me that neither of us is appreciated.'

'But we are quite aware of it ourselves, mother!' said father-stork.

'But you can't hang that on you,' said mother-stork. 'It neither gives us fair wind nor food.'

And so they flew.

The little nightingale, that sang in the tamarind-bush, also wished to start for the north immediately. Little Helga had often heard him up there near the moor; she wished to give him a message, for she understood the speech of birds when she flew in the swan's skin, and she had often since that time used it with the stork and the swallow. The nightingale would understand her, and she asked him to fly to the beech-forest on the peninsula of Jutland, where she had erected the grave of stones and boughs; there she asked him to bid all the small birds to protect the grave, and always to sing their songs around it. And the nightingale flew – and time flew also.

The eagle stood on the pyramid in the autumn, and saw a magnificent array of richly laden camels, with armed men in costly clothing, on snorting Arabian steeds, shining as white as silver, and with red quivering nostrils, their heavy thick manes hanging down about their slender legs. Rich visitors, a royal prince from the land of Arabia, beautiful as a prince ought to be, came to that noble house, where the storks' nest now stood empty, its former occupants now far away in the northern land, but soon to return. And they came exactly on that day which was most filled with joy and mirth. There was a grand wedding, and little Helga was the bride arrayed in silk and jewels; the bridegroom was the young prince from the land of Arabia; and the two sat highest at the table between the mother and grand-father. But she did not look at the bridegroom's brown, manly cheek, where his black beard curled; she did not look at his dark, fiery eyes, which were fastened upon her; she looked outwards and upwards towards the twinkling, sparkling stars, which beamed down from heaven.

Then there was a rustling sound of strong wing-strokes outside in the air – the storks had returned; and the old couple, however tired they might be with the journey, and however much they needed rest, still flew on to the railing of the verandah immediately they were aware whose festivity it was. They had already heard, at the frontier of the country, that little Helga had allowed them to be painted on the wall because they belonged to her history.

'That is very nicely borne in mind,' said father-stork.

'It is very little!' said the stork-mother; 'she could not have done less.'

And when Helga saw them, she got up and went out into the verandah to them to pat them on the back. The old storks curtsied with their necks, and the youngest of their young ones looked on, and felt themselves honoured.

And Helga looked up to the bright stars which shone clearer and clearer; and between them and her a form seemed to move still purer than the air, and seen through it, that hovered quite near her – it was the dead Christian priest; so he came on the day of her festivity, came from the Kingdom of Heaven.

'The splendour and glory which are there surpass everything that earth knows!' he said.

And little Helga prayed gently and from her heart, as she had never prayed before, that she only for one single minute might dare to look within, might only cast one single glance into the Kingdom of Heaven, to the Father of all.

And he raised her into the splendour and glory, in one current of sounds and thoughts; it was not only round about her that it shone and sounded, but within her. No words are able to describe it.

'Now we must return; you are wanted!' he said.

'Only one glance more!' she entreated; 'only one short minute!'

'We must go back to the earth; all the guests have gone away.'

'Only one glance! the last –'

And little Helga stood outside in the verandah; but all the torches outside were extinguished, all the lights in the wedding chamber were gone, the storks were gone, no guests to be seen, no bridegroom; everything seemed to be blown away in three short minutes.

Then Helga was filled with terror, and she went through the great, empty hall, into the next room. Strange soldiers were sleeping there. She opened a side door that led into her apartment, and when she expected to stand there, she found herself outside in the garden; but it was not like this before – the heaven was red and shining, it was towards daybreak.

Only three minutes in Heaven, and a whole night had passed on the earth! Then she saw the storks; she cried to them, speaking their language, and father-stork turned his head, listened, and drew near her.

'You are speaking our language!' said he; 'what do you want? Why do you come here, you strange woman?'

360

'It is I! it is Helga! Don't you know me? Three minutes ago we were talking together, yonder in the verandah.'

'That is a mistake!' said the stork; 'you must have dreamt it!'

'No, no!' she said, and reminded him of the Viking's stronghold and the moor, and of the journey hither!

Then father-stork blinked his eyes: 'That is a very old story. I have heard it from my great-great-great-grandmother's time! Yes, certainly, there was such a princess in Egypt from the land of Denmark, but she disappeared on the night of her wedding many hundreds of years ago, and never came back again. That you may read for yourself on the monument in the garden; there are sculptured both swans and storks, and at the top you yourself stand in white marble.'

It was indeed so. Little Helga saw it, understood it, and fell on her knees. The sun broke forth, and as in former times at the touch of its beams the toad form disappeared and the beautiful shape was seen, so she raised herself now at the baptism of light in a form of brighter beauty, purer than the air, a ray of light – to the Father of all.

Her body sank in dust; there lay a faded lotus-flower where she had stood.

'Then that was a new ending to the story!' said the father-stork. 'I had not at all expected it! but I rather like it!'

'I wonder what my young ones will say about it!' said the mother-stork.

'Yes, that is certainly the principal thing!' answered the father.

She Was Good for Nothing

The mayor stood at the open window. He looked smart, for his shirt-frill, in which he had stuck a breast-pin, and his ruffles, were very fine. He had shaved his chin uncommonly smooth, although he had cut himself slightly, and had stuck a piece of newspaper over the place. "Hark 'ee, youngster!" cried he.

The boy to whom he spoke was no other than the son of a poor washer-woman, who was just going past the house. He stopped, and respectfully took off his cap. The peak of this cap was broken in the middle, so that he could easily roll it up and put it in his pocket. He stood before the mayor in his poor but clean and well-mended clothes, with heavy wooden shoes on his feet, looking as humble as if it had been the king himself.

"You are a good and civil boy," said the mayor. "I suppose your mother is busy washing the clothes down by the river, and you are going to carry that thing to her that you have in your pocket. It is very bad for your mother. How much have you got in it?"

"Only half a quartern," stammered the boy in a frightened voice.

"And she has had just as much this morning already?"

"No, it was yesterday," replied the boy.

"Two halves make a whole," said the mayor. "She's good for nothing. What a sad thing it is with these people. Tell your mother she ought to be ashamed of herself. Don't you become a drunkard, but I expect you will though. Poor child! there, go now."

The boy went on his way with his cap in his hand, while the wind fluttered his golden hair till the locks stood up straight. He turned round the corner of the street into the little lane that led to the river, where his mother stood in the water by her washing bench, beating the linen with a heavy wooden bar. The floodgates at the mill had been drawn up, and as the water rolled rapidly on, the sheets were dragged along by the stream, and nearly over-turned the bench, so that the washerwoman was obliged to lean against it to keep it steady. "I have been very nearly carried away," she said; "it is a good thing that you are come, for I want something to strengthen me. It is cold in the water, and I have stood here six hours. Have you brought any-thing for me?"

The boy drew the bottle from his pocket, and the mother put it to her lips, and drank a little.

"Ah, how much good that does, and how it warms me," she said; "it is as good as a hot meal, and not so dear. Drink a little, my boy; you look quite pale; you are shivering in your thin clothes, and autumn has really come. Oh, how cold the water is! I hope I shall not be ill. But no, I must not be afraid of that. Give me a little more, and you may have a sip too, but only a sip; you must not get used to it, my poor, dear child." She stepped up to the bridge on which the boy stood as she spoke, and came on shore. The water dripped from the straw mat which she had bound round her body, and from her gown. "I work hard and suffer pain with my poor hands," said she, "but I do it willingly, that I may be able to bring you up honestly and truthfully, my dear boy."

At the same moment, a woman, rather older than herself, came towards them. She was a miserable-looking object, lame of one leg, and with a large false curl hanging down over one of her eyes, which was blind. This curl was intended to conceal the blind eye, but it made the defect only more visible. She was a friend of the laundress, and was called, among the neighbours, "Lame Martha, with the curl." "Oh, you poor thing; how you do work, standing there in the water!" she exclaimed. "You really do need something to give you a little warmth, and yet spiteful people cry out about the few drops you take." And then Martha repeated to the laundress, in a very few minutes, all that the mayor had said to her boy, which she had overheard; and she felt very angry that any man could speak, as he had done, of a mother to her own child, about the few drops she had taken; and she was still more angry because, on that very day, the mayor was going to have a dinner party, at which there would be wine, strong, rich wine, drunk by the bottle. "Many will take more than they ought, but they don't call that drinking! *They* are all right, but you are good for nothing indeed!" cried Martha. "And so he spoke to you in that way, did he, my child?" said the washer-woman, and her lips trembled as she spoke. "He says you have a mother who is good for nothing. Well, perhaps he is right, but he should not have said it to my child. How much has happened to me from that house!"

"Yes," said Martha; "I remember you were in service there, and lived in the house when the mayor's parents were alive; how many years ago that is. Bushels of salt have been eaten since then, and people may well be thirsty," and Martha smiled. "The mayor's great dinner-party to-day ought to have been put off, but the news came too late. The footman told me the dinner was already cooked, when a letter came to say that the mayor's younger brother in Copenhagen is dead."

"Dead!" cried the laundress, turning pale as death.

"Yes, certainly," replied Martha; "but why do you take it so much to heart? I suppose you knew him years ago, when you were in service there?"

"Is he dead?" she exclaimed. "Oh, he was such a kind, good-hearted man, there are not many like him," and the tears rolled down her cheeks as she spoke. Then she cried, "Oh, dear me; I feel quite ill: everything is going round me, I cannot bear it. Is the bottle empty?" and she leaned against the plank.

"Dear me, you are ill indeed," said the other woman. "Come, cheer up; perhaps it will pass off. No, indeed, I see you are really ill; the best thing for me to do is to lead you home."

"But my washing yonder?"

"I will take care of that. Come, give me your arm. The boy can stay here and take care of the linen, and I'll come back and finish the washing; it is but a trifle."

The limbs of the laundress shook under her, and she said, "I have stood too long in the cold water, and I have had nothing to eat the whole day since the morning. O kind Heaven, help me to get home; I am in a burning fever. Oh, my poor child," and she burst into tears. And he, poor boy, wept also, as he sat alone by the river, near to and watching the damp linen.

The two women walked very slowly. The laundress slipped and tottered through the lane, and round the corner, into the street where the mayor lived; and just as she reached the front of his house, she sank down upon the pavement. Many persons came round her, and Lame Martha ran into the house for help. The mayor and his guests came to the window.

"Oh, it is the laundress," said he; "she has had a little drop too much. She is good for nothing. It is a sad thing for her pretty little son. I like the boy very well; but the mother is good for nothing."

After a while the laundress recovered herself, and they led her to her poor dwelling, and put her to bed. Kind Martha warmed a mug of beer for her, with butter and sugar – she considered this the best medicine – and then hastened to the river, washed and rinsed, badly enough, to be sure, but she did her best. Then she drew the linen ashore, wet as it was, and laid it in a basket. Before evening, she was sitting in the poor little room with the laundress. The mayor's cook had given her some roasted potatoes and a beautiful piece of fat ham for the sick woman. Martha and the boy enjoyed these good things very much; but the sick woman could only say that the smell was very nourishing, she thought. By-and-by the boy was put to bed, in the same bed as the one in which his mother lay; but he slept at her feet, covered with an old quilt made of blue and white patchwork. The laundress felt a little better by this time. The warm beer had strengthened her, and the smell of the good food had been pleasant to her.

"Many thanks, you good soul," she said to Martha. "Now the boy is asleep, I will tell you all. He is soon asleep. How gentle and sweet he looks as he lies there with his eyes closed! He does not know how his mother has suffered; and Heaven grant he never may know it. I was in service at the counsellor's, the father of the mayor, and it happened that the youngest of his sons, the student, came home. I was a young wild girl then, but honest; that I can declare in the sight of Heaven. The student was merry and gay, brave and affectionate; every drop of blood in him was good and honourable; a better man never lived on earth. He was the son of the house, and I was only a maid; but he loved me truly and honourably, and he told his mother of it. She was to him as an angel upon earth; she was so wise and loving. He went to travel, and before he started he placed a gold ring on my finger; and as soon as he was out of the house, my mistress sent for me. Gently and earnestly she drew me to her, and spake as if an angel were speaking. She showed me clearly, in spirit and in truth, the difference there was between him and me. 'He is pleased now,' she said, 'with your pretty face; but good looks do not last long. You have not been educated like he has. You are not equals in mind and rank, and therein lies the misfortune. I esteem the poor,' she added. 'In the sight of God, they may occupy a higher place than many of the rich; but here upon earth we must beware of entering upon a false track, lest we are overturned in our plans, like a carriage that travels by a dangerous road. I know a worthy man, an artisan, who wishes to marry you. I mean Eric, the glovemaker. He is a widower, without children, and in a good position. Will you think it over?' Every word she said pierced my heart like a knife; but I knew she was right, and the thought pressed heavily upon me. I kissed her hand, and wept bitter tears, and I wept still more when I went to my room, and threw myself on the bed. I passed through a dreadful night; God knows what I suffered, and how I struggled. The following Sunday I went to the house of God to pray for light to direct my path. It seemed like a providence that as I stepped out of church Eric came towards me; and then there remained not a doubt in my mind. We were suited to each other in rank and circumstance. He was, even then, a man of good means. I went up to him, and took his hand, and said, 'Do you still feel the same for me?' 'Yes; ever and always,' said he. 'Will you, then, marry a maiden who honours and esteems you, although she cannot offer you her love? but that may come.' 'Yes, it will come,' said he; and we joined our hands together, and I went home to my mistress. The gold ring which her son had given me I wore next my heart. I could not place it on my finger during the daytime, but only in the evening, when I went to bed. I kissed the ring till my lips almost bled, and then I gave it to my mistress, and told her that the banns were to be put up for me and the

glovemaker the following week. Then my mistress threw her arms round me, and kissed me. She did not say that I was 'good for nothing;' very likely I was better then than I am now; but the misfortunes of this world were unknown to me then. At Michaelmas we were married, and for the first year everything went well with us. We had a journeyman and an apprentice, and you were our servant, Martha."

"Ah, yes, and you were a dear, good mistress," said Martha, "I shall never forget how kind you and your husband were to me.

"Yes, those were happy years when you were with us, although we had no children at first. The student I never met again. Yet I saw him once, although he did not see me. He came to his mother's funeral. I saw him, looking pale as death, and deeply troubled, standing at her grave; for she was his mother. Sometime after, when his father died, he was in foreign lands, and did not come home. I know that he never married, I believe he became a lawyer. He had forgotten me, and even had we met he would not have known me, for I have lost all my good looks, and perhaps that is all for the best." And then she spoke of the dark days of trial, when misfortune had fallen upon them.

"We had five hundred dollars," she said, "and there was a house in the street to be sold for two hundred, so we thought it would be worth our while to pull it down and build a new one in its place; so it was bought. The builder and carpenter made an estimate that the new house would cost ten hundred and twenty dollars to build. Eric had credit, so he borrowed the money in the chief town. But the captain, who was bringing it to him, was shipwrecked, and the money lost. Just about this time, my dear sweet boy, who lies sleeping there, was born, and my husband was attacked with a severe, lingering illness. For three quarters of a year I was obliged to dress and undress him. We were backward in our payments, we borrowed more money, all that we had was lost and sold, and then my husband died. Since then I have worked, and toiled, and striven for the sake of the child. I have scrubbed and washed both coarse and fine linen, but I have not been able to make myself better off; and it was God's will. In His own time He will take me to Himself, but I know He will never forsake my boy." Then she fell asleep. In the morning she felt much refreshed, and strong enough, as she thought, to go on with her work. But as soon as she stepped into the cold water, a sudden faintness seized her; she clutched at the air convulsively with her hand, took one step forward, and fell. Her head rested on dry land, but her feet were in the water; her wooden shoes, which were only tied on by a wisp of straw, were carried away by the stream, and thus she was found by Martha when she came to bring her some coffee.

In the meantime a messenger had been sent to her house by the mayor, to say that she must come to him immediately, as he had something to tell her. It was too late; a surgeon had been sent for to open a vein in her arm, but the poor woman was dead.

"She has drunk herself to death," said the cruel mayor. In the letter, containing the news of his brother's death, it was stated that he had left in his will a legacy of six hundred dollars to the glovemaker's widow, who had once been his mother's maid, to be paid with discretion, in large or small sums to the widow or her child.

"There was something between my brother and her, I remember," said the mayor; "it is a good thing that she is out of the way, for now the boy will have the whole. I will place him with honest people to bring him up, that he may become a respectable working man." And the blessing of God rested upon these words. The mayor sent for the boy to come to him, and promised to take care of him, but most cruelly added that it was a good thing his mother was dead, for "she was good for nothing." They carried her to the churchyard, the chruchyard in which the poor were buried. Martha strewed sand on the grave and planted a little rose-tree upon it, and the boy stood by her side.

"Oh, my poor mother!" he cried, while the tears rolled down his cheeks. "Is it true what they say, that she was good for nothing?"

"No, indeed, it is not true," replied the old servant, raising her eyes to heaven; "she was worth a great deal; I knew it years ago, and since the last night of her life I am more certain of it than ever. I say she was a good and worthy woman, and God, who is in heaven, knows I am speaking the truth, though the world may say, even now, she was good for nothing."

The Shadow

In very hot climates, where the heat of the sun has great power, people are usually as brown as mahogany; and in the hottest countries they are negroes, with black skins. A learned man once travelled into one of these warm climates, from the cold regions of the north, and thought he could roam about as he did at home; but he soon had to change his opinion. He found that, like all sensible people, he must remain in the house during the whole day, with every window and door closed, so that it looked as if all in the house were asleep or absent. The houses of the narrow street in which he lived were so lofty that the sun shone upon them from morning till evening, and it became quite unbearable. This learned man from the cold regions was young as well as clever; but it seemed to him as if he were sitting in an oven, and he became quite exhausted and weak, and grew so thin that his shadow shrivelled up, and became much smaller than it had been at home. The sun took away even what was left of it, and he saw nothing of it till the evening, after sunset. It was really a pleasure, as soon as the lights were brought into the room, to see the shadow stretch itself against the wall, even to the ceiling, so tall was it; and it really wanted a good stretch to recover its strength. The learned man would sometimes go out into the balcony to stretch himself also; and as soon as the stars came forth in the clear, beautiful sky, he felt revived. People at this hour began to make their appearance in all the balconies in the street; for in warm climates every window has a balcony, in which they can breathe the fresh evening air, which is very necessary, even to those who are used to a heat that makes them as brown as mahogany; so that the street presented a very lively appearance. Here were shoemakers, and tailors, and all sorts of people sitting. In the street beneath, they brought out tables and chairs, lighted candles by hundreds, talked and sang, and were very merry. There were people walking, carriages driving, and mules trotting along, with their bells on the harness, "tingle, tingle," as they went. Then the dead were carried to the grave with the sound of solemn music, and the tolling of the church bells. It was indeed a scene of varied life in the street. One house only, which was just opposite to the one in which the foreign learned man lived, formed a contrast to all this, for it was quite still; and yet somebody dwelt there, for flowers stood in the balcony, blooming beautifully in the hot sun; and this could not have been unless they had been watered carefully. Therefore some one must be in the house to do this. The doors leading to the balcony were half opened in the evening; and although in the front room all was dark, music could be heard from the interior of the house. The foreign learned man considered this music very delightful; but perhaps he fancied it; for everything in these warm countries pleased him, excepting the heat of the sun. The foreign landlord said he did not know who had taken the opposite house – nobody was to be seen there; and as to the music, he thought it seemed very tedious, to him most uncommonly so.

"It is just as if some one were practising a piece that he could not manage; it was always the same piece. He thinks, I suppose, that he will be able to manage it at last; but I do not think so, however long he may play it."

Once the foreigner woke in the night. He slept with the door open which lead to the balcony; the wind had raised the curtain before it, and there appeared a wonderful brightness over all in the balcony of the opposite house. The flowers seemed like flames of the most gorgeous colours, and among the flowers stood a beautiful slender maiden. It was to him as if light streamed from her, and dazzled his eyes; but then he had only just opened them, as he awoke from his sleep. With one spring he was out of bed, and crept softly behind the curtain. But she was gone – the brightness had disappeared; the flowers no longer appeared like flames, although still as beautiful as ever. The door stood ajar, and from an inner room sounded music so sweet and so lovely, that it produced the most enchanting thoughts, and acted on the senses with magic power. Who could live there? Where was the real entrance? for, both in the street and in the lane at the side, the whole ground floor was a continuation of shops; and people could not always be passing through them.

One evening the foreigner sat in the balcony. A light was burning in his own room, just behind him. It was quite natural, therefore, that his shadow should fall on the wall of the opposite house; so that, as he sat amongst the flowers on his balcony, when he moved, his shadow moved also.

"I think my shadow is the only living thing to be seen opposite," said the learned man; "see how pleasantly it sits among the flowers. The door is only ajar; the shadow ought to be clever enough to step in and look about him, and then to come back and tell me what he has seen. You could make yourself useful in this way," said he, jokingly; "be so good as to step in now, will you?" and then he nodded to the shadow, and the shadow nodded in return. "Now go, but don't stay away altogether."

Then the foreigner stood up, and the shadow on the opposite balcony stood up also; the foreigner turned round, the shadow turned; and if any one had

372

observed, they might have seen it go straight into the half-opened door of the opposite balcony, as the learned man re-entered his own room, and let the curtain fall. The next morning he went out to take his coffee and read the newspapers.

"How is this?" he exclaimed, as he stood in the sunshine. "I have lost my shadow. So it really did go away yesterday evening, and it has not returned. This is very annoying."

And it certainly did vex him, not so much because the shadow was gone, but because he knew there was a story of a man without a shadow. All the people at home, in his country, knew this story; and when he returned, and related his own adventures, they would say it was only an imitation; and he had no desire for such things to be said of him. So he decided not to speak of it at all, which was a very sensible determination.

In the evening he went out again on his balcony, taking care to place the light behind him; for he knew that a shadow always wants his master for a screen; but he could not entice him out. He made himself little, and he made himself tall; but there was no shadow, and no shadow came. He said, "Hem, a-hem;" but it was all useless. This was very vexatious; but in warm countries everything grows very quickly; and, after a week had passed, he saw, to his great joy, that a new shadow was growing from his feet, when he walked in the sunshine; so that the root must have remained. After three weeks, he had quite a respectable shadow, which, during his return journey to northern lands, continued to grow, and became at last so large that he might very well have spared half of it. When this learned man arrived at home, he wrote books about the true, the good, and the beautiful, which are to be found in this world; and so days and years passed – many, many years.

One evening, as he sat in his study, a very gentle tap was heard at the door. "Come in," said he; but no one came. He opened the door, and there stood before him a man so remarkably thin that he felt seriously troubled at his appearance. He was, however, very well dressed, and looked like a gentleman. "To whom have I the honour of speaking?" said he.

"Ah, I hoped you would recognise me," said the elegant stranger; "I have gained so much that I have a body of flesh, and clothes to wear. You never expected to see me in such a condition. Do you not recognise your old shadow? Ah, you never expected that I should return to you again. All has been prosperous with me since I was with you last; I have become rich in every way, and, were I inclined to purchase my freedom from service, I could easily do so." And as he spoke he rattled between his fingers a number of costly trinkets which hung to a thick gold watch-chain he wore round his neck. Diamond rings sparkled on his fingers, and it was all real.

"I cannot recover from my astonishment," said the learned man. "What does all this mean?"

"Something rather unusual," said the shadow; "but you are yourself an uncommon man, and you know very well that I have followed in your footsteps ever since your childhood. As soon as you found that I had travelled enough to be trusted alone, I went my own way, and I am now in the most brilliant circumstances. But I felt a kind of longing to see you once more before you die, and I wanted to see this place again, for there is always a clinging to the land of one's birth. I know that you have now another shadow; do I owe you anything? If so, have the goodness to say what it is."

"No! Is it really you?" said the learned man. "Well, this is most remarkable; I never supposed it possible that a man's old shadow could become a human being."

"Just tell me what I owe you," said the shadow, "for I do not like to be in debt to any man."

"How can you talk in that manner?" said the learned man. "What question of debt can there be between us? You are as free as any one. I rejoice exceedingly to hear of your good fortune. Sit down, old friend, and tell me a little of how it happened, and what you saw in the house opposite to me while we were in those hot climates."

"Yes, I will tell you all about it," said the shadow, sitting down; "but then you must promise me never to tell in this city, wherever you may meet me, that I have been your shadow. I am thinking of being married, for I have more than sufficient to support a family."

"Make yourself quite easy," said the learned man; "I will tell no one who you really are. Here is my hand, – I promise, and a word is sufficient between man and man."

"Between man and a shadow," said the shadow; for he could not help saying so.

It was really most remarkable how very much he had become a man in appearance. He was dressed in a suit of the very finest black cloth, polished boots, and an opera crush hat, which could be folded together so that nothing could be seen but the crown and the rim, besides the trinkets, the gold chain, and the diamond rings already spoken of. The shadow was, in fact, very well dressed, and this made a man of him. "Now I will relate to you what you wish to know," said the shadow, placing his foot with the polished leather boot as firmly as possible on the arm of the new shadow of the learned man, which lay at his feet like a poodle dog. This was done, it might be from pride, or perhaps that the new shadow might cling to him, but the prostrate shadow remained quite quiet and at rest, in order that it might listen, for it wanted to know how a shadow could be sent away by its master, and become a man itself. "Do you know," said the shadow, "that in the house opposite to you lived the most glorious creature in the world? It was poetry. I remained there three weeks, and it was more like three thousand years, for I read all that has ever been written in poetry or prose; and I may say, in truth, that I saw and learnt everything."

"Poetry!" exclaimed the learned man. "Yes, she lives as a hermit in great cities. Poetry! Well, I saw her once for a very short moment, while sleep weighed down my eyelids. She flashed upon me from the balcony like the radiant aurora borealis, surrounded with flowers like flames of fire. Tell me, you were on the balcony that evening; you went through the door, and what did you see?"

"I found myself in an ante-room," said the shadow. "You still sat opposite to me, looking into the room. There was no light, ar at least it seemed in partial darkness, for the doors of a whole suite of rooms stood open, and they were brilliantly lighted. The blaze of light would have killed me, had

I approached too near the maiden herself; but I was cautious, and took time, which is what every one ought to do."

"And what didst thou see?" asked the learned man.

"I saw everything, as you shall hear. But – it really is not pride on my part, as a free man and possessing the knowledge that I do, besides my position, not to speak of my wealth – I wish you would say *you* to me, instead of *thou*."

"I beg your pardon," said the learned man; "it is an old habit, which it is difficult to break. You are quite right; I will try to think of it. But now tell me everything that you saw."

"Everything," said the shadow; "for I saw and know everything."

"What was the appearance of the inner rooms?" asked the scholar. "Was it there like a cool grove, or like a holy temple? Were the chambers like a starry sky seen from the top of a high mountain?"

"It was all that you describe," said the shadow; "but I did not go quite in – I remained in the twilight of the ante-room – but I was in a very good position, – I could see and hear all that was going on in the court of poetry."

"But what did you see? Did the gods of ancient times pass through the rooms? Did old heroes fight their battles over again? Were there lovely children at play, who related their dreams?"

"I tell you I have been there, and therefore you may be sure that I saw everything that was to be seen. If you had gone there, you would not have remained a human being, whereas I became one; and at the same moment I became aware of my inner being, my inborn affinity to the nature of poetry. It is true I did not think much about it while I was with you, but you will remember that I was always much larger at sunrise and sunset, and in the moonlight even more visible than yourself, but I did not then understand my inner existence. In the ante-room it was revealed to me. I became a man; I came out in full maturity. But you had left the warm countries. As a man, I felt ashamed to go about without boots or clothes, and that exterior finish by which man is known. So I went my own way; I can tell you, for you will not put it in a book. I hid myself under the cloak of a cake woman, but she little thought who she concealed. It was not till evening that I ventured out. I ran about the streets in the moonlight. I drew myself up to my full height upon the walls, which tickled my back very pleasantly. I ran here and there, looked through the highest windows into the rooms, and over the roofs. I looked in, and saw what nobody else could see, or indeed ought to see; in fact, it is a bad world, and I would not care to be a man, but that men are of some importance. I saw the most miserable things going on between husbands and wives, parents and children, – sweet, incomparable children. I have seen what no human being has the

power of knowing, although they would all be very glad to know – the evil conduct of their neighbours. Had I written a newspaper, how eagerly it would have been read! Instead of which, I wrote direct to the persons themselbes, and great alarm arose in all the towns I visited. They had so much fear of me, and yet how dearly they loved me. The professor made me a professor. The tailor gave me new clothes; I am well provided for in that way. The overseer of the mint struck coins for me. The women declared that I was handsome, and so I became the man you now see me. And now I must say adieu. Here is my card. I live on the sunny side of the street, and always stay at home in rainy weather." And the shadow departed.

"This is all very remarkable," said the learned man.

Years passed, days and years went by, and the shadow came again. "How are you going on now?" he asked.

"Ah!" said the learned man, "I am writing about the true, the beautiful, and the good; but no one cares to hear anything about it. I am quite in despair, for I take it to heart very much."

"That is what I never do," said the shadow; "I am growing quite fat and stout, which every one ought to be. You do not understand the world; you will make yourself ill about it; you ought to travel; I am going on a journey in the summer, will you go with me? I should like a travelling companion; will you travel with me as my shadow? It would give me great pleasure, and I will pay all expenses."

"Are you going to travel far?" asked the learned man.

"That is a matter of opinion," replied the shadow. "At all events, a journey will do you good, and if you will be my shadow, then all your journey shall be paid."

"It appears to me very absurd," said the learned man.

"But it is the way of the world," replied the shadow, "and always will be." Then he went away.

Everything went wrong with the learned man. Sorrow and trouble pursued him, and what he said about the good, the beautiful, and the true, was of as much value to most people as a nutmeg would be to a cow. At length he fell ill. "You really look like a shadow," people said to him, and then a cold shudder would pass over him, for he had his own thoughts on the subject.

"You really ought to go to some watering-place," said the shadow on his next visit. "There is no other chance for you. I will take you with me, for the sake of old acquaintance. I will pay the expenses of your journey, and you shall write a description of it to amuse us by the way. I should like to go to a watering-place; my beard does not grow as it ought, which is from weakness, and I must have a beard. Now do be sensible and accept my proposal; we shall travel as intimate friends."

And at last they started together. The shadow was master now, and the master became the shadow. They drove together, and rode and walked in company with each other, side by side, or one in front and the other behind, according to the position of the sun. The shadow always knew when to take the place of honour, but the learned man took no notice of it, for he had a good heart, and was exceedingly mild and friendly.

One day the master said to the shadow, "We have grown up together from our childhood, and now that we have become travelling companions, shall we not drink to our good fellowship, and say *thee* and *thou* to each other."

"What you say is very straightforward and kindly meant," said the shadow, who was now really master. "I will be equally kind and straightforward. You are a learned man, and know how wonderful human nature is. There are some men who cannot endure the smell of brown paper; it makes them ill. Others will feel a shuddering sensation to their very marrow, if a nail is scratched on a pane of glass. I myself have a similar kind of feeling when I hear any one say *thou* to me. I feel crushed by it, as I used to feel in my former position with you. You will perceive that this is a matter of feeling, not price. I cannot allow you to say *thou* to me; I will gladly say it to you, and therefore your wish will be half fulfilled." Then the shadow addressed his former master as *thou*.

"It is going rather too far," said the latter, "that I am to say *you* when I speak to him, and he is to say *thou* to me." However, he was obliged to submit.

They arrived at length at the baths, where there were many strangers, and among them a beautiful princess, whose real disease consisted in being too sharp-sighted, which made every one very uneasy. She saw at once that the new comer was very different to every one else. "They say he is here to make his beard grow," she thought; "but I know the real cause, he is unable to cast a shadow." Then she became very curious on the matter, and one day, while on the promenade, she entered into conversation with the strange gentleman. Being a princess, she was not obliged to stand upon much ceremony, so she said to him without hesitation, "Your illness consists in not being able to cast a shadow."

"Your royal highness must be on the high-road to recovery from your illness," said he. "I know your complaint arose from being too sharp-sighted, and in this case it has entirely failed. I happen to have a most unusual shadow. Have you not seen a person who is always at my side? Persons often give their servants finer cloth for their liveries than for their own clothes, and so I have dressed out my shadow like a man; nay, you may observe that I have even given him a shadow of his own; it is rather expensive, but I like to have things about me that are peculiar."

"How is this?" thought the princess; "am I really cured? This must be the best watering-place in existence. Water in our times has certainly wonderful power. But I will not leave this place yet, just as it begins to be amusing. This foreign prince – for he must be a prince – pleases me above all things. I only hope his beard won't grow, or he will leave at once."

In the evening, the princess and the shadow danced together in the large assembly rooms. She was light, but he was lighter still; she had never seen such a dancer before. She told him from what country she had come, and found he knew it and had been there, but not while she was at home. He had looked into the windows of her father's palace, both the upper and the lower windows; he had seen many things, and could therefore answer the princess, and make allusions which quite astonished her. She thought he must be the cleverest man in all the world, and felt the greatest respect for his knowledge. When she danced with him again she fell in love with him, which the shadow quickly discovered, for she had with her eyes looked him through and through. They danced once more, and she was nearly telling him, but she had some discretion; she thought of her country, her kingdom, and the number of people over whom she would one day have to rule. "He is a clever man," she thought to herself, "which is a good thing, and he dances admirably, which is also good. But has he well-grounded knowledge? That is an important question, and I must try him." Then she asked him a most difficult question, she herself could not have ansered it, and the shadow made a most unaccountable grimace.

"You cannot answer that," said the princess.

"I learnt something about it in my childhood," he replied; "and believe that even my very shadow, standing over there by the door, could answer it."

"Your shadow," said the princess; "indeed that would be very remarkable."

"I do not say so, positively," observed the shadow; "but I am inclined to believe that he can do so. He has followed me for so many years, and has heard so much from me, that I think it is very likely. But your royal Highess must allow me to observe, that he is very proud of being considered a man, and to put him in a good humour, so that he may answer correctly, he must be treated as a man."

"I shall be very pleased to do so," said the princess. So she walked up to the learned man, who stood in the doorway, and spoke to him of the sun, and the moon, of the green forests, and of people near home and far off; and the learned man conversed with her pleasantly and sensibly.

"What a wonderful man he must be, to have such a clever shadow!" thought she. "If I were to choose him it would be a real blessing to my country and my subjects, and I will do it." So the princess and the shadow were soon engaged to each other, but no one was to be told a word about it, till she returned to her kingdom.

"No one *shall* know," said the shadow; "not even my own shadow;" and he had very particular reasons for saying so.

After a time, the princess returned to the land over which she reigned, and the shadow accompanied her.

"Listen, my friend," said the shadow to the learned man; "now that I am as fortunate and as powerful as any man can be, I will do something unusually good for you. You shall live in my palace, drive with me in the royal carriage, and have a hundred thousand dollars a year; but you must allow every one to call you a shadow, and never venture to say that you have been a man. And once a year, when I sit in my balcony in the sushine, you must lie at my feet as becomes a shadow to do; for I must tell you I am going to marry the princess, and our wedding will take place this evening."

"Now, really, this is too ridiculous," said the learned man. "I cannot, and will not, submit to such folly. It would be cheating the whole country, and the princess also. I will disclose everything, and say that I am the man, and that you are only a shadow dressed up in men's clothes."

"No one would believe you," said the shadow; "be reasonable, now, or I will call the guards."

"I will go straight to the princess," said the learned man.

"But I shall be there first," replied the shadow, "and you will be sent to prison." And so it turned out, for the guards readily obeyed him, as they knew he was going to marry the king's daughter.

"You tremble," said the princess, when the shadow appeared before her. "Has anything happened? You must not be ill to-day, for this evening our wedding will take place."

"I have gone through the most terrible affair that could possibly happen," said the shadow; "only imagine, my shadow has gone mad; I suppose such a poor, shallow brain, could not bear much; he fancies that he has become a real man, and that I am his shadow."

"How very terrible," cried the princess; "is he locked up?"

"Oh yes, certainly; for I fear he will never recover."

"Poor shadow!" said the princess; "it is very unfortunate for him; it would really be a good deed to free him from his frail existence; and, indeed, when I think how often people take the part of the lower class against the higher, in these days, it would be policy to put him out of the way quietly."

"It is certainly rather hard upon him, for he was a faithful servant," said the shadow; and he pretended to sigh.

"Yours is a noble character," said the princess, and bowed herself before him.

In the evening the whole town was illuminated, and cannons fired "boom," and the soldiers presented arms. It was, indeed a grand wedding. The princess and the shadow stepped out on the balcony to show themselves, and to receive one cheer more. But the learned man heard nothing of all these festivities, for he had already been executed.

The Buckwheat

As you go by a field of buckwheat after a thunderstorm, you will often notice that the buckwheat has been scorched quite black. It's just as though a flame had passed over it, and then the farmer says, "It's got that from the lightning." But how has it happened? I will tell you what the sparrow told me, and the sparrow heard it from an old willow tree that stood – and is still standing – by the side of a field of buckwheat. It's quite a venerable great willow, but wrinkled and aged, with a crack down the middle – and grass and brambles growing out of the crack! The tree leans forward, and the branches hang right down to the ground like long green hair.
In all the fields round about there was corn growing, rye and barley and oats – yes, the lovely oats that has the appearance, when it's ripe, of a whole string of little yellow canaries on a bough. The corn was a wonderful sight; and the heavier the crop, the deeper it stooped in meck humility.

But there was also a field of buckwheat, it was just in front of the old willow. The buckwheat didn't stoop, like the other corn; it held itself up proudly and stiffly.

"I must be just as rich as the grain," it said, "and I'm much better-looking. My blossoms are beautiful, like apple-blossoms; it's quite a pleasure to look upon me and mine. Do you know anyone finer, my dear willow?"

The willow tree nodded his head as if to say, "You may be sure I do!"

But the buckwheat was simply bursting with pride and said, "The stupid tree! He's so old that his stomach has grass growing on it."

And now a terrible storm blew up. All the flowers in the field folded their leaves or bent their delicate heads while the storm passed over them. But the buckwheat stood up straight in its pride.

"Stoop down like us!" cried the flowers.

"No need whatever for me to!" answered the buckwheat.

"Stoop down like us!" cried the corn. "Here comes the angel of the storm in full flight. He has wings that reach from the clouds right down to the earth; he will strike straight over you, before you can cry for mercy."

"Very well, but I refuse to stoop," said the buckwheat.

"Shut up your blossoms and bend down your leaves!" said the old willow. "Don't look up at the lightning, when the cloud bursts; even mankind daren't do that, for in the lightning one may see into God's heaven. But

384

even man can be blinded by the sight of that; what ever would happen to us plants, if we dared so much – we who are far inferior?"

"Far inferior?" said the buckwheat. "Well now, I'm going to look into God's heaven"; and in arrogance and pride it did. The lightning was so fierce that the whole earth seemed to be wrapped in flame.

When the storm had passed away, there in the pure still air stood flowers and corn, all refreshed by the rain; but the buckwheat had been scorched coal-black by lightning. It was a dead useless weed on the field.

And the old willow stirred his branches in the wind, and big drops of water fell from his green leaves, just as though the tree were crying. And the sparrows asked, "What are you crying for? It's so lovely here. Look how the sun is shining, how the clouds are sailing by. Can't you smell the perfume of flowers and bushes? Why should you cry, dear willow?"

Then the willow tree told them about the buckwheat's pride and arrogance – and punishment, for that always follows. I, who tell the tale, I heard it from the sparrows. It was they who told it me, one evening when I begged them for a story.

The Most Incredible Thing

The one who could do the most incredible thing was to have the King's daughter and half the kingdom.

The young men – and the old ones, too – strained every thought, muscle and sinew: two of them killed themselves by overeating, and another drank himself to death, trying, each according to his lights, to do the most incredible thing. But that wasn't how it was to be done. Little street-boys practised spitting on their own backs; they considered that the most incredible thing.

On a fixed day a display was to be given of what each one had to show as the most incredible thing. The judges appointed ranged from children of three up to people in their nineties. There was a whole exhibition of incredible things, but everyone soon agreed that the most incredible was a huge clock in its case, most cunningly contrived both in and out. At every hour living pictures appeared, showing which hour had struck; altogether, there were twelve representations with moving figures that sang or spoke.

"Yes, that was the most incredible thing," people said.

The clock struck one, and Moses stood on the mountain and wrote down on the Tables of the Law the first Commandment: "Thou shalt have none other gods but me."

The clock struck two, and the Garden of Eden was seen, where Adam and Eve met, both happy without so much as a wardrobe; they didn't need one.

On the stroke of three the three Wise Men appeared, one of them was coal-black, but he couldn't help that – he had been blackened by the sun. On the stroke of four came the four seasons: spring with the cuckoo in the fresh foliage of a beech tree, summer with a grasshopper on the ripe ear of corn, autumn with an empty stork's nest from which the bird had flown,

winter with an old crow who could tell stories in the chimney-corner, memories of the past.

As it struck five, there came the five senses: sight as an optician, hearing as a coppersmith; smell sold violets and sweet woodruff, taste was a cook, and feeling an undertaker with mourning cape down to his heels.

The clock struck six. There sat a gambler, throwing dice; the die showed its highest face, and it was "six".

Then came the seven days of the week – or the seven deadly sins – people couldn't agree about that, for they went together and weren't easy to tell from each other.

Next, a choir of monks came and sang eight o'clock matins.

On the stroke of nine appeared the nine Muses, one engaged in astronomy, another as a keeper of historical documents, while the others belonged to the theatre.

On the stroke of ten Moses stepped forward again with the Tables of the Law, on which were all the commandments of God, and they were ten.

The clock struck again, and little boys and girls came skipping out; they were playing a game, at which they sang:

"Three, four, five, six, seven –
the clock has struck eleven".
Finally, the clock struck twelve, and the watchman stepped forward with
fur cap and halberd; he sang the old song of the watchman:
"Twas at the hour of midnight
our Saviour he was born".
and, as he sang, roses sprang up and turned to angel-heads borne on rain-
bow-coloured wings.
It was charming to hear, and delightful to see. The whole contrivance was
a matchless work of art; everyone declared that *this* was the most incredible
thing. The artist was a young man, kind-hearted and happy as a child, a
faithful friend and good to his badly-off parents. Yes, he deserved the
Princess and half the kingdom.
The day of decision had arrived. It was a fête day for the whole city, and the
Princess sat on the royal throne, which had been newly stuffed with horse-
hair but wasn't any more comfortable for that. The judges all round looked

390

knowingly across at the likely winner, who stood there confident and happy; his success was certain, for he had done the most incredible thing. "No, no! I shall do that" suddenly shouted a gaunt, lanky giant of a fellow. "I am the man for the most incredible thing." And he swung a great axe at the work of art.

"Crash! Bash! Bang!" – there lay the whole contrivance. Wheels and springs flew all over the place. Everything was dashed to pieces.

"That was what I could do," said the man. "My deed has beaten his and beaten you all. I have done the most incredible thing."

"To destroy such a work of art!" said the judges. "Yes, that was the most incredible thing."

All the people said the same, and so the man was to have the Princess and half the kingdom; for a law is a law, even if it is the most incredible thing. From the ramparts and all the towers in the city it was proclaimed by trumpet that the wedding was to take place. The Princess wasn't at all pleased; still, she looked charming and was gorgeously dressed. The church was ablaze with candles; late at night they are seen at their best. The noble young girls of the city sang and led the bride forward; the knights sang and escorted the bridegroom, who strutted as *he* could never be broken in two. Now the singing stopped, and the church became so silent that you could have heard a pin fall. But, in the midst of the silence, with rolling and rumbling the great churchdoor flew open and boom! boom! all the works of the clock came marching up the middle aisle and stood in between bride and bridegroom. Dead men can't walk again – we know that well enough – but a work of art can. The body had been dashed to pieces, but not the spirit. The spirit of great art haunted the place; there wasn't the ghost of a doubt about that.

The work of art stood there exactly as it was when it was new and un- touched. The clock struck the hours, one after the other, up to twelve, and the figures came swarming out. First, Moses; flames or fire seemed to blaze from his forehead, as he hurled the heavy stone Tables of the Law on to the bridegroom's feet and pinned them to the floor of the church.

"I cannot lift them up again," said Moses. "You have knocked off my arms. Stand as you are!"

Next came Adam and Eve, the Wise Men from the east and the four seasons; each told him unpleasant truths – "shame upon you!"

But he felt no shame.

All the figures that had to appear at the stroke of each hour now stepped out of the clock and all increased terribly in size, till there hardly seemed room for the real people. And when at the stroke of twelve the watch- man stepped out with fur cap and halberd, there was a rare to-do. The watchman went straight up to the bridegroom and bashed him on the head with his halberd.

"Lie there!" he cried. "Measure for measure! Now we're avenged, and our young master, too. We vanish."

And then the whole contrivance disappeared. But the candles all over the church turned into great flowers of light, the gilded stars under the roof threw out long luminous beams, and the organ played of itself. All the people said that this was the most incredible thing they had ever known.

"Then please to summon the right one!" said the Princess. "He that made the work of art – let him be my lord and husband."

And he stood in the church with all the people around him. All rejoiced and wished him well. There wasn't one who was jealous – and that was the most incredible thing of all.

The Butterfly

There was once a butterfly who wished for a bride; and, as may be supposed, he wanted to choose a very pretty one from among the flowers. He glanced, with a very critical eye, at all the flower-beds, and found that the flowers were seated quietly and demurely on their stalks, just as maidens should sit before they are engaged; but there was a great number of them, and it appeared as if his search would become very wearisome. The butterfly did not like to take too much trouble, so he flew off on a visit to the daisies. The French call this flower "Marguerite," and they say that the little daisy can prophesy. Lovers pluck off the leaves, and as they pluck each leaf, they ask a question about their lovers; thus: "Does he or she love me? – Ardently? Distractedly? Very much? A little? Not at all?" and so on. Every one speaks these words in his own language. The butterfly came also to Marguerite to inquire, but he did not pluck off her leaves; he pressed a kiss on each of them, for he thought there was always more to be done by kindness. "Darling Marguerite daisy," he said to her, "you are the wisest woman of all the flowers. Pray tell me which of the flowers I shall choose for my wife. Which will be my bride? When I know, I will fly directly to her, and propose." But Marguerite did not answer him; she was offened that he should call her a woman when she was only a girl; and there is a great difference. He asked her a second time, and then a third; but she remained dumb, and answered not a word. Then he would wait no longer, but flew away, to commence his wooing at once. It was in the early spring, when the crocus and the snow-drop were in full bloom.

"They are very pretty," thought the butterfly; "charming little lasses; but they are rather formal."

Then, as young lads often do, he looked out for the elder girls. He next flew to the anemones; these were rather sour to his taste. The violet, a little too sentimental. The lime-blossoms, too small; and besides, there was such a large family of them. The apple-blossoms, though they looked like roses, bloomed to-day, but might fall off to-morrow, with the first wind that blew; and he thought that a marriage with one of them might last too short a time. The pea-blossom pleased him most of all; she was white and red, graceful and slender, and belonged to those domestic maidens who have a pretty appearance, and can yet be useful in the kitchen. He was just about to make her an offer, when, close by the maiden, he saw a pod, with a withered flower hanging at the end. "Who is that?" he asked.

"That is my sister," replied the pea-blossom.

"Oh, indeed; and you will be like her some day," said he; and he flew away directly, for he felt quite shocked. A honeysuckle hung forth from the hedge, in full bloom; but there were so many girls like her, with long faces and sallow complexions. No; he did not like her. But which one did he like? Spring went by, and summer drew towards its close; autumn came; but he had not decided. The flowers now appeared in their most gorgeous robes, but all in vain; they had not the fresh, fragrant air of youth. For the heart asks for fragrance, even when it is no longer young; and there is very little of that to be found in the dahlias or the dry chrysanthemums; therefore the butterfly turned to the mint on the ground. You know, this plant has no blossom; but it is sweetness all over, – full of fragrance from head to foot, with the scent of a flower in every leaf.

"I will take her," said the butterfly; and he made her an offer. But the mint stood silent and stiff, as she listened to him. At last she said, –

"Friendship, if you please; nothing more. I am old, and you are old, but we may live for each other just the same; as to marrying – no; don't let us appear ridiculous at our age."

And so it happened that the butterfly got no wife at all. He had been too long choosing, which is always a bad plan. And the butterfly became what is called an old bachelor. It was late in the autumn, with rainy and cloudy weather. The cold wind blew over the bowed backs of the willows, so that they creaked again. It was not the weather for flying about in summer clothes; but fortunately the butterfly was not out in it. He had got a shelter by chance. It was in a room heated by a stove, and as warm as summer. He could exist here, he said, well enough.

"But it is not enough merely to exist," said he; "I need freedom, sunshine, and a little flower for a companion."

Then he flew against the window-pane, and was seen and admired by those in the room, who caught him, and stuck him on a pin, in a box of curiosities. They could not do more for him.

"Now I am perched on a stalk, like the flowers," said the butterfly. "It is not very pleasant, certainly; I should imagine it is something like being married; for here I am stuck fast." And with this thought he consoled himself a little.

"That seems very poor consolation," said one of the plants in the room, that grew in a pot.

"Ah," thought the butterfly, "one can't very well trust these plants in pots; they have had too much to do with mankind."

The Wild Swans

Far away in the land to which the swallows fly when it is winter, dwelt a king who had eleven sons, and one daughter, named Eliza. The eleven brothers were princes, and each went to school with a star on his breast, and a sword by his side. They wrote with diamond pencils on gold slates, and learnt their lessons so quickly and read so easily that every one might know they were princes. Their sister Eliza sat on a little stool of plate-glass, and had a book full of pictures, which had cost as much as half a kingdom. Oh, these children were indeed happy, but it was not to remain so always. Their father, who was king of the country, married a very wicked queen, who did not love the poor children at all. They knew this from the very first day after the wedding. In the place there were great festivities and the children played at receiving company; but instead of having as usual, all the cakes and apples that were left, she gave them some sand in a tea-cup, and told them to pretend it was cake. The week after, she sent little Eliza into the country to a peasant and his wife, and then she told the king so many untrue things about the young princes, that he gave himself no more trouble respecting them.

397

"Go out into the world and get your own living," said the queen. "Fly like great birds who have no voice." But she could not make them ugly as she wished, for they were turned into eleven beautiful wild swans. Then, with a strange cry, they flew through the windows of the palace, over the park, to the forest beyond. It was yet early morning when they passed the peasant's cottage, where their sister Eliza lay asleep in her room. They hovered over the roof, twisted their long necks and flapped their wings, but no one heard them or saw them, so they were at last obliged to fly away, high up in the clouds; and over the wide world they flew till they came to a thick, dark wood, which stretched far away to the seashore. Poor little Eliza was alone in her room playing with a green leaf, for she had no other playthings, and she pierced a hole through the leaf, and looked through it at the sun, and it was as if she saw her brothers' clear eyes, and when the warm sun shone on her cheeks, she thought of all the kisses they had given her. One day passed just like another; sometimes the winds rustled through the leaves of the rose-bush, and would whisper to the roses, "Who can be more beautiful than you?" But the roses would shake their heads, and say, "Eliza is." And when the old woman sat at the cottage door on Sunday, and read her hymn-book, the wind would flutter the leaves, and say to the book, "Who can be more pious than you?" and then the hymn-book would answer "Eliza." And the roses and the hymn-book told the real truth. At fifteen she returned home, but when the queen saw how beautiful she was, she became full of spite and hatred towards her. Willingly would she have turned her into a swan, like her brothers, but she did not dare to do so yet, because the king wished to see his daughter. Early one morning the queen went into the bath-room; it was built of marble, and had soft cushions, trimmed with the most beautiful tapestry. She took three toads with her, and kissed them, and said to one "When Eliza comes to the bath, seat yourself upon her head, that she may become as stupid as you are." Then she said to another. "Place yourself on her forehead, that she may become as ugly as you are, and that her father may not know her." "Rest on her heart," she whispered to the third, "then she will have evil inclinations, and suffer in consequence." So she put the toads into the clear water, and they turned green immediately. She next called Eliza, and helped her to undress and get into the bath. As Eliza dipped her head under the water, one of the toads sat on her hair, a second on her forehead, and a third on her breast, but she did not seem to notice them, and when she rose out of the water, there were three red poppies floating upon it. Had not the creatures been venomous or been kissed by the witch, they would have been changed into red roses. At all events they became flowers, because they had rested on Eliza's head, and on her heart. She was too good and too innocent for witchcraft to have any power over

398

her. When the wicked queen saw this, she rubbed her face with walnut-juice, so that she was quite brown; then she tangled her beautiful hair and smeared it with disgusting ointment, till it was quite impossible to re-cognise the beautiful Eliza.

When her father saw her, he was much shocked, and declared she was not his daughter. No one but the watchdog and the swallows knew her; and they were only poor animals, and could say nothing. Then poor Eliza wept, and thought of her eleven brothers, who were all away. Sorrowfully she stole away from the palace, and walked, the whole day, over fields and moors, till she came to the great forest. She knew not in what direction to go; but she was so unhappy, and longed so for her brothers, who had been, like herself, driven out into the world, that she was determined to seek them. She had been but a short time in the wood when night came on, and she quite lost the path; so she laid herself down on the soft moss, offered up her evening prayer, and leaned her head against the stump of a tree. All nature was still and the soft, mild air fanned her forehead. The light of hundreds of glow-worms shone amidst the grass and the moss, like green fire; and if she touched a twig with her hand, ever so lightly, the brilliant insects fell down around her, like shooting-stars.

All night long she dreamt of her brothers. She and they were children again, playing together. She saw them writing with their diamond pencils on golden slates, while she looked at the beautiful picture-book which had cost half a kingdom. They were not writing lines and letters, as they used to do; but descriptions of the noble deeds they had performed, and of all they had discovered and seen. In the picture-book, too, everything was living. The birds sang, and the people came out of the book, and spoke to Eliza and her brothers; but, as the leaves turned over, they darted back again to their places, that all might be in order.

When she awoke, the sun was high in the heavens; yet she could not see him, for the lofty trees spread their branches thickly over her head; but his beams were glancing through the leaves here and there, like a golden mist. There was a sweet fragrance from the fresh green verdure, and the birds almost perched upon her shoulders. She heard water rippling from a number of springs, all flowing into a lake with golden sands. Bushes grew thickly round the lake, and at one spot an opening had been made by a deer, through which Eliza went down to the water. The lake was so clear that, had not the wind rustled the branches of the trees and the bushes, so that they moved, they would have appeared as if painted in the depths of the lake; for every leaf was reflected in the water, whether it stood in the shade or the sunshine. As soon as Eliza saw her own face, she was quite terrified at finding it so brown and ugly; but when she wetted her little hand, and rubbed her eyes and forehead, the white skin gleamed forth once more; and, after she had undressed, and dipped herself in the fresh water, a more beautiful king's daughter could not be found in the wide world. As soon as she had dressed herself again, and braided her long hair, she went to the bubbling spring, and drank some water out of the hollow of her hand. Then she wandered far into the forest, not knowing whither she went. She thought of her brothers, and felt sure that God would not forsake her. It is God who makes the wild apples grow in the wood, to satisfy the hungry, and He now led her to one of these trees, which was so loaded with fruit, that the boughs bent beneath the weight. Here she held her midday meal, placed props under the boughs, and then went into the gloomiest depths of the forest. It was so still that she could hear the sound of her own footsteps, as well as the rustling of every withered leaf which she crushed under her feet. Not a bird was to be seen, not a sunbeam could penetrate through the large, dark boughs of the trees. Their lofty trunks stood so close together, that, when she looked before her, it seemed as if she were enclosed within

400

trellis-work. Such solitude she had never known before. The night was very dark. Not a single glow-worm glittered in the moss.

Sorrowfully she laid herself down to sleep; and, after a while, it seemed to her as if the branches of the trees parted over her head, and that the mild eyes of angels looked down upon her from heaven. When she awoke in the morning, she knew not whether she had dreamt this, or if it had really been so. Then she continued her wandering; but she had not gone many steps forward, when she met an old woman with berries in her basket, and she gave her a few to eat. Then Eliza asked her if she had not seen eleven princes riding through the forest.

"No," replied the old woman, "but I saw yesterday eleven swans, with gold crowns on their heads, swimming on the river close by." Then she led Eliza a little distance farther to a sloping bank, and at the foot of it wound a little river. The trees on its banks stretched their long leafy branches across the water towards each other, and where the growth prevented them from meeting naturally, the roots had torn themselves away from the ground, so that the branches might mingle their foliage as they hung over the water. Eliza bade the old woman farewell, and walked by the flowing river, till she reached the shore of the open sea. And there, before the young maiden's eyes, lay the glorious ocean, but not a sail appeared on its surface, not even a boat could be seen. How was she to go farther? She noticed how the countless pebbles on the sea-shore had been smoothed and rounded by the action of the water. Glass, iron, stones, everything that lay there mingled together, had taken its shape from the same power, and felt as smooth, or even smoother than her own delicate hand. "The water rolls on without weariness," she said, "till all that is hard becomes smooth; so will I be unwearied in my task. Thanks for your lessons, bright rolling waves; my heart tells me you will lead me to my dear brothers." On the foam-covered sea-weed, lay eleven white swan feathers, which she gathered up and placed together. Drops of water lay upon them; whether they were dew-drops or tears no one could say. Lonely as it was on the sea shore, she did not observe it, for the ever-moving sea showed more changes in a few hours than the most varying lake could produce during a whole year. If a black heavy cloud arose, it was as if the sea said, "I can look dark and angry too;" and then the wind blew, and the waves turned to white foam as they rolled. When the wind slept, and the clouds glowed with the red sunlight, then the sea looked like a rose leaf. But however quietly its white glassy surface rested, there was still a motion on the shore, as its waves rose and fell like the breast of a sleeping child. When the sun was about to set, Eliza saw eleven white swans with golden crowns on their heads, flying towards the land, one behind the other, like a long white ribbon. Then Eliza went down the slope from the shore, and hid herself behind the bushes. The swans alighted quite close to her, and flapped their great white wings. As soon as the sun had disappeared under the water, the feathers of the swans fell off, and eleven beautiful princes, Eliza's brothers, stood near her. She uttered a loud cry, for, although they were very much changed, she knew them immediately. She sprang into their arms, and called them each by name. Then, how happy the princes were at meeting their little sister again, for they recognised her, although she had grown so tall and beautiful. They laughed, and they wept, and very soon understood how wickedly their mother had acted to them all. "We brothers," said the eldest, "fly about as wild swans, so long as the sun is in the sky; but as soon as it sinks behind the hills, we recover our human shape. Therefore we must always be near a resting place for our feet before sunset; for if we should be flying towards the clouds at the time we recovered our natural form as men, we should sink deep into the sea. We do not dwell here, but in a land just as fair, that lies beyond the ocean, which we have to cross for a long distance; there is no island in our passage upon which we could pass the night; nothing but a little rock rising out of the sea, upon which we can scarcely stand with safety, even closely crowded together. If the sea is rough, the foam dashes over us, yet we thank God even for this rock; we have passed whole nights upon it, or we should never have reached our beloved fatherland, for our flight across the sea occupies two of the longest days in the year. We have permission to visit our home once in every year, and to remain eleven days, during which we fly across the forest to look once more at the palace where our father dwells, and where we were born, and at the church, where our mother lies buried. Here it seems as if the very trees and bushes were related to us. The wild horses leap over the plains as we have seen them in our childhood. The charcoal burners sing the old songs, to which we have danced as children. This is our fatherland, to which we are drawn by loving ties; and here we have found you, our dear little sister. Two days longer we can remain here, and then must we fly away to a beautiful land which is not our home; and how can we take you with us? We have neither ship nor boat."

"How can I break this spell?" said their sister. And then she talked about it nearly the whole night, only slumbering for a few hours. Eliza was awakened by the rustling of the swans' wings as they soared above. Her brothers were again changed to swans, and they flew in circles wider and wider, till they were far away; but one of them, the youngest swan, remained behind, and laid his head in his sister's lap, while she stroked his wings; and they remained together the whole day. Towards evening, the rest came back, and as the sun went down they resumed their natural forms. "To-morrow," said one, "we shall fly away, not to return again till a whole year has passed. But we cannot leave you here. Have you courage to go with us? My arm is strong enough to carry you through the wood; and will not all our wings be strong enough to fly with you over the sea?"

"Yes, take me with you," said Eliza. Then they spent the whole night in weaving a net with the pliant willow and rushes. It was very large and strong. Eliza laid herself down on the net, and when the sun rose, and her brothers again became wild swans, they took up the net with their beaks, and flew up to the clouds with their dear sister, who still slept. The sunbeams fell on her face, therefore one of the swans soared over her head, so that his broad wings might shade her. They were far from the land when Eliza woke. She thought she must still be dreaming, it seemed so strange to her to feel herself being carried so high in the air over the sea. By her side lay a branch full of beautiful ripe berries, and a bundle of sweet roots; the youngest of her brothers had gathered them for her, and placed them by her side. She smiled her thanks to him; she knew it was the same who had hovered over her to shade her with his wings. They were now so high, that a large ship beneath them looked like a white sea-gull skimming the waves. A great cloud floating behind them appeared like a vast mountain, and upon it Eliza saw her own shadow and those of the eleven swans, looking gigantic in size. Altogether it formed a more beautiful picture than she had ever seen; but as the sun rose higher, and the clouds were left behind, the shadowy picture vanished away. Onward the whole day, they flew through the air like a winged arrow, yet more slowly than usual, for they had their sister to carry. The weather seemed inclined to be stormy, and Eliza watched the sinking sun with great anxiety, for the little rock in the ocean was not yet in sight. It appeared to her as if the swans were making great efforts with their wings. Alas! she was the cause of their not advancing more quickly. When the sun set, they would change to men, fall into the sea, and be drowned. Then she offered a prayer from her inmost heart, but still no appearance of the rock. Dark clouds came nearer, the gusts of wind told of a coming storm, while from a thick, heavy mass of clouds the lightning burst forth flash after flash. The sun had reached the edge of the sea, when the swans darted down so swiftly, that Eliza's head trembled; she believed they were falling, but they again soared onward. Presently she caught sight of the rock just below them, and by this time the sun was half hidden by the waves. The rock did not appear larger than a seal's head thrust out of the water. They sank so rapidly, that at the moment their feet touched the rock, it shone only like a star, and at last disappeared like the last spark in a piece of burnt paper. Then she saw her brothers standing closely round her with their arms linked together. There was but just room enough for them, and not the

smallest space to spare. The sea dashed against the rock, and covered them with spray. The heavens were lighted up with continual flashes, and peal after peal of thunder rolled. But the sister and brothers sat holding each other's hands, and singing hymns, from which they gained hope and courage. In the early dawn the air became calm and still, and at sunrise the swans flew away from the rock with Eliza. The sea was still rough, and from their high position in the air, the white foam on the dark green waves looked like

millions of swans swimming on the water. As the sun rose higher, Eliza saw before her, floating in the air, a range of mountains, with shining masses of ice on their summits. In the centre, rose a castle apparently a mile long, with rows of columns rising one above another, while, around it, palm-trees waved and flowers bloomed as large as mill wheels. She asked if this was the land to which they were hastening. The swans shook their heads, for what she beheld were the beautiful ever-changing cloud palaces of the "Fata Morgana," into which no mortal can enter. Eliza was still gazing at the scene, when mountains, forests, and castles melted away, and twenty stately churches rose in their stead, with high towers and pointed gothic windows. Eliza even fancied she could hear the tones of the organ, but it was the music of the murmuring sea which she heard. As they drew nearer to the churches, they also changed into a fleet of ships, which seemed to be sailing beneath her; but as she looked again, she found it was only a sea mist gliding over the ocean. So there continued to pass before her eyes a constant change of scene, till at last she saw the real land to which they were bound, with its blue mountains, its cedar forests, and its cities and palaces. Long before the sun went down, she sat on a rock, in front of a large cave, on the floor of which the over-grown yet delicate green creeping plants looked like an embroidered carpet. "Now we shall expect to hear what you

405

dream of to-night," said the youngest brother, as he showed his sister her bedroom.

"Heaven grant that I may dream how to save you," she replied. And this thought took such hold upon her mind that she prayed earnestly to God for help, and even in her sleep she continued to pray. Then it appeared to her as if she were flying high in the air, towards the cloudy palace of the "Fata Morgana," and a fairy came out to meet her, radiant and beautiful in appearance, and yet very much like the old woman who had given her berries in the wood, and who had told her of the swans with golden crowns on their heads. "Your brothers can be released," said she, "if you have only courage and perseverance. True, water is softer than your own delicate hands, and yet it polishes stones into shapes; it feels no pain as your fingers would feel, it has no soul, and cannot suffer such agony and torment as you will have to endure. Do you see the stinging nettle which I hold in my hand? Quantities of the same sort grow round the cave in which you sleep, but none will be of any use to you unless they grow upon the graves in a churchyard. These you must gather even while they burn blisters on your hands. Break them to pieces with your hands and feet, and they will become flax, from which you must spin and weave eleven coats with long sleeves; if these are then thrown over the eleven swans, the spell will be broken. But remember, that from the moment you commence your task until it is finished, even should it occupy years of your life, you must not speak. The first word you utter will pierce through the hearts of your brothers like a deadly dagger. Their lives hang upon your tongue. Remember all I have told you." And as she finished speaking, she touched her hand lightly with the nettle, and a pain, as of burning fire, awoke Eliza.

It was broad daylight, and close by where she had been sleeping lay a nettle like the one she had seen in her dream. She fell on her knees and offered her thanks to God. Then she went forth from the cave to begin her work with her delicate hands. She groped in amongst the ugly nettles, which burnt great blisters on her hands and arms, but she determined to bear it gladly if she could only release her dear brothers. So she bruised the nettles with her bare feet and spun the flax. At sunset her brothers returned and were very much frightened when they found her dumb. They believed it to be some new sorcery of their wicked step-mother. But when they saw her hands they understood what she was doing on their behalf, and the youngest brother wept, and where his tears fell the pain ceased, and the burning blisters vanished. She kept to her work all night, for she could not rest till she had released her dear brothers. During the whole of the following day, while her brothers were absent, she sat in solitude, but never before had the time flown so quickly. One coat was already finished and she had begun the second, when she heard the huntsman's horn, and was struck with fear. The sound came nearer and nearer, she heard the dogs barking, and fled with terror into the cave. She hastily bound together the nettles she had gathered into a bundle and sat upon them. Immediately a great dog came bounding towards her out of the ravine, and then another and another; they barked loudly ran back, and then came again. In a very few minutes all the huntsmen stood before the cave, and the handsomest of them was the king of the country. He advanced towards her, for he had never seen a more beautiful maiden.

"How did you come here, my sweet child?" he asked. But Eliza shook her head. She dared not speak, at the cost of her brothers' lives. And she hid her hands under her apron, so that the king might not see how she must be suffering.

"Come with me," he said; "here you cannot remain. If you are as good as you are beautiful, I will dress you in silk and velvet, I will place a golden crown on your head, and you shall dwell, and rule, and make your home in my richest castle." And then he lifted her on his horse. She wept and wrung her hands, but the king said, "I wish only your happiness. A time will come when you will thank me for this." And then he galloped away over the mountains, holding her before him on his horse, and the hunters followed behind them. As the sun went down, they approached a fair, royal city, with churches and cupolas. On arriving at the castle, the king led her into marble halls, where large fountains played, and where the walls and the ceilings were covered with rich paintings. But she had no eyes for all these glorious sights, she could only mourn and weep. Patiently she allowed the women to array her in royal robes, to weave pearls in her hair, and draw soft gloves over her blistered fingers. As she stood before them in all her rich dress, she looked so dazzlingly beautiful that the court bowed low in her presence. Then the king declared his intention of making her his bride, but the archbishop shook his head, and whispered that the fair young maiden was only a witch who had blinded the king's eyes and bewitched his heart. But the king would not listen to this; he ordered the music to sound, the daintiest dishes to be served, and the loveliest maidens to dance. Afterwards he led her through fragrant gardens and lofty halls, but not a smile appeared on her lips or sparkled in her eyes. She looked the very picture of grief. Then the king opened the door of a little chamber in which she was to sleep; it was adorned with rich green tapestry, and resembled the cave in which he had found her. On the floor lay the bundle of flax which she had spun from the nettles, and under the ceiling hung the coat she had made. These things had been brought away from the cave as curiosities by one of the huntsmen.

"Here you can dream yourself back again in the old home in the cave," said the king; "here is the work with which you employed yourself. It will amuse you now in the midst of all this splendour to think of that time." When Eliza saw all these things which lay so near her heart, a smile played around her mouth, and the crimson blood rushed to her cheeks. She thought of her brothers, and their release made her so joyful that she kissed the king's hand. Then he pressed her to his heart. Very soon the joyous church bells announced the marriage feast, and that the beautiful dumb girl out of the wood was to be made the queen of the country. Then the archbishop whispered wicked words in the king's ear, but they did not sink into his heart. The marriage was still to take place, and the archbishop himself had to place the crown on the bride's head; in his wicked spite, he pressed the narrow circlet so tightly on her forehead that it caused her pain. But a heavier weight encircled her heart – sorrow for her brothers. She felt not bodily pain. Her mouth was closed; a single word would cost her brothers their lives. But she loved the kind, handsome king, who did everything to make her happy, more and more each day; she loved him with her whole heart, and her eyes beamed with the love she dared not speak. Oh! if she had only been able to confide in him and tell him of her grief. But dumb she must remain till her task was finished. Therefore at night she crept away into her little chamber, which had been decked out to look like the cave, and quickly wove one coat after another. But when she began the seventh she found she had no more flax. She knew that the nettles she wanted to use grew in the churchyard, and that she must pluck them herself. How should she get out there? "Oh, what is the pain in my fingers to the torment which my heart endures?" said she. "I must venture, I shall not be denied help from heaven." Then with a trembling heart, as if she were about to perform a wicked deed, she crept into the garden in the broad moonlight, and passed through the narrow walks and the deserted streets, till she reached the churchyard. Then she saw on one of the broad tombstones a group of ghouls. These hideous creatures took off their rags, as if they intended to bathe, and then clawing open the fresh graves with their long, skinny fingers, pulled out the dead bodies and ate the flesh! Eliza had to pass close by them, and they fixed their wicked glances upon her, but she prayed silently, gathered the burning nettles, and carried them home with her to the castle. One person only had seen her, and that was the archbishop – he was awake while everybody was asleep. Now he thought his opinion was evidently correct. All was not right with the queen. She was a witch, and had bewitched the king and all the people. Secretly he told the king what he had seen and what he feared, and as the hard words came from his tongue, the carved images of the saints shook their heads as if they would say, "It is not so. Eliza is innocent."

But the archbishop interpreted it in another way; he believed that they witnessed against her, and were shaking their heads at her wickedness. Two large tears rolled down the king's cheeks, and he went home with doubt in his heart, and at night pretended to sleep, but there came no real sleep to his eyes, for he saw Eliza get up every night and disappear in her own chamber. From day to day his brow became darker, and Eliza saw it and did not understand the reason, but it alarmed her and made her heart tremble for her brothers. Her hot tears glittered like pearls on the regal velvet and diamonds, while all who saw her were wishing they could be queens. In the mean time she had almost finished her task; only one coat of mail was wanting, but she had no flax left, and not a single nettle. Once more only, and for the last time, must she venture to the churchyard and pluck a few handfuls. She thought with terror of the solitary walk, and of the horrible ghouls, but her will was firm, as well as her trust in Providence. Eliza went, and the king and the archbishop followed her. They saw her vanish through the wicket gate into the churchyard, and when they came nearer they saw the ghouls sitting on the tombstone, as Eliza had seen them, and the king turned away his head, for he thought she was with them – she whose head had rested on his breast that very evening. "The people must condemn her," said he, and she was very quickly condemned by every one to suffer death by fire. Away from the gorgeous regal halls was she led to a dark, dreary cell, where the wind whistled through the iron bars. Instead of the velvet and silk dresses, they gave her the coats of mail which she had woven to cover her, and the bundle of nettles for a pillow; but nothing they could give her would have pleased her more. She continued her task with joy, and prayed for help, while the street-boys sang jeering songs about her, and not a soul comforted her with a kind word. Towards evening, she heard at the grating the flutter of a swan's wing, it was her youngest brother – he had found his sister, and she sobbed for joy, although she knew that very likely this would be the last night she would have to live. But still she could hope, for her task was almost finished, and her brothers were come. Then the archbishop arrived, to be with her during her last hours, as he had promised the king. But she shook her head, and begged him, by looks and gestures, not to stay; for in this night she knew she must finish her task, otherwise all her pain and tears and sleepless nights would have been suffered in vain. The archbishop withdrew, uttering bitter words against her; but poor Eliza knew that she was innocent, and diligently continued her work.

The little mice ran about the floor; they dragged the nettles to her feet, to help as well as they could; and the thrush sat outside the grating of the window, and sang to her the whole night long, as sweetly as possible, to keep up her spirits.

It was still twilight, and at least an hour before sunrise, when the eleven brothers stood at the castle gate, and demanded to be brought before the king. They were told it could not be, it was yet almost night, and as the king slept they dared not disturb him. They threatened, they entreated. Then the guard appeared, and even the king himself, inquiring what all the noise meant. At this moment the sun rose. The eleven brothers were seen no more, but eleven wild swans flew away over the castle.

And now all the people came streaming forth from the gates of the city, to see the witch burnt. An old horse drew the cart on which she sat. They had dressed her in a garment of coarse sackcloth. Her lovely hair hung loose on her shoulders, her cheeks were deadly pale, her lips moved silently, while her fingers still worked at the green flax. Even on the way to death, she would not give up her task. The ten coats of mail lay at her feet, she was working hard at the eleventh, while the mob jeered her and said, "See the witch, how she mutters! She has no hymnbook in her hand. She sits there with her ugly sorcery. Let us tear it in a thousand pieces."

And then they pressed towards her, and would have destroyed the coats of mail, but at the same moment eleven wild swans flew over her, and alighted on the cart. Then they flapped their large wings, and the crowd drew on one side in alarm.

"It is a sign from heaven that she is innocent," whispered many of them; but they ventured not to say it aloud.

As the executioner seized her by the hand, to lift her out of the cart, she hastily threw the eleven coats of mail over the swans, and they immediately became eleven handsome princes; but the youngest had a swan's wing, instead of an arm; for she had not been able to finish the last sleeve of the coat.

"Now I may speak," she exclaimed. "I am innocent."

411

Then the people, who saw what happened, bowed to her, as before a saint; but she sank lifeless in her brothers' arms, overcome with suspense, anguish, and pain.

"Yes, she is innocent," said the eldest brother; and then he related all that had taken place; and while he spoke there rose in the air a fragrance as from millions of roses. Every piece of faggot in the pile had taken root, and threw out branches, and appeared a thick hedge, large and high, covered with roses; while above all bloomed a white and shining flower, that glittered like a star. This flower the king plucked, and placed in Eliza's bosom, when she awoke from her swoon, with peace and happiness in her heart. And all the church bells rang by themselves, and the birds came in great flocks. And a marriage procession returned to the castle, such as no king had ever before seen.

The Shepherdess and the Sweep

—

Have you ever seen an old wooden cupboard quite black with age, and ornamented with carved foliage and curious figures? Well, just such a cupboard stood in a parlour, and had been left to the family as a legacy by the great-grandmother. It was covered from top bottom with carved roses and tulips; the most curious scrolls were drawn upon it, and out of them peeped little stag's heads, with antlers. In the middle of the cupboard door was the carved figure of a man most ridiculous to look at. He grinned at you, for no once could call it laughing. He had goat's legs, little horns on his head, and a long beard; the children in the room always called him, "Major-general-field-sergeant-commander Billy-goat's-legs." It was certainly a very difficult name to pronounce, and there are very few who ever receive such a title, but then it seemed wonderful how he came to be carved at all; yet there he was, always looking at the table under the looking-glass, where stood a very pretty little shepherdess, made of china. Her shoes were gilt, and her dress had a red rose for an ornament. She wore a hat, and carried a crook, that were both gilded, and looked very bright and pretty. Close by her side stood a little chimney-sweep, as black as a coal, and also made of china. He was, however, quite as clean and neat as any other china figure; he only represented a black chimney-sweep, and the china workers might just as well have made him a prince, had they felt inclined to do so. He stood holding his ladder quite handily, and his face was as fair and rosy as a girl's; indeed, that was rather a mistake, it should have had some black marks on it. He and the shepherdess had been placed close together, side by side; and, being so placed, they became engaged to each other, for they were very well suited, being both made of the same sort of china, and being equally fragile. Close to them stood another figure, three times as large as they were, and also made of china. He was an old Chinaman, who could nod his head, and used to pretend that he was the grandfather of the shepherdess, although he could not prove it. He however assumed authority over her, and therefore when "Major-general-field-sergeant-commander Billy-goat's-legs" asked for the little shepherdess to be his wife, he nodded his head to show that he consented. "You will have a husband," said the old Chinaman to her, "who I really believe is made of mahogany. He will make you the

413

lady of Major-general-field-sergeant-commander Billy-goat's-legs. He has the whole cupboard full of silver plate, which he keeps locked up in secret drawers."

"I won't go into the dark cupboard," said the little shepherdess. "I have heard that he has eleven china wives there already."

"Then you shall be the twelfth," said the old cupboard, you shall be married, as true as I am Chinaman;" and then he nodded his head and fell asleep.

Then the little shepherdess cried, and looked at her sweetheart, the china chimney-sweep. "I must entreat you," said she, "to go out with me into the wide world, for we cannot stay here."

"I will do whatever you wish," said the little chimney-sweep; "let us go immediately: I think I shall be able to maintain you with my profession."

"If we were but safely down from the table!" said she; "I shall not be happy till we are really out in the world."

Then he comforted her, and showed her how to place her little foot on the carved edge and gilt-leaf ornaments of the table. He brought his little ladder

to help her, and so they contrived to reach the floor. But when they looked at the old cupboard, they saw it was all in an uproar. The carved stags pushed out their heads, raised their antlers, and twisted their necks. The major-general sprung up in the air, and cried out to the old Chinaman, "They are running away! they are running away!" The two were rather frightened at this, so they jumped into the drawer of the window-seat. Here were three or four packs of cards not quite complete, and a doll's theatre, which had been built up very neatly. A comedy was being performed in it, and all the queens of diamonds, clubs, and hearts, and spades, sat in the first row fanning themselves with tulips, and behind them stood all the knaves, showing that they had heads above and below as playing cards generally have. The play was about two lovers, who were not allowed to marry, and the shepherdess wept because it was so like her own story. "I cannot bear it," said she, "I must get out of the drawer;" but when they reached the floor, and cast their eyes on the table, there was the old China-man awake and shaking his whole body, till all at once down he came on the

415

floor, "plump." "The old Chinaman is coming," cried the little shepherdess in a fright, and down she fell on one knee.

"I have thought of something," said the chimney-sweep; "let us get into the great pot-porri jar which stands in the corner; there we can lie on rose-leaves and lavender, and throw salt in his eyes if he comes near us."

"No, that will never do," said she, "because I know that the Chinaman and the pot-pourri jar were lovers once, and there always remains behind a feeling of good-will between those who have been so intimate as that. No, there is nothing left for us but to go out into the wide world."

"Have you really courage enough to go out into the wide world with me?" said the chimney-sweep; "have you thought how large it is, and that we can never come back here again?"

"Yes, I have," she replied.

When the chimney-sweep saw that she was quite firm, he said, "My way is through the stove and up the chimney. Have you courage to creep with me through the fire-box, and the iron pipe? When we get to the chimney I shall know how to manage very well. We shall soon climb too high for any one to reach us, and we shall come through a hole in the top out into the wide world." So he led her to the door of the stove.

"It looks very dark," said she; still she went in with him through the stove and through the pipe, where it was as dark as pitch.

"Now we are in the chimney," said he; "and look, there is a beautiful star shining above it." It was a real star shining down upon them as if it would show them the way. So they clambered, and crept on, and a frightfully steep place it was; but the chimney-sweep helped her and supported her, till they got higher and higher. He showed her the best places on which to set her little china foot, so at last they reached the top of the chimney, and sat themselves down, for they were very tired, as may be supposed. The sky, with all its stars, was over their heads, and below were the roofs of the town. They could see for a very long distance out into the wide world, and the poor little shepherdess leaned her head on her chimney-sweep's shoulder, and wept till she washed the gilt off her sash; the world was so different to what she expected. "This is too much," she said; "I cannot bear it, the world is too large. Oh, I wish I were safe back on the table again, under the looking-glass; I shall never be happy till I am safe back again. Now I have followed you out into the wide world, you will take me back, if you love me."

Then the chimney-sweep tried to reason with her, and spoke of the old Chinaman, and of the Major-general-field-sergeant-commander Billy-goat's-legs; but she sobbed so bitterly, and kissed her little chimney-sweep till he was obliged to do all she asked, foolish as it was. And so, with

a great deal of trouble, they climbed down the chimney, and then crept through the pipe and stove, which were certainly not very pleasant places. Then they stood in the dark fire-box, and listened behind the door, to hear what was going on in the room. As it was all quiet, they peeped out. Alas! there lay the old Chinaman on the floor; he had fallen down from the table as he attempted to run after them, and was broken into three pieces; his back had separated entirely, and his head had rolled into a corner of the room. The major-general stood in his old place, and appeared lost in thought.

"This is terrible," said the little shepherdess. "My poor old grandfather is broken to pieces, and it is our fault. I shall never live after this;" and she wrung her little hands.

"He can be riveted," said the chimney-sweep; "he can be riveted. Do not be so hasty. If they cement his back, and put a good rivet in it, he will be as good as new, and be able to say as many disagreeable things to us as ever."

"Do you think so?" said she; and then they climbed up to the table, and stood in their old places.

"As we have done no good," said the chimney-sweep, "we might as well have remained here, instead of taking so much trouble."

417

"I wish grandfather was riveted," said the shepherdess. "Will it cost much, I wonder?"

And she had her wish. The family had the Chinaman's back mended, and a strong rivet put through his neck; he looked as good as new, but he could no longer nod his head.

"You have become proud since your fall broke you to pieces," said Major-general-field-sergant-commander Billy-goat's-legs. "You have no reason to give yourself such airs. Am I to have her or not?"

The chimney-sweep and the little shepherdess looked piteously at the old Chinaman, for they were afraid he might nod; but he was not able: besides, it was so tiresome to be always telling strangers he had a rivet in the back of his neck.

And so the little china people remained together, and were glad of the grandfather's rivet, and continued to love each other till they were broken to pieces.

It's Absolutely True

It's terrible affair!« said a hen – speaking, too in quite another part of
the town from where it all happened. "It's a terrible affair about that chicken-house. I daren't sleep alone tonight. It's a good thing there are so
many of us roosting together." And then she told them her story, which
made the other hens' feathers stand on end and even set the cock's comb
drooping. It's absolutely true!

But let's begin at the beginning. It was in a chicken-house at the other end
of the town. The sun went down, and the hens flew up. One of them was a
white short-legged bird, who regularly laid her eggs and was altogether a
most respectable hen. When she got to her perch she preened herself with
her beak, and a little feather came out and went fluttering down. "So much
for that one!" she said. "The more I preen, the lovelier I shall grow, no
doubt" Of course it was only said in fun, because she was the fun-maker

419

among the hens, though in other ways (as you've just heard) most respectable. After that, she went off to sleep.

All about was quite dark; hen sat with hen, but the one next to her was still awake. She heard, and had not heard – as you must often do in this world, if you are to live in peace and quiet. And yet she couldn't help saying to the hen perched on the other side of her, "Did you hear that? I give no names, but there is a hen who means to pluck out her feathers for the sake of her looks. If I were a cock, I'd simply despise her."

Now directly above the hens sat the owl, with her owl husband and her owl children. They had sharp ears in that family; they could hear every word their hen neighbour said; and they rolled their eyes, and the owl mother fanned herself with her wings. "Don't take any notice – but of course you heard what she said, didn't you? I heard it with my own ears, and they're going to hear a lot before *they* drop off. One of the hens has so far forgotten what is fit and proper for a hen that she's calmly plucking out all her feathers in full view of the cock."

"Prenez garde aux enfants!" said the father owl. "Not in the children's hearing!"

"But I must tell the owl over the way; she's so highly respected in our set." And away flew the mother.

"Tu-whit, tu-who!" they both hooted, and it carried right down to the doves in the dovecot across the yard. "Have you heard, have you heard? Tu-who! There's a hen that's plucked out all her feathers for the sake of the cock. She'll freeze to death, if she isn't dead already, tu-who!"

"Where, ooh, where?" cooed the doves.

"In the yard opposite. I as good as saw it with my own eyes. Really the story's almost too improper to repeat; but it's absolutely true."

"Tr-rue, tr-rue, every wor-rd!" said the doves; and they cooed down to their hen-run, "There's a hen, some say there are *two*, who have plucked out all their feathers so as to look different from the others and to attract the attention of the cock. It's a risky thing to do; suppose they catch cold and die of fever ... Yes, they're dead – *two* of them."

Then the cock joined in: "Wake up, wake up!" he crowed, and flew up on to the wooden fence. His eyes were still sleepy, but he crowed away all the same; "Three hens have died of love for a cock; they had plucked out all their feathers. It's a horrible story – I don't want it – pass it on!" "Pass it on!" squeaked the bats; and the hens clucked and the cocks crowed, "Pass it on, pass it on!" And so the story flew from one hen-house to another, till at last it came back to the place where it had really started.

"There are five hens" – that's how it ran – "who have all plucked out their feathers to show which of them had got thinnest for love of the cock. Then

they pecked at each other till the blood came and they all fell down dead, to the shame and disgrace of their family and the serious loss of their owner.'' The hen that had lost the one loose little feather didn't of course recognize her own story and, as she was a respectable hen, she said, "How I despise those hens! – though there are plenty more just like them. That's not the kind of thing to be hushed up, and I shall do my best to get the story into the papers, so that it may go all over the country. It'll serve those hens right, and their family too.''

And into the papers it came – all there in print – and it's absolutely true: *"One little feather can easily become five hens!"*

The Fir-Tree

Far down in the forest, where the warm sun and the fresh air made a sweet resting-place, grew a pretty little fir-tree; and yet it was not happy, it wished so much to be tall like its companions – the pines and firs which grew around it. The sun shone, and the soft air fluttered its leaves, and the little peasant children passed by, prattling merrily, but the fir-tree heeded them not. Sometimes the children would bring a large basket of raspberries or strawberries, wreathed on a straw, and seat themselves near the fir-tree, and say, "Is it not a pretty little tree?" which made it feel more unhappy than before. And yet all this while the tree grew a notch or joint taller every year; for by the number of joints in the stem of a fir-tree we can discover its age. Still, as it grew, it complained, "Oh! how I wish I were as tall as the other trees, then I would spread out my branches on every side, and my top would overlook the wide world. I should have the birds building their nests on my boughs, and when the wind blew, I should bow with stately dignity like my tall companions." The tree was so discontented, that it took no pleasure in the warm sunshine, the birds, or the rosy clouds that floated over it morning and evening. Sometimes, in winter, when the snow lay white and glittering on the ground, a hare would come springing along, and jump right over the little tree; and then how mortified it would feel! Two winters passed, and when the third arrived, the tree had grown so tall that the hare was obliged to run round it. Yet it remained unsatisfied, and would exclaim, "Oh, if I could but keep on growing tall and old! There is nothing else worth caring for in the world!" In the autumn, as usual, the woodcutters came and cut down several of the tallest trees, and the young fir-tree, which was now grown to its full height, shuddered as the noble trees fell to the earth with a crash. After the branches were lopped off, the trunks looked so slender and bare, that they could scarcely be recognised. Then they were placed upon waggons, and drawn by horses out of the forest. "Where were they going? What would become of them?" The young fir-tree wished very much to know; so in the spring, when the swallows and the storks came, it asked, "Do you know where those trees were taken? Did you meet them?" The swallows knew nothing; but the stork, after a little reflection, nodded his head, and said, "Yes, I think I do. I met several new ships when I flew from Egypt, and they had fine masts that smelt like fir. I think these must have been the trees; I assure you they were stately, very stately."

"Oh, how I wish I were tall enough to go on the sea," said the fir-tree. "What is this sea, and what does it look like?"

"It would take too much time to explain," said the stork, flying quickly away.

"Rejoice in thy youth," said the sunbeam; "rejoice in thy fresh growth, and the young life that is in thee."

And the wind kissed the tree, and the dew watered it with tears; but the fir-tree did not notice them.

Christmas-time drew near, and many young trees were cut down, some even smaller and younger than the fir-tree who enjoyed neither rest nor peace with longing to leave its forest home. These young trees, which were chosen for their beauty, kept their branches, and were also laid on waggons and drawn by horses out of the forest.

"Where are they going?" asked the fir-tree. "They are not taller than I am: indeed, one is much less; and why are the branches not cut off? Where are they going?"

"We know, we know," sang the sparrows, "we have looked in at the windows of the house in the town, and we know what is done with them. They are dressed up in the most splendid manner. We have seen them standing in the middle of a warm room, and adorned with all sorts of beautiful things, – honey cakes, gilded apples, playthings, and many hundreds of wax tapers."

"And then," asked the fir-tree, trembling through all its branches, "and then what happens?"

"We did not see any more," said the sparrows; "but this was enough for us."

"I wonder whether anything so brilliant will ever happen to me," thought the fir-tree. "It would be much better than crossing the sea. I long for it almost with pain. Oh! when will Christmas be here? I am now as tall and well grown as those which were taken away last year. Oh! that I were now laid on the waggon, or standing in the warm room, with all that brightness and splendour around me! Something better and more beautiful is to come after, or the trees would not be so decked out. Yes what follows will be grander and more splendid. What can it be? I am weary with longing. I scarcely know how I feel."

"Rejoice with us," said the air and the sunlight. "Enjoy thine own bright life in the fresh air."

But the tree would not rejoice, though it grew taller every day; and, winter and summer, its dark-green foliage might be seen in the forest, while passers-by would say, "What a beautiful tree!"

A short time before Christmas, the discontented fir-tree was the first to fall.
As the axe cut through the stem, and divided the pith, the tree fell with a
groan to the earth, conscious of pain and faintness, and forgetting all its
anticipations of happiness, in sorrow at leaving its home in the forest. It
knew that it should never again see its dear old companions, the trees, nor
the little bushes and many-coloured flowers that had grown by its side;
perhaps not even the birds. Neither was the journey at all pleasant. The
tree first recovered itself while being unpacked in the courtyard of a house,
with several other trees; and it heard a man say, "We only want one, and
this is the prettiest."

Then came two servants in grand livery, and carried the fir-tree into a large
and beautiful apartment. On the walls hung pictures, and near the great
stove stood great china vases, with lions on the lids. There were rocking-
chairs, silken sofas, large tables, covered with pictures, books, and playthings, worth a great deal of money, – at least, the children said so. Then the
fir-tree was placed in a large tub, full of sand; but green baize hung all round
it, so that no one could see it was a tub, and it stood on a very handsome
carpet. How the fir-tree trembled! "What was going to happen to him now?"
Some young ladies came, and the servants helped them to adorn the tree.
On one branch they hung little bags cut out of coloured paper, and each
bag was filled with sweetmeats; from other branches hung gilded apples

425

and walnuts, as if they had grown there; and above, and all around, were hundreds of red, blue, and white tapers, which were fastened on the branches. Dolls, exactly like real babies, were placed under the green leaves, – the tree had never seen such things before, – and at the very top was fastened a glittering star, made of tinsel. Oh, it was very beautiful!

"This evening," they all exclaimed, "how bright it will be!" "Oh, that the evening were come," thought the tree, "and the tapers lighted, then I shall know what else is going to happen. Will the trees of the forest come to see me? I wonder if the sparrows will peep in at the windows as they fly? shall I grow faster here, and keep on all these ornaments during summer and winter?" But guessing was of very little use; it made its bark ache, and this pain is as bad for a slender fir-tree, as headache is for us. At last the tapers were lighted, and then what a glistening blaze of light the tree presented! It trembled so with joy in all its branches, that one of the candles fell among the green leaves and burnt some of them. "Help! help!" exclaimed the young ladies, but there was no danger, for they quickly extinguished the fire. After this, the tree tried not to tremble at all, though the fire frightened him; he was so anxious not to hurt any of the beautiful ornaments, even while their brilliancy dazzled him. And now the folding doors were thrown open, and a troop of children rushed in as if they intended to upset the tree; they were followed more slowly by their elders. For a moment the little ones stood silent with astonishment, and then they shouted for joy, till the room rang, and they danced merrily round the tree, while one present after another was taken from it.

"What are they doing? What will happen next?" thought the fir. At last the candles burnt down to the branches and were put out. Then the children received permission to plunder the tree.

Oh, how they rushed upon it, till the branches cracked, and had it not been fastened with the glistening star to the ceiling, it would have been thrown down. The children then danced about with their pretty toys, and no one noticed the tree, except the children's maid, who came and peeped among the branches to see if an apple or a fig had been forgotten.

"A story, a story," cried the children, pulling a little fat man towards the tree.

"Now we shall be in the green shade," said the man, as he seated himself under it, "and the tree will have the pleasure of hearing also, but I shall only relate one story; what shall it be? Ivede-Avede, or Humpty Dumpty, who fell downstairs, but soon got up again, and at last married a princess."

"Ivede-Avede," cried some. "Humpty Dumpty," cried others, and there was a fine shouting and crying out. But the fir-tree remained quite still, and thought to himself, "Shall I have anything to do with all this?" but he had

426

already amused them as much as they wished. Then the old man told them the story of Humpty Dumpty, how he fell downstairs, and was raised up again, and married a princess. And the children clapped their hands and cried, "Tell another, tell another," for they wanted to hear the story of "Ivede-Avede;" but they only had "Humpty Dumpty." After this the fir-tree became quite silent and thoughtful; never had the birds in the forest told such tales as "Humpty Dumpty," who fell downstairs, and yet married a princess.

"Ah! yes, so it happens in the world," thought the fir-tree; he believed it all, because it was related by such a nice man. "Ah! well," he thought, "who knows? perhaps I may fall down too, and marry a princess;" and he looked forward joyfully to the next evening, expecting to be again decked out with lights and playthings, gold and fruit. "To-morrow I will not tremble," thought he; "I will enjoy all my splendour, and I shall hear the story of Humpty Dumpty again, and perhaps Ivede-Avede." And the tree remained quiet and thoughtful all night. In the morning the servants and the house-maid came in. "Now," thought the fir, "all my splendour is going to begin again." But they dragged him out of the room and upstairs to the garret, and threw him on the floor, in a dark corner, where no daylight shone, and there they left him. "What does this mean?" thought the tree, "What am I to do here? I can hear nothing in a place like this," and he leant against the wall, and thought and thought. And he had time enough to think, for days and nights passed and no one came near him, and when at last some-body did come, it was only to put away large boxes in a corner. So the tree was completely hidden from sight as if it had never existed. "It is winter now," thought the tree, "the ground is hard and covered with snow, so that people cannot plant me. I shall be sheltered here I dare say, until spring comes. How thoughful and kind everybody is to me! Still I wish this place were not so dark, as well as lonely, with not even a little hare to look at. How pleasant it was out in the forest while the snow lay on the ground, when the hare would run by, yes, and jump over me too, although I did not like it then. Oh! it is terribly lonely here."

"Squeak, squeak," said a little mouse, creeping cautiously towards the tree; then came another and they both sniffed at the fir tree and crept between the branches.

"Oh, it is very cold," said the little mouse, "or else we should be so com-fortable here, shouldn't we, you old fir-tree?"

"I am not old," said the fir-tree, "there are many who are older than I am."

"Where do you come from and what do you know?" asked the mice, who were full of curiosity. "Have you seen the most beautiful places in the world, and can you tell us all about them? and have you been in the store-room, where cheeses lie on the shelf, and hams hang from the ceiling? One can run about on tallow candles there, and go in thin and come out fat."

"I know nothing of that place," said the fir-tree, "but I know the wood where the sun shines and the birds sing." And then the tree told the little mice all about its youth. They had never heard such an account in their lives; and after they had listened to it attentively, they said, "What a number of things you have seen! You must have been very happy."

"Happy!" exclaimed the fir-tree, and then as he reflected upon what he had been telling them, he said, "Ah, yes! after all, those were happy days." But when he went on and related all about Christmas-eve, and how he had been dressed up with cakes and lights, the mice said, "How happy you must have been, you old fir-tree."

"I am not old at all," replied the tree, "I only came from the forest this winter, I am now checked in my growth."

"What splendid stories you can relate," said the little mice. And the next night four other mice came with them to hear what the tree had to tell. The more he talked, the more he remembered, and then he thought to himself, "Those were happy days, but they may come again. Humpty Dumpty fell downstairs, and yet he married the princess; perhaps I may marry a princess too." And the fir-tree thought of the pretty little birch-tree that grew in the forest, which was to him a real beautiful princess.

"Who is Humpty Dumpty?" asked the little mice. And then the tree related the whole story; he could remember every single word, and the little mice were so delighted with it, that they were ready to jump to the top of the tree. The next night a great many more mice made their appearance, and on Sunday two rats came with them; but they said, it was not a pretty story at all, and the little mice were very sorry, for it made them also think less of it.

"Do you know only one story?" asked the rats.

"Only one," replied the fir-tree; "I heard it on the happiest evening in my life; but I did not know I was so happy at the time."

"We think it is a very miserable story," said the rats. "Don't you know any story about bacon, or tallow in the storeroom.'

"No," replied the tree.

"Many thanks to you then," replied the rats, and they marched off.

The little mice also kept away after this, and the tree sighed, and said, "It was very pleasant when the merry little mice sat round me and listened while I talked. Now that is all past too. However, I shall consider myself happy when some one comes to take me out of this place." But would this ever happen? Yes; one morning people came to clear out the garret, the boxes were packed away, and the tree was pulled out of the corner, and thrown roughly on the garret floor; then the servant dragged it out upon

the staircase where the daylight shone. "Now life is beginning again, said the tree, rejoicing in the sunshine and fresh air. Then it was carried downstairs and taken into the courtyard so quickly, that it forgot to think of itself, and could only look about, there was so much to be seen. The courtyard was close to a garden, where everything looked blooming. Fresh and fragrant roses hung over the little palings. The linden-trees were in blossom; while the swallows flew here and there, crying. "Twit, twit, twit, my mate is coming," but it was not the fir-tree they meant. "Now I shall live," cried the tree joyfully spreading out its branches; but alas! they were all withered and yellow, and it lay in a corner amongst weeds and nettles. The star of gold paper still stuck in the top of the tree and glittered in the sunshine. In the same courtyard two of the merry children were playing who had danced round the tree at Christmas, and had been so happy. The youngest saw the gilded star, and ran and pulled it off the tree. "Look what is sticking to the ugly old firtree," said the child, treading on the branches till they crackled under his boots. And the tree saw all the fresh bright flowers in the garden, and then looked at itself, and wished it had remained in the dark corner of the garret. It thought of its fresh youth in the forest, of the merry Christmas evening, and of the little mice who had listened to the story of "Humpty Dumpty." "Past! past!" said the old tree; "Oh, had I but enjoyed myself while I could have done so! But now it is too late." Then a lad came and chopped the tree into small pieces, till a large bundle lay in a heap on the ground. The pieces were placed in a fire under the copper, and they quickly blazed up brightly, while the tree sighed so deeply that each sigh was like a little pistol-shot. Then the children, who were at play, came and seated themselves in front of the fire, and looked at it, and cried, "Pop, pop." But at each "pop," which was a deep sigh, the tree was thinking of a summer day in the forest, or of some winter night there, when the stars shone brightly; and of Christmas evening, and of "Humpty Dumpty," the only story it had ever heard or knew how to relate, till at last it was consumed. The boys still played in the garden, and the youngest wore the golden star on his breast, with which the fir-tree had been adorned during the happiest evening of its existence. Now all was past; the tree's life was past, and the story also, – for all stories must come to an end at last.

The Happy Family

The largest green leaf in this country is certainly the burdock-leaf. If you hold it in front of you, it is large enough for an apron; and if you hold it over your head, it is almost as good as an umbrella, it is so wonderfully large. A burdock never grows alone; where it grows, there are many more, and it is a splendid sight; and all this splendour is good for snails. The great white snails, which grand people in olden times used to have made into fricassees; and when they had eaten them, they would say, "Oh, what a delicious dish!" for these people really thought them good; and these snails lived on burdock-leaves, and for them the burdock was planted.

There was once an old estate where no one now lived to require snails; indeed, the owners had all died out, but the burdock still flourished; it grew over all the beds and walks of the garden – its growth had no check – till it became at last quite a forest of burdocks. Here and there stood an apple or a plum-tree; but for this, nobody would have thought the place had ever been a garden. It was burdock from one end to the other; and here lived the last two surviving snails. They knew not themselves how old they were; but they could remember the time when there were a great many more of them, and that they were descended from a family which came from foreign lands, and that the whole forest had been planted for them and theirs. They had never been away from the garden; but they knew that another place once existed in the world, called the Duke's Palace Castle, in which some of their relations had been boiled till they became black, and were then laid on a silver dish; but what was done afterwards they did not know. Besides, they could not imagine exactly how it felt to be boiled and placed on a silver dish; but no doubt it was something very fine and highly genteel. Neither the cockchafer, nor the toad, nor the earth-worm, whom they questioned about it, would give them the least information; for none of their relations had ever been cooked or served on a silver dish. The old white snails were the most aristocratic race in the world, – they knew that. The forest had been planted for them, and the nobleman's castle had been built entirely that they might be cooked and laid on silver dishes.

They lived quite retired and very happily; and as they had no children of their own, they had adopted a little common snail, which they brought up

as their own child. The little one would not grow, for he was only a common snail; but the old people, particularly the mother-snail, declared that she could easily see how he grew; and when the father said he could not perceive it, she begged him to feel the little snail's shell, and he did so, and found that the mother was right.

One day it rained very fast. "Listen, what a drumming there is on the burdock-leaves; tum, tum, tum; tum, tum, tum," said the father-snail.

"There come the drops," said the mother; "they are trickling down the stalks. We shall have it very wet here presently. I am very glad we have such good houses, and that the little one has one of his own. There has been really more done for us than for any other creature; it is quite plain that we are the most noble people in the world. We have houses from our birth, and the burdock forest has been planted for us. I should very much like to know how far it extends, and what lies beyond it."

"There can be nothing better than we have here," said the father-snail; "I wish for nothing more."

"Yes, but I do," said the mother; "I should like to be taken to the palace, and boiled, and laid upon a silver dish, as was done to all our ancestors; and you may be sure it must be something very uncommon."

"The nobleman's castle, perhaps, has fallen to decay," said the snail-father, "or the burdock wood may have grown over it, so that those who live there cannot get out. You need not be in a hurry; you are always so impatient, and the youngster is getting just the same. He has been three days creeping to the top of that stalk. I feel quite giddy when I look at him."

"You must not scold him," said the mother-snail; "he creeps so very carefully. He will be the joy of our home; and we old folks have nothing else to live for. But have you ever thought where we are to get a wife for him? Do you think that farther out in the wood there may be others of our race?"

"There may be black snails, no doubt," said the old snail; "black snails without houses; but they are so vulgar and conceited too. But we can give the ants a commission; they run here and there, as if they all had so much business to get through. They, most likely, will know of a wife for our youngster."

"I certainly know a most beautiful bride," said one of the ants; "but I fear it would not do, for she is a queen."

"That does not matter," said the old snail; "has she a house?"

"She has a palace," replied the ant, – "a most beautiful antpalace with seven hundred passages."

"Thank you," said the mother-snail; "but our boy shall not go to live in an ant-hill. If you know of nothing better, we will give the commission to the white gnats; they fly about in rain and sunshine; they know the burdock wood from one end to the other."

"We have a wife for him," said the gnats; "a hundred man-steps from here there is a little snail with a house, sitting on a gooseberry-bush; she is quite alone, and old enough to be married. It is only a hundred man-steps from here."

"Then let her come to him," said the old people. "He has the whole burdock forest; she has only a bush."

So they brought the little lady-snail. She took eight days to perform the journey; but that was just as it ought to be; for it showed her to be one of the right breeding. And then they had a wedding. Six glow-worms gave as much light as they could; but in other respects it was all very quiet; for the old snails could not bear festivities or a crowd. But a beautiful speech was made by the mother-snail. The father could not speak; he was too much overcome. Then they gave the whole burdock forest to the young snails as an inheritance, and repeated what they had so often said that it was the finest place in the world, and that if they led upright and honourable lives, and their family increased, they and their children might some day be taken to the nobleman's palace, to be boiled black, and laid on a silver dish. And when they had finished speaking, the old couple crept into their houses, and came out no more; for they slept.

The young snail pair now ruled in the forest, and had a numerous progeny. But as the young ones were never boiled or laid in silver dishes, they concluded that the castle had fallen into decay, and that all the people in the world were dead; and as nobody contradicted them, they thought they must be right. And the rain fell upon the burdock-leaves, to play the drum for them, and the sun shone to paint colours on the burdock forest for them, and they were very happy; the whole family were entirely and perfectly happy.

The Leaping Match

The flea, the grasshopper, and the frog once wanted to try which of them could jump highest; so they invited the whole world, and anybody else who liked, to come and see the grand sight. Three famous jumpers were they, as was seen by every one when they met together in the room.

'I will give my daughter to him who shall jump highest,' said the King; 'it would be too bad for you to have the trouble of jumping, and for us to offer you no prize.'

The flea was the first to introduce himself; he had such polite manners, and bowed to the company on every side, for he was of noble blood; besides; he was accustomed to the society of man, which had been a great advantage to him.

Next came the grasshopper; he was not quite so slightly and elegantly formed as the flea; however, he knew perfectly well how to conduct himself, and wore a green uniform, which belonged to him by right of birth. Moreover, he declared himself to have sprung from a very ancient and honourable Egyptian family, and that in his present home he was very highly esteemed, so much so, indeed, that he had been taken out of the field and put into a card-house three stories high, built on purpose for him, and all of court-cards, the coloured sides being turned inwards: as for the doors and windows in his house, they were cut out of the body of the Queen of Hearts. 'And I can sing so well,' added he, 'that sixteen parlour-bred crickets, who have chirped and chirped ever since they were born and yet could never get anybody to build them a cardhouse, after hearing me have fretted themselves ten times thinner than ever, out of sheer envy and vexation!' Both the flea and the grasshopper knew excellently well how to make the most of themselves, and each considered himself quite an equal match for a princess.

The frog said not a word; however, it might be that he thought the more, and the house-dog, after going snuffing about him confessed that the frog must be of a good family. And the old councillor, who in vain received three orders to hold his tongue, declared that the frog must be gifted with the spirit of prophecy, for one could read on his back whether there was to be a severe or a mild winter, which, to be sure, is more than can be read on the back of the man who writes the weather almanack.

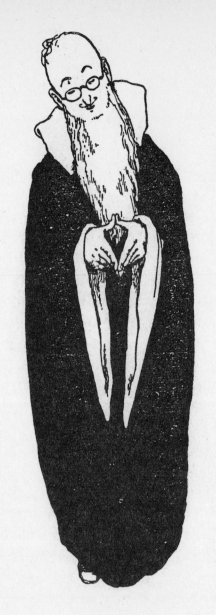

'Ah, I say nothing for the present!' remarked the old King, 'but I observe everything, and form my own private opinion thereupon.' And now the match began. The flea jumped so high that no one could see what had become of him, and so they insisted that he had not jumped at all, 'which was disgraceful, after he had made such a fuss!'

The grasshopper only jumped half as high, but he jumped right into the King's face, and the King declared he was quite disgusted by his rudeness.

The frog stood still as if lost in thought; at last people fancied he did not intend to jump at all.

436

'I'm afraid he is ill!' said the dog; and he went snuffing at him again, when lo! all at once he made a little side-long jump into the lap of the Princess, who was sitting on a low stool close by.

Then spoke the King: 'There is nothing higher than my daughter, therefore he who jumps up to her jumps highest; but only a person of good understanding would ever have thought of that, and thus the frog has shown us that he has understanding. He has brains in his head, that he has!'

And thus the frog won the Princess.

'I jumped highest for all that!' exclaimed the flea. 'But it's all the same to

437

me; let her have the stiff-legged, slimy creature, if she like him! I jumped
highest, but I am too light and airy for this stupid world; the people can
neither see me nor catch me; dulness and heaviness win the day with them!'
And so the flea went into foreign service, where, it is said, he was killed.
And the grasshopper sat on a green bank, meditating on the world and its
goings on, and at length he repeated the flea's last words – 'Yes, dulness and
heaviness win the day! dulness and heaviness win the day!' And then he
again began singing his own peculiar, melancholy song, and it is from him
that we have learnt this history; and yet, my freind, though you read it here
in a printed book, it may not be perfectly true.

Auntie Toothache

Where the story comes from – you want to know that, do you? We got it from the butter cask, the one with the old papers in it.

Many a good and rare book has gone to the grocer's and the provison dealer's, not for reading, but as something that may come in handy. They must have paper to make bags for starch and coffee-beans, paper to wrap up bloaters, butter and cheese. Handwritten documents can also be used.

Things often go into the tub that oughtn't to go into the tub.

I know a grocer's boy who's the son of a provision dealer. He has risen from the store-room to the front shop; a young man well up in paper-bag literature, whether printed or in manuscript. He has an interesting collection, including several important documents from the waste-paper basket of some bewildered overworked official, secret notes between lady friends; bits of scandal that mustn't go further or be mentioned to a soul. He's a walking salvage store for a large range of literature; and he has a big field to work in, for he has the shops of his parents and of his employer. He has rescued many a book or page of a book that might well deserve a second reading.

He has shown me his collection of printed and written things from the tub, chiefly from the grocer's. There were a few pages from a biggish exercise book, and the particularly fine clear handwriting at once caught my attention.

"That was written by the student," said the young man; "the student who lived just opposite and died a month ago. He must have suffered a lot from toothache. It's well worth reading. There's only a little left here of what he wrote – originally a complete book and some more besides. My parents gave half a pound of green soap for it to the student's landlady. Here's what I manage to rescue."

I borrowed it and read it, and now I'll pass it on to you. The title was:

Auntie Toothache
I

My aunt used to give me sweets when I was small. My teeth held out and weren't ruined. Now I'm older and have left school. She still spoils me with sweets and says I'm a poet.

There is something of the poet in me, though not enough. Often, as I walk through the streets of the town, I feel as if I was in a large library. The hauses are bookcases, every storey a shelf with books. Here is a tale of everyday life, there a good old play and scientific works on every subject, and there again reading pleasant and unpleasant. All that literature is for me to dream and philosophize over.

Yes, I've got something of the poet in me, but not enough. Lots of people must have just as much as I have – and yet have no badge or title to the name of poet.

To them and to me is given a gift from God, a boon big enough for oneself, but far too small to be parcelled out again among others. It comes like a ray from the sun, filling mind and soul; it comes like the scent of a flower, or a melody one has heard but cannot remember where.

The other evening, as I sat in my room longing to read, but without book or paper to look at, all at once a fresh green leaf dropped down from the lime tree, and a puff of air blew it in to me through the window.

I was looking at all the branching veins on the leaf, when a little insect crawled across it, just as though it wanted to make a close study of the leaf. That set me thinking about human wisdom. We, too, crawl about on a leaf, knowing nothing but that, and then proceed to give a lecture on the whole great tree – root, trunk and summit – the whole great tree, that's to say, God, the world and immortality ... And all we know of the whole thing is on a little leaf.

As I sat there, I had a visit from Auntie Millie. I showed her the leaf with the insect, told her what had come into my mind, and her eyes shone.

"You're a poet!" she exclaimed. "Perhaps the greatest we have. If I should live to see that, I would go happy to my grave. You have always, ever since Brewer Rasmussen's funeral, astonished me by your tremendous imagination."

So said Auntie Millie and kissed me.

Now, who was this Auntie Millie, and who was Brewer Rasmussen?

II

Mother's aunt was always called "Auntie" by us children; we had no other name for her.

She gave us sugar and jam, although this was very bad for our teeth, but she was weak with the dear children, she said; it was so cruel to deny them the little bit of sweet stuff they were so fond of.

And that made us very fond of Auntie. She was an old maid – always old, as far back as I can remember. Her age stood still.

In earlier years she suffered a lot from toothache and was always talking about it; that's why her friend, Brewer Rasmussen, called her for a joke "Auntie Toothache."

He didn't do any brewing in his later years, but lived on his dividends; he often came to see Auntie and was older than she was. He had no teeth at all, only a few black stumps.

As a child he had eaten too much sugar, he told us children, and that's what happened to your teeth. Auntie can't ever in her childhood have eaten sugar; she had the loveliest white teeth. She saved them, too – said Brewer Rasmussen – by not sleeping with them at night!

We children knew that was very naughty of him, but Auntie said he didn't mean anything by it.

One morning, at breakfast, she told us of a nasty dream she had had in the night: one of her teeth had fallen out. "That means I shall lose a true friend," she said. "Was it a false tooth?" asked the brewer with a chuckle. "Then it may only mean that you'll lose a false friend!"

"You're a rude old gentleman," said Auntie, more angry than I've ever seen her before or since.

But later on she said that her old friend was only teasing; he was the most generous man on earth and, when he came to die, he would become one of God's little angels in heaven.

I puzzled a lot over this tranformation and wondered whether I should ever be able to recognize him in his new shape.

When Auntie was young and he too was young, he proposed to her. She hesitated too long, was slow in making up her mind, was *much too* slow in making up her mind; and so she always remained an old maid, yet always a faithful friend.

And then Brewer Rasmussen died.

He was driven to his grave in the most expensive hearse and was accompanied by a large number of people in uniform and decorations.

Dressed in mourning, Auntie stood at the window with all of us children – except for the little brother that the stork had brought a week before.

When the hearse and all the mourners had gone by and the street was empty, Auntie wanted to leave, but I didn't want to. I was waiting for the angel, Brewer Rasmussen; for, of course, he had now become a little winged child of God and must show up.

"Auntie," I said, "don't you think he'll come now, nor maybe when the stork brings us another little brother he'll bring us Angel Rasmussen?"

My imagination quite took Auntie's breath away, and she said, "That child will be a great poet"; and she kept on saying this all through my schooldays, even after I was confirmed, right down to my present years as a student.

She was and is my most sympathetic friend both in the throes of writing and the throes of toothache. You see, I have attacks of both.

"Write down all your thoughts, that's all," she said, "and then put them away in a drawer. Jean Paul did that, and became a great writer, who as a matter of fact I'm not very fond of. He doesn't thrill. You must thrill – and you will thrill!"

The night after this conversation I lay in longing and agony with a deep desire to become the great writer that Auntie could see in me. I was aching to be a poet. But there is a worse ache than that – toothache. It smashed me and hashed me; I became a writhing worm with a hot poultice and blistering Spanish beetles.

"Yes, I know all about that!" said Auntie.

There was a sad smile about her mouth; her teeth shone so very white.

But here I must begin a new chapter in my aunt's history and in my own.

III

I had moved into new lodgings and had been living there for a month. I was chatting with Auntie about this.

"I'm living (I said) with a quiet family. They don't worry about me, even when I ring three times. Otherwise, it's a regular house of din with all the hubbub of wind and weather and people. My room is right over the entrance; every cart that comes out or in sets the pictures swinging on the wall. The banging of the gate shakes the house as if there was an earthquake. If I'm lying in bed, the shocks go right through me, though it's all supposed to strengthen the nerves. If it's windy – and it's always windy in this country – then the long window-catches outside swing to and fro and knock against the wall. The gate bell to the yard next-door peals with every gust of wind.

The lodgers in our house come home in driblets, late at night, well into the small hours. The lodger immediately above me, who by day gives lessons on the trombone, is the last home, and before he gets into bed he has a little midnight walk up and down, with heavy steps and hobnailed boots.

There are no double windows, but there is a broken pane which the landlady has stuck paper over; all the same, the wind blows in through the crack and produces a sound like a buzzing hornet. That's my lullaby.

443

When I do at last fall asleep, I'm soon woken up by a cock crowing. Both cock and hen announce from the cellarman's chicken-house that it will soon be morning. The little Norwegian ponies, which have no stable but are tethered in the cubby hole under the stairs, kick on the door and skirting as they stretch their legs.

The day dawns. The concierge, who sleeps with his family in the attic, goes stamping downstairs; the clogs clatter, the door slams, the house trembles and, when that's all over and done with, the lodger overhead begins to do his morning exercises, lifting with each hand a heavy dumb-bell which he cannot hold on to – it keeps falling. Meanwhile the young people of the house, who are off to school, come rushing screaming downstairs. I go to the window and open it to get some fresh air – and it is refreshing, as long as I can get it and the young woman in the backhouse isn't washing gloves in her chemicals, which is how she gets a living. Otherwise, it's a nice house and I'm living with a quiet family."

Well, that's the account I gave Auntie of the place where I lodged. Only I made it livelier, for a description by word of mouth is more vivid than it is in writing.

"You're a poet!" cried Auntie. "Only write your talk down, and you'll be as good as Dickens. In fact, you interest me much more. You paint, when you talk. You describe your house so that one sees it, and shudders! Go on writing – about something that's alive – about people; best of all, about unhappy people!"

As for the house, I really did write it down, with all its din and drawbacks, but only with myself in it. There was no action; that came later.

IV

It was during winter, late in the evening, after the theatre; with terrible weather – a snowstorm – so that you could hardly get along.

Auntie had been at the theatre, and I was there to take her home; but it was hard enough to get along yourself, let alone take others with you. The cabs were all engaged. Auntie lived a long way out, whereas my lodgings were close to the theatre; but for that we might have stood sheltering till further notice.

We stumbled ahead in the deep snow with the snowflakes whirling around us. I lifted her, I supported her, I pushed her forward. We only fell twice, but we fell softly.

We approached my gate, where we shook ourselves. Again, on the steps,

we shook ourselves, and even then we took in enough snow with us to cover the floor of the entrance-hall.

We took off overcoats and undercoats and any other things that could be taken off. The landlady lent Auntie dry stockings and a dressing-gown; this was necessary, said the landlady, and added – truly enough – that auntie couldn't possibly go home that night. She invited her to make shift with her sitting room; she would make up a bed for her on the sofa in front of the permanently locked door into my room. And this was done.

The fire was burning in my stove, the tea things were laid on the table, and it was very cosy in the little room – even though hardly as cosy as at Auntie's where in the winter there are thick curtains on the door, thick curtains on the windows, double carpets on the floor with three layers of thick paper underneath. You sit there as if you were in a well-corked bottle with warm air; and yet, as I said just now, it was also very cosy in my room, with the wind whistling outside.

Auntie talked and talked. Her young days came back to her; the brewer, too, came back, and old memories.

She could remember me cutting my first tooth and how delighted the family was.

The first tooth! The tooth of innocence, shining like a little white drop of milk: the milk tooth.

There came one, there came several, a whole row, side by side, above and below, the loveliest child's teeth; and yet these were only the advance troops, not the real ones that must last right through life.

Then they too arrived and the wisdom-teeth as well, fuglemen in the ranks, born in pain and great trouble.

They leave you again, everyone of them. They go before their period of service has run out; even the last one goes, and that's no day of rejoicing; it's a day of sadness.

And then you're old, even if your heart is young.

Conversation and thoughts like that are hardly amusing, and yet we came to talk of all that; we came back to the years of childhood, talked and talked, and the clock struck twelve before Auntie retired to rest in the room next to mine.

"Good night, my dear child," she called out. "Now I shall sleep as if I lay in my own chest of drawers!" And she settled down to sleep in peace.

But no peace was to be found either in the house or outside. The gale shook the windows, flogged the long dangling window-catches, rang the neighbour's door-bell in the yard behind the house. The lodger overhead had come home; once more he took his little nightly stroll up and down, then he flung his boots on to the floor and laid himself to rest. But his snoring is so loud that it can easily be heard through the ceiling.

There was no rest or peace for me, and the weather didn't settle down either; it was abominably active. The wind whizzed and sang in its own way; my teeth also began to be active, and whizzed and sang in their own way. It was the signal for a full-dress toothache.

There was a draught from the window. The moon shone in across the floor. The glimmer came and went as the clouds came and went in the gale. There was a restless light and shadow, but at last the shadow on the floor began to look like something. I stared at this moving object ... and I felt my blood run cold.

On the floor sat a figure, long and thin, just as when a child draws with a pencil on its slate something resembling a person. A single thin stroke

446

makes the body, another and another are the arms; the legs are also each done in one stroke, and the head is a polygon.

Presently the shape grew more distinct, wearing some sort of drapery, very thin and delicate; but this showed that it belonged to one of the female sex. I heard a droning sound. Was it her, or was it the wind humming like a hornet through the window-crack?

No, it was Madame Toothache herself, her infernal Satanic Frightfulness – heaven preserve us from a visit from her!

"It's good to be here," she droned. "This is a good neighbourhood: marshy, boggy ground. The mosquitoes have buzzed here with poison in their sting; now I have the sting. It must be sharpened on human teeth. They're shining so white on this fellow in bed. They have defied sweet and sour, hot and cold, nutshells and pulm stones; but I'll take them and shake them, nourish their roots with draughts, let the cold in their stumps."

This was a terrible speech, from a terrible visitor.

"Dear, dear, so you're a poet, are you?" she said. "Very well. I'll compose tortures for you in every metre. I'll give you iron and steel in your body, new fibres in all your nerves."

I felt as if a red-hot gimlet was piercing my cheekbone; I writhed and squirmed.

"A capital toothache!" she said. "Quite an organ to play on. Concert on the Jew's harp – magnificent – with trumpets and kettledrums, piccolos, and a trombone in the wisdom-tooth. Great poet – great music!"

And she struck up – no doubt about that – and her appearance was frightful, even though you could hardly see more of her than her hand, that shadowy ice-cold hand with the long skinny fingers. Each of them was an instrument of torture. Thumb and first finger had forceps and screw, the second finger ended as a sharp-pointed awl, the ring finger was a gimlet and the little finger squirted mosquito poison.

"I'll teach you metrics!" she said. "A big poet must have a big toothache, a little poet a little toothache."

"Please let me be little," I begged. "Don't let me be anything! I'm no poet I only have fits of writing, like fits of toothache. Do go away!"

"Will you admit, then, that I'm more powerful than poetry, philosophy, mathematics and all music?" she asked. "More powerful than all those impressions in paint and in marble? I'm older than the whole lot of them. I was born near the Garden of Eden, just outside, where the wind blew and the damp toadstools were growing. I got Eve to wear clothes in the cold weather, and Adam too. Believe me, there was strength in the first toothache."

"I believe everything you say," I replied. "But do go away!"

447

"Very well. If you will give up being a poet, never write down a single verse on paper, slate or any other kind of writing material, then I'll leave you. But I shall come back, if you start writing."

"I swear!" I answered. "All I ask is never to see you or meet you again."

"But you *shall* see me, only in an ampler form, one dearer to you than mine is at present. You shall see me as Auntie Millie; and I shall say, 'Write, my dear boy! You're a great poet, maybe the greatest we have'. But, believe me, if you start writing I shall set your poems to music and play them on your Jew's harp, you darling child! Remember me, when you see Auntie Millie." And she vanished.

As a parting gift I got a red-hot stab in the cheekbone, but it was soon lulled. I seemed to glide on smooth water and to see the white water-lilies with their broad green leaves give way and sink beneath me, then wither and dissolve, and I sank with them and faded away in rest and peace ...

"Die, melt away like snow," came the sound of singing in the water. "Vanish in the cloud, sail away like the cloud ..."

Down to me through the water came shining large luminous names inscribed upon floating banners of victory, the patent of immortality written on the may-fly' wings.

I slept deeply, a sleep without dreams. No longer I heard the whistling wind, the banging door, the clanging bell at the neighbour's entrance, nor the clumsy exercises of the lodger.

How heavenly!

Suddenly there came a gust of wind, and the locked door into Auntie's room flew open. Auntie jumped up, slipped on clothes and shoes, and came in to me.

I was sleeping like an angel, she said, and she hadn't the heart to wake me.

I awoke of my own accord, opened my eyes and had quite forgotten that Auntie was in the house. But then presently I remembered it, remembered my toothache apparition. Dream and reality became mingled together.

"I suppose you didn't write something last night, after we had said goodnight?" she asked. "If only you had! You are my poet, and you'll always be that."

Her smile seemed to me so crafty. I wasn't sure whether it was the good-natured Auntie Millie who loved me, or the terrible one I had given my promise to last night.

"Have you written anything, dear child?"

"No, no!" I cried. "You *are* my Auntie Millie, aren't you?"

"Who else?" she said. And it was Auntie Millie. She kissed me, got into a cab and drove home.

449

I wrote down what is written here. It's not in verse and it shall never be printed ...

Well, that's where the manuscript stopped. My young friend, the future grocer's apprentice, couldn't lay his hands on the part that was missing; it had gone out into the world as paper to wrap up bloaters, butter and green soap. It had fulfilled its destiny.

The brewer is dead; Auntie is dead; the student is dead, the sparks of whose spirit went into the tub. That's the end of my story – the story of Auntie Toothache.

The High Jumpers

The flea, the grasshopper and the skipjack* once wanted to see which of them could jump the highest. So they invited the whole world, and anyone else who liked, to come and watch the sport. They were three first-class jumpers; you could see that as they came into the room together.

"Now, the one that jumps highest shall have my daughter," said the King; "for it seems so shabby that these gentlemen should have nothing to jump for."

The first to make his bow was the flea. He really had perfect manners, with greetings for everyone; he had of course gentle blood in his veins and was accustomed to mix only with mankind, and that does make such a difference.

Next came the grasshopper, who it's true was a good deal stouter than the flea and yet by no means lacking in polish; he was wearing his native green uniform. This gentleman, moreover, said that he came of a very old family in Egypt and that here at home he was held in high esteem; he had been brought straight from the fields and put into a house of cards, three storeys high, built of nothing but court-cards with their picture sides facing inwards, and with doors and windows that were cut out of the waist of the Queen of Hearts. "I can sing so well," he told them, "that sixteen native crickets, who've been chirping ever since they were small and yet never been given a house of cards, have become so nettled at hearing me that they've grown even thinner than they were to begin with."

In this way each one of them, both the flea and the grasshopper, gave a full account of himself and why he felt that he had every right to marry a princess.

The skipjack said nothing, but it was reckoned that he thought the more; and the Court dog had only to sniff at him to be able to answer for the skipjack's coming of a good family. The old alderman, who had been decorated three times for holding his tongue, declared that he was certain the skipjack was endowed with second sight: you could tell from his back whether it was going to be a mild or a hard winter, and that's a thing you can't even tell from the back of the man who writes the almanac.

* A skipjack is a toy made from the merrythought of a goose or duck. With the aid of an elastic fastened to one end of a peg which is stuck into a lump of cobbler's wax fixed under the wish-bone, it can be made to leap into the air.

"Well, for the moment I shan't say a thing," said the old King. "I'll just bide my time, as it were, and keep my thoughts to myself."

Now the jumping had to begin. The flea jumped so high that no one could see him, and so they protested that he hadn't jumped at all, and that was a mean trick.

The grasshopper only jumped half as high, but he jumped straight into the King's face, and the King said it was disgusting.

The skipjack stood still for some time hesitating, till at last people began to think that he couldn't jump at all.

"I hope he isn't unwell," said the Court dog, and it took another sniff at him ... flip! went the skipjack with a little sidelong jump right into the Princess's lap as she sat on her low gold stool.

Then the King declared, "The highest jump is the jump up to my daughter – that's a very subtle thing to do. But a good headpiece is wanted for an idea like that, and the skipjack has shown that he has a good headpiece. He has strength of mind."

And so he won the Princess.

"All the same, I jumped the highest," said the flea. "What does it matter, though? Let her take that goose-fellow by all means, with his peg and his cobbler's wax. Anyhow, my jump was the highest. The trouble is that in this world it's size that counts, to make sure of being seen."

And, with that, the flea went abroad on foreign service, where he is said to have been killed.

The grasshopper went and sat in a ditch, pondering on the way of the world, and he too remarked, "Yes, size is the thing, size is the thing!" And then he sang his own mournful little song, and that's where this story comes from. But even though it's been printed, it's not absolutely certain that it's true.

452

The Snow Man

" It is so delightfully cold," said the Snow Man, "that it makes my whole body crackle. This is just the kind of wind to blow life into one. How that great red thing up there is staring at me!" He meant the sun, who was just setting. "It shall not make me wink. I shall manage to keep the pieces."

He had two triangular pieces of tile in his head, instead of eyes; his mouth was made of an old broken rake, and was, of course, furnished with teeth. He had been brought into existence amid the joyous shouts of boys, the jingling of sleigh-bells, and the slashing of whips. The sun went down, and the full moon rose, large, round, and clear, shining in the deep blue.

"There it comes again, from the other side," said the Snow Man, who supposed the sun was showing himself once more. "Ah, I have cured him of staring, though; now he may hang up there, and shine, that I may see myelf. If I only knew how to manage to move away from this place, I should so like to move. If I could, I would slide along yonder on the ice, as I have seen the boys do; but I don't understand how; I don't even know how to run."

"Away, away," barked the old yard-dog. He was quite hoarse, and could not pronounce "Bow wow" properly. He had once been an indoor dog, and lay by the fire, and he had been hoarse ever since. "The sun will make you run some day. I saw him, last winter, make your predecessor run, and his predecessor before him. Away, away, they all have to go."

"I don't understand you, comrade," said the Snow Man. "Is that thing up younder to teach me to run? I saw it running itself a little while ago, and now it has come creeping up from the other side."

"You know nothing at all," replied the yard-dog; "but then, you've only lately been patched up. What you see yonder is the moon, and the one before it was the sun. It will come again tomorrow, and most likely teach you to run down into the ditch by the well; for I think the weather is going to change. I can feel such pricks and stabs in my left leg; I am sure there is going to be a change."

"I don't understand him," said the Snow Man to himself; "but I have a feeling that he is talking of something very disagreeable. The one who stared so just now, and whom he calls the sun, is not my friend; I can feel that too."

"Away, away," barked the yard-dog, and then he turned round three times, and crept into his kennel to sleep.

There was really a change in the weather. Towards morning, a thick fog covered the whole country, and a keen wind arose, so that the cold seemed to freeze one's bones; but when the sun rose, the sight was splendid. Trees and bushes were covered with hoar frost, and looked like a forest of white coral; while on every twig glittered frozen dew-drops. The many delicate forms concealed in summer by luxuriant foliage, were now clearly defined, and looked like glittering lace-work. From every twig glistened a white radiance. The birch, waving in the wind, looked full of life, like trees in summer; and its appearance was wondrously beautiful. And where the sun shone, how everything glittered and sparkled, as if diamond dust had been strewn about; while the snowy carpet of the earth appeared as if covered with diamonds, from which countless lights gleamed, whiter than even the snow itself.

"This is really beautiful," said a young girl, who had come into the garden with a young man; and they both stood still near the Snow Man, and contemplated the glittering scene. "Summer cannot show a more beautiful sight," she exclaimed, while her eyes sparkled.

"And we can't have such a fellow as this in the summer-time," replied the young man, pointing to the Snow Man; "he is capital."

The girl laughed, and nodded at the Snow Man, and then tripped away over the snow with her friend. The snow creaked and crackled beneath her feet, as if she had been treading on starch.

"Who are these two?" asked the Snow Man of the yard-dog. "You have been here longer than I have; do you know them?"

"Of course I know them," replied the yard-dog; "she has stroked my back many times, and he has given me a bone of meat. I never bite those two."

"But what are they?" asked the Snow Man.

"They are lovers," he replied; "they will go and live in the same kennel by-and-by, and gnaw at the same bone. Away, away!"

"Are they the same kind of beings as you and I?" asked the Snow Man.

"Well, they belong to the same master," retorted the yard-dog. "Certainly people who were only born yesterday know very little. I can see that in you. I have age and experience. I know every one here in the house, and I know there was once a time when I did not lie out here in the cold, fastened to a chain. Away, away!"

"The cold is delightful," said the Snow Man; "but do tell me, tell me; only you must not clank your chain so; for it jars all through me when you do that."

"Away, away!" barked the yard-dog; "I'll tell you: they said I was a pretty little fellow once; then I used to lie in a velvet-covered chair, up at the master's house, and sit in the mistress's lap. They used to kiss my nose, and wipe my paws with an embroidered handkerchief, and I was called 'Ami, dear Ami, sweet Ami.' But after a while I grew too big for them, and they sent me away to the hosekeeper's room; so I came to live on the lower storey. You can look into the room from where you stand, and see where I was master once; for I was indeed master to the housekeeper. It was certainly a smaller room than those upstairs; but I was more comfortable; for I was not being continually taken hold of and pulled about by the children, as I had been. I received quite as good food, or even better. I had my own cushion, and there was a stove – it is the finest thing in the world at this season of the year. I used to go under the stove, and lie down quite beneath it. Ah, I still dream of that stove. Away, away!"

"Does a stove look beautiful?" asked the Snow Man; "is it at all like me?"

"It is just the reverse of you," said the dog; "it's as black as a crow, and has a long neck and a brass knob; it eats firewood, so that fire spurts out of its mouth. We should keep on one side, or under it, to be comfortable. You can see it through the window, from where you stand."

Then the Snow Man looked, and saw a bright polished thing with a brazen knob, and fire gleaming from the lower part of it. The Snow Man felt quite a strange sensation come over him; it was very odd, he knew not what it meant, and he could not account for it. But there are people who are not men of snow, who understand what it is. "And why did you leave her?" asked the Snow Man, for it seemed to him that the stove must be of the female sex. "How could you give up such a comfortable place?"

"I was obliged," replied the yard-dog. "They turned me out of doors, and chained me up here. I had bitten the youngest of my master's sons in the leg, because he kicked away the bone I was gnawing. 'Bone for bone,' I thought; but they were so angry, and from that time I have been fastened to a chain, and lost my bone. Don't you hear how hoarse I am. Away, away! I can't talk any more like other dogs. Away, away, that is the end of it all."

But the Snow Man was no longer listening. He was looking into the house-keeper's room on the lower storey, where the stove stood on its four iron legs, looking about the same size as the Snow Man himself. "What a strange crackling I feel within me," he said. "Shall I ever get in there? It is an innocent wish, and innocent wishes are sure to be fulfilled. I must go in there and lean against her, even if I have to break the window."

"You must never go in there," said the yard-dog, "for if you approach the stove, you'll melt away, away."

"I might as well go," said the Snow Man, "for I think I am breaking up as it is."

During the whole day the Snow Man stood looking in through the window, and in the twilight hour the room became still more inviting, for from the stove came a gentle glow, not like the sun or the moon; no, only the bright light which gleams from a stove when it has been well fed. When the door of the stove was opened, the flames darted out of its mouth; this is customary with all stoves. The light of the flame fell directly on the face and breast of the Snow Man with a ruddy gleam. "I can endure it no longer," said he; "how beautiful it looks when it stretches out its tongue!"

The night was long, but it did not appear so to the Snow Man, who stood there enjoying his own reflections, and crackling with the cold. In the morning, the window-panes of the housekeeper's room were covered with ice. They were the most beautiful ice-flowers any Snow Man could desire, but they concealed the stove. These window-panes would not thaw, and he could see nothing of the stove, which he pictured to himself, as if it had been a lovely human being. The snow crackled and the wind whistled around him; it was just the king of frosty weather a Snow Man might thoroughly enjoy. But he did not enjoy it; how, indeed, could he enjoy anything when he was "stove sick?"

"That is a terrible disease for a Snow Man," said the yard-dog; "I have suffered from it myself, but I got over it. Away, away," he barked, and then he added, "the weather is going to change." And the weather did change; it began to thaw. As the warmth increased, the Snow Man decreased. He said nothing, and made no complaint, which is a sure sign. One morning he broke, and sunk down altogether; and, behold, where he had stood, something like a broomstick remained sticking up in the ground. It was the pole round which the boys had built him up. "Ah, now I understand why he had such a great longing for the stove," said the yard-dog. "Why, there's the shovel that is used for cleaning out the stove, fastened to the pole." The Snow Man had a stove scraper in his body; that was what moved him so. "But it's all over now. Away, away." And soon the winter passed. "Away, away," barked the hoarse yard-dog. But the girls in the house sang,

"Come from your fragrant home, green thyme;
  Stretch your soft branches, willow-tree;
The months are bringing the sweet spring-time,
  When the lark in the sky sings joyfully.
Come, gentle sun, while the cuckoo sings,
And I'll mock his note in my wanderings."

And nobody thought any more of the Snow Man.

The Puppet Show Man

On board a steamer I once met an elderly man, with such a merry face
that, if it was really an index of his mind, he must have been the happiest
fellow in creation; and indeed he considered himself so, for I heard it from
his own mouth. He was a Dane, the owner of a travelling theatre. He had all
his company with him in a large box, for he was the proprietor of a puppet-
show. His inborn cheerfulness, he said, had been tested by a member of the
Polytechnic Institution, and the experiment had made him completely
happy. I did not at first understand all this, but afterwards he explained the
whole story to me; and here it is:

"I was giving a representation," he said, "in the hall of the posting-house
in the little town of Slagelse; there was a splendid audience, entirely juvenile
excepting two respectable matrons. All at once, a person in black, of stu-
dent-like appearance, entered the room, and sat down; he laughed aloud at
the telling points, and applauded quite at the proper time. This was a very

unusual spectator for me, and I felt anxious to know who he was. I heard that he was a member of the Polytechnic Institution in Copenhagen, who had been sent out to lecture to the people in the provinces. Punctually at eight o'clock my performance closed, for children must go early to bed, and a manager must also consult the convenience of the public.

"At nine o'clock the lecturer commenced his lecture and his experiments, and then I formed a part of his audience. It was wonderful both to hear and to see. The greater part of it was beyond my comprehension, but it led me to think that if we men can acquire so much, we must surely be intended to last longer than the little span which extends only to the time when we are hidden away under the earth. His experiments were quite miracles on a small scale, and yet the explanations flowed as naturally as water from his lips. At the time of Moses and the prophets, such a man would have been placed among the sages of the land; in the middle ages they would have burnt him at the stake.

"All night long I could not sleep; and the next evening, when I gave another performance and the lecturer was present, I was in one of my best moods.

"I once heard of an actor, who, when he had to act the part of a lover, always thought of one particular lady in the audience; he only played for her, and forgot all the rest of the house, and now the Polytechnic lecturer was my *she*, my only auditor, for whom alone I played.

"When the performance was over, and the puppets removed behind the curtain, the Polytechnic lecturer invited me into his room to take a glass of wine. He talked of my comedies, and I of his science, and I believe we were both equally pleased. But I had the best of it, for there was much in what he did that he could not always explain to me. For instance, why a piece of iron which is rubbed on a cylinder, should become magnetic. How does this happen? The magnetic spark comes to it, – but how? It is the same with people in the world; they are rubbed about on this spherical globe till the electric spark comes upon them, and then we have a Napoleon, or a Luther, or some one of the kind.

"'The whole world is but a series of miracles,' said the lecturer, 'but we are so accustomed to them that we call them everyday matters.' And he went on explaining things to me till my skull seemed lifted from my brain, and I declared that were I not such an old fellow, I would at once become a member of the Polytechnic Institution, that I might learn to look at the bright side of everything, although I was one of the happiest of men.

"'One of the happiest!' said the lecturer, as if the idea pleased him; 'are you really happy?'

"'Yes,' I replied; 'for I am welcomed in every town, when I arrive with my company; but I certainly have one wish which sometimes weighs upon my

cheerful temper like a mountain of lead. I should like to become the manager of a real theatre, and the director of a real troupe of men and women.'

"'I understand,' he said; 'you would like to have life breathed into your puppets, so that they might be living actors, and you their director. And would you then be quite happy?"

"I said I believed so. But he did not; and we talked it over in all manner of ways, yet could not agree on the subject. However, the wine was excellent, and we clanked our glasses together as we drank. There must have been magic in it, or I should most certainly have become tipsy; but that did not happen, for my mind seemed quite clear; and, indeed, a kind of sunshine filled the room, and beamed from the eyes of the Polytechnic lecturer. It made me think of the old stories of when the gods, in their immortal youth, wandered upon this earth, and paid visits to mankind. I said so to him, and he smiled; and I could have sworn he was one of these ancient deities in disguise, or, at all events, that he belonged to the race of the gods. The result seemed to prove I was right in my suspicions; for it was arranged that my highest wish should be granted, that my puppets were to be gifted with life, and that I was to be the manager of a real company. We drank to my success, and clanked our glasses. Then he packed all my dolls into the box, and fastened it on my back, and I felt as if I were spinning round in a circle, and presently found myself lying on the floor. I remember that quite well. And then the whole company sprang from the box. The spirit had come upon us all; the puppets had become distinguished actors – at least, so they said themselves – and I was their director.

"When all was ready for the first representation, the whole company requested permission to speak to me before appearing in public. The dancing lady said the house could not be supported unless she stood on one leg; for she was a great genius, and begged to be treated as such. The lady who acted the part of the queen expected to be treated as a queen off the stage, as well as on it, or else she said she should get out of practice. The man whose duty it was to deliver a letter gave himself as many airs as he who took the part of first lover in the piece; he declared that the inferior parts were as important as the great ones, and deserving equal consideration, as parts of an artistic whole. The hero of the piece would only play in a part containing points likely to bring down the applause of the house. The 'prima donna' would only act when the lights were red, for she declared that a blue light did not suit her complexion. It was like a company of flies in a bottle, and I was in the bottle with them; for I was the director. My breath was taken away, my head whirled, and I was as miserable as a man could be. It was quite a novel, strange set of beings among whom I now found myself. I only wished I had them all in my box again, and that I had never been their director. So I told them roundly that, after all, they were nothing but puppets; and then they killed me. After a while I found myself lying on my bed in my room; but how I got there, or how I got away at all from the Polytechnic professor, he may perhaps know, I don't. The moon shone upon the floor, the box lay open, and the dolls were all scattered about in great confusion; but I was not idle. I jumped off the bed, and into the box they all had to go, some on their heads, some on their feet. Then I shut down the lid, and seated myself upon the box. 'Now you'll just have to stay,' 'and I shall be cautious how I wish you flesh and blood again.'

"I felt quite light, my cheerfulness had returned, and I was the happiest of mortals. The Polytechnic professor had fully cured me. I was as happy as a king, and went to sleep on the box. Next morning – correctly speaking, it was noon, for I slept remarkably late that day – I found myself still sitting in happy consiousness that my former wish had been a foolish one. I inquired for the Polytechnic professor; but he had disappeared like the Greek and Roman gods; from that time I have been the happiest man in the world. I am a happy director; for none of my company ever grumble, nor the public either, for I always make them merry. I can arrange my pieces just as I please. I choose out of every comedy what I like best, and no one is offended. Plays that are neglected now-a-days by the great public were run after thirty years ago, and listened to till the tears ran down the cheeks of the

audience. These are the pieces I bring forward. I place them before the little ones, who cry over them as papa and mamma used to cry thirty years ago. But I make them shorter, for the youngsters don't like long speeches; and if they have anything mournful, they like it to be over quickly."

Dad's always Right

Now listen! I'm going to tell you a story I heard when I was a boy. Since then the story seems to have become nicer every time I've thought about it. You see, stories are like a good many people – they get nicer and nicer as they grow older, and that is so pleasant.

Of course you've been in the country, haven't you? You know what a real old farmhouse looks like, with a thatch roof all grown over with moss and weeds and a stork's nest perched on the ridge – we can't do without the stork – and crooked walls and low-browed windows, only one of which will open. The oven pokes out its fat little stomach; and the elder-bush leans over the fence, where there's a little pond with a duck or some ducklings, just under the wrinkled willow-tree. Yes, and then there's a dog on a chain that keeps barking at all and sundry.

Well, that's just the sort of farmhouse there was out in the country, and two people lived in it, a farmer and his wife. They had little enough of their own, and yet there was one thing they could do without: that was a horse which used to graze along the roadside ditch. Father would ride it into town, the neighbours would borrow it, and of course one good turn deserved another; and yet they felt it would pay them better to sell the horse or to change it for something alse that might be still more use to them. But whatever was it to be?

"You'll know best, Dad!" said his wife. "It's market-day today, so you just ride into town and get some money for the horse or else change it for something good. What you do is always right. Now ride along to market!"

And then she tied on his necktie – she knew how to do that better than he did – and she tied it in a double bow; it did look smart. And she brushed his hat with the flat of her hand and gave him a nice warm kiss, and then away he rode on the horse that he was either to sell or exchange. Yes, depend upon it, Dad knew.

There was a burning sun and not a cloud in the sky. The road was full of dust, there were such a lot of people driving and riding to market or going there on Shanks' pony. It was scorching hot, and there wasn't a scrap of shade on the road.

A man came along driving a cow – you couldn't imagine a finer cow. "I'll bet she gives lovely milk," said the farmer to himself, thinking what a good exchange it would make. "I say, you with the cow," he called out, "I'd like to have a word with you. Now look here, I suppose a horse is really worth more than a cow. But, never mind, I've more use for a cow. Will you change over?"

"You bet I will!" said the man with the cow. And so they changed over.

Well, now the deal was done, and the farmer might just as well have turned back. After all, he had done what he wanted; but then, you see, he had made up his mind to go to market, and so to market he would go, if only to have a look at it. So on he went with his cow. He quickened his pace, and so did the cow, and presently they found themselves walking alongside a man who was driving a sheep. It was a good sheep, in good condition and with a good fleece.

"I could do with that sheep, I could," thought the farmer. "It would find plenty of grazing at the side of our ditch, and in the winter we could bring it into the house. Really, when you come to think of it, we'd do better to keep a sheep than a cow. Shall we do a swop?" he asked.

Yes, the man who had the sheep was quite ready to do that; and so the bargain was struck, and the farmer went on with his sheep down the road. There, by a stile, he saw a man with a big goose under his arm.

"That's a plump'un you've got there!" said the farmer. "It's got both feathers and flesh; that'd look well if we kept it by our little pond. It'd be something Mother could save her scraps for. She's often said: 'If only we had a goose!' Well, now she can have one – and she *shall* have one! Will you do a swop? I'll give you the sheep for the goose – and a thankee as well." The other man said yes, he didn't mind if he did, and so they made the exchange; the farmer got the goose.

As he neared the town, the traffic on the road got bigger and bigger; there was a swarm of people and cattle, stretching over road and ditch right up to the toll-keeper's potatoes, where his hen was kept shut in so as not to take fright and go astray and get lost. It was a bob-tailed, good-looking hen, that winked with one eye. "Cluck, cluck!" she said. What her idea may have been, I can't say; but the farmer's idea, when he saw her, was: "she's the finest hen I've ever seen; she's finer than Parson's broodhen. I could do with that hen, I could. A hen will always find a bit o' corn; she can almost take care of herself. I reckon it's a good exchange if I get her for the goose. "What do you say to a swop?" he asked. "Swop?" answered the other. "Why, yes, that's not at all a bad idea." And so they changed over; the toll-keeper got the goose, and the farmer got the hen.

He had done such a lot of things on his way to town, and it was a warm

day and he was tired. He felt he could do with a drop to drink and a morsel to eat. He had now reached the inn and, just as he was about to enter, there was the ostler coming out, and he met him right in the doorway carrying a bag that was brimful of something.

"What's that you-ve got there?" asked the farmer.

"Rotten apples," answered the ostler. "A whole sackful for the pigs."

"Why, what a tremendous lot! I do wish Mother could see that. Last year we only had one solitary apple on the old tree by the coal-shed. That apple had to be kept, and it lay on the chest of drawers till it burst. 'That looks so prosperous', said Mother. Well, here's a prosperous sight for her – how I wish she could se it!"

"What'll you give me?" asked the ostler.

"Give? I'll give you my hen in exchange."

And so he gave him the hen, got the apples in exchange and went into the taproom straight up to the bar. His sack with the apples he leaned against the stove, without noticing that the fire was alight. He found a number of

strangers in the room – horsedealers, cattledealers and two Englishmen; these two were so rich that their pockets were bursting with gold. And the way they bet – you just listen to this.

S-s-s-! S-s-s! What was that they could hear beside the stove? The apples were beginning to roast. "Whatever is it?" they asked. Well, they very soon heard. They were given the whole story of the horse which was changed for the cow, and so on right down to the rotten apples.

"Well, well! Your missus'll warm your ears for you, when you get home!" said the Englishmen; "there'll be a fine set-out."

"No, she won't, she'll give me a kiss," said the farmer. "She'll say: Dad's always right!"

"Shall we have a bet?" they asked. "Golden sovereigns by the barrel – a hundred pounds to the hundredweight!"

"Make it a bushel – that'll be enough," said the farmer; "I can only put up a bushel of apples, with myself and the missus thrown in. After all, that's more than full measure – that's heaped measure."

"Done!" they ansered, and the bet was made.

The innkeeper brought out his cart; the Englishmen got in, the farmer got in, the rotten apples got in, and soon they all came to the farmer's house.

468

"Good evening, Mother."

"Good evening, Dad!"

"Well, I've done the deal."

"Ay, you're the one for that," said the wife and, heeding neither bag nor strangers, she gave him a hug.

"I exchanged the horse for a cow."

"Thank goodness for some milk!" said the wife; "now we can have milkpuddings and butter and cheese to eat. What a lovely exchange!"

"Well, but I swopped the cow again for a sheep."

"There, that's better still," she replied; "You think of everything. We've got plenty of grazing for a sheep. Now we can have ewe's milk and cheese and woolen stockings, yes, and woolen night-clothes – the cow couldn't give us that; it sheds its hair ... You really are a considerate husband."

"But I swopped the sheep for a goose."

"My dear Dad, do you mean to say we shall have Michaelmas goose this year? You're always thinking how you can give me pleasure. What a lovely idea of yours! We can tether the goose and fatten it up for Michaelmas."

"But I swopped the goose for a hen," said the husband.

"A hen? That was a good exchange," said the wife. "The hen will lay eggs and hatch them out; we shall get chicks and a fowlrun. That's just what I've always wanted."

"Yes, but I swopped the hen for a bag of rotten apples."

"Why, now you must have a kiss," said the wife. "Thank you, dear husband o' mine. And now I've got something for you to hear. While you were away, I thought of a really nice meal to cook you when you got back: omelette flavoured with onion. I had the eggs, but no onions. So I went across to the schoolmaster's; they grow chives there, I know. But his wife's stingy, the mealymouthed vixen! I asked her to lend me – 'Lend?' she repeated. 'Nothing grows in our garden, not so much as a rotten apple. I couldn't even lend you that.' Well, now I can lend her ten – in fact, a whole bagful! What a lark, Father!" And then she gave him a kiss right on the mouth.

"I do like that," cried the Englishmen together. "Always going downhill and never downhearted. It's worth the money." And with that they counted out a hundredweight of gold coins to the farmer who was not scolded but kissed.

Yes, it always pays for the wife to admit freely that 'Dad' knows best and that what he does is right.

Well, what do you think of that for a story? I heard it as a child and now you have heard it, too, and realize that Dad's always right.

The Sunbeam and the Captive

It is autumn. We stand on the ramparts, and look out over the sea. We look at the numerous ships, and at the Swedish coast on the opposite side of the Sound, rising far above the surface of the waters which mirror the glow of the evening sky. Behind us the wood is sharply defined; mighty trees surround us, and the yellow leaves flutter down from the branches. Below, at the foot of the wall, stands a gloomy looking building enclosed in palisades. The space between is dark and narrow, but still more dismal must it be behind the iron gratings in the wall which cover the narrow loopholes or windows, for in these dungeons the most depraved of the criminals are confined. A ray of the setting sun shoots into the the bare cells of one of the captives, for God's sun shines upon the evil and the good. The hardened criminal casts an impatient look at the bright ray. Then a little bird flies towards the grating, for birds twitter to the just as well as to the unjust. He only cries, "Tweet, tweet," and then perches himself near the grating, flutters his wings, pecks a feather from one of them, puffs himself out, and sets his feathers on end round his breast and throat. The bad, chained man looks at him, and a more gentle expression comes into his hard face. In his breast there rises a thought which he himself cannot rightly analyse, but the thought has some connection with the sunbeam, with the bird, and with the scent of violets, which grow luxuriantly in spring at the foot of the wall. Then there comes the sound of the hunter's horn, merry and full. The little bird starts, and flies away, the sunbeam gradually vanishes, and again there is darkness in the room and in the heart of that bad man. Still the sun has shone into that heart, and the twittering of the bird has touched it.

Sound on, ye glorious strains of the hunter's horn; continue your stirring tones, for the evening is mild, and the surface of the sea, heaving slowly and calmy, is smooth as a mirror.

The Shirt Collar

There was once a fine gentleman who possessed among other things a boot-jack and a hair-brush; but he had also the finest shirt collar in the world, and of this collar we are about to hear a story. The collar had become so old that he began to think about getting married; and one day he happened to find himself in the same washing-tub as a garter. "Upon my word," said the shirt collar, "I have never seen anything so slim and delicate, so neat and soft before. May I venture to ask your name?"

"I shall not tell you," replied the garter.

"Where do you reside when you are at home?" asked the shirtcollar. But the garter was naturally shy, and did not know how to answer such a question.

"I presume you are a girdle," said the shirt collar, "a sort of under girdle. I see that you are useful, as well as ornamental, my little lady."

"You must not speak to me," said the garter; "I do not think I have given you any encouragement to do so."

"Oh, when any one is as beautiful as you are," said the shirt collar, "is not that encouragement enough?"

"Get away; don't come so near me," said the garter, "you appear to me quite like a man."

"I am a fine gentleman certainly," said the shirt collar, "I possess a boot-jack and a hair-brush." This was not true, for these things belonged to his master; but he was a boaster.

"Don't come so near me," said the garter; "I am not accustomed to it."

"Affectation!" said the shirt collar.

Then they were taken out of the wash-tub, starched, and hung over a chair in the sunshine, and then laid on the ironing-board. And now came the glowing iron. "Mistress widow," said the shirt collar, "little mistress widow, I feel quite warm. I am changing, I am losing all my creases. You are burning a hole in me. Ugh! I propose to you."

"You old rag," said the flat-iron, driving proudly over the collar, for she fancied herself a stream-engine, which rolls over the railway and draws carriages. "You old rag!" said she.

The edges of the shirt collar were a little frayed, so the scissors were brought to cut them smooth. "Oh!" exclaimed the shirt collar, "what a first-rate dancer you would make; you can stretch out your leg so well. I never saw anything so charming; I am sure no human being could do the same."

"I should think not," replied the scissors.

"You ought to be a countess," said the shirt collar; "but all I possess consists of a fine gentleman, a boot-jack, and a comb. I wish I had an eastate, for your sake."

"What! is he going to propose to me?" said the scissors, and she became so angry that she cut too sharply into the shirt collar, and it had to be thrown away as useless.

"I shall be obliged to propose to the hair-brush," thought the shirt collar; so he remarked one day, "It is wonderful what beautiful hair you have, my little lady. Have you never thought of being engaged?"

"You might know I should think of it," answered the hairbrush; "I am engaged to the boot-jack."

"Engaged!" cried the shirt collar, "now there is no one left to propose to;" and then he pretended to despise all love-making.

A long time passed, and the shirt collar was taken in a bag to the paper-mill. Here was a large company of rags, the fine ones lying by themselves, separated from the coarser, as it ought to be. They all had many things to relate, especially the shirt collar, who was a terrible boaster. "I have had an

immense number of love affairs," said the shirt collar, "no one left me any peace. It is true I was a very fine gentleman; quite stuck up. I had a bootjack and a brush that I never used. You should have seen me then, when I was turned down. I shall never forget my first love; she was a girdle, so charming, and fine, and soft, and she threw herself into a washing tub for my sake. There was a widow too, who was warmly in love with me, but I let her alone, and she became quite black. The next was a first-rate dancer; she gave me the wound from which I still suffer, she was so passionate. Even my own hair-brush was in love with me, and lost all her hair through neglected love. Yes; I have had great experience of this kind, but my greatest grief was for the garter – the girdle I meant to say – that jumped into the wash-tub. I have a great deal on my conscience, and it is really time I should be turned into white paper."

And the shirt collar came to this at last. All the rags were made into white paper, and the shirt collar became the very identical piece of paper which we now see, and on which this story is printed. It happened as a punishment to him, for having boasted so shockingly of things which were not true. And this is a warning to us, to be careful how we act, for we may some day find ourselves in the rag-bag, to be turned into white paper, on which our whole history may be written, even its most secret actions. And it would not be pleasant to have to run about the world in the form of a piece of paper, telling everything we have done, like the boasting shirt collar.

Table of Contents